THE WITNESSES

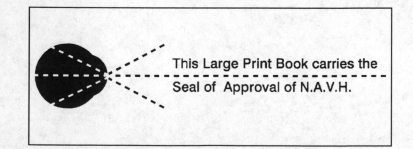

This Large Print Book carries the
Seal of Approval of N.A.V.H.

THE WITNESSES

ROBERT WHITLOW

THORNDIKE PRESS

A part of Gale, Cengage Learning

Farmington Hills, Mich • San Francisco • New York • Waterville, Maine
Meriden, Conn • Mason, Ohio • Chicago

GALE
CENGAGE Learning

LIBRARY OF CONGRESS CATALOGING-IN-PUBLICATION DATA

Names: Whitlow, Robert, 1954– author.
Title: The witnesses / by Robert Whitlow.
Description: Large print edition. | Waterville, Maine : Thorndike Press, 2016. |
    Series: Thorndike Press large print Christian mystery
Identifiers: LCCN 2016023464| ISBN 9781410492036 (hardcover) | ISBN 1410492036
    (hardcover)
Subjects: LCSH: Large type books. | GSAFD: Legal stories. | Christian fiction.
Classification: LCC PS3573.H49837 W58 2016b | DDC 813/.54—dc23
LC record available at https://lccn.loc.gov/2016023464

Published in 2016 by arrangement with Thomas Nelson, Inc., a division of HarperCollins Christian Publishing, Inc.

Printed in Mexico
1 2 3 4 5 6 7 20 19 18 17 16

TO THOSE WHO ARE CALLED
TO WITNESS THE FUTURE
AND GUIDE THE PRESENT

I have set watchmen upon thy walls,
O Jerusalem.

— ISAIAH 62:6

CHAPTER 1

Germany-Belgium Border, 1939

Franz Haus entered the small chapel. The dark stone walls were bare, and the windows were narrow slits that hearkened back to the days when archers defended a monastery from military attack. Light from the windows cast sharp, distinct lines on the stone floor. A junior officer in the German Wehrmacht, Franz's high black boots clicked against the floor of the church as he walked slowly down the aisle.

"Hello!" he called out in German.

No one answered, and Franz stepped up to the altar rail that separated the common from the holy. To the left was a wooden pulpit made of dark wood that shone with a deep luster. A massive Bible lay open on a broad table directly across the railing. Glancing over his shoulder to make sure he was alone, Franz opened a small gate in the railing and approached the table. The Holy

9

Book was a work of art with gilted edges. The first letter of each chapter was embellished by fantastic creatures from land and sea. The Bible was open to 2 Kings 6. Franz read the words translated from Hebrew into classic German by Martin Luther. When he reached verses 8 through 12, his heart started beating so hard he thought it might jump out of his chest:

Then the king of Syria warred against Israel, and took counsel with his servants, saying, "In such and such a place shall be my camp." And the man of God sent unto the king of Israel, saying, "Beware that thou pass not such a place; for thither the Syrians are coming down." And the king of Israel sent to the place of which the man of God told him and warned him, and saved himself there, not once nor twice. Therefore the heart of the king of Syria was sore troubled by this thing; and he called his servants and said unto them, "Will ye not show me which of us is for the king of Israel?" And one of his servants said, "None, my lord, O king; but Elisha, the prophet who is in Israel, telleth the king of Israel the words that thou speakest in thy bedchamber."

Elisha was a witness to what no one else could see, and the prophet's secret knowledge turned the tide of battle for his nation. To reveal the unseen, to protect the fatherland, was a noble calling. Franz put his hand in his pocket and felt the Iron Cross awarded to his grandfather for extraordinary valor during the Franco-Prussian War in 1870–1871. This was Franz's hour, his time to step into his destiny.

Turning around, he left the church.

Southwestern Germany, 1944

There was a sharp knock on the door. Hauptmann Franz Haus hastily folded the letter and slipped it into the inner pocket of his military jacket. He neatly draped the jacket bearing the insignia of a captain over a plain wooden chair.

"Come in," he said crisply.

The door opened, and a soldier entered who looked so much like Franz's younger brother, Wilhelm, that Franz suddenly wondered if he'd stepped into the unseen realm. The soldier's salute and "Heil Hitler" banished any doubt of present reality.

"General Berg will see you in fifteen minutes in the library of the main house, sir. You will then accompany him to the briefing."

11

"Thank you, Private. You're dismissed."

The soldier didn't move. "He ordered me to accompany you, sir," he continued.

Franz's mouth suddenly went dry. It was his job, not that of his commanding officer, to discern secret thoughts and plans.

"Very well. Please wait outside. I'll be ready in a few minutes."

The soldier turned on his heel. Franz waited until the door closed, then retrieved the letter he had written to his father in Dresden. He read it again. The vision that prompted the words had been clear. In his mind's eye he'd witnessed the horror of the all-consuming flames and could almost feel the searing heat. However, Franz had been mistaken in the past in interpreting what he saw.

Sitting in a simple wooden chair, Franz polished his dress boots with an oily rag and made up his mind. Better to warn of danger and be wrong than to keep silent and bear the guilt of disaster. Seeing the resemblance between the private and Wilhelm strengthened Franz's resolve to act. Overcoming his father's doubts would be as hard as dislodging an entrenched enemy from a well-fortified position, but the last blood Franz wanted on his conscience was that of his family. Perhaps his father would at least discuss the letter with Franz's mother. She would act.

Tossing the rag in the corner of the room, Franz stood and slipped on his jacket. It was not typical military protocol for a twenty-three-year-old without any military pedigree to receive regular access to the commander of an infantry division in a German army group. But Franz was no ordinary soldier. He inspected himself in the hand-held mirror that was part of his dopp kit. He kept his light brown hair cut close to his scalp, masking the tight curls his mother had loved since his hair first sprouted. He had a square jaw and clear blue eyes. The ability of those eyes to see what others could not caused General Berg to call him "the Aryan Eagle." Franz hated the label.

A shade under six feet tall with a slender build, Franz rubbed his hands across the front of his uniform. When he did, he noticed a dark spot left from a wine spill the previous day. He didn't worry about the spot. One welcome perk he enjoyed because of General Berg's favor was a pass from close inspection of his appearance or quarters, a privilege that drove Major Deigel, his immediate commander, to red-faced distraction. Deigel may have been Franz's superior on an organizational chart, but not

13

in practice.

Franz opened the door and the private snapped to attention. He followed the soldier down a narrow hallway in the former dormitory of an abandoned school at the edge of the estate. They stepped outside into the sleepy warmth of an early-summer afternoon. Linden, beech, and Norway spruce trees, the same trees that covered the nearby Black Forest, surrounded the buildings. The linden trees were Franz's favorite. On a class trip when he was seven years old, he'd had his picture taken in front of the squat, gnarly trunk of the Kaditzer Linde, the oldest tree in his hometown of Dresden.

"Private, what sort of trees grow where you live?" Franz asked.

The soldier glanced over his shoulder. Outside, he looked even younger — a boy who should be kicking a soccer ball, not carrying a rifle.

"I'm from Kiel, sir. There is a big maple tree in my aunt's yard. It turns bright red in the fall."

Kiel was a major port on the Baltic Sea and home to people with a mix of German and Viking heritage.

"Why didn't you join the navy?" Franz asked.

14

"I tried to, sir, but I was sent to the army."

"Is this your first assignment?"

"Yes, sir. I arrived last week."

They turned toward the chateau and stepped onto a narrow stone walkway rubbed smooth by years of countless footsteps. Bits of moss peeked from the cracks between the stones. They reached the front door where two guards with machine guns stood on either side of the entrance.

"Thank you, Private," Franz said.

The freshly minted soldier delivered another smart salute and a "Heil Hitler."

Franz casually reciprocated. The young man turned to leave.

"Oh, one other thing," Franz said, causing the soldier to stop and face him.

Franz looked into the private's eyes and knew the young man had not yet seen or smelled death.

"If an opportunity to join another unit in the north comes up, don't accept it, even though it might look like a chance to be closer to home."

The soldier's eyes widened. "My uncle is an oberst with the Army Group North and is trying to arrange a transfer."

"Respectfully ask him to stop."

The private opened his mouth, then closed it without speaking. Franz turned away and

15

walked up the steps toward the chateau. One of the guards opened the door for him. Franz didn't look back. He doubted the young man from Kiel would heed his warning.

Faded Oriental carpets that whispered of their former glory covered the marble floor of the expansive foyer. Inside the library eight or nine senior officers were sitting in leather chairs. A thin haze of cigarette smoke hung in the air. General Berg hadn't arrived. No one paid any attention to Franz, who slipped to the side of the room. Many of the volumes on the shelves were in French. He thumbed through *Germinal,* a novel by Émile Zola about the brutal life of coal miners in northern France in the 1860s. Franz had read parts of the novel in French class in school, but he couldn't remember much about it beyond the difficulty he had conjugating the verbs.

"Zola?" a man's voice said. "That's trash, Hauptmann. Don't waste your time."

Franz turned and faced a middle-aged oberst with red cheeks and a thin goatee.

"He's the Jew-lover who came to the defense of Dreyfus," the officer continued, referring to the Jewish French officer convicted of spying for Germany in the 1890s. "It turned out he was innocent, of course,

16

but it took the French years to sort it out. However, no Jew can be trusted. It's not in their nature to love any country."

As a boy Franz was friends with two Jewish brothers. Their father served in the German army during the Great War and received the Iron Cross first-class. It was hard to imagine anyone more patriotic than the boys' father, who proudly displayed his service medals in a case on the wall in the foyer of the family home. Franz had lost track of the brothers when he joined the army. He returned the book to its place on the shelf.

Every man sitting in the room suddenly jumped to his feet as General Berg entered. The general, a short man with thinning gray hair and a paunch caused by a lifelong love of sweet pastries, quickly made his way around the room. Flanked by three aides, the general stopped in front of Franz, who stood ramrod-straight.

"Hauptmann Haus, come with me."

Franz saw a puzzled look cross the face of the oberst who'd spoken to him about Zola and felt the eyes of other officers in the room on his back as he followed the general from the room. Army Group G, tasked with defending southern France from an anticipated Allied invasion, was a recent creation,

17

and few officers knew that Franz had long been a part of General Berg's inner circle.

"We can't talk in there," the general said when they reached the door. "It's smokier than an Egyptian coke factory. Apparently they haven't gotten the word about no smoking in my presence."

Franz followed the general down a hallway, up a half flight of stairs, and around a corner into a small windowless room with white cabinets on the walls.

"Leave us," the general said to his aides, who backed out of the room and closed the door.

"A footman's antechamber," Berg said, opening the door to an empty cabinet. "These cabinets should be filled with silver serving platters."

The senior commander coughed into the back of his hand. Berg was more likely to die from emphysema than to fall in battle.

"I sent your report on the Allied invasion to a senior officer I know on General Von Rundstedt's staff. Are you one hundred percent sure the landings at Normandy aren't a feint, with the real invasion to take place at Pas de Calais? I'm sticking my neck into someone else's fight, and I don't want to get it chopped off."

Franz licked his lips. "As sure as I was

18

about the enemy's intentions southeast of Sedan," he replied.

Sedan, on the France-Belgium border, was the site of a major battle in May 1940. Franz, a junior lieutenant at the time, made an unorthodox tactical recommendation to his captain, who reported it to General Berg. The general summoned a trembling Franz to his headquarters for a fuller explanation. Reconnaissance confirmed Franz's hunch, and the resulting victory boosted General Berg's career and cemented the relationship between him and the fresh-faced lieutenant.

Franz's mind flashed back to the carnage after the battle was over. The bodies of enemy soldiers lay contorted and dismembered throughout the woods. Although he'd not fired a single shot, Franz knew he was connected to every corpse. Since then he'd seen thousands of dead bodies: German, French, Italian, British, and American displayed in a macabre mural of untimely death.

Inwardly, Franz trembled at the horror of war. His toughest struggle was trying to erase from his memory individual faces, comrades he knew from the mess hall and unknown enemies whose countenances, for one reason or another, remained imprinted on his mind.

Two specific events — a mission in Siena in northern Italy and the treatment of resistance fighters in a nearby French village — had undermined Franz's loyalty to the German cause. And he was still reeling from a terrifying dream of tornadoes he saw sweeping toward Germany from the east at the time of the invasion of the Soviet Union. Franz's homeland had sown to the wind and was now reaping the whirlwind. The Allied invasion of France would succeed unless immediately repulsed. Without question, Germany was on the verge of losing the war, and there was nothing he or any other loyal soldier could do to stop it.

"Have you considered asking General Blaskowitz to exert his influence?" he asked. General Johannes Blaskowitz was the supreme commander of Army Group G. His headquarters lay ten kilometers to the west. Franz had not yet met him.

"General Blaskowitz is a soldier first with little interest in politics. He spent a couple of years in internal exile after complaining about the conduct of SS units during the invasion of Poland. Now that he has a command again, he's not going to cross Berlin when the big shots are wedded to a Calais invasion. And I'm not sure I want to tell him about you. Not yet, maybe never."

The general coughed again. Franz could hear the older man wheeze as he took in his next breath.

"At any rate, he'll be here this evening for a formal reception," the general continued. "I want you to evaluate him and let me know what you think."

"Yes, sir."

"Do you have anything new to tell me?" the general asked, clearing his throat.

The question was always part of their conversations. Franz kept his hand from going to the letter in his pocket. Dresden was hundreds of kilometers to the east. What happened there had no relevance to Army Group G.

"No, sir."

"If something comes to you, I'll need it prior to the reception. It's supposed to be a social event, but I anticipate General Blaskowitz will pull General Kittel and myself aside for a private conversation."

"Yes, sir."

"Oh, one other thing," the general said. "There's a possibility General Krieger will be here next week."

Franz shifted on his feet. The powerful staff officer from Berlin had visited General Berg when the division was in the Tuscany region of Italy and was the person who ordered the mission to Siena. Young for a general, the ambitious Krieger was cold-blooded, cruel, and greedy.

"Do you know why he's coming?" Franz asked nervously.

"It probably has to do with this." The general rubbed his thumb against his fingers. "We're close to France, and the general is always on the lookout for something of value. He appreciates what we did for him in Siena."

Franz's mouth went dry. "Herr General," he began but then stopped.

"Out with it," Berg ordered. "Don't waste my time."

Franz took a deep breath and licked his lips. "Do you think General Krieger may transfer me to Berlin?" he asked.

The general swore. Franz stepped back.

"It's possible," the general growled. "And I'm not sure I could stop him, especially if the high command wants you there."

"I want to remain on your staff, sir," Franz said, trying to keep the panic out of his voice.

"Of course you do. But if duty calls . . ." The general paused. "Maybe Krieger won't show. The adjunct who contacted me said it was only a possibility."

They left the antechamber. Franz lagged behind the general's entourage as they made their way to the large dining room where the briefing and reception would take place. The threat of a transfer to Berlin was real. Anxious thoughts began racing through Franz's mind. A soldier stepped in front of him. Franz almost ran into him.

"Hauptmann Haus, a telegram for you," the young man said, holding out his hand.

Franz wasn't expecting a message. Shaking his head to clear it, he took the telegram into the dining room. An enormous chandelier filled the room with a stunning display of reflected light. Stepping into a corner, he opened the message. It was from his aunt. As the impact of the words hit him, the lights of the chandelier blurred, and his concerns about General Krieger vanished.

Franz's family was dead.

CHAPTER 2

Franz held the telegram tightly in his right hand as he blinked and tried to refocus on the room. He saw one of General Berg's aides standing a few feet away and stepped over to him.

Keeping his gaze lowered, he spoke in a hoarse whisper. "If he asks, please tell the general I don't feel well and went to my quarters."

Not waiting for a response, Franz walked rapidly from the room. By the time he reached the smooth stone pathway outside, tears had begun to fall down his cheeks.

His father, mother, brother, and little sister lived in a modest working-class neighborhood in one of the industrial areas surrounding Dresden. Two nights earlier, a solitary bomb had scored a direct hit on the house, killing everyone instantly. His family was most likely asleep when they died.

Franz made it back to his room, closed

the door, and leaned against it. Why hadn't he received the warning about coming destruction sooner? Why would he write a letter begging them to relocate before Christmas when they were dead before he put pen to paper? He wiped his eyes with the back of his hand as another wave of sorrow hit him. Franz wanted to run from the dormitory and not stop until his lungs were burning and his legs gave out.

He began to pace back and forth across the room. Franz had always considered himself a loyal soldier who would perform his duty as long as it was humanely possible, but the things he witnessed and reported no longer had the ability to do anything except delay an inevitable result. The mission of Army Group G to defend southern France would ultimately become a tactical retreat. Suddenly he stopped in his tracks. And he couldn't go to Berlin. Closing his eyes, Franz saw himself in a room with Krieger and a group of high-ranking officers. Someone turned off the lights, and he was plunged into total darkness. The scene vanished; Franz shivered. His Germany was gone. And he couldn't stay in the one that was left.

An odd calm descended on the numbness of his broken heart. He quickly threw his personal belongings in a knapsack and slowly opened the door. The private who had accompanied him earlier to the chateau turned around.

"Are you feeling better, sir?" he asked. "One of the general's aides asked me to either bring a medic if needed or accompany you back to the meeting if you are able to join them."

"No, I'm going to remain in my quarters for the rest of the evening," Franz responded. "You may resume your duties."

"My orders are to stay here."

"Suit yourself." Franz shrugged as he closed the door.

Franz sat down in his chair and stared at the wall. The presence of the unwanted soldier was a roadblock, but it forced Franz to realize that he needed a strategy, especially for something dangerously foolish.

Franz waited two hours until the lights from the chateau twinkled between the tree trunks in the dusky light. Then, carefully raising the window, he slipped outside. With his knapsack slung over his right shoulder, he started to walk up a small hill behind the building and looked back as General Blaskowitz's motorcade made its way onto the property. Franz's timing was perfect. It was best to leave when the commotion surrounding the supreme commander's arrival was at its height.

Franz continued to climb the hill. Coming to a clearing, he had a panoramic view of the estate, which was lit up as if for a holiday. Inside the main house the wine would be flowing, and the officers would be congregating in small groups to chat and act important. Franz disliked receptions and the constant download of information that forced its way into his consciousness. At some point in the evening General Berg would notice Franz's absence and send another soldier to check on him. If the general discovered Hauptmann Haus was missing, he would take immediate action to locate his Aryan Eagle.

Then the lights across the chateau suddenly began to disappear as blackout curtains were lowered. Franz listened for the drone of approaching airplanes but heard nothing. Perhaps General Blaskowitz's security detail had wisely decided to squelch the public display of a large military gathering.

Franz climbed toward his goal, a paved road that crossed the crest of the hill. The road would give him an opportunity to catch a ride in the direction of the town of Freiburg and the Black Forest. He'd already prepared his story for any motorist who stopped — he was an officer needing to meet friends in town. Nearing the top of the hill, he saw a tiny glowing light and slipped into the shadows. Peering around a tree, he saw a solitary soldier smoking a cigarette. The man was on guard duty at the precise spot where the road to town came out of the trees. Beside him was a motorcycle.

Franz lowered his hand to the Luger strapped to his hip. He was a staff officer, not a combat soldier, and he'd never fired his weapon except as part of a training exercise. Also, the guard was a fellow German, not an enemy combatant. Standing at the edge of the hill looking down at the chateau, the soldier had taken off his helmet and placed it on the seat of the motorcycle. Franz crept closer, raised his gun, and pointed it at the guard's back. From this distance he couldn't miss. And if he fired a shot it would only be one more pebble added to the mountain of guilt already charged to Franz's account.

Suddenly the soldier let out a loud belch followed by a second, softer one. It was such a basic human sound that it caused Franz to freeze. And in that instant he knew something about the guard. The man came from a long generation of Bavarian dairy farmers, and Franz could see the soldier standing in an idyllic pasture in the late-afternoon sunlight as a herd of cows walked down a flower-strewn hill toward a stone barn. Franz lowered his pistol. He couldn't shoot a man he knew.

Taking a deep breath, Franz ran as fast as he could and crashed into the man's back. The guard grunted, lost his footing, and rolled down the hill into the darkness. Turning away, Franz didn't check to see where the soldier landed.

The man's motorcycle was a lightweight DKW RT 125. Early in his army career, Franz had awkwardly ridden one of the bikes in the courtyard of a military barracks while stationed in Belgium. He touched the engine. It was still warm. Then, out of the darkness, the guard called for help. Following the man's cry was the sound of a gunshot.

Franz jumped on the motorcycle. He kick-started the single-cylinder motor that sputtered to life with a staccato sound. Hoping it was in gear, he released the clutch. The motorcycle shot forward about ten feet then died. Franz could hear the guard's voice as the soldier scrambled up the hill. Restarting the engine, Franz let out the clutch, and with a herky-jerky motion the motorcycle lurched forward to the edge of the road. Franz opened the throttle without shifting gears, and the engine screamed in protest. The bike jumped over the edge of the pavement and onto the roadway. He shifted gears and heard a loud *pop.* Glancing over his shoulder, he saw the guard standing at the edge of the road with his pistol pointing in Franz's direction. Franz stopped the motorcycle, turned, and gave a crude "Heil Hitler" salute. The salute seemed to puzzle the guard, and Franz didn't hear another shot as the motorcycle pulled away and rounded a bend into the forest.

It was ten kilometers to Freiburg. The dairy farmer turned soldier could run down the hill and report the assault and theft of the motorcycle by a crazy officer in less than ten minutes. Franz's plan of a secret getaway was blown. He opened the throttle wider, and the motorcycle shot around a corner so fast that he almost lost control and skidded into the trees. Fighting panic, Franz slowed and tried to match his reflexes to the gray pavement illuminated by the dim headlamp. Over the next few minutes he encountered two cars going in the opposite direction. There was no sign or sound of pursuit from behind.

It took fifteen minutes to reach the outskirts of Freiburg. Franz rode toward the medieval center of the city. Stopping on a side street near a streetlight, he turned off the engine. He ripped a twig from a nearby tree, opened the fuel tank, and lowered the stick. When he raised it up, he was relieved to see that it was damp halfway from the top. The lightweight motorcycle was stingy with petrol. He had plenty of fuel.

A door opened, and a group of German officers stepped from a nearby beer garden. Franz ducked his head as if inspecting the motorcycle. He was about to kick-start the engine when he felt a hand on his arm.

"Haus?" a voice asked.

Franz looked up into the faces of Hauptmann Koenig, an officer who had joined the division the previous week, and Hauptmann Dietz, a short, chubby man who had served on General Berg's staff for over a year. They were accompanied by two officers Franz didn't know.

"You could have ridden in the car with us," Koenig said. "How did you know we were here?"

"Haus knows everything," said Dietz, who was obviously intoxicated. "He's General Berg's soothsayer."

Without responding, Franz made another

move to start the engine.

"Let me take it for a ride?" the drunk officer said, stepping closer. Franz could smell the beer on the man's breath. "I need the fresh air on my face."

"No." Koenig held out his hand. "You don't want to wrap yourself around a pole or crash your face into a wall. And wrecking a motorcycle would get you a quick trip to the eastern front."

Dietz roughly pushed away Koenig's hand.

"Why aren't you at the reception for General Blaskowitz?" Dietz asked Franz. "He keeps you around like a pet puppy."

"Why aren't you?" Franz countered, trying to sound bolder than he felt.

"It doesn't take a fortune-teller to know that," Dietz retorted.

The drunk officer stepped off the curb, tripped, and crashed into Franz, knocking him and the motorcycle to the pavement. Dietz swore. Koenig grabbed Dietz by the arm and picked him up in the air, depositing him on his rear end on the sidewalk. The other officers laughed.

"You don't need weights to work out, Gerhardt," one of the officers said. "Dietz is your dumbbell."

Franz righted the motorcycle. There was a small rip in his trousers.

"If you don't want to join us, I'll understand," Koenig said. "See you at the barracks."

Dietz tried to stand up, but Koenig placed his hand on top of the smaller man's head and kept him pinned to the ground.

"Heil Hitler," Franz replied and then started the engine.

He drove slowly down the street without shifting gears. After he'd gone a hundred meters, he glanced over his shoulder. The group was turning into a side street. Franz's heart was pounding. He rode three blocks toward the main square before turning southeast in the direction of the Black Forest.

The dense woodlands and high mountains of the Black Forest weren't Franz's ultimate destination. His original plan had been to pretend he was on a short leave, spend the night in Freiburg, and then catch a train going south sixty kilometers to the Rhine. On the other side of the Rhine was Basel, Switzerland, where Franz and his family had vacationed on a couple of occasions when he was a boy. However, that plan didn't make it past his encounter with the Bavarian guard at the crest of the hill overlooking the chateau. Now time was Franz's enemy and the motorcycle his only friend.

As part of General Berg's staff, Franz had studied maps of the area and knew there was a road running south along the edge of the forest. The moon was full, and when he reached the edge of town Franz could make out the brooding peak of Feldberg, the highest mountain in Germany outside the Alps. He headed south, slowing several times when he reached crossroads. None of the intersections had signs, and making an incorrect turn would cost valuable time and be disastrous. He tried to discern the direction of the main highway.

The road entered the edge of the woods. The Black Forest hadn't been truly dark and foreboding since the Middle Ages, but the combination of firs and pines did become thicker and the moonlight dimmed. Franz tried to stay calm and focused. He approached another crossroads and saw a sign he'd been seeking: "Basel 70 Kilometers."

Franz turned right and accelerated. He buzzed past farmhouses and vineyards. War was a time when darkness reigned, and good people stayed inside once the sun set. There was virtually no traffic on the road. Alone on the motorcycle, he found his thoughts returning to his family. The reality that they were gone was as hard to grasp and hold on to as the air rushing by his ears. He tried to keep his mind focused on the dimly lit pavement illuminated by the lamp between the motorcycle's handlebars.

Twice, dogs charged out in warning but didn't pursue him. He scattered a small flock of chickens that had escaped their coop. The motorcycle's engine jangled like it was about to sputter and die, but that was its normal sound. He came to a larger village. In the center of the town, a sign announced that it was fifteen kilometers to Basel. Franz stopped and took a long drink of water from an aluminum dipper at a communal well.

The biggest question mark in his original plan had been how he would get across the Rhine. Whether by train or motorcycle, crossing the border would be difficult. All interaction between neutral Switzerland and the Third Reich was tightly controlled, and a German military officer like Franz couldn't casually saunter across one of the ancient bridges that spanned the river for a spontaneous Swiss holiday.

Franz returned the dipper to its place. Before starting the motorcycle, he checked the fuel level again with a stick. It was lower than he'd hoped. The final kilometers of his journey might have to be on foot. He rode slowly from town and onto the main road. Ten minutes later he saw a bright light in the distance. There was a wooden barricade across the road. When he came closer, he realized what barred his path.

It was a military checkpoint.

CHAPTER 3

In his pocket Franz had a general authorization to travel signed by General Berg. The document allowed Hauptmann Haus to conduct wide-ranging reconnaissance. Franz rarely used the permit and never at nighttime near a foreign border. A long wooden plank painted white and red blocked the road. Franz slowed to a stop and turned off the motorcycle's engine. Two soldiers came out of a guard shack. Next to the small building was a large motorcycle with a sidecar.

"Heil Hitler," said one of the soldiers, a burly sergeant.

Franz reciprocated. "I'm on General Berg's staff with the 114th Division stationed near Freiburg," he said.

"And where are you going this evening, Hauptmann?" the sergeant asked.

"I cannot reveal my destination," Franz replied, reaching into his pocket for the authorization. He handed it to the sergeant. "This is signed by General Berg and gives me permission to pass."

The sergeant stood up straighter at the mention of the general and returned to the lighted guard shack with the paper in his hand. The other soldier, a corporal, stayed near Franz. The corporal had a mustache exactly like that of the führer. He walked around the motorcycle as if considering a purchase. Franz ignored him. Through the open door of the guard shack, Franz could see the sergeant studying the document. The sergeant picked up a phone, and Franz's heart sank.

"Do you need any petrol, sir?" the corporal asked.

"Yes."

The corporal left. Franz kept his eyes on the sergeant, who held the phone receiver to his ear as he yawned. The corporal returned with a gray metal can. Franz stayed on the motorcycle while the corporal unscrewed the fuel tank and poured in the petrol.

"Thank you, Corporal," Franz said when the young man finished.

The sergeant left the guard shack and returned with Franz's authorization in his hand. He stifled another yawn.

"Hauptmann Haus, I couldn't reach anyone at General Berg's headquarters who could verify your paperwork."

"That's because General Blaskowitz, the commander of Army Group G, is there for a reception."

Franz shouldn't have revealed the information to a common soldier, but he felt he had to say something impressive. Dropping the name of an even more important general would make the sergeant think twice about delaying him.

"I gave the captain some petrol," the corporal volunteered.

The sergeant looked at his subordinate, and Franz knew he was about to receive permission to proceed.

"Raise the barricade," the sergeant said with a shrug to the corporal.

Franz started the motorcycle's engine and moved forward; however, he didn't give the engine enough fuel, and it died as soon as he passed the barrier. Without looking back, he kick-started it again and drove off, badly missing the shift from first to second gear, which caused the engine to rev to a high rpm and scream in pain.

It was a terrible performance and made Franz cringe. Only after he'd gone a couple of kilometers did he begin to relax. Then, glancing over his shoulder, he saw a single light on the road behind him. It had to be another motorcycle. Pressing his lips together, he accelerated, but the other motorcycle continued to gain ground. Driving too fast would cause Franz to either wreck or attract too much attention. He throttled back and waited for the other motorcycle to come up to him. When it came close enough to get a better look, he recognized the sergeant from the checkpoint with the corporal in the sidecar. The sergeant raised his arm and lowered it in a clear sign to stop.

Franz opened the throttle as wide as it would go, and the motorcycle shot forward. His pursuers accelerated as well. Franz kept his attention focused on the road ahead and hoped the corporal in the sidecar wouldn't try to fire his gun at him. But there was no way he could outrun the more powerful machine. Franz came around a corner and saw a narrow dirt road to the right. He slammed on the brakes and barely maintained control of the motorcycle as he swerved onto the unpaved track. Within fifty meters the narrow road became little more than a dirt path. Franz bounced over some tree roots and nearly crashed into a tree. He looked back and saw that the sidecar on the other motorcycle prevented the soldiers from following him into the woods. However, the corporal was already out of the sidecar and running toward him.

Franz jerked the handlebars of the motorcycle to the left and made his way around the tree. He continued to bounce up the path as it climbed a hill. He didn't look back but knew he was going faster than a man could run in the dark. The path suddenly ended, and he burst into a meadow. In the headlamp he saw several Holstein cattle that looked up in curious surprise. Franz continued across the meadow and onto the path the cows probably took to and from the meadow. He stopped just inside the trees and turned off the engine to listen. There was no sound of pursuit. He restarted the motorcycle and continued down the trail, not sure where it might lead.

Ten minutes later the bumpy path spilled out onto a paved road. It was narrower than the main road he'd been on, but at least it seemed to run north and south. Franz headed south and hoped the road wouldn't be a dead end. He was encouraged when he passed several darkened farmhouses. He came to a crossroads with a sign that pointed to the right for Basel. He wasn't sure exactly where he was but knew he couldn't be far from the Rhine. He took the road for a kilometer, then turned onto a rutted dirt track that curved around and through the trees. Even going slow, it was a jarring ride. The trees got thicker and the road narrower. If this was the way to Basel, not many people used it. He came around a sharp bend and stopped.

He'd reached the Rhine.

This close to its headwaters in the Swiss Alps, the river looked deceptively easy to cross; however, after the recent rains the current was strong, and Franz was an average swimmer without any floatation device. He looked to the left and saw the outline of one of the several bridges that spanned the river in the vicinity of Basel. He couldn't be sure, but he guessed it was the Schwarzwalkbrucke, the Black Forest Bridge. Serving as both a train bridge and a roadway bridge, it would be heavily guarded.

A narrow path ran along the river. Franz turned away from the bridge and rode along the path in hopes he could find a small boat. He rode several hundred meters and came into a clearing. On the right was a small, dilapidated wooden structure, and beside the river on the left was a large boat. It was a ferry crossing. On the far side of the clearing was a narrow paved road running along the bank.

Franz turned off the motorcycle, leaned it against a tree, and walked down to the ferry. The twenty-passenger ferry wasn't motorized and made the short trip attached to a cable strung across the river between two telegraph poles. Franz couldn't steal something as large as the ferry but suspected there might be other small boats in the area. He stepped away from the dock and heard a deep growl. Turning around, he was suddenly knocked to the ground by a large dog that stuck its muzzle close to his face and bared its teeth. It was an enormous Rottweiler.

"Bruno!" a man called out. "Heel!"

Still showing its fangs, the dog slowly backed away. A man with a workman's cap on his head and carrying a kerosene lamp approached. He held the lamp so it illuminated Franz. When he realized Franz was a German officer, he backed up, and Franz could see fear in his eyes.

"Hauptmann," the man said. "I'm sorry."

Franz scrambled to his feet. The man grabbed the dog by its collar and attached a stout leash. The animal panted, and its eyes glowed yellow in the reflected light from the lamp.

"He was only doing his duty," Franz said,

trying to sound military.

"We've had a problem with thieves," the man explained, reaching down to pat the dog on the top of its head.

As he watched the gesture, Franz knew what he wanted to do. "Are you the ferryman?" he asked.

"Yes, sir."

"I'd like to cross."

The man stared at Franz and then looked over his shoulder at the path.

"I'm alone," Franz replied. "I came on a motorcycle from Freiburg. I'll show you."

Franz led him to the spot where he'd left the motorcycle. The man nervously glanced down the footpath.

"I found out this afternoon that all my family was killed by a bomb in Dresden," Franz continued. "My war is over. Take me across the river, and I'll give you the motorcycle. You can sell it to your friend in Basel. You know, the one who buys the goods you smuggle."

The man eyed Franz with suspicion.

"I also have money," Franz continued, pulling out a small roll of reichsmarks and handing them to the ferryman.

The man quickly counted the money in the light of the lamp.

44

"You will need clothes," he replied. "Come inside."

Leaving the dog to guard the ferry, they went inside the building. The front room was bare except for a few chairs where people could sit while waiting for a ride. The man opened a door that led to two rooms that were filled with cans of food, clothes, furniture, and a broad selection of junk and other items that might be valuable, especially during wartime rationing. The ferryman began sorting through a pile of clothes.

"Are you going to be a businessman?" he asked in an excited voice. "I have a nice suit that would fit you perfectly. Or would you prefer to blend in as a farmer? That might be better. However, your accent is going to give you away as soon as you open your mouth."

The man held up a dark red woolen shirt and dark pants.

"It's too warm for that," Franz noted.

The man tossed the clothes over his shoulder.

"Here you go!" he exclaimed.

He held up a green shirt and light brown pants. Franz did a double take when he saw the outfit. It looked almost identical to something his father had worn.

"Yes," he said. "I'll take that."

"Excellent. Leave your uniform with me. It can be reconditioned into civilian clothes."

Franz took off his uniform and put on the green shirt and brown pants. He stuck the Luger inside his trousers. The ferryman looked at him with approval.

"A farmer come to town for a holiday! Now all you need is a pretty girl on your arm."

Franz ignored the comment. He looked at his watch. "Let's go."

"As soon as I hide the motorcycle."

"No!" Franz replied immediately. "Leave it until you return."

He knew success depended on the ferryman's motivation to make a quick trip across the river. The man hesitated but then shrugged.

"Follow me," he said.

They went down to the ferry. The man carried the lamp. The dog pattered along after them.

"Stay inside the shelter," the ferryman said to Franz, pointing to a small enclosed space in the center of the boat. "The last patrol checked the river about half an hour ago. I thought you were part of their group. You're lucky they didn't spot you. If some-

46

one hails me, I'll tell them I'm bringing the boat over for repairs before the morning shift. The guys on the Swiss side are friends."

The man stepped into the boat and the dog jumped in behind him. Franz paused and tried to figure out if he was overlooking something.

"Come, come," the man said, gesturing.

It was all the encouragement Franz needed. He got into the boat. The man cast off and let the boat drift into the river. The connecting cable became taut, and the force of the current caused the boat to slide along the thick wire toward the other side. It was an ingenious method of navigating.

Halfway across the river, Franz pulled out the Iron Cross his grandfather had given him and held it loosely in his hand over the edge of the railing. To drop it would sever all links to his past. Knowing he no longer deserved to possess it, Franz let his fingers run over the edges of the military medal. He pulled back his arm to throw the medal into the dark water, but an unseen force stayed his hand. He struggled for a moment but slipped the medal into the pocket of his new pants.

They neared the opposite bank.

"Do you want me to introduce you —"

the ferryman began.

"No," Franz interrupted. "Return as fast as you can and hide the motorcycle. Hurry, in case another patrol comes along the path."

"I told you. The evening patrol already came."

"Believe me."

In the light of the lamp, the ferryman's eyes widened. "Will they be looking for you?"

Franz didn't answer. As soon as they reached the dock, he leapt from the boat. "Go!" he hissed. "Don't start the motorcycle. Push it out of sight."

The ferryman used a long pole to reposition the ferry so the current could push the boat across the river. Franz sat in the shadows on the bank and watched as the boat slowly moved away and then picked up speed. The ferry completed the crossing, and Franz saw the light of the lantern bob toward the motorcycle before it moved slowly toward the building. The light disappeared. A few moments later he heard the Rottweiler barking furiously as a group of soldiers with flashlights entered the clearing. A shot rang out, and Franz knew Bruno was dead.

He wasn't sure why, but the end of the

dog's life saddened him. Perhaps his real hurt was so numbingly deep that all he could feel in the moment was the death of a creature to whom he had no real emotional attachment. He watched as the lights continued toward the run-down building. The door opened, and he could see the ferryman standing in the entrance. Then he saw a large, furry flash run past him and disappear inside.

Bruno was alive.

Franz had been wrong. And he was glad. He scrambled to his feet and brushed off his pants. He didn't know where to go, what to do, or what lay ahead of him. And he would be content to keep it that way. All that his access to secret knowledge had produced thus far in his life was death to the enemies of a dying Thousand-Year Reich and failure to save his own family from fiery destruction. He walked up the bank away from the river.

CHAPTER 4

New Bern, North Carolina, 2003
Parker House ran his fingers through his
curly brown hair and straightened his yellow tie. As the only associate attorney at
Branham and Camp, he had been responsible for bringing over the large cardboard
banker's box containing the paper file on
the case. Now the lanky young lawyer sat at
the end of the counsel table while the firm's
two partners, Greg Branham and Dexter
Camp, pored over the notes they'd taken
during voir dire questioning of potential
jurors. The members of the jury pool had
retired to a waiting area while the attorneys
decided whom to cut and whom to keep.
While his bosses talked, Parker held his new
BlackBerry phone beneath the edge of the
table. The phone represented the cutting
edge of technology in 2003, and Parker's
thumbs had rapidly become adept at pounding out messages on the miniature keyboard

beneath the screen.

Today he was checking on players to pick up for his fantasy football team. Parker was desperate. His best wide receiver had gone down the previous Sunday with a season-ending knee injury. He made a selection and glanced up. Greg was furiously scribbling notes on a legal pad. A former all-conference wrestler in high school, Parker's boss had been practicing law for eight years and considered every case a chance to grapple with the opposing lawyer until he applied a match-ending choke hold.

"Mr. Foxcroft, the guy who works for the gas company, has got to go," Greg said to Dexter. "One bad apple can spoil the whole barrel."

Greg had an unshakable penchant for clichés and never tired of trotting one out from his vast repertoire. Dexter squinted and pushed his rimless glasses higher up the bridge of his nose. The younger of the two partners felt more comfortable analyzing the merits of a shopping center lease than assisting in a jury trial, but Mr. Nichols was Dexter's client, and Dexter had to show up and pretend he knew his way around a courtroom.

"I'm not so sure," he replied. "He'll understand the purpose for an easement.

The gas company has to get them all the time so it can run lines beneath an owner's property."

"But the easement issue isn't the key to the case," Greg responded with exasperation. "We've got to prove an unfair and deceptive business practice to open the door for treble damages and attorney's fees. Otherwise we're wasting two lawyers' time" — he paused and motioned toward Parker — "two and a half lawyers' time. We need jurors who will have the guts to sock it to the lumber company. I can see Foxcroft getting in the jury room and arguing that a verdict against a major employer is going to be bad for the community. Didn't he say he was a member of the Kiwanis Club?"

"Yes," Dexter replied and then turned to Parker. "What do you think?"

Not expecting to be invited into the conversation, Parker quickly glanced down at the practice notes he'd jotted on a legal pad. For some unexplainable reason he'd put a star beside one name.

"Uh, the key person to get on the jury is Layla Donovan, the photographer."

"You've got to be kidding!" Greg snorted. "The blonde? How old is she? Twenty-six? She's total filler."

"I'm twenty-six," Parker replied.

"I rest my case," Greg answered. "How about Ms. Hamrick, the chubby lady who owns the beauty shop on Spencer Avenue?"

"It's not a beauty shop," Parker replied. "They have both men and women customers. That's where I get my hair cut."

"My wife goes there too," Dexter added. "I think we should leave her on if we can. I hear she's scatterbrained."

"From the way she talks at the salon, I think she'll form an opinion and stick to it," Parker said. "That will be great if she's for us but could be a disaster if she's not."

Greg quickly made another note on his legal pad. "I'll make that call if she's still on the panel when we reach her," he said. "Let's get back to Mr. Foxcroft, the gas company manager."

"I have him as a coin flip," Parker said.

"What does that mean?" Greg asked.

"He'll go with the majority so he can get out of here as soon as possible."

"That makes sense to me," Dexter said. "Remember, he asked the judge what constituted a legal excuse to avoid serving."

"Yeah," Greg grunted. "I'd forgotten about that."

"What about Donovan, the pretty photographer?" Dexter asked. "Parker wants to keep her."

"I'm going to cut her if I have a strike left when we get to her," Greg said. "I can tell by the look in her eyes that she's an airhead."

"I disagree," Parker said, rising to the young woman's defense.

"Why?" Greg shot back. "Did she offer to give you a discount on a glamour portrait in return for getting a chance to serve on our jury?"

Parker couldn't come up with an appropriate, nonsarcastic response. "No," he replied. "But I think she looks smart."

Thirty minutes later the judge brought the jurors back into the courtroom for the winnowing process. Twenty minutes after that, twelve men and women took their seats in the jury box. Mr. Foxcroft wasn't among them, but Ms. Hamrick, the beautician whose hair featured three subtle shades of highlighting, was juror number eight, and Layla Donovan, the blond photographer with bright red fingernails, squeaked by as juror number twelve.

"Gentlemen," the judge said to the lawyers, "is that your jury?"

"Yes, Your Honor," Greg said as he rose to his feet.

"Yes, sir," responded the defense lawyer, a young man from a large firm in Raleigh.

"We'll take a ten-minute break before we begin with opening statements," the judge said.

The judge and jury left. Parker glanced over his shoulder and saw a distinguished-looking man in his early fifties with a full head of carefully groomed gray hair sitting on the opposite side of the courtroom.

"Who's that?" he asked Greg, pointing. "I don't recognize him as one of their witnesses."

Greg turned in his chair. His eyes widened.

"That's Thomas Blocker, the trial lawyer from Wilmington. He must have something he needs to talk to Judge Murray about."

"Then why didn't he follow the judge into his chambers?"

"I don't know." Greg shrugged. "But he's not here to help us try this case. Go back to the office and double-check the outline I prepared for my cross-examination of Buck Jenkins, the corporate representative for the defendant. We won't get to him until mid-afternoon at the earliest. Make sure I didn't miss anything."

"Could I stay and listen to the opening statements first?"

"Why? You've already heard mine five times."

"I'd like to see the jury's reaction."

"Okay."

The judge returned to the courtroom and everyone stood. Parker glanced over at Thomas Blocker. The trial lawyer caught his eye, nodded, and smiled. Parker quickly looked away.

"Proceed for the plaintiff," the judge said to Greg.

Greg stepped forward and began his opening statement. Even though Parker had never delivered an opening statement in a real case, he'd been a member of his law school's mock trial team. In that role, he'd spent hundreds of hours focused on how to be effective in the courtroom, and he'd drawn on some of that experience to circumspectly critique his boss's opening statement. He wanted to see how it went.

One of the first things Greg did was place a large aerial photograph of Mr. Nichols's property on an easel and position it in front of the jury. Hiring a pilot to take the photo had been Parker's suggestion. He'd argued it would transport the jury away from the courtroom to the formerly beautiful tract of land ruined by the actions of the defendant. Greg had barely begun to describe the land when the defense lawyer objected, a rare occurrence during the normally benign opening-statement phase of a trial.

"Use of a demonstrative aid whose admissibility at trial will be in dispute is not proper during an opening statement," the lawyer said.

Greg was startled and so was Parker, who'd made two trips to a local print shop to make sure the photo was the right size and mounted on a sturdy foam board.

"The appearance of the property is not in issue," Greg responded. "This case has to do with a dispute over what rights were granted to the defendant by the plaintiff and whether the defendant made false representations about those rights that resulted in damages to our client."

"That's very succinct, Mr. Branham," the judge observed wryly. "And you don't need a disputed exhibit to tell that to the jury. If the photograph is ultimately admitted into evidence, you may refer to it during closing argument."

Greg picked up the photo and put it behind Dexter at the counsel table. In the process, he glared at Parker, who knew that as soon as Greg had a chance he would chew him out. Parker listened to a few more sentences, but there was no question Greg had lost his rhythm. It was a painful performance to watch. Parker slipped from his seat and walked quickly up the aisle. As he did, he noticed that Thomas Blocker was no longer in the courtroom.

Built in 1883, the Craven County Courthouse, with its mansard rooflines and ornate decorative ironwork, was one of the best remaining examples of French Second Empire architecture in the southeastern United States. Parker walked west down Broad Street toward the firm's office on Metcalfe Street.

Even if he would later be ripped by Greg for the fiasco with the photograph, Parker was happy. Landing a job in his hometown of New Bern, North Carolina, after graduating from law school had been a dream. It didn't matter that his salary was less than that of Creston Keller, his best friend, who taught math at a local high school. Parker had wedged his foot in the legal door, and the certificate on his wall made him just as much a lawyer as the most senior partner in the biggest firm in Charlotte.

Branham and Camp occupied the second floor of a Victorian-era residence turned into office space. The first-floor tenant was a mortgage company that specialized in refinancing. The law firm and the mortgage company shared a conference room on the first floor. When the mortgage business was booming, it was hard to schedule a time for the lawyers to use the converted dining room, which often forced Greg and Dexter to meet with clients upstairs.

Parker climbed a narrow wooden staircase that creaked with each step. The firm's reception area was at the top of the stairs. Greg's office was in a former bedroom to the right, and Dexter's office was in an identical room on the left. The partners shared a secretary whose desk was crammed into a former linen closet that had just enough room for Dolly Vargas, a petite, attractive brunette in her midtwenties, to squeeze into a small chair and face her computer screen.

"How's the trial going?" asked Vicki Satterfield, a stocky woman in her late fifties who served triple duty as the law firm's receptionist, bookkeeper, and office manager.

Parker repeated what he'd seen and heard. Vicki had worked in several law offices during the past thirty-five years. Landing someone with her experience had been a coup for Greg and Dexter.

"He'll bounce back," Vicki replied, jutting out her jaw. "A trial is like a fistfight. Once the first blow lands, you don't feel anything that follows."

Parker wasn't so sure about her comparison, but after eight months at the firm, he'd learned that an argument with Vicki should be undertaken only when the stakes were high and worth the pain.

"He wants me to look over his cross-examination questions for Mr. Jenkins," Parker said.

Vicki nodded. "Good idea. I've known Buck Jenkins for years. He's so pompous he'll self-destruct if Greg keeps him on the stand for more than half an hour."

"Then I'll try to pad the first section of his questioning."

"Make me a copy of his notes, and I'll jot down a few ideas too."

Having worked in law offices her whole career, Vicki fancied herself a pseudolawyer. Dolly rolled her eyes while Parker waited for Vicki to photocopy the notes. Dolly had a steady boyfriend, which took the pressure off Parker to decide whether it would be smart to date her.

Parker's office was in a smaller bedroom across the stairwell and shared a common wall with Greg's office. Occasionally he could hear the senior partner shouting at someone on the phone. It was a shock the first time he heard Greg launch into a screaming rant. Parker had stepped from his office and glanced at Vicki, who didn't seem to be fazed by the yelling. Greg emerged seconds later, handed something to her, and politely thanked her in a normal tone of voice. When Greg returned to his office, Vicki looked up and saw Parker staring wide-eyed at her.

"Did you hear him talking to that insurance adjuster?" Vicki asked.

Parker nodded. "Yes. Although I wouldn't describe it as talking."

"Don't worry, it's all for show," Vicki said and shrugged. "Greg wants to make sure he gets his point across."

"Will he ever yell at me like that?"

"Possibly," Vicki said. "Just consider it part of your training. But if he did that to me, he knows I'd quit."

"Me too," Dolly chimed in.

"And I can't quit?" Parker asked.

Vicki smiled. "You'll have to decide that for yourself when the time comes."

Vicki was already revising the cross-examination notes for Buck Jenkins as Parker turned toward his office. On the credenza behind his desk was a photograph of his parents taken at the beach on Ocracoke Island a month before they were killed in an automobile collision with a drunk driver.

Parker was seventeen at the time of their deaths and spent his senior year of high school living with his paternal grandfather, a retired commercial fisherman. Leaving New Bern for college had been an escape from indescribable pain, returning to work in his hometown eight years later an act of courage.

Parker's desktop computer was positioned so he could see out his office window. An older couple lived in the house next door, and Parker often enjoyed watching the antics of their small dog that ran around a fenced-in backyard. After Parker mentioned his interest in the dog to the woman, she came over to the office a few days later and gave him a small bag of fresh tomatoes that tasted better than candied apples.

Parker read through Greg's cross-examination questions. His boss's strength was homing in on the important facts, but he often rushed there too quickly and didn't take time to lay possible traps for a hostile witness. Vicki was right. Buck Jenkins needed time to become impatient on the witness stand. The trick would be whether Greg could be patient enough to make that happen.

Two hours later, Parker put the finishing touches on the supplemental questions and printed them off. He'd incorporated them into Greg's outline but also retained the original list. It was 11:45 a.m. Knowing he'd be in court that day, he'd worn his best suit.

"Here are my notes for the cross-examination," Vicki said when she saw Parker.

He'd forgotten that the receptionist was going to prepare something and casually held out his hand. She gave him three sheets of paper.

"I'll pass them along to Greg."

"No, he'll trash them if he knows they're from me. It would be better if you work them into your memo."

Parker checked his watch.

"They never break exactly at noon," Vicki continued in anticipation of his objection. "Judge Murray always likes to finish a major witness at the end of the morning session even if it runs over. You've got time."

"Okay," Parker replied, tight-lipped.

He trudged back into his office, catching a smirk on Dolly's face. He sat down and began reading. Vicki's ideas weren't bad. In fact, she'd suggested a line of additional questions identical to one Parker had come up with. He reopened the file and inserted a smattering of her input in appropriate spots. It was exactly noon when he finished.

"That was helpful," he told Vicki when he emerged. "Especially about allowing Jenkins to build himself up before Greg tears him down. I had the same thought."

"It won't take much to encourage Buck to brag about what an awesome manager he is, and then Greg can show he's a crook who'll lie to make extra bucks," Vicki said with a short laugh. "Get it? Buck is only interested in bucks. What do you think about that as a tagline for the closing argument?"

Parker managed a wry smile. "That sounds like something Greg would say."

Vicki's face fell. Parker left.

It was early fall, and the stifling hot, humid heat that pressed down like a sizzling waffle iron on the North Carolina coast from May to September was gone. It was a pleasant return trip to the courthouse. On his way, Parker passed two of the ubiquitous, brightly painted, ceramic black bears that inhabited virtually every corner of the city. Inspired by the famous bears of Bern, Switzerland, New Bern had adopted a much tamer version. There was Captain Black Beared, Brier Bear, and the favorite of the local bar association — Bearly Legal.

Parker eased open the rear door of the

64

courtroom as the judge stood and left the bench. Greg and Dexter immediately huddled with Mr. Nichols and continued to talk as Parker approached. Greg glanced up and saw him.

"The case is going faster than anticipated," he said. "Jenkins could be the first witness after lunch."

Parker handed him the folder. "Here are some suggestions."

"I'll look them over at the restaurant."

Parker waited in the hope that he'd be included in the tactical discussion.

"Anything else?" Greg asked.

"I'd be glad to go over my ideas during lunch."

"Not necessary."

Parker wasn't going to retreat so easily. "How's the trial going?" he asked.

"Better after we were able to get the aerial photograph admitted. You should have anticipated an objection if I tried to use it during the opening statement."

Parker didn't point out the obvious truth that Greg had been trying cases for eight years; Parker had been practicing law for eight months.

"Yeah," he said. "I blew it, but I'm glad it got in."

Dexter and Nichols began moving away

from the table.

"Go ahead," Greg said to Dexter. "I'll meet you at the Franklin House. Order the Wednesday special for me — meat loaf with mashed potatoes and candied carrots. I don't want to pass out from hunger during my cross-examination of Jenkins."

Greg waited until the other two men were out of earshot before he turned to Parker. "But I can't figure out the defense strategy," he said. "Except for a couple of easy questions, he virtually gave our client a free pass."

Parker listened as his boss summarized the testimony.

"Maybe he's trying to come off nice and make you look like —" Parker stopped.

"A jerk?" Greg bristled. "All I'm doing is fighting for my client."

"I know, I know," Parker quickly backpedaled. "Are you getting any sense of how the jury is responding to the evidence?"

"Not really. As soon as we started the case, the blond photographer put on a pair of glasses and has been constantly scribbling ever since. Ms. Donovan is either a compulsive note taker or she's working on her next novel."

"Will you give the closing arguments today?"

"Probably. Judge Murray will push through with the evidence and make us finish even if the jury comes back in the morning to begin deliberation."

"I'd like to come back and listen to the arguments."

"Not unless you finish the memo I need in the Bontemps case. Remember, I'm meeting with the client on Friday," he said.

Parker cringed. It was a massive project that required evaluation of several hundred pages of documents for business transactions in several states with conflicting local laws.

"That will take the rest of the day and all day tomorrow."

"Then get to it. And don't forget to bill every second. That's not a contingency case, and the client can pay the freight."

Greg began packing up his briefcase. Parker turned and walked up the aisle. As he reached the door, another thought about Buck Jenkins's testimony hit him. He stopped and started to go back and tell Greg, but his boss had already disappeared through the exit door used by lawyers near the judge's bench.

Parker could swing by the restaurant that was three blocks in the opposite direction from the office. But he knew his uninvited appearance would only irritate Greg at a moment when a trial lawyer didn't need it. Parker returned to the office and ate a sandwich he'd brought from home.

With each bite, he fought the feeling that he'd made a big mistake not talking to Greg.

CHAPTER 5

The Bontemps file had more twists and turns than a law school exam question prepared by a sadistic professor. It combined complex conflict-of-laws principles with interpretation of ambiguous contract provisions. Greg had warned Parker that the client didn't want an opinion letter that sounded like a politician avoiding a direct answer to a question. But it was hard turning play dough into bricks. By 5:00 p.m., Parker had settled on a strategy that gave percentages to different scenarios and would give the practically minded client a quick way to assess his risks without binding the law firm to a specific recommendation that might come back to bite them.

Glancing out his office window, he saw Greg, Dexter, and Mr. Nichols walking down the sidewalk. Parker couldn't tell anything about how the day had gone from their facial expressions. He cracked open his door so he would hear them when they reached the top of the stairs. Whatever the status of the trial, Greg would broadcast the news to Vicki.

When he didn't hear anything, Parker tried to resume his research on the Bontemps file, but his concentration was shot. Giving up any pretense of work, he approached Vicki.

"Any word from Greg or Dexter?" he asked.

"No, I think they're meeting with the client in the downstairs conference room."

"Maybe they didn't finish the evidence, and they're talking about tomorrow," Parker guessed.

"I don't know. Maude from the mortgage company buzzed me when they got back from the courthouse. I'd told her I wanted a heads-up."

"Do you think I can crash the meeting?"

"Not without an excuse."

Parker started to turn away.

"And here's your excuse," Vicki added and held out her hand.

"What is it?" Parker took a sheet of paper from her.

"A fax just came in that Greg's been waiting for all week. He needs to send a response in the next ten minutes. I was going to take it to him, but if you're willing to be my messenger boy —"

"Thanks," Parker said, not waiting for Vicki to finish.

He bounded down the stairs. The conference room to the left of the foyer had been the parlor when the house was a private residence. Parker knocked on the door and barged in without permission. The lawyers were standing up and each shook Mr. Nichols's hand.

"We'll be in touch as soon as the thirty-day time period ends," Dexter said to the client.

"Just a minute," Greg said to Parker when he saw him. "We're almost finished."

Parker stepped aside as the client left. "Thirty days?" he asked as soon as Nichols was gone.

"For the defendant to appeal!" Greg clapped his hands together. "The judge charged the jury and sent them out to elect a foreman before wrapping up for the day. They returned in thirty minutes after doing a lot more than electing a foreman."

"Forewoman," Dexter corrected.

"Yeah," Greg said. "The photographer you have a crush on, Ms. Donovan, was the forewoman. The jury answered all three questions in our favor, including the finding that will support treble damages. Everyone in the courtroom was in shock, especially me after I got blindsided by Buck Jenkins."

"What did he do that caught you off guard?" Parker asked, his mouth suddenly dry.

"Testified about a conversation he had with our client after Jenkins's deposition. I have no idea why Nichols didn't think it might be important to let us know that he'd seen Jenkins at the marina where they both keep boats. They talked about settling the case before incurring the costs of trial."

"And because it didn't take place between the lawyers, it wasn't protected by the attorney-client privilege," Parker mumbled.

"Yeah, they taught me the same thing in law school," Greg replied.

It wasn't exactly the concern that had crossed Parker's mind at the back of the courtroom, but he had remembered from the deposition testimony that the two men occasionally saw each other socially and he'd wanted to remind Greg of the possibility.

"But in the end it didn't matter," Greg continued. "I tried to grab Ms. Donovan before she bolted out the door, but she was gone before I got to her. However, one of the other jurors, a retired army staff sergeant

I'd pegged as most likely to be chosen foreman, said she gave a summary of the evidence as soon as they hit the jury room, and no one disagreed with her opinion and conclusions."

"Do you think the lumber company will appeal?" Parker asked.

"Sure, but they'll also try to settle since the clock will be ticking on postjudgment interest. I anticipate an offer before we argue their motion for new trial."

"Oh." Parker suddenly remembered the fax Vicki gave him as his excuse to barge into the meeting. "This just came in."

Greg quickly read it. "Why didn't you give this to me as soon as you walked through the door?" he asked irritably.

Before Parker could offer an explanation, his boss brushed past him and headed toward the stairs.

"Sorry," Parker said to Dexter.

"Ignore him," Dexter replied. "He's working through the fact that he hit a home run in a case he didn't want to take when Mr. Nichols first contacted me. I had to agree that all the expenses would come out of my pocket if we lost."

"Do you get a greater share of the recovery?"

Dexter smiled. "Are you going to get a

bonus because you lobbied to keep Ms. Donovan on the jury? The best thing I did all day was back you up when it came time to exercise our last strike. Greg only went along because he was convinced she was filler who wouldn't move the meter."

Parker and Dexter left the conference room together.

"Don't get me wrong," Dexter continued as they climbed the stairs. "Greg did a nice job, especially with Buck Jenkins. If that had happened to me, I would have frozen up and started wishing it was time to go home on Friday afternoon."

Dexter stopped to tell Vicki about the trial. Parker continued to his office where he printed out his research in the Bontemps matter. Even though he'd not been directly involved in the trial, he felt vindicated that his instincts about juror Donovan had proved accurate and relieved that his failure to warn Greg about Buck Jenkins's testimony hadn't been fatal to the case.

Most days Parker tried not to be the first lawyer to leave the office for home. Dexter, who was married and had two small children, usually left in time to make it home for supper. Greg was divorced and married to his career. He worked extra-long hours. Vicki appeared in the open door of Parker's office. It was past time for her to leave for the day.

"Hey, I was downstairs talking to Marge when an older gentleman came in asking for you," Vicki said, then glanced down at a slip of paper in her hand. "He's looking for someone named Franz Haus."

Parker sat up straighter in his chair.

"He has a thick German accent," Vicki continued. "He's elderly, and I didn't think it was a good idea to ask him to climb the stairs, so I asked him to write down his name on a slip of paper."

She handed the paper to Parker. Written in carefully formed letters was the name *Conrad Mueller*.

"Thanks, I'll be right down."

Vicki didn't move, and Parker knew he had to toss her a bone to satisfy her curiosity.

"The family name was changed from Haus to House when my grandfather immigrated to the US after World War II. Franz Haus is my grandfather."

"Your grandfather was German?"

"He came from Switzerland," Parker replied evasively.

"Oh," Vicki said.

Parker didn't wait for her to ask another question and stepped past her.

"Marge offered him a glass of water," Vicki called after him.

Descending the stairs, Parker saw a man with thinning white hair and an angular frame sitting stiffly in a chair.

"Mr. Mueller," Parker said as he extended his hand. "I'm Parker House."

The man stood, closely eyed Parker, and then shook his hand. When he did, Parker glanced at Mueller's left hand and saw the German was missing the index and middle fingers.

"Is Hauptmann Franz Haus alive?" Mueller asked.

Parker glanced at Marge, who was clearly going to eavesdrop and scoop up every morsel of conversation.

"Let's go someplace where we can talk privately," he said to the older man.

Parker heard Marge huff as they left the building. Mr. Mueller walked with a distinct limp, favoring his left leg as he moved across the porch and slowly descended the stairs to the sidewalk. There was a coffee shop on the next block where Parker could engage in a gentle inquiry into Mueller's interest in his grandfather. Normally Parker would walk there. Seeing Mueller's limp, he decided to drive.

Parker knew his grandfather had fled to

Switzerland after deserting from the German army in 1944 and felt an obligation to protect his opa's privacy. He led the way to his car parked down the street from the office.

"This is my vehicle," he said. "Would you like some coffee?"

"Is Hauptmann Haus alive?" Mueller asked again.

Parker stopped and faced him. "Haus is a common name, and I'm sure there were a lot of captains with that name who served in the army. Why do you think the one you're looking for lives here in New Bern?"

"Did your grandfather serve on the staff of General Berg, whose division was part of Army Group G in 1944?"

"I have no idea," Parker answered truthfully.

"Then the only way for me to find out if he's the right man is for me to ask him myself."

"Why do you want to find out?" Parker persisted.

Mueller looked at Parker and touched the place where his fingers were missing on his left hand.

"He told me something that saved my life."

CHAPTER 6

Frank cut the motor on the twenty-two-foot skiff and let it drift to the end of the rickety dock that precariously stuck its nose into the broad flow of the Neuse River. In the boat's fish well was the afternoon's catch of croaker, a bony fish that derived its name from the plaintive sound it made when pulled from the water. It was spawning season, and the croaker had turned a deep golden color. Leonard "Lenny" Blackstock was sitting in the front of the boat. He leaned over so he could loop a yellow rope around a gray wooden post and then pulled the skiff close and made it fast.

"What are you going to do with your mess of fish?" he asked Frank.

"Fry 'em," Frank replied.

Even the clipped pronunciation of the two little words revealed the man's German accent. Almost six decades in the southeastern United States hadn't sanded the crisp

Teutonic edge from his speech. Frank picked up the bucket containing his fish and, with a surprisingly limber motion for an eighty-two-year-old man, swung it onto the dock. Lenny grabbed his bucket and did the same. Each year, countless croaker, flounder, speckled trout, striped bass, and more exotic fish, like mature red drum and tarpon, swam, spawned, and grew in the shallow waters protected by the Outer Banks archipelago. Several miles downstream from the dock, the Neuse and Trent Rivers ended their separate journeys and flowed into Pamlico Sound. Frank paid rent to the owner of the dock for the right to leave his boat there and avoid having to take it in and out of the water each time he wanted to use it.

Lenny was a retired firefighter in his late fifties. The Vietnam War veteran had salt-and-pepper hair maintained in an old-fashioned flattop. He stepped onto the dock and held his broad hand out to Frank. The older man hesitated.

"Take it," Lenny commanded. "I don't want you falling and busting your lip again."

"That day it was wet and blowing so hard the boat had trouble fighting through the waves."

Lenny continued to extend his hand.

Frank took it, and Lenny hoisted him roughly onto the dock.

"Be gentle," Frank complained, rubbing his right shoulder. "I'm not a fish on a hook."

"And I don't want you to get away. How else will I know where the fish are biting?"

"You put us onto the best spot today," Frank said. "I haven't thought about heading up that little creek all season."

Frank looked up at the cloudless sky and took in a deep breath of the salt-tinged air. The only sound on the river was the gentle lapping of the water against the boat. With the cooler weather, it was past the season for enormous swarms of mosquitoes. Their tackle in one hand and the bucket of fish in the other, the two men walked side by side along the dock and onto the sandy soil.

"And don't be running out on the water by yourself tomorrow," Lenny said. "Call me. It's supposed to be a clear day, and we can head down past Oriental. I'd be willing to bet a few giant drum are still hanging around down there."

"Maybe," Frank replied.

They reached Lenny's vehicle, an older-model pickup truck that was fighting a losing battle against saltwater rust.

"Any chance you'd go to church with

Mattie and me tonight after you eat your supper?" Lenny asked. "There's a gospel group coming over from Engelhard, and I've heard they're real lively. I could pick you up and bring you home when it's over."

Lenny never tired of inviting Frank to attend a meeting. The last time Frank accepted was for a Christmas Eve service to watch his fishing buddy's three grandchildren in a Nativity skit.

"Not tonight," Frank replied slowly. "I'm feeling caught between the past and the present."

Lenny gave Frank an odd look. "What on earth does that mean?" Lenny asked as he started the truck's motor, which rumbled noisily due to tiny holes in the muffler.

Frank was silent for a moment before he spoke. "I was feeling down this afternoon even though we were catching a lot of fish. Do you ever think the distant past is a nightmare that didn't really happen, but you know it did?"

Lenny put the truck in gear, and they started moving forward. "Yeah, every time I have a bad dream about rice paddies, monsoon rainstorms, and the men who never came home."

"Yes," Frank said as he stared out the window. "That's what I mean."

They rode in silence. It was less than a mile from the river to the secluded bungalow Frank had bought two years after his wife died. Getting away from town after her death enabled him to at least separate himself from constant reminders of his family. However, today on the river, it was remote memories of war that unsettled his soul.

A thick mixture of crushed seashells on the driveway crunched beneath the tires of Lenny's truck. The two-bedroom house, built of cedarwood planks now turned dark by age and sun, looked like it had sprouted from the sandy soil. A small tributary creek ran along the edge of the property. The large screened-in porch on the rear of the house gave Frank a view of the backyard. A previous owner had planted spiny cocklebur cactus, native to the Outer Banks, to mark the property line. When a cactus died, Frank didn't bother replacing it, and what had once been an orderly barrier was now a gap-toothed grin.

Frank retrieved his tackle and fish bucket from the truck bed.

"Remember, call me in the morning if you want to go fishing," Lenny called out through the open window of the truck. "If you don't, Mattie is going to put me to work."

Frank watched for a moment as Lenny backed out of the driveway and then walked around the house to a wooden shed where he kept his fishing tackle. The modest contents of the shed were a far cry from the extensive gear he'd owned when he captained the *Aare,* a commercial fishing vessel named after the scenic Alpine river that flowed through Bern, Switzerland.

Because it was built as a fishing retreat, the bungalow featured a utility sink in one corner of the porch. Croaker could be cooked whole, but Frank had enough fish that he could cut thin fillets and avoid the hassle of dealing with a labyrinth of tiny bones. He expertly sliced the pale flesh from one side of the fish, separated it from the skin, and cut out a narrow remaining strip of rib bones. It didn't take him long to build a neat pile of twelve fillets on a cutting board. The phone in the kitchen rang. Wiping his hands on a paper towel, he went inside and picked up the beige receiver.

It was Parker, his grandson.

While he listened, Frank once again found himself suspended between the past and the present; the name Conrad Mueller, however, had no connection in either world.

"Is that all he wants to do?" he asked Parker. "To thank me?"

"Yes, Opa. He claims you saved his life. If you don't want to see him, I can tell him no. He may have the wrong Franz Haus."

"But he called me Hauptmann Haus? You're sure of it?"

"Yes, and he mentioned that the Franz Haus he's looking for served on the staff of a General Bergen or something like that."

"Berg," Frank said softly.

"Yes," Parker replied quickly. "So, he really is looking for you?"

"Did he say he served in the army?" Frank asked, avoiding an answer.

"I didn't ask him. Do you want me to find out?"

Frank hesitated. He'd left the German army behind when the ferryman took him across the Rhine at Basel. There wasn't a Luger in his house or a closet filled with wartime memorabilia. If a program or movie about World War II came on the television, Frank changed the channel. The years 1939–1944 remained a closed, locked book, and he knew of no good reason to open it.

"No," Frank replied. "I don't want to see him, whatever the reason."

"Will do. Did you go fishing today?"

Frank told him about the mess of croaker he and Lenny caught.

"Awesome," Parker replied. "I'll talk to you later."

The call ended. Frank took the fish pieces into the kitchen. He would cook four in a skillet and freeze the rest. He divided the fish into three sections and put the pieces to freeze in plastic bags. He was also in the mood for okra and tomatoes to complement his fish.

Frank opened a bag of frozen okra from Lenny's garden. There were three ripe tomatoes on the windowsill above the kitchen sink. Putting the okra in a pot over low heat, Frank added salt, pepper, a half cup of chicken stock, and a thick pat of butter. After dicing and stirring in the tomatoes, he turned up the heat. His phone rang again. Two calls in one night was a rare occurrence. But it was Parker again.

"Opa, I'm sorry to bother you, but you really should talk to Mr. Mueller. He's totally convinced you saved his life toward the end of the war."

"I heard you the first time, but that's not possible," Frank replied irritably. "I was a junior staff officer."

"I don't think he's going to take no for an answer, and he doesn't need me to find out where you live. He can do that by asking around town, especially now that he knows you've changed your name to House. Mr. Mueller came all the way from Germany to see you and seems like a nice old gentleman."

Frank grunted. Someone who met him for five minutes might say he was a nice old gentleman, too, but he knew the truth that lay behind the eyes that faced him each morning in the mirror.

"I'm fixing supper," he replied.

"What are you having?"

Frank told him. Parker was silent for a moment, then spoke.

"That sounds good to me," he said. "I was going to have to go to the grocery store and pick up a frozen TV dinner. I'm not sure what Mr. Mueller is going to eat, but he looks hungry too."

"Okay, bring him," Frank replied grumpily. "I have extra fillets and can add more okra. But I'm out of fresh tomatoes."

"I can bring some. The lady who lives next to the office gave me a bag of a late-season variety yesterday. We'll be there in twenty minutes."

The call ended. Frank turned down the okra and tomatoes to simmer slowly. He'd cook white rice and fry the fish after Parker and Mr. Mueller arrived.

Frank ate his meals at a tiny table in the kitchen or sitting on the back porch, but the front of the house was a combination living room/dining room that he kept neat. The day's mail lay unopened on the corner of the dining room table. He sorted it and put what he needed to keep in a rolltop desk. The living room contained a brown leather couch and a matching leather chair where Frank would sit and read during the few months of cold weather that blew frost across the eastern North Carolina coast. The rest of the year he preferred a well-padded lounge chair on the back porch where his time with a book, in German or English, could be serenaded by chirping crickets and evening calls from night herons or an occasional owl.

While he straightened up the house, Frank racked his brain trying to remember Conrad Mueller. There were hundreds of faces in his mental scrapbook of his years in the army. Only a few still had names: serious, clean-cut young men, many of whom didn't survive the war. Other faces were faded and washed out like an old picture left in a shirt pocket and run through a clothes washer.

General Berg died in 1946 from emphysema, a fact Frank learned decades later when he researched his former commander's name on the Internet. After that discovery, he'd not dug further into the past. As for Mueller, he was beyond the reach of natural memory or long-dormant revelation.

Thinking about former comrades in arms troubled Frank afresh and made him mad at the unwelcome visitor for tracking him down. It could all be a mistake, of course, but even if it wasn't, Frank had no interest in reminiscing about a period of his life during which he'd been so efficient in helping kill men whose cause he now believed more just than his own. The postwar revelation of the death camps in eastern Germany and Poland had shaken Frank deeply. Glorifying the horror of war by either the winning or the losing side was, to him, a sign of insanity.

Returning to the kitchen, he vigorously stirred the okra and tomatoes. He heard the sound of Parker's car crunching the seashells as he pulled into the driveway. Placing the large spoon on the counter beside the stove, Frank went to the front door and prepared to reluctantly welcome an unknown face from the past.

CHAPTER 7

"Hauptmann Haus," Mueller said respectfully in German after he looked Frank up and down. "Do you remember me?"

Frank looked into the man's blue eyes. No recognition came. Parker stood beside the sofa and watched.

"No," Frank responded in the same language. "And I haven't been a hauptmann for a long time."

"Thank you for agreeing to see me and inviting me to your home," Mueller replied.

Parker cleared his throat. "If you're going to speak in German, how am I going to understand what you're talking about?"

Frank turned to his grandson. "Do you finally regret not studying harder when you took German in high school and refused my offer to tutor you?"

"Yes, but you can't hold that against me now."

"My English is not good," Mueller said

with an apologetic look at Parker.

"That's okay," Parker answered, raising his hand. "This is your rodeo. I'll go into the kitchen and finish preparing supper."

"Rodeo?" Mueller asked.

"It's an American idiom for our having a private conversation," Frank explained in German.

"I recognized American," Parker said.

"And if you discover a new interest in learning German, we'll explore that later," Frank said. "The okra and tomatoes are stewing, and the fish need to be fried. The seasoned cornmeal is in the cupboard. Do you want rice too?"

"Yes, I'll take care of it."

Parker started moving toward the rear of the house.

"And there's a new container of oil next to the toaster," Frank called after him. "Use that, please."

Frank and Mueller sat down across from each other in the side chairs.

"Your English is excellent," Mueller said. "And your tall grandson is a lawyer. Congratulations."

"He's a good boy and busy with his new job. But I enjoy it when he has time for me."

"I have several grandchildren," Mueller replied, rubbing his chin with his left hand.

Frank noticed the missing fingers.

"Do you remember me?" Mueller asked again.

"No." Frank shook his head. "I met so many men during the war, and I've not kept in touch with anyone from those days."

"It's understandable. I was a lowly private when we met. You were an officer on General Berg's staff."

As he listened, Frank suspected that Mueller didn't know Frank had deserted. He relaxed. Mueller placed his right hand over his left one as he spoke.

"I was born in Kiel, and after completing basic training, I was assigned to Army Group G in June 1944. One afternoon I escorted you to a meeting with General Berg at the chateau where he had his headquarters."

Frank took in a sharp breath. It was the day he'd deserted. Mueller paused.

"You remember," Mueller said.

"Yes."

Not only did Mueller escort him to the chateau, but he was also the young soldier on duty when Frank slipped out the window and deserted. Frank shifted nervously in his chair.

"Before we parted at the chateau, you spoke kindly to me, not as an officer to a new recruit, but man-to-man," Mueller continued.

"I don't remember a conversation," Frank replied, trying to keep his voice calm.

"Understandable. A captain and a private lived in different worlds. Anyway, you told me not to seek a transfer for duty in the north, closer to my home. At that time, my uncle was an oberst who could have arranged an assignment to a regiment that was doing guard duty for the shipyards. However, within a few months his regiment was rolled into a division sent to Estonia, where it was trapped in the Courland Peninsula. Over 150,000 men in the northern army group died there, with the remainder surrendering to the Russians. Many of those who surrendered, including my uncle, never returned."

Casualty numbers that large were always too much for Frank to absorb. His burden was the faces of individual men he'd known who lay broken and twisted on a battlefield.

"Hauptmann Haus, please listen to me."

Frank hadn't realized his daydream had played out on his face. He blinked his eyes.

"Go ahead."

"I never transferred to the north. Today I have three children and six grandchildren." Mueller leaned forward. "For many years I thought you knew something about the central command's overall military strategy because of your relationship with General Berg and you gave me an inside tip. That alone deserved my thanks. But then I read a blog on the Internet about an officer on General Berg's staff who knew where the enemy would be and how to defeat them without conducting reconnaissance. The blogger didn't know the officer's name, but he said the general called him the 'Aryan Eagle.' When I heard that, I immediately thought about you. Were you the Aryan Eagle?"

Although relieved Mueller hadn't brought up their interaction at the dormitory, Frank flinched at the mention of the moniker General Berg had hung around his reluctant neck.

"Opa!" Parker called, sticking his head through the opening to the kitchen. "I can't find the cornmeal."

"I need to help prepare the dinner," Frank said, standing up. "Please, wait here."

Frank retreated to the kitchen. He'd put the box of seasoned cornmeal in the cabinet next to the peanut butter. He took it out and placed it on the counter.

"What's going on?" Parker asked, peering past Frank toward the opening to the living area. "I could tell Mr. Mueller was telling you a story. Were you able to figure out where your paths crossed?"

"I'll batter the fish," Frank replied. "How long has the rice been cooking?"

"Less than a minute. Are you going to answer me or am I going to have to use my lawyer skills to dig it out of you?"

Frank lifted a large skillet from a hook above the stove and grabbed the jug of cooking oil.

"We served for a short time in the same unit," he said.

"How did you save his life?"

"I gave him some advice," Frank replied as he turned up the heat for the oil. "He thinks it was important."

"It must have been very good advice," Parker replied. "Especially if it convinced him to come all the way to America to thank you."

"Maybe it was, but he's also bringing up things I don't want to talk about."

"Did he tell you how he lost his fingers? Was that a wartime injury? He has a bad limp too."

"No, and I didn't ask him."

"Does he know you deserted and fled to Switzerland?" Parker asked, lowering his voice.

Frank shook his head. "I don't think so, but he saw me the day I left."

"Wow," Parker replied. "Did you tell him to desert too?"

"No!" Frank answered sharply. "And I don't want to be cross-examined by you or anyone else! When we sit down at the table, I'm going to change the subject. And as soon as we've finished eating, you're going to take Mr. Mueller back to town. Is my English clear?"

"Okay, okay." Parker took a step back.

Frank turned away, dragged a croaker fillet through the batter, and dropped it in the oil where it sizzled. Three others quickly joined it. The delicate fish needed to cook only long enough for the coating to turn a crispy brown. Frank placed a few sheets of paper towel on a plate and scooped the fish from the oil. He added four more fillets to the skillet. Parker stirred the okra and tomatoes that were melding together.

"Our law firm won a case in court today," he said. "And it was my suggestion about a member of the jury that made a huge difference."

Frank looked up from the skillet. "What do you mean?"

Parker told him about lobbying for the young photographer.

"Was it because she was a pretty girl?" Frank asked, glad for a change in subject.

"No," Parker said, pointing to his chest. "Something in here told me that getting the photographer on the jury was critically important if we wanted to win the battle."

Frank was about to turn over a fillet in the hot oil. His hand froze. "Did you say 'win the battle'?"

"Yeah, I guess I have war on the brain. Anyway, a trial is a form of civilized warfare. Strategy at all points of the case is crucial because it will influence who wins and who loses. Selecting the right jury is a huge part of it."

Frank grunted and refocused his attention on the fish.

"What else do you know about this woman photographer?" he asked after a few moments passed. "Did you have any other thoughts about her?"

"No, but she took extensive notes during the testimony that convinced everyone else to go along with what she thought the verdict should be."

Frank stared unseeing at the fish in the skillet.

"Opa!" Parker said. "Aren't those fillets done?"

Frank shook his head and then quickly

scooped out the remaining pieces of fish and put them on the paper towels. Parker took the rice off the burner and poured the okra and tomatoes into a glass serving dish.

"I'm glad you went to Switzerland," Parker said. "If you hadn't, I wouldn't be here."

When they sat down at the table, Parker prepared to be excluded from an ongoing conversation in German between the two older men.

"Please, let's be polite to my grandson and speak English while we eat," Frank said to Mueller.

"This meal is his rodeo," Mueller said with a smile.

Parker laughed. As they ate, Mr. Mueller asked simple questions about Frank's life. None of the information was new to Parker. His grandfather had arrived in the United States in 1946, and after living in Norfolk, Virginia, for six months moved to New Bern where he got a job working in a lumberyard. He married Parker's grandmother, the daughter of a local butcher who'd emigrated from Germany in the 1920s. They had two children, a daughter first and then, eight years later, Parker's father. Parker's aunt lived near Orlando. He braced for his grandfather to reveal the death of Parker's parents in the car wreck, but he didn't. Instead, he used family pictures lined up in a row on a cupboard next to the dining room table to illustrate the story of his children and grandchildren. Mueller brought out photos of his family from an envelope in his pocket. When he did, the two men lapsed into German for several minutes until Mueller looked up at Parker.

"I apologize," he said. "It is easier to tell about my family in German."

"Of course," Parker said. "That's fine."

"Do you want more fish, Herr Mueller?" Frank asked.

"Yes. It is very good. And I like the other dish. What do you call it?"

"Okra and tomatoes. I'll bring that too."

Frank left the table and went into the kitchen.

"At first I thought the okra was . . . ," Mueller began to say to Parker but paused.

"Slimy," Parker suggested.

"What is slimy?"

"The okra sticks together as if held by tiny strings that feel slippery inside your mouth."

"But if you bite down it is good with the taste of tomatoes."

"That's why the two are often married together," Parker said.

Mueller gave him a puzzled look.

"They are cooked in the same pot," Parker explained. "Like peas and carrots."

"I will tell my wife about this and show her pictures on the Internet."

"Do you spend a lot of time on the computer?" Parker asked, putting a piece of fish in his mouth.

"Some. That's where I found out about your grandfather. To be so young, he was a high-ranking officer who often talked to a general."

"A general?"

Frank returned with more fillets and the pot of okra and tomatoes and said something to Mueller in German. Parker didn't ask any follow-up questions about the general while they ate a second round.

"You stay here, and I'll clean the dishes," Parker said when they finished the meal.

"You know how I like to put the dishes in the washer —" Frank began.

"Yes, Opa," Parker responded. He then looked at Mueller. "Does everyone in Germany load the dishwasher the same way?"

Mueller gave him a puzzled look for a moment and then smiled. "Yes, it must be done perfectly. Ubung macht den Meister."

"What does that mean?" Parker asked his grandfather.

"It's a German proverb: 'Practice is what makes a master.' "

"That's what I thought."

Parker gathered up the dirty plates and eating utensils and carried them into the kitchen. The two older men began talking softly in German. Hearing them, Parker wondered if his grandfather ever longed for fellowship with people from his native land. If so, he never mentioned it.

As he rinsed the plates, Parker began to daydream about taking a trip to Germany with Opa as soon as Parker had enough vacation time accumulated at the law firm to do so. It would be fascinating to view the country and people through his grandfather's eyes.

Parker thoroughly rinsed the dirty dishes and carefully lined them up in the dishwasher. Using a steel wool pad, he scrubbed the pots used for the okra and tomatoes and the rice before placing them in the top rack. He separated the forks, knives, and serving spoons into their own sections, placing the fork tines and knives up so they would receive maximum spray. The remaining area in the upper rack would hold the glasses. Sometimes when opening his grandfather's dishwasher it was hard to tell if the dishes were dirty or clean. Finally, Parker wiped off the stove, removing all splatter from the oil in the skillet.

"All done," he said, sticking his head through the opening. "Sorry, but there's no strudel for dessert."

Frank looked at him and rubbed his eyes. If he thought it possible, Parker would have suspected his grandfather had been crying.

Parker watched as Mueller and his grandfather solemnly shook hands at the bottom of the steps leading into the house. It was late dusk, when evening hovers at the edge of the rapidly fading light. The night insects were already in full-throated song.

"Thank you for seeing me," Mueller said in English.

Frank spoke several sentences in German. Mueller looked at Parker and nodded his head. Frank turned away and walked up the steps without looking back. Parker and Mueller got in the car.

"What did he say to you there at the end?" Parker asked as he started the car.

"He asked me not to tell you," Mueller replied, staring straight ahead.

Parker left the driveway and turned onto the paved road. It was half a mile to a four-way stop. Parker slowed and stopped to wait for a truck to pass through.

"Why was my grandfather crying after supper?" he asked. "Can you tell me that?"

"Seeing me made him think about the war. It was a hard time. He lost many friends."

"He never talks about it."

Mueller turned slightly in the passenger seat. "It is not a story to tell. Does that make sense?"

"Yes," Parker replied. "Words can bring back bad memories."

They rode in silence. Mueller was staying in a hotel near the regional airport. Parker pulled into the parking lot.

"Can you at least tell me what you found out about my grandfather on the Internet?" he asked, turning off the car's engine. "You said he was a high-ranking officer for his age. Is there a reason? And who was the general you mentioned?"

"I can see you are a good lawyer who never gives up," Mueller said with a smile. "But I am not the person to ask about the past."

"I can do my own search." Parker shrugged.

Mueller reached out and touched Parker on the arm. "Be careful. You may find something you don't want to know. Your grandfather and I are old men who need to sleep in peace and rest. Give him that gift."

Parker sat in his car and watched Mueller

walk slowly through the automatic doors of the hotel lobby. Something stirring inside made Parker want to ignore the old man's simple request.

Parker lived in a one-room efficiency apartment on the second floor of a brick home built in the 1940s. The house was located in a transitional neighborhood, and it was a matter of local debate whether the neighborhood was transitioning up or down. Parker didn't care about the sketchy aspects of the area. He liked the eight-minute commute to the office.

Access to the apartment was via an exterior metal staircase on the back of the house. A young couple with two small children and one large dog rented the main floor of the home. Because the couple used the single-car garage for their minivan, Parker kept his car on the street. When he opened the gate in the chain-link fence that surrounded the yard, Bosco, the couple's black Lab, greeted him excitedly. Parker kept a bag of dog treats in his car and slipped one into his pocket when he got out of the car. He tossed the treat toward the rear of the lot. Bosco raced after it past a wooden swing set while Parker climbed the stairs and unlocked his door.

Originally the apartment had been the house's attic, and the steeply sloping roofline forced Parker to walk toward the middle of the long room. The lower walls held shelving, an entertainment center, and the headboard for his bed. A kitchenette filled one end of the space with the bathroom occupying the other. There was a single dormer on the front side of the house where Parker kept a small desk for use when he needed to work at home. From the dormer he could see across the street to a vacant wooded lot.

When he got home, Parker unwound by doing passive resistance exercises followed by several variations of push-ups. He could maintain a static plank for several minutes and moved smoothly from one position to another. Tonight the time with his grandfather had provided a buffer from work, and he did only a few stretches. Plopping into a secondhand recliner, he powered up his laptop and typed in "Hauptmann Franz Haus." The results were a German-language jumble of obituaries and hits on Hauptmann, Franz, and Haus. The foreign-language maze was as impenetrable as an Amazonian rain forest, and after less than half an hour Parker gave up. If he wanted to find out something specific about his grandfather's war record, he was going to have to narrow his search, just like he did when researching an obscure principle of law.

Frank sat on the screened-in porch in the dark and let his thoughts stew like the okra and tomatoes he'd eaten for supper. He heard an unfamiliar sound in the yard and peered into the darkness. A few moments of silence passed, and he tried to settle back in his chair. For many years fear had not been his regular companion, but tonight it slithered across the sandy soil and tried to wrap itself around his soul.

He lived in an isolated, rural area of the county, but the absence of neighbors didn't normally worry him. The only security system he had was the crushed shells of his driveway that announced the approach of vehicles, and he rarely bothered to lock his front door. During the cooler months of the year, he slept with his windows open, a flimsy screen the only thing separating him from the outside world. But tonight the peace Frank normally felt at the end of a long day vanished with the final rays of the sun.

He knew the source of his unease. Initially he'd been relieved when Mueller didn't indicate knowledge of Frank's desertion, but the former private's mention of the Aryan Eagle caused the sinister nature of Frank's past to creep from the shadows. This many years after the end of the war, the label should have faded like a wartime ribbon abandoned in the sunny corner of a rarely used bedroom. Frank never directly answered Mueller's question, but in the depths of his being he knew that somewhere, someone was intent on tracking him down.

His last words to Mueller had been a plea to keep their reunion a secret. Frank had couched his request in terms of the desire to live out the remainder of his life uninterrupted by painful memories, and his old comrade reassured him that his only purpose in coming to America was to thank him for the crucial warning years before. Frank didn't know if Mueller would keep his word or not. Even if he did, it didn't remove the threat of discovery. If Conrad Mueller could find him, so could someone else.

Frank heard another unfamiliar sound in the direction of the creek and shifted in his chair. Getting up, he went to the front door, locked it, and flipped the dead bolt. Tonight he'd sleep with the windows closed.

CHAPTER 8

Southern France, 1944

The two officers stood on a slight rise overlooking a tiny French village in the soft light of a midsummer dawn. The senior officer, Oberst Gottfried, lowered the binoculars from his eyes.

"Are you sure that's the place, Hauptmann Haus?"

"Yes, sir." Franz ran his fingers through his hair. The sleepy village was exactly as he'd seen it when he was lying in his bunk in the dormitory near the chateau where their division of Army Group G had its headquarters. Franz was a careful witness. He'd waited two days before saying anything to General Berg. One of the maxims he'd scrupulously stuck to since the early days of the war was to never tell all he knew until he was sure it was all he would receive. Otherwise there was a danger his imagination would take over and lead him down a detour that could mean life-or-death consequences for the men in the division.

No one moved between the buildings. No dogs barked. The company of select infantry supported by a machine gun and mortar unit held the element of surprise. Franz took a deep breath.

"Remember, the stone barn with the thatched roof is the primary target," he said.

"I see it," Oberst Gottfried replied irritably.

The senior officer motioned with his right hand, and one of four privates assigned to him as runners ran up.

"Begin the attack," he said.

The soldier left. Less than a minute later Franz heard the muffled retort caused by a mortar. He and Gottfried watched as a puff of smoke and tiny flash of light marked where the mortar shell had landed. Others quickly followed. They peppered the open ground in front of the barn. Franz heard the colonel mutter impatiently as the soldiers adjusted the trajectory of the shells. By the time the battery fired a second volley, at least twenty men, some carrying rifles, were running from the barn.

Gottfried swore. "We had them trapped, and they're getting away."

He summoned a second soldier. "Tell

Hauptmann Kolb to send in the infantry."

Franz looked to the places where soldiers lay waiting to attack the village from three directions. It was a risky strategy because of cross fire, but it was the only way to try to trap and destroy the unit of French resistance fighters who had been harassing military rail shipments and ambushing isolated patrols for the past few weeks. Franz could see the soldiers moving quickly from the shelter of the trees toward the buildings. The crackle of small arms fire reached their ears on the small hill. Gottfried called over another private.

"I want the name of every man in the mortar unit," the colonel said to the enlisted man. He then growled at Franz, "They should have covered three times as much ground with their initial salvo."

Franz didn't respond. His job for the day was to provide information about the target and the enemy forces they faced, not implement a battle plan. Now he was nothing more than an observer. However, both he and Oberst Gottfried knew that General Berg would ask Franz to debrief him when Franz returned to headquarters. Field commanders both welcomed and hated the sight of Franz.

Franz raised the binoculars that hung

around his neck. Bodies of German soldiers and French fighters lay on the ground. The sight of battlefield death had sickened him when he first saw the carnage of war four years earlier during the invasion of Belgium. And he'd never gotten used to it. Over the next few minutes the sound of gunshots slowed before finally stopping. A soldier ran up to their position and saluted.

"The town is secured, Herr Oberst," he said with a smart salute.

"Prisoners?" Gottfried asked.

"Yes, sir. Almost twenty."

"Excellent. Bring my vehicle."

An armored car sputtered onto the ridge and they got in. In combat situations many officers preferred the protection of a vehicle with a machine gun on a turret. They rumbled down the hill and onto the narrow road leading into the village. Franz counted the bodies of four German soldiers and six French fighters. Several German soldiers were receiving treatment at a hastily constructed medical tent on the outskirts of town. They reached the center of the village. A group of forlorn and dejected-looking Frenchmen, some wounded, sat or lay huddled on the ground surrounded by guards with automatic rifles. The car stopped, and Oberst Gottfried got out.

"Stay here," he said to Franz. "And keep your head down in case there's a sniper. I don't want to report your death to General Berg."

Franz cautiously eyed the blank windows of the houses surrounding the center of town. Suddenly he heard the sound of a gunshot and a puff of dirt appeared at Gottfried's feet. The colonel was quickly hustled back inside the armored car while a squad of soldiers rushed into a nearby house.

"Did you see that coming and neglect to tell me?" Gottfried asked Franz, his eyes blazing.

"No, Herr Oberst."

A few minutes later the soldiers emerged from the house dragging what appeared to be a ten- or eleven-year-old boy between them. A woman, who Franz guessed was the boy's mother, was crying and screaming. They brought the boy up to the armored car, and a sergeant showed Gottfried an antique hunting rifle.

"He fired the shot, and he's proud of it, sir," the sergeant said.

"Put him with the men," Gottfried said.

"He's only a boy," Franz objected.

"When he fired that shot, he became a resistance fighter," Gottfried replied brusquely. "And he'll share their fate."

While Franz watched, the sergeant dragged the boy over to the group and threw him to the ground. A man who'd been wounded in the shoulder came over to the youngster. Franz could see the family resemblance of father and son. The father began to berate his son in rapid French until one of the guards ordered them to be quiet. The father then put his good arm around his son, who was now crying. The boy's mother continued to wail from the doorstep of the house.

"Hauptmann Haus," Gottfried said. "You're no longer needed here. A jeep will return you to General Berg's headquarters."

While they waited for the jeep, there was a commotion in the direction of a side street, and several soldiers appeared with another group of ten or twelve teenage boys walking in front of them. Franz saw two girls in the group as well. A soldier from the group came over to the armored car.

"We found them hiding in an outbuilding behind the barn," he said.

"Did they have any weapons?" Franz asked.

"They were near the barn," Gottfried replied, giving Franz a cold look. "That was the target you identified. And young fighters are just as dangerous as older ones. We lost two men last month who were killed by a woman hiding a grenade in a handbag."

"But Herr Oberst —" Franz began.

Gottfried turned his back to Franz and began speaking to another officer. The jeep arrived, and the oberst faced Franz.

"Hauptmann Haus," Gottfried said, "give my regards to General Berg. I'll include your vital contribution to this successful operation in my report."

Glancing one last time at the group of men, boys, and two girls now seated in the center of the village, Franz got in the jeep. When they neared the turnoff for the observation point, he touched the driver on the arm.

"Private, take me to the top of the hill for a moment."

The driver slowed to a stop but stayed in the middle of the road. "Oberst Gottfried ordered me to take you directly to headquarters, sir."

"Where I will tell General Berg you disobeyed a command if you don't do as I say."

The driver jerked the wheel of the jeep to the left and they drove to the hilltop. Franz got out and raised the binoculars to his eyes. He could see the group of resistance fighters moving down the road in the direction of the barn. The coming execution of members of the French Underground was as certain as the death of the German soldiers the French fighters ambushed along the roadways. But the presence of the teenage boys and the two girls greatly troubled Franz. Oberst Gottfried followed the group of prisoners in his armored car. When they reached the barn, the soldiers herded the captured fighters inside. Franz saw the man hold the hand of his son as they passed through the double doors together. The other boys also entered the barn. At the last second, a sergeant pulled the two girls from the group and made them stand across the barnyard. Franz could no longer see the mother of the boy who'd fired the shot at Gottfried.

When all of the men and boys were inside the barn, a soldier closed the doors and placed a metal rod through the handles to lock them in. He stepped back, and two other soldiers came forward with something Franz couldn't see in their hands. A few seconds later they were holding torches that slowly flickered to life. Franz suddenly felt sick to his stomach.

The two soldiers looked at each other, nodded, and simultaneously tossed their torches onto the thatched roof of the barn. Flames quickly shot up from the dry, densely packed grass. The faint sound of shouts drifted across the fields surrounding the village and up the hill to the place where Franz watched. As the flames grew higher, the shouts turned to screams. The smell of smoke began to reach the hilltop. Soldiers fired shots at the windows of the barn as men and boys tried to jump out.

Franz had seen more than enough. He got in the jeep and left.

Frank involuntarily jerked in his bed as the memory of long-ago flames shot through his mind in a searing nightmare. He sat bolt upright, breathing heavily. The smoke no longer lingered except in the crevices of his soul. For a few moments he tried to remember the name of the village with the burning barn, but he quickly gave up. Nothing could be undone.

At 8:00 a.m., Frank got out of bed. It had been over a year since his last nightmare, and he suspected the trigger for the latest installment was the visit from Conrad Mueller. Needing to banish the apprehensive melancholy of the previous evening and the harsh memories that jerked him awake, Frank brewed a pot of coffee and sat on the porch sipping a cup. Within a few hours Conrad Mueller would be on a plane leaving town. Hopefully the dark memories his presence awakened would go with him.

The sound of an approaching vehicle on his driveway caused Frank to sit up straight. He knew who it was. Mueller had caught a cab and was returning with more questions Frank didn't want to answer. Frank shuffled into the living room and peeked through the window near the front door. Cowardly as it might be, he could always hide in his bedroom and not answer the doorbell.

It was Lenny.

Most people equate mistake with failure, but relief washed over Frank that he was wrong. What had once been an accurate, precise ability to see into the unseen and witness what would happen in the future had been dulled by age and neglect. And he was glad. He held open the door for his friend, who'd parked his truck beneath the low-spreading branches of a live oak tree that stood as a sentinel in the front yard.

"I didn't want you to head downriver without me," Lenny said as he climbed the steps.

"I thought Mattie had chores for you to do."

"Her sister from Buxton is driving over for a visit, so I was only going to be in the way." Lenny pointed at the sky. "And on a

116

day like this, is there anything better to do on God's earth than cruise to Oriental? I thought we might even stick our nose into the Sound."

Frank hesitated. "I don't know . . ."

"What?" Lenny asked in surprise. "Are you sick?"

"No."

"What are you going to do all day? Your house stays neater than ours when Mattie and I finish mopping the kitchen and vacuuming the carpets. I'll pay for the gas."

"You always pay for the gas because we use my boat."

"And I want you to appreciate my generosity."

Lenny pushed past Frank into the living room. "Any coffee left?" he asked. "I brought my travel mug just in case. I don't understand why people stand in line to pay five bucks for a cup of burnt coffee when they can get the real thing for pennies. Did you grind the beans this morning?"

"Left over from yesterday."

"Still better than anything I could get in downtown New Bern."

Frank led the way into the kitchen while Lenny continued to chatter. It had taken Frank years to adjust to the random thoughts that poured out of gregarious

Americans. For Lenny, talking was a by-product of breathing.

"How was your fish dinner last night?" Lenny asked. "Mattie kissed both my cheeks just like you Europeans do after she tasted the fish. Did you fillet yours?"

"Yes, and I fixed okra and tomatoes with some of the okra you gave me. Parker ate with me" — Frank paused — "and brought someone with him."

"The dark-haired girl he dated when he was in law school?" Lenny asked. "Mattie was asking me about her the other day. Didn't she get a job in Raleigh with some kind of marketing company? The girl has a great personality. I don't think she's ever met a stranger."

"It wasn't Catelyn," Frank said as he refilled his own cup of coffee. "They haven't dated in months."

Lenny veered off onto another subject, the dating adventures of Chris, his youngest son who had followed in his father's footsteps as a firefighter. Lenny liked Chris's current girlfriend, but Mattie wasn't so sure. Frank and Lenny went out to the shed and began putting together the tackle for the day. Frank let Lenny talk, which allowed him to keep his mouth shut.

"I have a couple of rods in the back of my

truck," Lenny said. "Including a stiff stick in case we go after any larger drum still hanging around."

They loaded everything into the back of Lenny's truck. It could be windy on the water even on a clear day, and Frank brought an insulated windbreaker. Leaving the house, they stopped at a bait shop that also sold prepackaged sandwiches, which nobody but a fisherman would eat. They filled their cooler with ice and fresh mullet and shrimp for bait and drove to the dock.

"So, who did Parker bring to supper last night?" Lenny asked as he lifted the cooler from the rear of the truck. "You never did tell me."

Frank put on the floppy hat he used to protect his head from the sun and leaned against the side of the truck. "A man I knew during the war."

"Really?" Lenny raised his eyebrows. "I want to hear about that."

Parker spent his morning grinding out research in one of Greg's cases and proofreading a commercial lease for Dexter. Shortly before noon, he heard Greg talking to Vicki. Getting up to stretch his legs, Parker stepped from his office and went up to his boss, who was standing at the receptionist's desk flipping through messages.

"How did the motion hearing go in the Mitchell case?" Parker asked, referring to litigation for which he'd written the brief.

Greg glanced up but ignored him while he read two more messages. He handed one of the slips back to Vicki.

"Call Mr. Chet Ferguson and schedule an initial appointment as soon as possible," he said, holding up one of the slips of paper. "I don't want to miss a chance to grab his case if he's going down a list of lawyers to interview."

"Already done," Vicki replied with satisfaction. "He'll be here at one o'clock."

"Nice," Greg replied with a smile before turning to Parker. "Would you like to sit in on the interview? This could be huge."

"Sure. What's it about?"

"Wrongful death of his wife. She was hit by a drunk driver."

"Any kids?" Parker managed.

"A daughter, age eight, was in the backseat," Vicki replied. "She was banged up but not seriously injured."

"Except for the psychological trauma of seeing her mother killed," Greg added. "You can see why I want to get the father in as soon as possible. Every personal injury lawyer from here to Raleigh would salivate over a claim like this."

CHAPTER 9

Frank and Lenny anchored at the mouth of a small creek and ate lunch on the boat. A breeze blowing up from the Sound kept the insects at bay and served as free air-conditioning on their faces. Lenny took a long drink of water.

"So would you like to give the Sound a try?" he asked.

"Yeah, we brought the bait and tackle. And it can't be worse than our luck this morning."

They'd caught a few small fish that they threw back to grow bigger. Lenny pinched off a piece of bread and dropped it into the water. It floated away in the current until it was about fifteen feet from the boat and then disappeared as a fish swirled to the surface and inhaled it.

"Maybe we should switch to dough balls," he said, pointing to the ripples left by the fish.

"That's what I used to do with Parker when he was little," Frank replied. "He'd be extra careful to mash the bread around his hook to hide it. He's always wanted to do things perfectly."

Lenny took a bite of his sandwich. "Who'd he get that from?" Lenny asked with a smile.

Frank grunted. "May he only inherit the little good that's in me and none of the bad."

Sitting in the boat as it gently rocked in the current, Frank watched the sun sparkle on the water.

"Tell me more about the fellow who ate supper with you and Parker last night," Lenny said.

Frank's chest suddenly tightened. He put his hand on his heart and took a deep breath, but the pressure didn't go away.

"Are you okay?" Lenny asked.

Frank took a couple more deep breaths and sighed three times. The tightness finally lifted.

"I think so," he replied. "It felt like there was a band wrapped around my chest for a few seconds."

"Let's go back," Lenny said, quickly screwing the top on his water bottle. "We don't need to go all the way to the Sound. It's not a good idea to —"

"Be too far from the hospital in case I keel

over with a heart attack," Frank said, finishing the thought. "We're already pretty far from civilization, but I'm going to be okay."

Lenny didn't look convinced, so Frank pulled the key from the ignition and put it in his pocket.

"There, we're only going where I want to go," Frank said.

"If the pain comes back —" Lenny began.

"I'll let you know and you can drive the boat."

"Okay." Lenny settled back in his seat.

Frank took another sip of water. "My visitor was a private assigned to my unit toward the end of the war. He grew up in Kiel, a coastal city in northern Germany on the Baltic."

"And he came all the way from Germany to see you?" Lenny's eyes widened.

"Yeah."

"Why?"

"He wanted to thank me for saving his life." Frank briefly told Lenny about the wartime advice he'd given Mueller.

"War is hell, and I'm not pretending to be a good guy," Frank said as he finished. "People watch documentary shows on TV or go to movies and think they have an idea what it was like." He stopped as he remembered the fiery barn and distant screams.

"But they don't."

"You don't have to convince me," Lenny replied. "I know exactly what you mean, especially when it comes to the smells."

The two men finished eating their sandwiches in silence. Lenny reached over and put the wrapper from Frank's sandwich in the small trash bag they kept in the boat.

"For years, what bothered me the most about my time in Vietnam was a nagging fear that I'd killed one of my own guys by mistake in the middle of a firefight when bullets were flying everywhere and people were running all over the place. I don't know for sure that it happened, but I couldn't shake the thought that it did. You know, a man who's been in combat can go nuts if he lives it over and over again."

"Do you still think about the battles?" Frank asked.

"Not the same way."

"Why not?"

"I've asked God to forgive my sins, even those I'm not sure I committed. When the old guilty thoughts dance around the edges of my mind, I tell them to beat it. Ultimately, the power of life and death isn't in my hands anyway; it's in his."

Lenny spoke with conviction, but his words didn't make sense to Frank. Sometimes German logic and American reasoning didn't follow the same path.

"I'm not sure," Frank replied, shaking his head. "And I don't want to try to convince myself of something unless I know it's true."

"You're making it depend on you," Lenny replied gently. "It doesn't work that way. God reaches out; you respond. It's a lot like keeping your hook in the water even if the fish haven't been biting. Just be ready when they do."

Frank didn't say anything. He took the key from his pocket and placed it in the ignition. Starting the motor, he turned the boat into the wind.

"Let's run down to the Sound," he said.

Most days Parker didn't go out for lunch but worked while eating at his desk. Today he spent the time before the scheduled meeting with Mr. Ferguson reviewing the possible causes for a wrongful death action in a drunk-driving case. He'd received nothing from the death of his parents. The man who hit them didn't have insurance and lived in a dilapidated shack in a poor part of town.

Vicki buzzed Parker's office. "Mr. Ferguson is here," she said.

Parker took a last glance at the photo of

his parents on his credenza. Beside it was a picture of Parker and his grandfather on the *Aare.* The photo was taken the summer after Parker graduated from high school when he worked as a deckhand on the boat. It had been a time of bonding in common grief for both of them, and an opportunity for salt breezes to touch their faces and the winds of healing to blow over their souls.

"Let's go," Greg said when Parker approached Vicki's desk. "Don't say anything. I only want you there to give the impression that Ferguson is hiring a law firm, not just a lawyer."

"Just be pretty," Vicki said with a smile.

"That comes naturally," Parker replied with a wink.

He followed Greg downstairs to the main floor where Chet Ferguson was waiting in the conference room. Before opening the door, Greg turned again to Parker and put his index finger to his lips. The potential client was standing at the end of the long table staring at a bookcase partially filled with legal books that were becoming obsolete with the advent of computer research.

"Mr. Ferguson," Greg said brightly when they entered. "I'm Greg Branham, and this is one of our associate lawyers, Parker House."

Chet Ferguson turned around. He was in his midthirties with sandy hair and blue eyes. His broad shoulders revealed a man who worked out at the gym. He pressed his lips together and stepped forward to shake their hands. His grip was firm, and he looked directly into Parker's eyes in a way that was unsettling.

"Have a seat," Greg said to Ferguson. "Thanks for contacting our firm to discuss your situation."

"I have a stack of letters from scores of lawyers wanting to represent me," Ferguson replied. He then pointed at Parker. "But doing my own research I saw that you were working here and remembered what happened to your parents several years ago. I figured you'd understand better than anyone what my family is going through."

Parker's jaw dropped open. "I don't remember meeting you," he said.

"You didn't. But I was one of the EMTs that responded to the accident when your parents were killed. I wanted to come to the funeral, but I had to work and couldn't get off."

Greg shifted his attention back and forth from Ferguson to Parker as they talked. He cleared his throat and spoke.

"Uh, I've brought Parker in at this early

stage because he's uniquely qualified to assist in your case."

"I believe that," Ferguson replied, opening a manila folder he had in his right hand. "Here's a copy of the accident report."

Frank and Lenny had an uneventful run along the western edge of Pamlico Sound, which at eighty miles long and thirty miles wide was the largest lagoon on the East Coast. Most of the large red drum fish had already spawned and returned to the ocean on the other side of the Outer Banks, but there was a chance stragglers remained, and Lenny was a determined angler. After several hours, Frank stowed his rod and patiently waited for Lenny to give up.

"One more cast to starboard, Captain," Lenny said, reeling in his line. "I've got a good feeling about this one."

Frank began putting items away in a storage bin. He glanced up as Lenny cast the bait, let it sink, and began his retrieve. Within forty-five seconds his pole suddenly bent sharply forward.

"Fish on!" he cried out.

Frank stopped and watched as the fish stripped line off Lenny's reel. The Sound had a reputation for the best red drum fishing in the world, and a skillful angler could catch a fish over forty inches long and weighing fifty pounds or more. Frank peered across the water and then examined the bend in Lenny's rod.

"It's a big one," he said.

"My arms are telling me that," Lenny responded, leaning backward against the pull of the fish. "Can you fire up the boat and help me out a little bit?"

Frank started the motor and slowly maneuvered the boat to keep steady pressure on the fish. When there was a momentary lapse in the fight, Lenny managed to crank a few rounds on the reel. Twenty minutes later a swirl in the water beside the boat gave them their first glimpse of their prey. Frank reached into the bottom of the boat for a large net at the end of an aluminum pole.

"Bring him back around to port, and I'll try to net him," Frank said. "But I'm not sure I can bring him into the boat without help."

"I need to do more push-ups," Lenny grunted. "This is supposed to be fun, but my arms are about to fall off."

It took two tries to get the fish into a good position for Frank to scoop it with the net. Together they lifted the gleaming silver fish into the boat. It was a mature adult with only a hint of reddish color on its side.

"Wow," Lenny said. "Let's measure and weigh him."

Lenny held up the fish, and Frank took out a tape measure. It was forty-three inches long. Suspended from a handheld scale, the fish weighed slightly over fifty-five pounds.

"How old do you think he is?" Lenny asked.

"At least thirty years old, maybe closer to forty," Frank replied.

Frank took several pictures of the fish with a waterproof camera they kept on the boat before they lowered the fish into the water. Lenny held it between his hands while the brackish water of the Sound washed over its gills. After a few moments passed, the fish swished its tail twice and moved away with easy grace.

"Was it a successful day on the water?" Lenny asked, looking up.

"Yes." Frank nodded.

"Like I said earlier, sometimes you have to leave the hook in the water a long time before you catch the big fish," Lenny said with a grin.

Parker made two trips up and down the stairs to bring paperwork for Chet Ferguson to sign.

"What if the insurance company for the driver agrees to pay the policy limits without having to file suit?" Ferguson asked after reading the standard form contingency fee contract Greg placed in front of him. "Will you still charge a twenty-five percent attorney fee if all you have to do is send a demand letter?"

"We never know what's involved in a case," Greg replied confidently. "The contingency fee protects you from paying us a bunch of money if things get complicated and we have to spend hundreds of hours on the file. You don't get billed for that time."

Ferguson pushed the agreement away from him. "I'll take my chances on an hourly rate up to the point of filing suit, then switch to a contingency fee if the insurance company refuses to pay the policy limits."

Parker could see the veins in Greg's neck stand out.

"There's also the possibility of a dramshop claim," Parker interjected. "From what you told us, Mr. Drew admitted to the officer on the scene that he left the Calloway Club fifteen minutes before the accident. If it was obvious that Drew was intoxicated, the bartender should have stopped serving him liquor."

"I can sue the tavern?" Ferguson asked.

"Yes, that's a possibility," Greg replied, cutting his eyes toward Parker. "But those cases can be hard to prove."

Ferguson paused for a moment. "Why don't we do that case on a contingency basis and the claim against Drew's insurance company on an hourly basis?"

Greg hesitated for a moment. "Are you prepared to pay a five-thousand-dollar deposit in the case against the driver's insurance company?"

"Yes. Jessica had a small life insurance policy, and the company sent me a check last week."

"And if there's anything left, that money can help defray out-of-pocket costs in the dramshop case," Parker added.

"That sounds fair to me," Ferguson replied.

"It will take more than that to finance the litigation against the Calloway Club," Greg said, shaking his head.

"Just let me know so we discuss and make a wise decision," Ferguson responded. "I want to be fair to you and Parker."

"Okay," Greg replied and then turned to Parker. "Take the agreement upstairs to Dolly so she can modify it to include the dramshop claim."

"What hourly rate shall I put down for the liability case?" he asked.

"The usual for both of us," Greg answered, pointing his thumb toward the ceiling.

Five minutes later Parker returned with the modified documents, which Ferguson signed. The firm was now representing Chet Ferguson and the Estate of Jessica Ferguson against both Walter Drew and the Calloway Club.

"This will also cover the claims of your daughter, Candace," Greg said as Ferguson signed the documents.

"Does Josiah have a case?" Ferguson asked, referring to his ten-year-old son, who was at home with his father when the wreck occurred.

Greg glanced at Parker, who gave him an imperceptible shake of the head.

"No," Greg replied.

"That would occur only if you and Jessica were divorced and the court didn't allow you to proceed on behalf of your wife's estate," Parker added. "In that case, another person like a grandparent might take over."

Ferguson didn't react, but Parker knew he'd touched a sensitive nerve.

"Thanks for coming in," Greg said, standing up. "We'll get right to work."

"I'll drop off a check for the five-thousand-dollar deposit tomorrow afternoon," Ferguson replied.

After Ferguson left, Greg and Parker went upstairs in silence.

"Come into my office," Greg said when they reached the landing.

Not sure what to expect, Parker followed the senior partner into his office.

CHAPTER 10

Lenny tied off the boat when they reached the dock.

"How many pictures are left on that camera?" he asked. "That red drum grew bigger and bigger in my mind on the way back from the Sound, and I don't want my head to explode."

Frank retrieved the camera from the console. "We've taken twenty-two photos, which means two are left," he said. "I think we started using this camera on the trip when we caught a bunch of speckled trout."

"That was last year!" Lenny exclaimed. "The camera may be waterproof, but salt water eventually gets into everything. Give it to me, and I'll pay the developing fee. I also want to have proof to back up my bragging about the flounder I hooked a few months ago near the rock jetty."

"Suit yourself," Frank replied, handing the camera to his friend. "But I'll recognize the fish I caught. The flounder I landed at the sandbar near Little Creek was the biggest one of the season."

"That was a fantastic fish," Lenny admitted. "I'll get double prints. I want to put my hand on the photo of your flounder and ask the Lord to let me catch a bigger one."

Frank handed the gear from the boat to Lenny, who stood on the dock. After they loaded everything into the bed of Lenny's truck, they drove to Frank's house.

"Do you want me to help you put away the tackle in your shed?" Lenny asked as he pulled into the driveway.

"No thanks. I'll take my time and do it myself," Frank replied.

"How are you feeling?"

"Okay. Seeing you catch that big drum was medicine to my soul."

"If you decide you want to go to church Sunday for a real dose of soul medicine, let me know," Lenny said. "Mattie will let you come to the house for Sunday dinner as a reward."

"That's tempting," Frank answered. "If I decide to come, I'll let you know."

Parker sat across from Greg's desk and steeled himself for the explosion he knew was coming. He was about to find out how he would react when his boss yelled at him. Greg stared at him for several seconds and let him inwardly squirm.

"Well done," Greg said after several more moments passed.

"What do you mean?" Parker managed.

"You convinced Chet Ferguson to trust us faster than I would have thought possible. From here on out, he'll go along with my recommendations without raising a whimper."

"How can you be so sure?" Parker asked, mystified.

"Give me some credit for experience and instinct," Greg replied, pointing his finger at Parker's chest. "Time will prove me right."

"You're not mad about having to take the liability claim on an hourly basis?"

"For about two seconds. One essential trait of a trial lawyer is the ability to adapt in the moment. We had to pivot, and capturing the dramshop case was the reward. What made you think about that?"

"It came to mind during lunch. Have you handled one before?"

"No, so there will be a learning curve for both of us. But it's not that complicated. Ferguson likes you, so I'm going to keep you in the center of the storm. Begin by drafting a demand letter for policy limits from the driver's insurance company. I bet they'll roll over and surrender without a fight. We'll make sure Mr. Drew isn't independently wealthy before we cut him loose. I'm glad you picked up on my signal to put our highest hourly rate in the contract. Your input for the jury in the Nichols case was on target. Now this. We're beginning to flow together."

Five minutes later Parker left Greg's office not sure if he felt good or bad about getting in the flow with his boss.

Even though it was Saturday, Parker went into the office early to bill a few hours before leaving for the wedding of a friend from high school. The word *weekend* wasn't in an associate attorney's vocabulary, and he worked diligently through lunch until he put memos on both Greg's and Dexter's desks. After straightening up his office, he returned home to shower and put on a suit and tie. The wedding was at a popular waterfront location on the Neuse River. Parker saw Creston Keller entering the lot and waited for his friend to pull in beside him.

When they were in high school, Creston had been a track star. Now, in addition to teaching math, algebra, and geometry, he coached the boys' and girls' cross-country teams at their alma mater. Shorter than Parker, he had a lean, wiry build and closely cut black hair. The largest muscles in his body were his heart and his calves.

"Where's Catelyn?" Creston asked when they got out of their cars. "I thought you were going to invite her to the wedding so you could reignite her romantic feelings for you."

"We're done by mutual agreement," Parker replied. "Now my only goal in life is to be your wingman."

"Unselfish is your new middle name. But you're too late to protect me. I have a date tonight with a woman I met the other day during a training run with the boys' team from school. She was very impressed that I wanted to invest my life in molding young men."

"What impressed you about her?"

"Her 1600-meter time, of course. I took her word for it, but I'm looking forward to timing her myself."

They walked along a short path to a large open-air pavilion surrounded by lush grass and flowering plants. Rows of white chairs were set up for the guests, and an arch covered with fresh flowers embellished the front. A massive three-tier wedding cake rested on a round table in the middle of a gazebo to the right of the pavilion.

"That's a bigger cake than the one at Chip's first wedding," Creston said in a low voice, pointing it out to Parker.

"Yeah, I hope this marriage will last."

"That wasn't Chip's fault. Hillary left him."

Parker had heard other reasons for the breakup, but to talk about it at the moment seemed like bad luck.

"Anyway, Chip is happy," he said. "And Kelsey is a cool girl. We hung out a few weeks ago at his aunt's place on the Intracoastal Waterway. Kelsey is laid-back, which is what he needs. Hillary was as amped up as Chip."

"If opposites attract, does that mean I shouldn't ask out a girl who's a runner?"

"You're weird enough that any girl is going to be your opposite."

Creston laughed and punched Parker in the arm. Two other high school classmates joined them, and they made their way to seats on the groom's side of the gathering. Chip had a lot of relatives, and the space was filling up rapidly.

The wedding music, provided by a violin, flute, and cello trio, began and the crowd grew quiet. Chip, his best man, the minister, and four groomsmen stepped to the front. To the left of the group, Parker saw the wedding photographer, crouching down to take pictures.

It was Layla Donovan.

The blond photographer was wearing gray slacks and a light blue top. Her hair was pulled away from her face in a long braided ponytail. She held a large black camera in her hands with another slung over her shoulder. The designer-frame glasses she'd worn during the trial were gone. Parker watched as she moved gracefully across the front of the pavilion snapping photos of the groom's party. If she wasn't so attractive, she would have blended into the background. The music shifted, and the bridesmaids began to walk down the aisle. Parker nudged Creston.

"Do you see the blond photographer?" he whispered.

"Uh, yeah. Who hasn't been eyeing her?"

"She was on the jury for a case our firm tried this week."

All conversation ended as they stood for the entrance of the bride. Parker had a good view of Chip's face, and his friend looked down the aisle with the excited anticipation reserved for grooms at the altar. Parker didn't get a good look at Kelsey as she passed, but her father was a large man with a thick neck and a full head of gray hair. Layla Donovan snapped pictures until the bride reached the flowery arch. She then slipped to a corner where she still had a clear view of the couple over the minister's shoulder.

Since he'd graduated from high school, Parker had been to so many weddings that he considered himself an expert. He liked this one because it wasn't drawn out with a bunch of extra songs, the minister's remarks were succinct, and the wedding vows stuck to the traditional script. Throughout the service, Parker kept glancing at Layla Donovan until she moved to the rear in preparation for the newly joined couple's walk down the aisle.

"When you come to a wedding, do you think about what you'd like to include in your ceremony?" Creston asked Parker when everyone stood.

Parker eyed his friend suspiciously.

"That's all I need to know," Creston said and held up his hand. "The answer is yes."

They made their way to a large open area behind the chairs that would soon become the dance floor after a band finished setting up. The wedding party and the photographer returned to the front of the room for more pictures. Parker left his friends and eased over to a spot where he could watch. Layla Donovan orchestrated the group like a conductor, which didn't surprise him since she'd done the same thing with the jury. Completely focused on her work, Layla didn't notice Parker watching her. When she finished and the wedding party moved toward the open area, Parker approached her as she was scrolling through her pictures.

"Hi," Parker said, clearing his throat.

The photographer looked up, and Parker saw her eyes had a greenish tint. Her fingernails were the same bright red as on the day of the trial.

"I'm Parker House. I was one of the lawyers who represented Benjamin Nichols in the case against the lumber company. You're Layla Donovan, right?"

"Yes." The photographer eyed him closely. "But I don't remember you."

"I'm an associate and was only there for voir dire. But I told the partner trying the case to make sure he left you on the jury."

"And you want me to thank you?" she asked, raising her eyebrows. "I made twenty-five dollars sitting there all day when I had four hundred photos to edit sitting in my computer for a job that was past due."

"No, no. I want to thank you. And I'm sorry about the inconvenience, although having you on the jury made a huge difference for our client."

"He deserved justice, even if your boss did as much to hurt his case as he did to help it."

Parker cringed. He didn't automatically feel the need to defend Greg, but it hurt to hear a sharp, stinging critique.

"I'd like to hear what worked and what didn't."

"And you want me to tell you now?"

Parker suspected the photographer had a strong personality. However, he had a persistent streak of his own.

"I know you're working now, but the jury reached a verdict so quickly that I'm sure you have insights that would be helpful to hear."

The photographer eyed him a second time. "Fair enough. Are you going to stay until the bride and groom ride off in a limo for a lifetime of marital bliss?"

Parker had planned on leaving sooner but immediately changed his plans.

"Yes," he replied.

"Okay. I'll see you then."

Layla moved to the side of the pavilion and began snapping pictures of the guests.

Parker returned to his friends.

"What's up with the photographer?" Creston asked.

"Remember, I told you she was on a jury in a case our firm handled earlier this week. I'm doing follow-up research. We're going to talk later."

"Research?"

"Yes, that's what lawyers do with jurors so we can learn what works and what doesn't."

"Right," Creston replied with a skeptical look and moved away toward the food table. "I'm going to hit the shrimp before the other sharks start a feeding frenzy."

As with most weddings, the celebration dragged on much longer than the ceremony. Thankfully, the hors d'oeuvres were top-notch. Creston could consume an enormous quantity of shrimp. Parker preferred tiny crab cakes with rémoulade sauce. Together with their other friends, they plowed diligently through the food offerings.

"My grandfather uses shrimp as bait," Parker said when Creston returned carrying a third plate of pink shrimp with a large dollop of cocktail sauce in the middle.

"Which is why it would be a mistake to invite me on a fishing trip. I'd eat the bait." Creston ate a plump shrimp and a blissful look crossed his face. "If Kelsey's father has another daughter, I'd like an invitation to her wedding too. He knows how to do it right."

The band began to play, and after the obligatory dances by the newlyweds and their parents, the younger guests crowded onto the dance floor. At one point, Parker ended up facing one of Chip's cousins, an eight-year-old girl with braces on her teeth who was amazingly coordinated. Once, when he spun her around, he glanced up and saw Layla Donovan snapping their picture. Finally, Chip and Kelsey received a send-off in the early evening through a tunnel of sparklers.

"Ready to go?" Creston asked Parker. "I have a stack of papers to grade before going out on my date, but you could talk me out of it with just about any suggestion for something to do."

"Remember, I'm meeting with the photographer to talk about the jury." Parker gestured toward Layla, who was getting a few last shots.

"How long is that going to take?"

"I don't know." Parker smiled. "But if you need an excuse to take the rest of the day off, I can certify that anyone who sweats like you do when you dance is in no shape to grade math papers. You'll need to take an extra-long shower before picking up Runner Girl."

Creston put his finger on Parker's chest. "Next wedding, I'm going to challenge you to a dance-off."

Creston left, and Parker held back while Layla continued to take pictures. When she finished, he walked over to her. She was standing beside a round table covered with dirty plates.

"Would you like to go someplace and talk?" he asked. "There's a coffee shop not far —"

"No, let's sit here," she cut in. "A piece of wedding cake is calling my name."

Parker sat down and moved some plates out of the way. Layla returned with a thick slab of wedding cake on a clear plastic plate.

"It's crazy, but I love this stuff," she said, plopping down in the chair. "I usually max out my quota of sweets for the week in one sitting if I have a wedding on the books."

The photographer seemed more relaxed now that her work was complete. She took a big bite of the cake that Parker had found dry.

"Do you want something to drink?" he asked. "A water?"

Her mouth full, Layla nodded. Parker went to an ice bucket and grabbed one of the last remaining bottles of water and handed it to her. She opened it and took a long drink.

"Thanks," she said. "I got a good photo of you dancing with the little girl. Who is she?"

Parker told her. Layla took another bite of cake that she chased with a sip of water.

"Was the cake this dry when you ate it?" she asked.

Parker nodded. Layla sighed and pushed her cake plate next to the other dirty dishes.

"All right," she said. "You want to know the secret to persuading a jury to rule in your favor?"

"Not exactly. I'm not expecting you to —"

"Remember how you felt when you were dancing with the little girl?" Layla interrupted.

"Huh?"

"What were you thinking about?"

Parker paused. "Making sure she was having fun."

"Were you self-conscious because you were dancing with a child?"

"No."

"I agree, and the camera, which doesn't lie, will confirm it. You were acting naturally while focused on someone else, not yourself and your performance. That's what will work with a jury. The jury knows you're there to represent your client. You don't have to convince them of that. But if they think your goal is to help them understand the case so they can do the right thing, it will go a long way toward building the kind of trust you want them to feel toward you and, vicariously, your client. Greg what's-his-name spent so much time preening and strutting around the courtroom that it became almost laughable. However, the defense lawyer was so snooty and arrogant that it was a draw as far as the lawyers were concerned."

Parker realized his mouth was hanging open, and he quickly closed it. Layla was brutally accurate in her analysis of Greg.

"You're right about Greg," he said with a shrug, "but I don't think I can put that in a memo to him."

"Too bad. He's got a bulldog personality that could work if he channeled it as a humble champion." Layla paused and checked her watch. "Anything else you want to ask me?"

"Yes. How did you convince the other jurors to go along with you so quickly? I know you took notes during the trial."

"I didn't bully them, if that's what you're asking. I did the same thing I'm suggesting to you. I came in with an attitude to help, and they appreciated it. Once we decided who was most likely telling the truth, the result was clear, and everybody signed off on it."

Listening to her, Parker realized that the insightful photographer could be a helpful resource for the law firm in the future.

"Would you be willing to critique the lawyers in our firm and evaluate our witnesses when we're preparing for trial in the future? Kind of a one-person mock jury. You'd be paid, of course."

"No," Layla said as she shook her head. "If I wanted to be involved in the courtroom on a regular basis, I would have gone to law school."

Layla stood up and brushed a stray strand of hair from her face. Confident he could pry more information from the photographer, Parker wasn't ready to part ways.

"Would you like to go out to dinner with me?" he blurted out and then watched Layla's eyes widen in surprise.

"Why?" she asked.

"Uh, I know a place that has really good cake for dessert."

CHAPTER 11

As he prepared for his date with Layla Donovan, Parker tried to decide if the meeting was more professional or personal. There was certainly more Layla could reveal about the inner workings of the jury, and he hadn't given up hope that she might reconsider serving as a low-level consultant for the law firm. Greg needed the help. On the other hand, the blond photographer was very attractive, and even if a dominant, opinionated woman wasn't normally his type, Parker was interested in learning more about her.

Layla insisted they meet at the restaurant, so instead of picking her up and finding out where she lived, Parker pulled into the sandy parking lot at 7:30 p.m. and went inside. Layla hadn't arrived. While he waited, Parker read the special entrées written on a blackboard in brightly colored chalk surrounded by freehand art. He was standing there when Layla walked through the door wearing a yellow-and-blue dress with a camera slung over her shoulder. Her hair hung down her back. With sandaled heels on her feet, her nose was level with his chin.

"Is this a working dinner?" Parker asked.

"Yes." Layla patted the camera. "Strictly professional."

His question answered, Parker followed Layla as the hostess led them to a table for two in a quiet corner of the noisy room. Layla slipped the camera from her shoulder and placed it on the table. Parker eyed it.

"Are you going to photograph our dinner?" he asked.

"Don't worry," Layla replied with a smile. "I won't take your picture without express permission."

A waitress arrived and took their drink orders.

"What do you recommend?" Layla asked Parker as she scanned the menu. "I've not been here before."

"The turtle stew is good even though they leave out the turtle meat. It's made with shrimp and andouille sausage in a spicy red sauce."

"Hmm," Layla replied as she read the

menu. "I'm leaning more toward the mango fish."

"I haven't tried it, but it sounds good and looks tasty."

"That settles it," Layla said as she closed the menu. "Presentation is huge to me."

The waitress returned with their drinks and took their food orders.

"Do you know the owner or manager of the restaurant?" Layla asked Parker when the waitress left.

"Is something wrong? They haven't even brought out our food."

"No, it has to do with this," Layla replied and touched her camera. "One of my specialties is photographing food for magazines and websites."

"Okay," Parker said slowly.

"But that's not what you wanted to talk about." Layla put her hands on the table. "You're interested in the law, and I won't make you cross-examine me. My father is a trial lawyer. We don't talk much, but he happened to phone me before I left my apartment, and I told him about our conversation. He was curious about you and wanted to know why you lobbied so hard for me to serve on the jury. Did you do background research on the members of the jury pool? I didn't say much during voir dire except my name and what I did for a living. In big cases my father puts together a dossier on every juror before he walks into the courtroom."

"Branham and Camp is a small law firm," Parker said, shaking his head. "We're not that sophisticated. I didn't know anything about you."

"Then what was it?" Layla persisted.

"I had a strong feeling that you would be an influential juror. It was a hunch, really."

"A hunch?"

"Yeah, I have good instincts about people."

Layla nodded. "An intuitive lawyer. Combine that with diligent preparation, and you could be a courtroom powerhouse."

Layla suddenly grabbed her camera and left the table. Parker watched as she approached a nearby couple who had just received their meals. Layla quickly took several pictures and returned to the table.

"Don't you agree that a gorgeous picture of food can make you want to take a bite out of the page of a magazine?" she asked.

"No." Parker laughed.

The waitress brought their dinners. Layla asked to speak to the manager and told her why.

"I'll let him know," the waitress promised

before she left.

"Don't touch anything!" Layla exclaimed when Parker picked up his spoon and prepared to take a bite of his turtle stew. "I need the bay leaves in one place for the best shot."

Slightly embarrassed, Parker pushed his chair away from the table and looked around as Layla positioned the large bowl and took several pictures. She then pointed the camera at her own dish, which had a yellowish-orange theme due to the mangoes.

"I love this restaurant," she said when she returned to her chair and put her napkin in her lap.

"You haven't eaten a bite yet."

"You know what I mean," Layla replied with another smile. "And thanks for being a good sport. I caught a glimpse of the dessert tray when I was at the other table. There were three kinds of cake. I hope they're as luscious as they look."

Parker ate a piece of shrimp immersed in the broth from the stew. The flavors were vivid.

"If a person loves something, there's no reason to hide it," Layla continued. "Photography and cake are two of my passions."

Parker suddenly wondered if the photographer liked to juggle. There were three small bread rolls in the center of the table, and he could see her grabbing them and tossing them in the air.

"What do you love?" Layla asked. "You know, what makes you get out of bed in the morning?"

Parker thought for a moment. "I know it sounds boring, but right now I guess it's figuring out how to be a good lawyer."

"There's nothing wrong with that so long as the rest of your life is in balance. What else do you love to do?"

"I like to work out. Several days a week I do something called parkour at a playground near where I live."

Parker then described the European exercise program that involved a fluid, unbroken circuit of jumping over picnic tables, swinging into trees from low-lying limbs, and using the metal supports on playground equipment for rudimentary gymnastic moves, all interspersed with pull-ups, push-ups, and burpees.

"I've never heard of it, but it sounds cool," Layla replied. "I'm a power walker myself, especially on the beach."

Parker suspected the long-legged photographer could rapidly cover a lot of ground.

"But if I take my camera on a walk, there are too many interruptions."

"I also like spending time with my grandfather," Parker said, taking a sip of water. "He's a retired commercial fisherman, and sport fishing with him is my favorite way to relax. He has a twenty-two-foot skiff that we take on the river or into the Sound."

"I haven't been on a boat since moving to New Bern," Layla replied. "What about the rest of your family?"

"My older sister lives in Florida with her husband and two kids." Parker paused. "My parents were killed almost nine years ago in a car wreck involving a drunk driver."

Layla's expression changed. Parker was used to similar reactions when he shared the tragic news.

"It's one of the reasons I decided to become a lawyer," he continued. "You know, so I could help people who've been hurt. Personal injury work is a growing part of our firm's practice."

They ate in silence. Parker glanced at Layla's left ring finger. He'd noticed it was bare at the wedding, but he suspected that hadn't always been the case. Suddenly Parker saw himself standing in the back of an unfamiliar courtroom as Layla and a tall man with dark hair stood before a female judge.

"The mangoes in this dish are perfect, not

too mushy even though they're cooked,"
Layla said. "Would you like a taste?"

"Sure," Parker said, shaking his head to
dispel what he was witnessing in the unfamiliar courtroom.

She deposited a generous portion on the
edge of his plate. Parker took a bite.

"It's good," he said with a nod.

They ate in silence for a few moments.

"I'm sorry about your parents," Layla said.

"I don't bring it up often, but you asked.
What about your family?"

"I'm an only child. My parents split when
I was twelve. My own divorce was finalized
fourteen months ago. That's when I moved
from Atlanta to New Bern and started the
photography business. I needed a change of
scene, and after growing up in Wilmington,
I've always loved being near the coast."

They finished the meal, and the waitress,
accompanied by the manager, brought out
a dessert tray.

"I can't make up my mind," Layla said to
the manager. "Should I have the carrot cake
or chocolate cake?"

"What was your entrée?" he asked.

Layla told him.

"Carrot cake pairs nicely with the mango
dish."

"Sounds good," she replied. "Would you

like to see some of the photos I took this evening?"

The manager stood behind Layla's shoulder as she scrolled through the pictures. Parker watched the man's eyes and the obvious interest revealed in his body language.

"I'd like to put together a portfolio for you," Layla said when she finished. "You could use it in advertising, especially online. A text-only menu is classier for diners who come into the restaurant, but people like a visual presentation when searching the Internet for a place to eat."

The manager left with Layla's card and a promise to call her within the next few days. The waitress brought a thick slice of carrot cake and a dish of raspberry sorbet for Parker. He started to bury his spoon in the sorbet and then stopped.

"Sorry," he said. "I guess you want a picture of the sorbet."

"No." Layla shook her head as she put the first bite of cake in her mouth. "It's too generic. And this carrot cake is scrumptious. Thanks for inviting me to dinner, but I'll pay for my meal since this evening is going to generate business."

Parker started to protest, but Layla Donovan seemed to have nonnegotiable reasons for what she said and did. After they finished dessert, Parker walked her to her car, a small imported sedan that looked like it had traveled a lot of miles.

"Oh," he said. "I forgot to ask. Where does your father practice law?"

"He's based in Wilmington where I grew up, but he travels all over the country," Layla replied. "His name is Thomas Blocker."

CHAPTER 12

Frank woke early Sunday morning. While waiting for his morning coffee to brew, he logged on to a computer Parker had helped him buy and set up for him. Frank rarely used the machine except to check the soccer scores for the German Bundesliga, the division in which the best teams competed. Frank played soccer as a boy and still considered it the purest form of competitive team sport. As usual, Bayern Munich occupied first place, but Frank always rooted for one of the underdog teams that might dethrone the perennial power. This year, that team was Wolfsburg in Lower Saxony. After finishing an article about a recent match, Frank checked his unread e-mails. Virtually all of them were advertisements, and he might go weeks between cleaning out the spam.

Frank clicked open his in-box and began deleting messages. Many of them were repeat offenders, and he resolved to ask Parker how to cut down on the volume of unsolicited inquiries. An e-mail from Germany caught his attention, and he opened it.

It was from Conrad Mueller.

The former soldier had returned to Germany and was thanking him again for seeing him. Frank wondered how Mueller got his e-mail address, but then he realized that Parker would have given it to him without asking questions. Included in the text was an invitation to attend a veterans' reunion for Army Group G the following spring in the Black Forest region with a link to find out more information and register for the event. Frank opened the link but didn't provide any personal information before closing it. He didn't want his Internet footprint to extend beyond the end of his driveway.

Logging off the computer, he stared at the blank screen. He had nothing to do at the house, and he didn't relish the prospect of staying inside the four walls all day. An unanticipated idea crossed his mind. He immediately dismissed it, but it popped back up like a bobber momentarily jerked underwater by a curious fish. Frank pushed his chair away from the computer and checked the time.

If he got ready quickly, he could go to church.

While shaving, Frank considered his options. Lenny's church was an obvious possibility, and Frank knew he had an open invitation to church followed by a delicious lunch. But if he went to the service it would create an expectation that he come back the following week. Better to go someplace where he could remain anonymous and uncommitted.

Frank owned a lonely dark suit that he wore to funerals. Putting it on with a white shirt and maroon tie, he got in his car, not sure where to go. However, the closer he drove to New Bern, the more options there'd be. He reached the outskirts of town and began passing churches familiar from his many years in the area. None of them called out to him. He stopped at an intersection and decided to turn right. Two blocks down the road, he saw an invitation in front of a new tan-and-brown metal building: "Looking for a church?"

He smiled to himself. His ability to see into the future was rusty, but even in his old age a sign could still be a sign.

This early on a Sunday morning, Parker had

the playground to himself. It was a cool day with low humidity, and he enjoyed moving rapidly from one activity to another. Today he added a few new wrinkles into his routine involving a fire hydrant and a brick wall.

After getting home from his dinner with Layla Donovan the night before, Parker had researched her father. Thomas Blocker went to college at UNC–Chapel Hill and then attended an Ivy League law school. Upon graduation, he returned to his hometown of Wilmington, where he joined a small firm. His courtroom reputation grew quickly, but instead of relocating to a metropolitan area or joining a big law firm, he stayed put and eventually went out on his own. Clients came from all over the country to hire him. Blocker practiced law on his own terms and made the rest of the world come to him. The Wilmington firm now had six partners and ten associates, with satellite offices in Raleigh and Atlanta. It was an impressive accomplishment. Nothing on the law firm website contained information about Blocker's family or personal life.

Parker was taking an exercise break to drink water from a large bottle when Creston Keller pulled into the parking lot.

"I thought I'd find you here," Creston said when he got out of the car. "I'm meeting

165

Melinda for a morning run in thirty minutes."

"Melinda?"

"The girl I took to dinner last night."

"This must be serious," Parker said, eyebrows raised. "An intimate, candlelight dinner is one thing; going out for a morning run takes things to another level. Are you moving too fast?"

"We'll find out when I start to push the pace about two and a half miles into the run. If she can still carry on a conversation without getting into oxygen debt, she may be the woman of my dreams."

"It's so easy for you to decide."

"What about the photographer?" Creston asked, stretching one of his legs by propping his foot on a wooden bench. "What's she like?"

Parker told him about the evening. Creston's eyes widened as he listened to the account of Layla flitting around the restaurant taking pictures of dinner entrées.

"If I didn't know better, I'd think you were making this up," he said when Parker finished.

"It was odd, but I liked her. She's different but interesting. And then, when she was about to get in her car to leave, I found out her father is a very successful trial lawyer in

Wilmington. He was in the courtroom when we selected the jury in the case she served on last week. At the time it didn't make any sense why he would be there. Now I guess he was watching out for his little girl."

"Whoa, an overprotective father who's a lawyer. You need to steer clear of this woman. He'll slap a restraining order on you if you splash water in her face while playing in the surf."

"I don't think so. There's distance between them, probably because her parents broke up when she was twelve." Parker paused. "And Layla's divorced too."

"Dude," Creston said as he changed legs and continued to stretch. "You're way too young to date a divorced woman. Don't take another step until you find out why they split."

Parker reached up and grabbed a pull-up bar. "You sound like a paranoid parent. Do you want to see if you can keep up with me on a circuit?"

"No, I'm not interested in playing Tarzan. I'd better get going. If you see a blur running down the river trail, it's me chasing Melinda."

"That will really motivate her to run faster."

Creston left, and Parker performed a different series of maneuvers that emphasized upper-body strength. After several minutes, he could feel the pleasant burn in his muscles that let him know he'd reached a training effect. He finished and jogged back to his apartment where he showered and read the news online until it was time to fix a sandwich for lunch. Checking his watch, he drove to the office. Greg's car was parked in its usual spot. Relieved that he'd decided to go to the office, Parker unlocked the door and went inside.

The only Christian meetings Franz attended as a child took place in his home in the 1920s, and it had been years since Franz had scrolled back in his mind to the informal gatherings that occurred when his grandfather came to town for a visit. Franz wasn't sure how the news went out that Herr Haus had arrived in Dresden, but on Friday or Saturday night a group of twenty to thirty people would cram into the house for a time of singing, praying, and listening to Franz's grandfather teach from the Bible. Franz would be hustled off to bed while the meetings continued into the night, but for the last two years of his grandfather's life, he was allowed to sit in the corner of the room so long as he didn't do anything to disrupt the gathering.

The most interesting part of the evenings would be the private, individual conversations people had with Franz's grandfather after the teaching ended. From his seat in the corner, Franz couldn't hear what was said, but the intense emotional reaction by the normally stoic Germans could be dramatic. Franz's mother reassured him that the tears were good tears and the occasional verbal outburst an expression of appreciation to God for his goodness in speaking to his people. None of it made sense to Franz, but he couldn't deny the goose bumps that would pop up on his own arms or the shivers that ran down his spine when his grandfather would place his hand on a person's head and begin to pray for them.

Franz's father always left the house before the meetings began. By the time he reached his teen years, Franz knew his father never warmed his hands at the fire of religious zeal, and any spiritual flame that flickered in the heart of Franz's mother was effectively squelched by her husband.

The worship music that came before the sermon at the start-up church in New Bern was unfamiliar to Frank. A woman with a guitar sat on a stool in front of a microphone and led the congregation of around 125 people in a series of praise songs with a solo ballad dropped into the middle. Frank didn't try to sing, and none of the people with their eyes closed and hands raised seemed to notice. As an elderly man wearing a dark suit, Frank stood out in the congregation like a solitary green apple in a bushel of red ones. There was no doubt he was the oldest, most formally attired person in attendance. When the music stopped, ushers passed small plastic buckets down the aisles for the offering. The church obviously needed money, and Frank, who always carried several hundred dollars in his wallet, folded up a crisp one-hundred-dollar bill and dropped it in.

The pastor of the church was a young man in his thirties named Eric. With his rimless glasses and prematurely bald head, the minister looked more like a college professor than a preacher. He spoke in a conversational tone with calm confidence that made it clear he believed he had something important to say.

The sermon topic of the day was forgiveness, and the message included a PowerPoint presentation, photos, and a humorous video clip. It was informative and entertaining, and Frank found himself enjoying the talk. When Eric discussed forgiveness, he didn't limit it to God forgiving the church-goers; he also emphasized the churchgoers' need to forgive those who'd wronged them. Holding grudges had never been a major problem for Frank. He'd seen too much during the war for a silly slight or minor dispute to sap his energy. If insulted or taken advantage of, he'd shrug his shoulders and go on. Eric closed the last slide, and Frank checked his watch. It was exactly twelve o'clock. Time to go.

But then, instead of praying, the minister continued to speak. His tone of voice became more authoritative.

"Unforgiveness is sin," he said. "And the presence of sin in our lives is the ground from which guilt and bitterness grow. Right now some of you are thinking about in-stances of unforgiveness, ongoing resent-ment, and the crushing weight these unseen burdens cause in your lives. I don't agree with the popular proverb; time doesn't heal wounds. It only causes them to fester longer and grow deeper."

At the mention of guilt and the long-term weight it placed on the human soul, Frank perked up and leaned forward in his chair.

"Guilt comes in many different shapes and forms. It has a thousand faces but only one solution, the blood of Jesus and the grace available through his sacrifice on the cross. Some people are understandably turned off by the idea of Jesus shedding his blood for our sins. It was a brutal and barbaric death that offends our sense of basic decency. But it also demonstrates the seriousness of our problem and the depth of God's love in providing a solution for it. If you've seen anything as remotely horrific as what Jesus suffered, it's not something you want to revisit."

Frank swallowed, but his mouth was dry. There was no shortage of dismembered and unrecognizable bodies of young men in his memory bank. Blood dominated many of those scenes. He blinked his eyes to dispel the images rapidly demanding his attention. The minister paused as Frank continued to fend off the mini flashbacks assaulting his brain.

"One of the most foolish things we could ever do is arrogantly reject God's offer of help. If you're willing to humble yourself, today is your opportunity to take a first step in the right direction from the wrong path you've been traveling and begin the process of true healing and freedom for your heart and soul. If these words are speaking to the depths of your heart, this can be a day of life-changing freedom for you. Reach out and receive what Jesus has done for you."

Frank now knew why he'd come to church. If younger, perhaps he would have debated what to do or tried to rationalize away the relevance of the minister's words. But Frank was an old man. There is a time for action in youth; there is a time for action in old age. The passage of decades removes the luxury of delay.

He slowly raised his right hand. With every fiber of his being he wanted to be forgiven and free of the guilt he'd carried for nearly sixty years. He sat completely still, acutely aware of each breath entering and leaving his lungs. He closed his eyes, but the images of the dead stubbornly held rank and refused to retreat.

Then, suddenly, the lifeless faces faded, replaced by a vision of a field of lush green grass with a bubbling stream flowing through it. Frank instantly knew it was a massive graveyard. And buried beneath the grass were those whose deaths were shackled to his heart by a massive chain of guilt. But no headstones reminding him of what he'd done marred the pristine landscape. The power of the guilt over the graves he'd helped to fill was gone. His culpability for all those lost lives so many years before could no longer haunt his present.

He was free.

As Frank continued to watch the peaceful scene, a single tear flowed from his right eye and down his cheek. And with that tear he understood the purpose of the stream. It was to restore his soul. More tears followed the first one. Sitting rigidly straight, with his arm extended in front of him, he let the tears fall from his eyes.

The minister prayed a benediction, but Frank didn't budge. He didn't want to think or move or do anything that would make him lose contact with the place God had provided for him. He lowered his hand but didn't stand up. People began to move out of the row. Frank bowed his head. The flow of tears slowed, then stopped. The vision faded, and he felt a gentle touch on his shoulder.

"Are you okay?" a woman asked him.

Frank turned and saw a young woman with blond hair sitting in the row behind him. He took out a carefully folded handkerchief and wiped his eyes.

"Yes," he replied.

"I couldn't help watching you," she continued. "Whatever was happening was beautiful."

Frank smiled slightly but didn't respond.

"Are you visiting the church for the first time?" she asked.

"Yes."

"Well, I'll leave you alone," the woman said, standing up. "God bless you."

CHAPTER 13

Greg's office door was closed, and Parker knocked lightly before opening it. His boss was staring at his computer.

"I just got an e-mail stating that Thomas Blocker is going to defend the Mixon arbitration case," Greg said, glancing up. "An associate in his office was handling the case, but for some reason Blocker wants to take over. That means we're going to have to ramp up our preparation and run down every rabbit about Robert Lipscomb, the stockbroker, and Chesterfield Consolidated, the company whose stock took a massive nosedive."

Several thoughts flashed through Parker's mind.

"Maybe that's why he was in the court-room the other day," Greg continued. "He wanted to evaluate me as a trial lawyer. I'm not sure when he left, but I think he was there long enough to see my fiasco during the opening statement."

"His daughter, Layla, was the photographer on the jury," Parker added, interrupting Greg's rambling.

"What?" Greg replied.

"That's a more likely explanation of why he was there. Her name is Layla Blocker Donovan. Not that it wouldn't be smart for her father to check you out so he can see who he's up against in the arbitration."

"Are you mocking me?" Greg's eyes narrowed.

"You're the one who said he's thorough," Parker replied, not cracking a smile.

"How did you find out the photographer is his daughter?"

"I took her to dinner last night after running into her at a friend's wedding."

"I knew you had an ulterior motive in lobbying for her to be on our jury." Greg nodded with satisfaction. "You have to be careful with that kind of thing. Just because a woman is attractive doesn't mean you should put her on a jury."

"That had nothing to do with it."

"And I don't believe you."

"Do you want me to help you prepare for the arbitration?"

"You read my mind about that." Greg picked up a piece of paper from his desk and handed it to Parker. "Read this. It's the exclusive remedy clause that mandates arbitration. Similar language is in every brokerage agreement in America. If an investor could go in front of a jury and complain every time he lost money and wanted to sue a stockbroker, it would be great for us but bad for them. An arbitrator isn't going to be swayed by sympathy and will factor in the risk inherent in all investing. I took the case hoping we could scare a small settlement from the company for cost of defense, but with Blocker on the scene, that's not going to happen."

"What do you want me to do?"

"Learn this stuff backward and forward. Don't worry about your time. We took it on contingency. No fee unless we win."

"And you'll be there to handle the arbitration, right?" Parker asked, suddenly suspecting that Greg was going to dump the case on him.

"I'm not going to throw you to the wolves alone, at least not yet. And I'm curious to watch Blocker work, even if he's trying to beat my brains out."

Parker took the file to his office. The clients were a retired husband and wife who alleged their stockbroker advised them to put a significant percentage of their portfolio in a volatile stock that quickly lost eighty percent of its value. The legal argument was straightforward — advising an older couple to buy a high-risk stock was contrary to a prudent investment strategy.

Three hours later there was a knock on his doorframe. It was Greg.

"Well?" his boss asked. "What do you think?"

"You're going to destroy Blocker, no doubt about it."

Greg rolled his eyes.

The following morning Parker arrived at work early to resume his work on the arbitration case. Thirty minutes later Dexter, a cup of coffee in his hand, came by to see him.

"What do you have going on tomorrow morning?" Dexter asked.

It was the kind of question an associate attorney hears frequently. There was only one acceptable answer.

"What do you need me to do?" Parker asked.

"DUI case. You know I don't handle them, and Greg's gotten too high and mighty to accept them. This one involves a close friend of my wife."

Parker felt his parents peering over his

shoulder from their photo on the credenza. He'd assumed Dexter knew about his family tragedy.

"Dexter," Parker began, "I'm not the right person to take on a DUI case —"

"It's only to enter a plea," Dexter interrupted as he handed Parker the citation. "Here's the ticket. It's a woman, and they nailed her. She was clearly intoxicated and had no business being on the road. Her name is Donna McAlpine, and she blew .19 on the Breathalyzer, which is over two times the legal limit."

"Who is Clarisse McAlpine?" Parker asked as he read the ticket.

"Her three-year-old daughter."

Parker looked up. "The little girl was in the car with her drunk mother?"

"Yeah." Dexter shrugged. "Donna is going through a rough stretch in her marriage and stopped off at a coworker's apartment one afternoon after picking Clarisse up from day care. They drank some fruity stuff the friend whipped up in the blender. It was only a couple of miles to Donna's house, but she didn't make it. The officer pulled her over in her driveway. I know there's nothing much you can do beyond hold her hand, but maybe you could talk to the DA about giving her a break on punishment."

"Why would I want to do that?"

Dexter nervously checked his watch. "Do me a favor so I can get my wife off my back about helping Donna."

There was look of quiet desperation in Dexter's eyes.

"Will you promise not to ask me to do this again and back me up with Greg if he wants to drag me into defending a DUI case in the future?" Parker asked.

"You got it."

"Okay."

"And don't bill your time. This is pro bono."

"Greg expects me to record every second."

"I'll say something to him," Dexter said with a vague wave of his hand. "This one is off the books."

"Will your wife be happy if Donna is found guilty?"

"Just treat Donna nice and act like you're fighting like crazy for her even if you don't have a chance. I'll keep working on world peace along the home front."

"Having the kid in the car . . ." Parker shook his head.

"I know. Missy has chewed her out repeatedly about that. Donna will be here in about an hour to meet with you."

After Dexter left, Parker shelved the

arbitration file and took a crash course in DUI law. When Vicki buzzed to let him know Donna McAlpine was in the downstairs waiting room, Parker avoided a final glance at the photo of his parents before leaving his office to meet with her.

If tearful remorse were a defense to drunk driving, Donna wouldn't have to worry. She went through so many tissues that Parker had to get a fresh box partway through the meeting. But tears weren't going to wash away the results of the Breathalyzer test or the fact that she'd had a previous driving-under-the-influence charge six years earlier. The new client had two aggravating factors — a prior DUI and a minor child in the car. The possibility of jail time was almost certain.

"Would it help if Jasmine testified for me?" Donna asked. "She knows I was fine when I left her apartment."

"No," Parker said with a shake of his head. "That might help a little, but we don't want to listen to ten minutes of detailed questioning by the DA about the drinks you had at her apartment and the amount of alcohol in them."

"Jasmine was just trying to cheer me up." Donna wiped her eyes with a tissue. "She and her husband have been good friends with Sean and me for a couple of years."

"She's done her damage, and coming to court won't fix it," Parker replied. "I'll try to catch the assistant DA in the morning and see what I can do. Be here at least thirty minutes before we have to be in court."

"If I go to jail, I'll get fired," Donna said through a final round of sniffles. "With Sean walking out on me, Clarisse and I could end up on the street."

Parker ushered Donna out after reassuring her of his commitment to fight as hard as he could for her. After she left, he felt like a hypocrite.

Late in the afternoon Vicki buzzed Parker. He'd spent hours staring at the computer doing research and was glad for an interruption. He rubbed his eyes before picking up the phone.

"Ms. Layla Donovan is here to see you," Vicki said in a soft voice. "She doesn't have an appointment."

"Is she downstairs?"

"No, standing in front of my desk," Vicki replied in a whisper.

"Okay, just a minute."

Parker saved his work and logged out of his research project. When he stepped out of his office, Layla was talking to Greg near Vicki's desk.

"I appreciate the feedback," Greg said to Layla. "Lawyers can get carried away with the performance aspect of a trial and forget it's about connecting with the people in the jury box at a basic level."

Parker slowed so he could hear Layla's response, but she turned toward him.

"Sorry to barge in unannounced," she said. "But I wanted to follow up on our conversation the other day about helping the firm with trial preparation."

"That would be great," Greg replied. "But there's one case you can't help us with."

Layla gave him a puzzled look.

"Your father is on the other side," Parker interjected.

"No one can help you beat him," Layla said seriously.

Parker suspected Layla was teasing but saw a surprised look cross Greg's face.

"Where's your office?" she asked Parker.

"Uh, this way," Parker replied.

They entered, but he left the door open.

"Were you joking about nobody beating your father?" he asked.

"Only if you outwork him, and I doubt Greg will do that." Layla glanced at the credenza. "Your parents?"

"Yes."

Layla stepped closer and inspected the

picture. "You have your mother's eyes and your father's curly hair. I'm not sure about the nose."

"It's never been the same since I broke it playing football in high school," Parker replied.

Layla reached over and picked up the photo of Parker and his grandfather on the *Aare.*

"My grandfather, the fisherman," Parker said.

"He looks vaguely familiar," Layla replied. "And that's a neat-looking boat with all the nets hanging down. I'd love to photograph a boat like that."

"Handling those nets was the hardest work I've ever done. The boat he has now is just for fun."

Standing beside Layla, Parker admired her profile in the light from his window.

"Would you like to go out on my grandfather's boat sometime?" he asked. "I'm sure we could find a few fishing vessels to photograph."

Layla faced him. "I'd like that very much."

CHAPTER 14

The next morning Parker hung up the phone after talking to the assistant district attorney assigned to Donna McAlpine's DUI case. Mercy was not going to be on the calendar when they appeared in court. Vicki buzzed him to let him know the client had arrived and was waiting in the downstairs conference room. Parker went out to the receptionist's desk.

"How did she look?" he asked.

"She has a box of tissues in her lap and is filling up the trash can in the conference room."

"I hope she brought a bag of personal items and toiletries."

"She's going to jail?" Vicki asked, her eyes opening wider.

"That's what the DA offered as a plea bargain."

"Good luck," Vicki replied with a shake of her head.

Parker went downstairs. His client was nervously wringing her hands. She'd put on a conservative navy blue outfit with a white blouse and looked like she was ready to make a marketing call on a corporate client. Parker sat down across the table from her. No course in law school had prepared him for what he had to do.

"Did you talk to the DA?" Donna asked before he could say anything. "I haven't slept more than a couple of hours for the past three days."

Parker could see the shadows of fatigue beneath his client's eye makeup.

"Yes, and it's not good news. Because Clarisse was in the car with you when you were pulled over, you're subject to a level-one punishment under Section 20–179(g), which means a fine of up to four thousand dollars and a maximum jail sentence of twenty-four months. It's worse because you've had a previous offense within the past seven years. The DA is willing to recommend a two-thousand-dollar fine and six months in jail if you plead guilty."

Donna stared at him with her mouth slightly open. "How can I do that?" she asked.

It wasn't a question Parker could answer.

"And what's going to happen to Clarisse?"

Donna continued, her voice rising to the edge of hysteria. "Who is going to take care of her?"

Steeling his jaw, Parker checked his watch. "We'll talk on our way to the courthouse," he said.

They left the office walking side by side. Donna kept her head bowed with a wad of tissues in her hand. They got in Parker's car.

"Once the DA gets a chance to see you, I'll make another run at a reduction in the sentence," he said.

"Let me tell the judge about Clarisse and how much she needs me," Donna replied between sniffles.

"I'm not sure that's a good idea," Parker said slowly.

"Why not?"

"Because one of the reasons behind the harsher sentence required by the law is her presence in the car. Trying to convince someone that you care about her —" Parker stopped.

He wanted to tell Donna she should be thankful she didn't kill herself, Clarisse, and some other innocent people, but he knew she wouldn't hear him. Donna buried her face in her hands. So far, Parker was failing miserably at satisfying Dexter's request that he reassure the client. The famous statue of justice might be blind, but in Donna's case the blindfold was lifted when she blew .19 on the Breathalyzer with a minor child in the car. They reached the courthouse.

"There are a number of cases on the docket," Parker said. "We'll have to wait our turn."

"Will the officer who gave me the ticket be here?"

"Yes. If we don't work out a deal with the DA, your case will be called for trial in front of the judge, and the deputy will testify."

Since he'd joined the firm, Parker had been to traffic court several times to represent people who'd received speeding tickets, but he'd never walked into the busy courtroom with bigger stakes on the line. People were milling about and chatting. There was a casual atmosphere among the lawyers who spent the bulk of their careers in traffic court. They were accustomed to moving rapidly from one case to another. Even more serious offenses like habitual DUI charges happened so often that they became routine. Parker knew it would never seem routine to him.

He found a place near the front of the courtroom where he sat down with Donna and waited for the arrival of the assistant

DA, a young woman named Julie Fletchall. She'd been easy to work with about speeding tickets but showed a much tougher side for the DUI charge.

"Who's on the bench?" Parker asked Julie when she arrived and began lining up files on the prosecution table.

"Judge Baldwin," the assistant DA replied, glancing over her shoulder.

Parker's previous experience with the female judge had been positive.

"And where's my case on the calendar?" he asked. "It's the only one I have."

"Did you talk to your client about the plea bargain?" Julie replied.

"Yes, she's thinking about it. I'd like the chance for you to meet her during a break so you can —"

"See what a nice person she is?" Julie cut in. "Save it, but her case isn't going to come up until the second half of the calendar. Maybe seeing what Judge Baldwin does in other DUI cases will help her make up her mind to accept my offer."

Parker returned to the bench and told Donna. A fresh wad of tissues emerged from her purse.

"Do you see the officer who gave you the ticket?" he asked when the sniffles momentarily slowed.

"That's him over there." Donna pointed to the upper left portion of the courtroom where five officers were huddled together. "He's the tall, skinny one with black hair."

"I'm going to talk to him before court gets started," Parker said.

Frank woke up later than usual. Taking a deep breath of fresh air, he let his head settle back into the pillow. He'd slept peacefully all night with the windows open and a breeze wafting through the screens. The image of the meadow and flowing stream remained, and he was able to meditate on the serene place while he sipped his morning coffee on the back porch. No tears came to his eyes, but an inner thankfulness welled up within him. Over and over he found himself saying, "Thank you, thank you, thank you." He then switched to German, "Danke, danke, danke sehr." The change in language touched him in a different way because it brought him closer to the world in which death had once reigned but did so no longer.

He took a sip of coffee and thought about all the men he'd known who needed a green field of forgiven graves. All casualties of war can't be counted on a calculator and recorded in a book of military history. Frank touched his chest. The wounds a man carried within could be as real as a severed limb.

After finishing his coffee, he decided to go for a walk. There was a narrow path beside the creek that ran along the edge of his property. He followed the creek for almost a mile until it spilled into a marshy area. There was enough breeze that the summer's remaining mosquitoes couldn't stay airborne, and Frank found a fallen log where he could sit and watch the marsh.

For a few minutes there was no sign of visible life, even though he knew the murky water was teeming with crabs, bait fish, and small crustaceans. A blue heron glided overhead and landed not far from where Frank was sitting. Balancing on one leg, the bird peered with dark eyes into the water. It was sight-fishing in its purest form. Frank waited along with the heron, which was more patient than most human fishermen. After several minutes passed, the bird's head suddenly knifed into the water and came up with a fish impaled on its sharp bill. The heron expertly transferred the fish to its mouth, where it made a final quick trip down the bird's neck and into its stomach. Frank started to get up and move on when he saw a swirl in the water to the right of the heron. The bird sensed it, too, and took off, awkwardly flapping its wings until the natural grace of flight took over. Frank watched the swirl in the water as the two nostrils of an alligator broke through the surface.

Alligators were occasional inhabitants of coastal areas as far north as New Bern and often hung out where they had access to an easy food source like garbage or discarded fish parts. When he ran his fishing boat, Frank would dump fish heads and guts in a spot frequented by a small band of gators. He enjoyed watching the babies snap their jaws and frantically scoop up the food as if it were their last chance on earth for a meal. This gator was no juvenile. It moved through the water with the easy confidence of a creature that knew it had no natural enemies.

Frank's eyes widened when the reptile turned toward him and raised its head above the water to inspect him. Big gators weren't common in North Carolina, but if the size of the alligator's head was any indication, this was one of the larger creatures Frank had seen. It opened its mouth in a massive yawn that revealed rows of pointed, yellow-tinged teeth.

"I'm impressed," Frank said to the gator.

"But I don't have any dead fish or spoiled chicken parts to feed you."

The gator turned to the side and exposed enough of its broad body to confirm Frank's suspicions about its size. The cold-blooded animal had spent the warm summer months feasting and storing up fat in advance of the fall and winter, when the temperatures would cause it to become lethargic and a less effective hunter.

As the gator moved away, Frank glanced down at the wrinkled hands that rested on his knees. He couldn't tie on a hook or fix a rip in a net as quickly as he could in years past. And there was no denying that Frank's time in life's pond was drawing close to the end, with way more water in his wake than in front of his bow. He'd survived the war, immigrated to America, and lived what most people would consider a full life, and now, at last, he'd made peace with the guilt of his past. The war years weren't erased, but they lay buried beneath a field of green grass that proclaimed the message of life covering death. He relaxed and let the tranquillity of the marsh wash over his soul.

Maybe, like the old gator, he could live out his days in peace.

Parker walked up to the group of deputies,

who didn't pay any attention to his approach.

"Officer Buchanan, may I speak with you for a minute?" he asked the deputy identified by Donna and listed on the ticket.

The officer held up his index finger. "Take a number, I'm finishing a story."

Parker took a step back and tried to keep his cool while Buchanan continued talking. While he waited, Parker thought of a question that might throw the deputy off his obviously confident demeanor. The other men laughed when Buchanan finished. He faced Parker.

"What do you want, Counselor?" he asked, looking Parker over.

"I'm Parker House, and I represent Donna McAlpine. I assume you're here to testify in her case."

"Affirmative. And I did that one by the book."

"I agree. Nice work."

Buchanan gave Parker a surprised look.

"How well do you know her husband?" Parker continued.

"We've met a time or two. Sean and I occasionally play pickup basketball at Twin Rivers YMCA."

"Did you talk to him the day you pulled

Donna over and gave her the ticket for DUI?"

"Why would I do that?" Buchanan looked past Parker and raised his hand in greeting to someone.

"Judge Baldwin is going to make you answer that question," Parker replied calmly. "And when you do, are you curious what I'm going to ask you next?"

"Not really." The deputy shrugged.

"You should be, because it has to do with Jasmine Vickers, the woman Donna stopped by to see on her way home from work the day you stopped her."

"What does she have to do with it?"

"Wasn't she more than just the person who gave Ms. McAlpine a few drinks on the way home from work? What will you tell the judge about her relationship with Sean McAlpine?"

Parker turned away and didn't wait for the deputy to respond. He returned to his place beside Donna.

"What did he say?" she asked.

"Not much. He doesn't have to talk to me."

The judge arrived, and they sat through the opening half of the calendar that was devoted to plea bargains and initial arraignments. The cases to be tried would begin after the 10:30 a.m. break. As soon as the judge left the courtroom, Parker saw Deputy Buchanan make a beeline for Julic Fletchall. While they talked, Julie glanced over her shoulder at Parker and Donna. The deputy backed away, and Julie motioned for Parker to come over.

"I can recommend thirty days in jail and a thousand-dollar fine for Ms. McAlpine on a guilty plea to a level-two offense under Section 20–179(h)."

Parker started to speak, but the DA cut him off. "No negotiation or counteroffers," Julie said. "Your so-called entrapment defense isn't going to work, but it's going to muddy the waters if we end up in front of a jury in superior court."

"I'll talk to my client," Parker said.

He returned to Donna and told her about the new offer. He didn't mention Julie's reference to an entrapment defense.

"I can't go to jail." Donna shook her head. "And where am I going to come up with a thousand dollars?"

Parker pressed his lips together tightly for a moment. His extremely limited bank of sympathy for his client was already overdrawn.

"You're not paying me an attorney fee," he said through clenched teeth, "which is saving you way more than a thousand dollars. There's no getting around Clarisse being in the car with you when you were stopped, and I don't have a way to attack the Breathalyzer test that proves you were way over the legal limit."

"It's not right," Donna replied in a whiny voice. "I didn't mean to do anything wrong, and my driving was fine. The deputy had no reason to stop me. It would be different if I'd been speeding or ran a red light or had a wreck."

"Yes, and those would be aggravating factors in addition to the ones you already have and make the deal I just communicated out of the question."

Donna bit her lower lip. "Who's going to take care of Clarisse if I go to jail for a month?"

"What about Dexter's wife, Missy? Aren't you good friends?"

"She and Jasmine have been my only friends. Missy's daughter and Clarisse go to the same preschool program. She'd probably do it."

"Well, this is the best I can do for you. Take the deal or tell me to turn it down so we can go to trial."

Donna didn't respond, and Parker waited. There was nothing more for him to say. He wanted to become a trial lawyer, but it would be hard to put his heart and soul into trying to beat a DUI charge for Donna McAlpine. He suddenly wondered if his lack of zeal meant he should withdraw from the case.

"I'll do it," Donna sighed.

"Are you sure?" Parker asked.

"Yeah."

After they finished entering the guilty plea, the judge gave Donna a day to make arrangements before reporting to the jail to begin her sentence. The tears that had dominated Parker's time with his client were gone. Either Donna was numb or the tears were a subterfuge. Parker didn't know or care.

"I may ask Jasmine to watch Clarisse," Donna said as they left the courthouse. "I've known her longer than Missy, and she's not so uptight."

"Are you sure Jasmine is a friend?" Parker asked.

"What do you mean?"

They stopped at a light and waited for it to turn red before continuing down the street.

"What kind of friend fixes you drinks on your way home from work when she knows you're going to have your little girl in the car?" he asked.

CHAPTER 15

That afternoon Parker was working in his office on the arbitration case when Dexter barged in without knocking.

"What happened in Donna McAlpine's case?" he demanded.

Parker outlined the plea bargain. "It was a phenomenal deal," he said when he finished. "Ask any lawyer who does that sort of thing for a living, and he'll back me up."

"That's not what I'm talking about. Is it true that Sean is having an affair with Jasmine Vickers and used her to get Donna drunk, then notified one of his buddies at the sheriff's department to pull her over?"

"It's possible, I guess."

"Donna thinks you knew and didn't tell her because you wanted her to plead guilty."

"No," Parker replied and then told Dexter exactly what he said to Deputy Buchanan. "After that, the deputy huddled up with the assistant DA, and we got a much better of-

201

fer. But what you're saying makes sense because Julie Fletchall claimed an entrapment defense wouldn't work in a DUI case. And she's right. Something seedy like that might generate sympathy in front of a jury but not enough to convince them to let a woman walk free who was driving with over twice the legal limit of alcohol in her system and a three-year-old child in the car."

"Okay," Dexter said. "But that doesn't make my job much easier on the home front. We're stuck babysitting Clarisse for a month, which is going to be a huge hassle, and Donna gets more hysterical every time she calls my wife."

Parker didn't doubt Donna's ability to ramp up the hysteria.

"Dexter, I did what I could," Parker said as calmly as possible. "Do you want me to go to the jail and talk to Donna? And how did she find out about her husband and her friend?"

"Sean blabbed about it, and it wasn't going to stay a secret, especially when Jasmine kicked her husband out of their apartment earlier today." Dexter paused. "But there's no need for you to meet with Donna at the jail. Anyone with half a brain knows you got her a great deal, and she's crazy to think dragging all their dirty domestic laundry out in public was going to work. But she's not going to be referring any cases to the firm in the future."

"Great."

When the day for the Mixon arbitration arrived, Parker put on his favorite yellow tie and carefully knotted it while standing in front of the bathroom mirror. He tried to strike a menacing pose, but it lacked ferocity and really didn't matter. Charlie Tompkins, the arbitrator from Washington, DC, wouldn't tolerate courtroom fisticuffs. He would want the facts topped with barely a smidgen of legal argument; however, Parker anticipated a smattering of fireworks from Thomas Blocker and a vigorous, if wild, response from Greg.

Full of nervous energy, Parker bounded up the steps to the office.

"You look like you're ready to climb a mountain," Vicki said in greeting.

"Then I'd better not have another cup of coffee. Is Greg here yet?"

"No, but he took the file home last night."

"How do you know?"

Vicki pointed to Dolly, who nodded her head. "He remotely sent in a bunch of dictation around midnight," the secretary responded.

"Did you confirm the date and time with the court reporter?" Parker asked Vicki.

"Yes, and I did the same thing last week when you asked me about it then."

"Okay, it's just that Greg gave me a logistic responsibility."

"Do you want me to order donuts and bagels?"

"No. What time are Mr. and Mrs. Mixon supposed to be here?"

"In fifteen minutes. Do you want me to call and make sure they've left home?"

Parker hesitated.

"Everything is going to be fine unless Greg messes up what you gave him," Vicki continued. "You've worked a ton on this case. Preparation wins."

Forty-five minutes later Parker was sitting in the front seat of Greg's car as they chauffeured Mr. and Mrs. Mixon to the federal courthouse on Middle Street. Mr. Mixon sat in the backseat reviewing revised questions hot off the printer connected to Dolly's computer. The previous afternoon they'd had a marathon session focused on the direct examination Parker prepared about their communication with Robert Lipscomb and the failed investment in Chesterfield Consolidated.

"Are you sure I have to testify too?" Mrs.

Mixon asked anxiously. "Mike handles all the finances."

"Which is the main point I want to make with you," Greg replied from the driver's seat. "We need to avoid a red herring defense built on innuendo that you were more investment-savvy than your husband."

Parker kept his mouth shut. He'd strongly recommended that Mrs. Mixon remain on the sidelines and avoid the risk of a deft cross-examination that might nudge her off the edge of a cliff. A reluctant witness was more likely to agree with a hostile lawyer in a vain attempt to ease the pain caused by more questions.

They arrived at the courthouse, an imposing Georgian Revival–style brick building built in the 1930s. The arbitration was going to be held in a conference room on the second floor. They lined up to go through the security checkpoint staffed by US marshals.

"There he is," Greg said to the clients when they reassembled beyond the security area. "Thomas Blocker is in the gray suit."

At the other end of the long, open space that had once been the lobby for the local US post office, Parker saw the trial lawyer. Beside him was a shorter, balding man in his forties wearing a tweed sport coat. Parker turned to Mr. Mixon.

"Is that Robert Lipscomb in the sport coat?"

"Yes," Mr. Mixon growled. "It's going to be hard for me to sit in the same room with that scoundrel."

Mrs. Mixon touched her husband's arm. "Please, honey."

They made their way to the stairway and climbed to the second floor.

"We're in room 212," Greg said when they assembled at the top. "It's down the hall and around the corner."

Parker could see the anticipation of the coming fight in his boss's eyes. It was a look that probably had intimidated his opponents across a high school wrestling mat, but Parker doubted it would faze Thomas Blocker. They reached the conference room and went inside.

Thomas Blocker had placed his briefcase on a long wooden table. Up close, Blocker had piercing blue eyes that instantly pulled everyone who made contact with them into his orbit. Parker could see physical traits inherited by Layla, particularly Blocker's well-shaped jaw and high forehead. Everyone shook hands except Mr. and Mrs. Mixon and Robert Lipscomb.

They set up on opposite sides of the table.

The arbitrator would sit at one end with a witness chair offset to his right.

"Where's the court reporter?" Greg whispered to Parker. "Did you confirm her appearance?"

"Yes."

He'd not been able to bring his Black-Berry into the federal courthouse, so there was no way Parker could contact the court reporting firm. He squirmed in his chair. A side door opened, and a bearded man in his midthirties stuck his head into the room.

"Is this the hearing in the arbitration case?" he asked.

"Yes," Greg and Blocker replied at the same time.

"I'm the court reporter," the man replied. "I wanted to make sure before I brought in my equipment."

Parker exhaled in relief. "Are you fine with a male court reporter?" he asked Greg. "I didn't specifically request a woman."

"Don't get smart with me," Greg grunted. "I can't chew you out here for making me sweat, but that won't stop me when we get back to the office."

Parker began laying out the exhibits he'd organized and labeled. The door opened again and the arbitrator, Charlie Tompkins, entered. Parker immediately stood up. Greg and Blocker stayed seated. Tompkins, an older man with wispy white hair, looked at Parker and smiled. Red-faced, Parker plopped down in his chair.

"Thank you, but I'm not a judge," Tompkins said. "And at this point in my career I have no interest in punching a ticket on that train."

Tompkins sat at the end of the table and opened a laptop.

"Good to see you again, Mr. Blocker," he said before turning to Greg. "And you must be Mr. Branham. Once I'm up and running, we'll get started."

A minute later the arbitrator looked up from his computer.

"Gentlemen, I'll make a few introductory remarks to your clients about our process and then turn it over to you."

Tompkins provided an overview of arbitration for the Mixons and Lipscomb. He emphasized the informal nature of the process and reassured the parties they would be able to present everything they wanted him to consider. He had a folksy way of communicating that seemed to make the Mixons relax.

"I've heard over a hundred of these types of cases, and I believe that will help me serve you better," Tompkins said in conclusion. He looked at the lawyers. "Are there any preliminary questions or matters for me to consider?"

"No," Greg replied.

"I'd like to reserve the right to cross-examine Mr. and Mrs. Mixon a second time after Mr. Lipscomb testifies," Blocker said.

"Objection," Greg replied sharply. "He only gets one bite at the apple. It's oppressive and redundant to subject my clients to multiple cross-examinations."

"Overruled," Tompkins replied. "But I'll restrict any additional questions to matters specifically raised in Mr. Lipscomb's testimony."

It was a unique trial strategy that Parker had never considered. It wasn't unusual for a lawyer to recall his or her own witness to the stand a second time to fill in gaps, but flipping it to an adverse party was a new idea. He could tell it caught Greg off guard, and Mr. and Mrs. Mixon exchanged an anxious look.

"Proceed, Mr. Branham," Tompkins said.

Mr. Mixon was the first witness, and Parker thought Greg did a good job settling the client down emotionally and drawing out the sequence of events about the stockbroker's recommendation and the disastrous results. During the testimony, Parker checked his notes to make sure Greg didn't skip an important point. As he did so, he paused over the names of the board of directors of the company. One, a man named Burt Woodlawn, caught his eye. He jotted it down and slipped a note to Greg telling him to ask Mr. Mixon if he knew him. The witness was in the middle of a long explanation of why he strongly emphasized to Lipscomb that preservation of his portfolio was vital to his retirement plans. Greg looked down at the question, glanced at Parker, and raised his eyebrows.

"Just ask him," Parker whispered.

Greg shook his head and continued down the planned path. During another long answer, Parker wrote down two more questions and tapped the paper again. Greg shook his head. Thirty minutes passed, and Parker gave up. He was already reviewing his notes about Mrs. Mixon's testimony when Greg asked a question that caused Parker to look up.

"Tell me what you know about Burt Woodlawn," Greg said. "He's on the board of directors for the company you invested in."

Mixon paused, a puzzled expression on his face, and looked at Lipscomb. Parker glanced at the stockbroker, who seemed to sit up a bit straighter in his chair.

"I'm not one hundred percent sure," the witness replied, "but Mr. Lipscomb may have mentioned his name."

"Objection as speculative," Blocker said.

"I'll give it the weight it deserves," the arbitrator said. "Go on."

"Did Mr. Lipscomb tell you about any conversations he had with Mr. Woodlawn prior to recommending you purchase stock in the company?"

"More speculation," Blocker interjected.

"Where are you going with this line of testimony?" the arbitrator asked Greg.

Greg glanced irritably at Parker, who rose to his feet. "To bring out evidence that Mr. Lipscomb's recommendation to our clients was influenced by self-interest and therefore a clear breach of Mr. Lipscomb's fiduciary duty."

It was an entirely new basis for the claim, and Greg stared openmouthed at him. Blocker leaned over and spoke to Lipscomb.

"Go ahead and answer," the arbitrator said to the witness.

Mr. Mixon nodded his head. "I remember now. Mr. Lipscomb had a photograph of some men on a fishing trip in his office. I asked him about it, and he mentioned that

Woodlawn caught the huge fish in the picture."

"Would it have affected your decision to buy the stock if you'd known Mr. Lipscomb had a conflict of interest due to close personal connections with a member of the board of directors?"

"Of course. I wouldn't have authorized the purchase and would have reported Mr. Lipscomb to his superiors in the company."

There wasn't another question on the sheet of paper. Parker held his breath as he waited to see what Greg would do next.

"That's all from this witness," Greg said.

The arbitrator checked his watch. "We'll take a ten-minute recess."

Blocker and Lipscomb stepped out of the conference room. The Mixons also left for a restroom break. As soon as they were alone, Greg spun around and faced Parker.

"Where did that come from?" he demanded. "Who is this Woodlawn guy and what does he have to do with anything?"

"He's on the board of directors, and I studied the company structure as part of my preparation."

"Which tells me nothing. Are we talking about insider information? That doesn't make sense because the stock tanked. What's the basis for a conflict of interest?

And if you suspected something like that occurred, why didn't you include it in your memo?"

"I didn't know for sure," Parker said, backpedaling. "But it looks like you struck a nerve we need to keep pressing."

"Without any evidence to back it up?" Greg raised his voice. "This isn't a TV show! Do you think Lipscomb is going to confess to something illegal when it's his turn to testify?"

"He doesn't know what we have."

"And neither do we. If you expect me to run a bluff and see how far it goes, you're nuts! Tompkins isn't going to be swayed by innuendos without proof. I've planted a seed of doubt about Lipscomb's honesty, but if I don't deliver the goods, it will make everything else we're arguing look ten times weaker."

Greg was right. Desperate, Parker tried to come up with a theory.

"The fishing photo shows they're friends, or at least know each other well enough to go on a junket together. You can ask Lipscomb who paid for the fishing trip. That would link them tighter."

Greg eyed Parker with intense suspicion that eroded the last thread of confidence Parker was holding on to.

"I'm heading to the restroom," Greg said. "And when I come back you'd better have something that has more than a snowball's chance in July."

Alone in the conference room, Parker took a deep breath. Lipscomb's reaction to the brief line of questioning made him think there might be truth to the allegation of impropriety. But without the benefit of pretrial discovery or taking Woodlawn's deposition, they were shooting in the dark at a target they couldn't see.

Then Parker had an idea.

Chapter 16

Frank got out of his car at Lenny's house. He'd called earlier to see if his friend wanted to go fishing and found out Lenny was spending the day renovating the bathroom in their guest bedroom. Frank knocked on the door, and Mattie answered.

"What are you doing here?" she asked, standing aside so he could step into the small foyer.

Frank pointed at his work jeans that were speckled with various colors of paint. "I don't want Lenny to mess up your guest bath. I'm much better at laying tile than he is. And everything has to be perfect when your future daughter-in-law comes for a visit."

"When is that going to be?" Mattie asked with a smile.

Suddenly there was a barely familiar stirring in Frank's chest that shot an unexpected thought into his mind.

"How long has it been since Jessie got married?" he asked, referring to Lenny and Mattie's oldest child, a daughter.

"Eight years and three grandchildren."

"Within the next twelve months you'll have another wedding," Frank said.

"You think so?" Mattie replied, her eyes wide. "Chris is dating a girl who works in human resources at the fire department, but I'm not sure she's the one for him."

"Is that Sally?" Frank asked.

"No, her name is Regina."

"Does he know a girl named Sally?"

Mattie thought for a moment. "The Hendersons have a daughter named Sally who lives in Wilmington. She's a year or two younger than Chris."

"That won't matter. Chris is immature for his age, just like Lenny."

Mattie laughed.

"Next time you have a big barbecue, maybe you should invite the Hendersons and see if Sally can come along," Frank continued. "It wouldn't hurt to let them meet."

"You know, I could see that myself. Sally is a real outdoors person. But I can't remember the last girl Chris asked out for a second date. I've told him nobody is perfect, and some of the best marriages are between opposites."

"Like you and Lenny," Frank replied. "You're sweet; he's sour."

"You shouldn't say that," Mattie scolded. "Even if it's true."

"And Chris needs to rip up the list he wrote down about his requirements in a wife and trust more in his heart than his head."

"Did Lenny tell you about that list?" Mattie asked. "I thought it was a terrible idea, but I kept my mouth shut because if I say something negative, he never listens."

"Just keep praying for him," Frank said.

"Praying?" Mattie replied with surprise.

"Isn't that what you and Lenny do?"

"Yeah, of course, but —"

"It sounds strange coming from me," Frank said to complete the thought. "I know. Let me sneak up on Lenny."

Frank left a puzzled Mattie in the foyer and made his way to the rear of the house. The bathroom was in the hallway next to the guest bedroom door. Lenny, his back to Frank, was on his hands and knees loosening the bolts that held down the toilet. A new toilet was in a box in the hallway.

"I should have waited until later," Frank said. "You're still in the demolition phase."

Lenny looked under his shoulder. "And

I'm not going to finish in time to go fishing today. This may stretch into a three-day job."

"It will go faster if I help."

Lenny put down his wrench and sat up. "That's nice of you to offer, Frank, but you don't need to be crawling around on the floor."

"At my age?"

"Well, yeah."

Frank stepped into the bathroom that had a modest single-sink vanity, toilet, and tub-shower combination.

"Are you pulling out the tub?" he asked.

"No, thank goodness Mattie likes the old-fashioned look, so all I have to do is clean it up." Lenny pointed to a pack of nonabrasive scouring pads. "I'm going to use those along with a bleach-based cleanser to remove the built-up gunk."

"No." Frank shook his head.

"Do you have a better idea?"

"Yes, I'm going to do it. Do you have a mask? I don't enjoy the smell of chlorine."

"Are you sure?" Lenny asked.

"Yes, I've really been into cleaning the past few days."

"What? Your place always looks spick and span to me."

"In here." Frank touched his heart.

"Your heart?" Lenny asked with concern. "Is there a problem with your arteries?"

"No, it's better than it's been in years."

Lenny shook his head and refocused on the toilet. They worked steadily for the next three hours. Frank had a patient eye for detail and restored the tub to a surprising level of sheen. Using a razor blade, he carefully removed bits of old caulking and laid down a fresh, uniform bead. He installed the new faucet handles and multifunction showerhead. Lenny carried out the toilet and vanity. He then pulled up the old tile and created a smooth surface for the new tile. The two men stood up to stretch. Lenny checked his watch.

"Are you hungry?" Lenny asked. "Mattie promised me a special lunch."

"She didn't know I was coming."

"I think she's probably added water to the soup to stretch it out." Lenny smiled.

They went into the kitchen to wash up. There was a large cast-iron Dutch oven on the stovetop.

Frank lifted the lid. "Is that what I think it is?" he asked.

Mattie came into the kitchen in time to hear his question. "Yep, it's fish stew."

"What kind of fish?" Frank asked.

"Snapper caught yesterday. Lenny and I

went down to the market yesterday afternoon and bought some from Jimbo Perkins."

Frank took a whiff of the simmering collaboration of chicken broth, celery, onions, garlic, peppers, tomatoes, spices, and several unidentified ingredients.

"The key is getting the roux right and then not overcooking the fish," Mattie said. "As much as I want you to keep working, I know you boys are hungry."

They sat at a small round table in the kitchen. In front of each of them was a steaming bowl of stew. In the center of the table was a loaf of homemade bread that was still hot enough to melt butter.

"I'll say a blessing," Lenny said, bowing his head.

"Could I do it?" Frank said before Lenny could begin.

Both Lenny and Mattie stared wide-eyed at Frank.

"I guess so," Lenny replied.

"And I want to do it in German first and then in English."

Lenny and Mattie exchanged a look.

"We won't understand a word of the German, but God will," Mattie said.

They bowed their heads and closed their eyes. Frank took a deep breath and tapped into the intimate level of expression where only heart knowledge of a native tongue can go. He referred to God as Grandfather, which he knew wasn't exactly true, but it made the most sense to him. He thanked his heavenly Opa for what had happened at the church and the peace it had brought to Frank's life. He expressed gratitude to God for his friendship with Lenny and Mattie and prayed a blessing over their household and their children. He turned the words he'd spoken to Mattie about Chris into a prayer. Finally, he asked God to guide the steps of each person sitting at the table. He paused and switched to English.

"Thank you, God, for this good food. Amen."

Lenny and Mattie were staring at him.

"That wasn't equal time," Lenny said.

"I recognized a few words," Mattie said. "Opa is what Parker calls you. And I recognized our names along with Chris's, who isn't here. What were you saying?"

Frank didn't answer but took a bite of stew. He swallowed it and licked his lips. "Something good, I hope, but not as perfect as this stew. Pass the bread, please."

Greg was the last person to return to the conference room.

"I'm going to leave and make a phone call," Parker said when his boss returned.

"Who are you going to call?"

"I need the car keys so I can go back to the office," Parker answered evasively.

"You may conduct your cross-examination of the witness," Tompkins said to Blocker.

Greg leaned over to Parker. "You can walk and don't bother coming back!" he hissed. "You're nothing but a distraction here."

Grabbing his notes, Parker left. It was normally a ten-minute walk from the courthouse to the law office. He cut the time to eight minutes.

"How's it going?" Vicki asked when he appeared at the top of the stairs. "Did you forget something?"

Ignoring her, Parker went into his office and shut the door. Logging on to the Internet, he located a business phone number for a Burt Woodlawn in Charleston, South Carolina. Then, taking a deep breath, he called Woodlawn's office. A woman answered.

"What is your fax number, please?" Parker asked.

After a brief pause, the woman gave it to him.

"I'm trying to reach Mr. Woodlawn," Parker continued. "Is he available?"

"May I ask who is calling?"

"Is he in the office?" Parker asked.

"Yes."

"I'm a lawyer in New Bern who is going to send him a fax in the next five minutes."

Parker hung up and went to Dolly's desk. "Prepare a notice to take a deposition in the Mixon arbitration case for a man named Burt Woodlawn. Set it for next Tuesday."

"Is the arbitrator going to leave the record open for a deposition?" Vicki called out from her desk. "They usually don't do that."

Parker watched as Dolly rapidly hit the keys on her computer. After less than a minute, the document rolled out of her printer.

"Here you go," she said.

"Thanks," Parker said as he took the piece of paper and handed it to Vicki. "Fax the notice to Woodlawn at this number with a cover page asking him to call me. I'll be in my office."

"What is going on?" Vicki demanded.

Parker didn't have the will or energy to explain or argue. "Just do it, or I'll start yelling like Greg on his worst day."

Vicki's eyes got big, and she turned around to the fax machine behind her desk. Parker returned to his office and sat in his chair to wait. He tried watching the dog in the next-door neighbor's yard, but there weren't any squirrels tormenting the little animal that lay in the sun on the back deck. He picked up the picture of him and his grandfather and studied it. Vicki buzzed him, and Parker grabbed the phone.

"It's Mr. Woodlawn."

Parker pushed the Receive button. "This is Parker House."

"Burt Woodlawn in Charleston. Before I call my lawyer, what's behind this notice to take a deposition that landed on my desk a few minutes ago?"

Parker sat up and cleared his throat. "Have you ever gone on a fishing trip with a stockbroker named Robert Lipscomb? I think you caught a nice blue marlin."

There was a brief pause. "Do you mean Bobby Lipscomb?"

"Yes."

"I've never heard anybody call him Robert," Woodlawn replied. "A mutual friend invited him to join us last year on a three-day trip to Roatán. That's where I caught the fish."

Parker looked at the clock on his credenza. "Lipscomb has been sued by our clients, an elderly couple who lost a bunch of money in Chesterfield Consolidated based on his recommendation to buy."

"So did I. What does that have to do with me?"

Parker swallowed nervously and tried to steady his voice. "That's what I want to ask you about in the deposition, but I'm not going to bother if you're going to plead the Fifth Amendment."

CHAPTER 17

There was silence on the phone for a few seconds. Parker could only hope he'd set a hook that would extract information from Woodlawn without scaring him into ending the call and telling Parker to talk to his lawyer.

"Why would I want to plead the Fifth Amendment?" Woodlawn asked, his voice getting louder. "Does Lipscomb claim I did something wrong?"

"If he did, what would you say about it?"

"That he's a liar!"

"So you didn't give him any insider information about the company?"

"Of course not. Whatever Lipscomb recommended to your clients wasn't based on any information from me. It came from someone else."

"Do you know who that might be?"

Woodlawn was silent for a moment. "I have a good guess."

"Do I have to take your deposition to find out?"

There was a long pause.

"Mr. Woodlawn, are you still there?" Parker asked.

"Yes, but unless you agree to let me record this conversation and promise not to use it in a court proceeding, I'm not going to say another word."

Parker tried to come up with a reason to disagree with the demand but couldn't. There was a slim-to-none chance that the arbitrator would leave the record open for a deposition, and even if he did, there was no guarantee the witness would provide something useful.

"Agreed, if I can record it too," Parker said. "Just so I don't misunderstand what you're saying."

"Okay, let's get this over with."

Woodlawn made Parker identify himself and state his consent not to use the conversation in court.

"One night on the fishing trip to Roatán, we all stayed up late drinking. Bobby told me that he had an opportunity to score some stock options in Chesterfield and wanted to know what I thought about investing in the company. I'm not stupid, and as a director I refused to comment. One of the other guys on the trip told me a few months later that Bobby bragged about collecting side commissions in the form of options from an officer at Chesterfield for recommending purchase of stock. My guess is Bobby thought he was going to make money for himself and everybody else. What he didn't know was that the company was having a serious liquidity problem due to an overseas manufacturing expansion that didn't work out. When that came to light, the stock tanked. The core business is solid, but it may take years to dig its way out."

"Who would have been in on this at Chesterfield?"

"My best guess is Brad Flanagan, the former CFO, and that's one reason why you can't quote me. I don't want to get sued for slandering him if I'm wrong. Anyway, he's no longer with the company. He was fired for padding his expense account way beyond what's normally allowed, so I wouldn't be surprised if he and Lipscomb came up with something crooked that created a conflict of interest for both of them. If you want hard facts, you're going to have to go after Flanagan, not me."

"Okay, thanks for talking to me," Parker said with relief.

"What about this notice to take a deposition?" Woodlawn asked. "If you come to Charleston next week, I'm not going to be here. I've been planning an anniversary trip with my wife for months. We're going to be out of the country visiting Machu Picchu in Peru."

"I'll withdraw the notice."

The phone call ended. Parker left for the courthouse.

When he slipped into the arbitration hearing, Thomas Blocker was questioning Mrs. Mixon. Greg turned sideways in his chair for an instant but then ignored Parker.

"Isn't it true that you obtained a degree in economics from Davidson College?" the lawyer asked Mrs. Mixon.

"Yes, but that was a long time ago."

"And that you graduated with honors?"

"Yes."

"In fact, you graduated magna cum laude, didn't you?"

"Yes."

Blocker lifted a sheet of paper from the table and held it up in his hand. "Mrs. Mixon, do you remember the topic for your honors thesis?"

"Uh, I'm not sure. That was forty years ago."

Blocker stepped forward and handed the

sheet of paper to her. "Are these the courses you took at Davidson?" he asked.

Parker couldn't believe the defense lawyer had a copy of the sixty-two-year-old witness's college transcript.

"Yes," she said.

"Please tell the arbitrator the subject for your honors thesis."

Mrs. Mixon studied the sheet for a moment. "It's not listed."

"And you don't remember?"

Mrs. Mixon looked sheepishly at her husband. "It had something to do with equity risk analysis."

Blocker returned to the table and picked up another sheet of paper. "Was the title 'Simulations, Decision Trees, and Scenario Analysis: Probabilistic Approaches to Risk'?"

"Yes, something like that."

Blocker shook his head. "I'm a small-town lawyer. Can you explain to me what in the world that means?"

"Uh, stocks."

"Would you agree that you conducted research about risk analysis in the equity markets?"

"That would have been part of it."

"Along with a whole lot more, correct?"

"Yes."

Blocker looked at the arbitrator. "No more questions of the witness."

"Any redirect?" Tompkins asked Greg.

"No."

"We'll take an hour break for lunch," Tompkins said. "Please return by one thirty."

Parker could tell that Mrs. Mixon was on the verge of tears as she stood up and approached her husband.

"I'm sorry," she began.

Parker didn't wait to listen. Instead, he stepped over to Thomas Blocker, who was talking to Lipscomb.

"Excuse me," Parker said to the lawyer. "When you finish, could I speak to you for a moment?"

"Certainly."

"Wait for me in the hallway," Blocker said to his client before turning his attention to Parker.

"Did Mr. Lipscomb tell you about the stock options he was promised in Chesterfield for recommending that clients invest in the company?"

Blocker eyed Parker curiously. Parker continued, "And if he didn't, ask him about his relationship with Brad Flanagan, the former CFO with the company."

"And what's that going to prove?" Blocker asked.

Out of the corner of his eye, Parker saw Greg approaching as Mr. and Mrs. Mixon left the room.

"Our case. And if we're successful, this is going to end up costing Lipscomb his career and your client a lot of money," Parker said.

"Parker!" Greg said sharply. "What are you doing?"

"He's forecasting his view of the evidence and asking me to consider it," Blocker replied smoothly.

The defense lawyer left, and Greg turned to Parker. "What did you tell him?"

Parker summarized his conversation with Burt Woodlawn. As Parker talked, Greg's hostility lessened.

"I wish we'd known about this before," he said. "But it may not matter. You heard the tail end of Mrs. Mixon's testimony. We're in trouble. Based on her college thesis, she's the definition of a sophisticated investor."

"We'll just have to see if what I said to Blocker worries him and Lipscomb more than Mrs. Mixon's testimony does us."

At lunch, Parker was too nervous to do more than nibble a few potato chips. Greg didn't seem to have any problem wolfing down a footlong sub sandwich with extra meat and cheese.

"How can you eat like that during a trial?" Parker asked.

"When I'm in a fight, I have to eat," Greg replied. "I hated having to make a certain weight when I was a wrestler in high school. At least when we go back to the courthouse I'm not going to have to step on a scale to see if I can continue."

"What is Thomas Blocker doing right now?"

"Shaking in his boots about the next curveball you're going to throw him in this case."

"Really?"

Greg shook his head. "No. You missed most of his performance. Blocker is the definition of smooth. He bludgeoned Mrs. Mixon with her educational background and toyed with Mr. Mixon before making him look like a bitter man who is looking for someone to blame for his financial problems. I didn't know it, but Mixon was receiving a buyout from a former employer that filed for bankruptcy last year, cutting off a big revenue stream for our clients. Blocker got him to admit that without an increase in his equity portfolio, Mixon's retirement would never sustain their life-style."

"That should help us," Parker said, confused.

"Not the way Blocker spun it. He made it look like Mixon needed to gamble in order to hit a home run and make up for his loss from his previous employer."

Parker ate a chip and took a sip of water. "Why didn't we know about that?" he asked.

"I don't ask a client what he ate for breakfast last week." Greg grunted. "And I don't think you're in great shape to criticize me for poor preparation when you're scrambling eggs on evidence you should have brought to my attention as soon as you dove into the case."

Parker shut his mouth and watched Greg finish the rest of his sandwich. His boss took a final swig of sweet tea.

"Okay, let's do this," Greg said.

"Are you going to ask Lipscomb about his relationship with Brad Flanagan and the kickback scheme for stock options?" Parker asked.

Greg looked Parker in the eye. "Would you do that without any evidence to back it up?"

"There's Burt Woodlawn."

Greg wiped his mouth with a flimsy napkin. "Who isn't within 150 miles of the courthouse and made you commit not to use the information he gave you. Run your questions by me."

"Uh, Mr. Lipscomb, isn't it true you had an arrangement with Brad Flanagan, the former CFO at Chesterfield, that resulted in your receiving stock options in the company if you convinced investors to buy common stock?"

"He denies it. What next?"

"A director of the company says you did."

"What's his name? Oh, you can't tell me. At that point, the arbitrator threatens to make me pay Blocker's attorney's fees for wasting everybody's time. Anything else?"

"No," Parker conceded.

They stood up.

"It's not a bad theory," Greg said. "But next time you have a brilliant investigative idea, tell me before we're in the middle of a trial. A general needs to know what lies ahead before the battle begins."

When they returned to the courthouse, Mr. and Mrs. Mixon were sitting in the hallway outside the courtroom.

"It's not going very well, is it?" Mrs. Mixon asked anxiously.

"We scored some points," Greg replied.

"But they did too," Mr. Mixon said. "It's

going to come down to what you can get out of Lipscomb."

Parker glanced at Greg to see how he would react to the client putting all the responsibility for the case on the lawyer's shoulders.

"I have plans for him."

"I want you to embarrass him like the other lawyer did me," Mrs. Mixon said. She pressed her lips together tightly for a moment. "I couldn't believe he brought up that paper I wrote in college. It was a group project with two other students. They did most of the work."

Parker stared at Mrs. Mixon and wondered why she didn't emphasize that tidbit of relevant information while she was on the witness stand. Greg told them what Parker had uncovered.

"What a crook," Mr. Mixon spit out. "I'd like to nail him to the wall."

Thomas Blocker and Lipscomb returned to the conference room, and the defense lawyer stepped over to them.

"Greg, may I speak with you for a moment in the hallway?" he asked.

Greg turned to leave.

"You too," Blocker said, motioning to Parker.

Greg glanced at Parker and nodded. They

236

stood in a circle in the vacant hallway.

"I'm not going to reargue my case and tell you the damage I've done to your clients during cross-examination, but before I begin my evidence, do you want to discuss settlement?" Blocker asked.

Parker knew his boss settled a lot of cases before they reached the courthouse steps, but not often after a trial began. Greg so immersed himself in the fight that he had trouble objectively evaluating which way the winds of evidence were blowing. His confidence helped him weather adverse storms but could blind him to a favorable resolution.

"What's your proposal?" Greg asked. "I've not discussed the possibility with my clients. They're ready to go to the mat."

Parker caught a hint of a smile at the corner of Blocker's mouth, but the more experienced lawyer was careful not to let it become a smirk.

"Twenty-five percent of their damage request, each side to bear an equal share of the costs of arbitration."

"No way." Greg shook his head.

"Talk to them and let me know," Blocker replied, unruffled. "I'll wait here with Mr. House, if it's okay."

Greg glanced at Parker. "No, he comes

with me."

Wondering why Thomas Blocker was interested in hanging out with him, Parker followed Greg into the conference room, where he quickly communicated the offer to the clients and his recommendation that they reject it.

"I'm ready to see if we can drag Lipscomb through the mud," Greg said. "He's a sleazy —"

"We'll take fifty percent and pay half the costs," Mr. Mixon said. "I'm afraid we're going to lose and end up owing all the costs."

Mrs. Mixon rapidly nodded her head up and down. "And we'll take their offer if they won't increase it."

"Are you sure this is —" Greg asked.

"Yes," Mr. Mixon interrupted.

The arbitrator reentered the room.

"Just a minute, Mr. Tompkins," Greg said. "We're having settlement discussions."

"Take your time," Tompkins replied with a wave of his hand.

Parker and Greg returned to the hallway.

"Seventy-five percent of the demand and your client pays the arbitrator," he said to Blocker.

"I called the home office during the lunch recess," Blocker replied. "We can split the difference at fifty percent of demand with each side bearing half the costs."

"We can't agree on splitting the costs," Greg replied.

"Yes, you can," Blocker answered decisively. "And I believe you will. Otherwise, we're moving forward."

Greg and Parker returned to the conference room. This was shuttle diplomacy at light speed.

"They'll do it," Greg said to the Mixons. "Half our demand and split the costs. Are you sure?"

"Yes," they both said.

"Okay," Greg sighed. "We have a chance —"

"Of losing more than we already have," Mr. Mixon interrupted again. "Accept the offer."

Once everyone was in the conference room, they went back on the record, and the lawyers quickly stated the terms of the settlement agreement, which included a confidentiality clause. Tompkins then turned to Mr. and Mrs. Mixon and asked each of them if this was what they wanted to do. He repeated the process with Lipscomb.

"That concludes the arbitration," Tompkins said. "My office will issue a statement for my services within the next seven to ten days. The court reporter will bill you directly for his appearance. I assume there's no need for preparation of a transcript."

Tompkins and the court reporter left, followed by Thomas Blocker and Robert Lipscomb. Greg held back so Mr. and Mrs. Mixon wouldn't have to be in close proximity to the stockbroker.

"Will anything happen to Lipscomb for what he did to us?" Mrs. Mixon asked.

"Nothing unless someone else files a claim against him and the lawyer uncovers it," Greg replied.

They exited the courthouse. Walking toward the car, Parker saw Thomas Blocker standing beside a long black Mercedes at the opposite end of the parking lot. Lipscomb wasn't with him. The lawyer gestured for them to come closer.

"What does he want?" Mr. Mixon asked.

"I'm not sure," Greg replied. "Parker, why don't you go over and ask him?"

Parker crossed the lot. Blocker put his briefcase in the backseat of his car.

"Did we forget to cover something?" Parker asked.

"Not about the case. And you're the one I want to talk to. Greg can leave."

CHAPTER 18

"Nice bluff," Blocker said to Parker as Greg drove away with the Mixons. "Only I guess it isn't a bluff when it convinces a corporate client to toss money on the table to settle a bogus claim."

Parker didn't respond.

"You're not going to disagree with me?" Blocker asked.

"I don't have to. Your client agreed to pay the money."

Blocker laughed. It was another similarity to Layla.

"Tell me a little bit about yourself," Blocker said, loosening his blue tie.

Parker provided the basic information about college, law school, and moving back to New Bern to work for Branham and Camp.

"I already know all that," Blocker said when he finished. "Tell me something I don't know."

Parker was surprised that Blocker had researched a junior associate's background prior to going to court in a low-dollar arbitration hearing. Then he realized the real reason for their conversation.

"Did you check me out because I took Layla to dinner after she served on our jury?" he asked.

"No, I didn't know about that, but anything that affects my little girl is important to me."

Parker suddenly felt like he was back in high school, awkwardly sitting in a living room with a date's father while he waited for the young woman to come downstairs.

"Uh, I wanted to talk to her about the trial and her impressions of the lawyers' performances. Also, she completely dominated the jury deliberations, and I was curious how that played out."

"Layla is smart and persuasive."

"Like her father."

"In more ways than she's willing to admit. Tell me about your family. House? Is that an English name?"

"Usually, but for us it's the anglicized version of Haus. My grandfather came to America from Switzerland after World War II and changed his name from Franz Haus to Frank House."

"Franz Haus? Is he still alive?"

"Yes, he's a retired commercial fisherman. He lives in a little house about a twenty-minute drive downriver."

"Interesting." Blocker nodded. "I'd like to meet him. We have a lot in common. My grandfather emigrated from Germany shortly after World War I. He fought against the Americans at Belleau Wood and received the Iron Cross second-class with several combat ribbons. After Germany lost the war, he was smart enough to seek a brighter future here. I assume your grandfather avoided World War II because he was Swiss German."

"What was your grandfather's surname?" Parker asked, avoiding the invitation to provide more information.

"Blocher. An immigration officer turned it into Blocker when my grandfather landed at Ellis Island. He worked in the Wilmington shipyards when they were still booming."

"I'm not very interested in genealogy," Parker replied as he started to move away.

"It's one of my passions."

A thought suddenly shot through Parker's mind, and he stopped in his tracks. "Did Layla's husband work for you?" he asked.

"Layla told you about that?" Blocker asked in surprise.

"No. It was a hunch."

"Like your insight at the arbitration today?" Blocker's eyes narrowed.

Parker now felt uncomfortable about the new direction of the conversation. "I need to get back to the office," he said.

"Having a son-in-law in the firm was bad for business and worse for Layla," Blocker continued. "He used both of us."

"I'm sorry," Parker replied, continuing to back away. "Nice talking to you."

"Until the next time."

Inspired by the bathroom remodeling project at Lenny's house, Frank was busy performing a few repairs on his house in anticipation of the coming winter. The greatest threat to his home wasn't from cold temperatures but rather the briny air that drifted in from the Sound. Since buying the house, Frank had changed out much of the hardware on the windows and doors and installed fixtures treated to resist the silent onslaught of salt.

He put down his electric screwdriver and checked a window latch to make sure it opened and shut smoothly. Hearing a car coming up his driveway, he went around to the front of the house as Lenny parked his truck beneath the live oak tree and got out with a brown paper sack in his hand.

"Fresh tomatoes!" Lenny said, raising the bag. "Some of the final stragglers of the season. My plants look like scarecrows on life support, but I was able to salvage a few decent ones. It's additional payment for helping me out the other day."

"That fish stew was more than enough," Frank replied. "I finished the last of the batch Mattie sent home with me last night for supper."

"Mine didn't last that long."

Frank held the door open for Lenny, who took the bag to the kitchen. There were five tomatoes in the bag.

"Tomato sandwiches for supper," Frank said, "on slices of Mattie's homemade bread."

Frank rinsed the tomatoes in the kitchen sink and handed them to Lenny, who dried them with a paper towel.

"Now that Mattie isn't around, are you going to clue me in on what's going on with you and God? I didn't know the two of you were on speaking terms, but then you show up at my house and talk to him in both German and English."

"I went to church. What more is there to tell?"

"Did it have anything to do with what we

talked about in the boat the other day? You know, about dealing with past regrets?"

"Yes," Frank said and nodded. "I'm thinking about the past and the future, which for me could be pretty short."

"Is anything wrong with you that you've not told me about?"

"No, but I'm certainly much closer to the end than I am the beginning."

They went onto the back porch. Frank grabbed two bottles of water from a mini-fridge in the corner and handed one to Lenny, who sat in a straw-backed rocking chair.

"Are there things Mattie and your kids don't know about your time in Vietnam?" Frank asked.

"Plenty. I've never been one of those guys who talk about the terrible stuff. I don't know any good reason to drag her or any of my kids through those dark times. I've told my boys some of the funny stories, and they know not to push me for anything else."

"I've kept quiet too," Frank said. "Maybe even more than you. What I told you the other day about having the ear of a general was more than I've mentioned to any other person."

The air on the porch suddenly seemed heavier than on the most humid day of the year. The two men sat in silence. Then Frank told Lenny what happened at the church and the sermon about forgiveness and freedom from shame and guilt.

"That sounds like a good message —" Lenny said.

"That's not all," Frank interrupted.

Frank took a deep breath and described the green field and flowing stream — the graveyard without headstones, the water that could cleanse the soul.

"Wow," Lenny said when Frank finished. "That's amazing. I could see it myself."

"I've been so grateful since Sunday that it's never been far from my thoughts."

"What's next?" Lenny asked.

Frank smiled slightly. "I guess it's not enough to make it through another day until I finally die."

"No," Lenny said. "There's more in your future than that."

Friday morning Parker was in his office with his door closed. After coming in early to finish an evidence summary Greg needed for depositions scheduled in a case the following week, he'd rewarded himself with a second cup of coffee. His feet propped on the corner of his desk, Parker took a sip of coffee and ran his fingers through his hair.

Without warning, the door opened. It was Greg. Parker's feet hit the floor, and his hand knocked the cup of coffee from the desk. Greg stared at him.

"Looks like you weren't expecting any feedback from me about the memo you wrote last week in the Ferguson case."

"Just taking a quick time-out," Parker replied as he leaned over to open the bottom drawer of his desk and retrieve some napkins that he then dropped into the pool of brown coffee on the floor. He glanced up at Greg. "But I guess you figured that out pretty quickly."

"Yeah, I know you came in early to crank out the evidence summary so I'd have it on my desk."

Parker mopped up most of the coffee. Greg sat down in the chair on the other side of Parker's desk.

"What do you think about asking Thomas Blocker if he'd be willing to join the fight as cocounsel?" the senior partner asked.

"Why would you want to do that?" Parker replied, raising his head to the level of his desk.

"Because my jury verdict research shows he was involved in four of the ten highest verdicts in dramshop cases in North Carolina over the past fifteen years. He knows this stuff better than anyone, and adding him to the pleadings might make the insurance company cough up a decent settlement and save us the risk of getting a goose egg in court. Splitting the fee with Blocker would be worth it."

Parker paused. Even though he'd been present for the initial interview with the client, it was odd that Greg was asking him about an important business decision for the firm instead of Dexter.

"What does Dexter think?"

"He's working on a lease or something," Greg said with a dismissive wave of his hand. "I want to know what you think."

"Uh, let me think about it. I mean, we'd learn a ton from seeing how Blocker prepares and tries a case. The client would have to approve bringing him on board. Have you heard anything from the driver's insurance company?"

"They were about to send a check directly to Ferguson for the policy limits, so I told them to forward it to us. And based on your memo, Walter Drew is judgment-proof. There's no use trying to squeeze anything from him. We'll bill Ferguson hourly and disperse the rest of the money to him, holding back fifteen thousand for costs in the dramshop case."

"I thought we were going to put five thousand dollars in trust."

"You know that won't cover the expenses, especially if we hire any expert witnesses."

"Yeah," Parker admitted. "It's just, we told Mr. Ferguson —"

"Don't worry," Greg cut in, dismissing Parker's objection. "I'll explain it to the client. And make sure I have all the time you spent on the memo. I'll bill that hourly against this initial payment."

"It's already in the system."

Greg turned toward the door. "Oh, and get back to me with your thoughts about associating Blocker. I wouldn't mind sending him your memo to show him we know what we're doing."

Parker sat in his chair for several moments. There was one person he could call who would have lifelong insight into the trial lawyer.

CHAPTER 19

"Layla, it's Parker House. Do you have a minute to talk?"

"Sure, I need to take a break from trying to make a grumpy groom look like he's having a good time at his wedding."

"Some clients won't be happy no matter the circumstances."

"In your business, but it's not supposed to be that way in mine. What's on your mind?"

Parker had a sudden change in plan for the conversation. "I'm calling to make you happy."

"I'm listening."

"Would you have time tomorrow for a photo shoot and fishing trip on my grandfather's boat?"

"That could work, so long as I'm here for a sunset photo shoot with a couple who's getting engaged."

Parker glanced at the paperwork piled on

his desk and hesitated. He'd planned on working in the morning, then spending no more than three hours on the water.

"Okay, I need a break from the office and my grumpy clients."

"Could we make it to Bath?" Layla asked.

Bath was the first settlement in North Carolina, and with its historic buildings and coastal charm, Parker could understand why Layla wanted to visit and take pictures. However, it was a long way by water to Bath from New Bern.

"To go to Bath we'd have to go down the Neuse and up the Pamlico River. That's a full day burning a lot of fuel with not much time to spare once we got there. From here it's really better to drive in a car than boat to Bath."

"How about Oriental?"

"That's about twenty miles on the water, which would give us time to fish in a nearby creek and see the town, although the big draw is the marinas. Oriental is one of the best places on the coast to see different kinds of sailboats. There would also be fishing vessels like the one my grandfather owned in the area."

"Could you pick me up around seven? The early-morning light is best for pictures."

"Yes. What's your address?"

Parker wrote it down.

"See you then," Layla said when she finished.

"Oh, there's one other thing I wanted to ask you about," Parker said before she could hang up. "I met your father the other day when we were on opposite sides of an arbitration hearing. The case settled, and afterward he wanted to talk to me."

"Did he say anything about me?"

"Uh, yes. We both think you're smart."

"I bet that's not all he said. I hope he didn't make you uncomfortable. My father is the ultimate control freak. He drives the other lawyers in his office crazy. Even now he wants to be in charge of my life and micromanage every detail."

"It was a brief conversation, mostly about genealogy," Parker replied.

"Ugh, I'm sorry. That stuff bores me to tears."

"And won't be a topic of conversation tomorrow. See you around seven o'clock."

"Perfect."

The call ended. Parker had his answer for Greg about Thomas Blocker without directly asking Layla.

Frank finished organizing the fishing tackle in the shed behind his house. He'd spent two hours making sure every hook, lure, weight, bobber, and pole was positioned exactly where he wanted it to be. The phone in the kitchen rang as he entered the back porch. It was Parker.

"Opa, could I borrow your boat tomorrow? I'd like to take a woman I met recently on a trip down to Oriental. She's a professional photographer and saw the photo of you and me on the *Aare.* She wants to take some boat pictures. I'll make sure and bring the skiff back full of gas."

Frank rubbed his chin. "Are you going to fish?"

"I'd like to," Parker replied. "I thought we could run up a creek and try to score some speckled trout."

"I know exactly where to go," Frank said.

Parker was silent for a moment.

"I don't want to trouble you if you're busy," Parker said.

"Not at all," Frank replied. "I'll be your guide. I don't have anything planned for tomorrow, and the weather should be perfect. Right before you called, I finished getting all my tackle situated. All we'll need is shrimp if you want to use live bait. I can pick some up or you can do it on your way to the house."

"Are you sure you want to go?" Parker asked.

"Absolutely. We ought to be on the water early."

"I'm picking up Layla at seven o'clock. I'll stop at a bait shop for shrimp. And she'll need a fishing license."

"Yeah, there's a chance we'll get checked by a fish and game warden if we're near Oriental. See you around seven thirty. I'll stay out of the way and make sure you and Layla have a good time."

After the call ended, Frank leaned against the kitchen counter and chuckled. He knew he'd thrown Parker a curveball by inviting himself on the boating trip. But as soon as his grandson started talking, Frank knew he wanted to meet this woman named Layla.

Still puzzled by his grandfather's response, Parker walked down the hall. Greg's office door was cracked open, and Parker entered. Greg was on the phone and motioned for Parker to sit.

"If you want to play hardball, I'll be happy to oblige," Greg said to the person on the other end of the line. "Threats like that are fuel to my fire."

Greg was silent for a moment. He looked at Parker and grinned.

"Bring it on," Greg said when the person on the call stopped talking. "If you want to swim with the sharks, you have to get in the ocean. I'll be waiting for your insured with my jaws wide open."

Greg hung up the phone. His grin widened. "Man, I love baiting insurance adjusters who spout off a bunch of nonsense about their statistical models for how much a case is worth. The value of a case is what a jury will award in a verdict."

"But it often makes sense to settle out of court."

"Of course it does, but in the meantime, can't I have fun convincing an adjuster that I'm crazy enough to try every case that walks through the door? They have to believe you'll go to the mat before they'll pay top dollar on a claim. That's my style; you'll have to find your own. What's up?"

"I've been thinking about whether to associate Thomas Blocker in the Ferguson case."

"And I'm waiting for him to call me back. I sent your memo to him as an e-mail attachment. Would you believe he responded in less than a minute and said he's very interested?"

"You already asked him to come in as co-counsel?"

"It's a no-brainer."

"Then why did you ask my opinion?"

Before Greg responded, his phone buzzed and Vicki spoke. "Thomas Blocker is returning your call," she said.

"See," Greg said to Parker, putting his hand over the receiver. "He is all over this."

"Which is exactly what will happen to the case if you associate him as cocounsel."

Greg dismissed Parker's comment with a wave of his hand. He pressed a button to put the call on speakerphone.

"Hello, Mr. Blocker. Thanks for calling."

"Excellent. And call me Tom," Blocker replied. "If we end up working together, it's best to drop the formalities."

"So what do you think about our dramshop case, Tom?" Greg asked.

"Before we get into that, there's a change coming your way in the settlement documents in the Mixon-Lipscomb arbitration. Paragraph six will reflect that the check will be issued by the E and O carrier for the brokerage firm."

"I thought a settlement this small would fall within the deductible," Greg replied.

"That's an issue I wrestled through with them. Anyway, a temp worker typed the documents, and I also caught typos in paragraphs nine and thirteen. Those will be corrected and the revised documents on their way to you by tomorrow morning."

Parker could see Greg looking down at his notes he retrieved from the corner of his desk. His boss spoke. "Uh, you also need to delete the provision in paragraph ten requiring my clients to terminate their relationship with the company, transfer their equity holdings to another broker, and agree never to apply to open an account in the future. We didn't agree to that on the day of the hearing."

"If that's a problem, it's a dealbreaker. My client isn't going to litigate with Mr. and Mrs. Mixon in the future. The money paid in this case is going to buy the peace, once and for all."

"I'll have to talk to my clients about it."

"Of course, but they already closed out all their accounts the day after the arbitration. They've done everything I'm asking except agree to work with someone else in the future."

Parker could tell from the look on Greg's face that he didn't know about the Mixons' actions. On his boss's desk was a stack of pink phone message slips. Parker suspected more than one might be from their client.

"Then I don't anticipate a problem," Greg replied, trying to sound confident. "Are you ready to move on to the dramshop case? Parker House is here with me."

"Greetings to you," Blocker said in German. "How are you doing today?"

Greg looked at Parker and raised his hands in bewilderment.

"Uh, fine, sir," Parker replied in English. "If I understood your question."

"Go ahead," Blocker said. "Tell me more about the dramshop case."

"Okay," Greg said, sitting up straighter in his chair. "Chet Ferguson will make a great witness. He's a thirty-six-year-old man who now has to be a single father to two children, ages eight and ten. The eight-year-old girl is the spitting image of her mother, so we've got to get her in front of the jury as much as possible. My client dropped off some family photos yesterday, and I have a picture of the mother when she was the same age that I'm going to blow up."

While Greg continued to talk, Parker couldn't help feeling that the discussion about Jessica Ferguson was disrespectful to the woman killed instantly on impact. He'd have been offended if someone had talked about his mother as if she were nothing more than a key piece of evidence.

"Sounds like you're off to a good start," Blocker said. "I'm not sure what I can bring to the table."

"He's right," Parker interjected as loudly as he dared.

"Your reputation in this type of litigation," Greg said, shaking his head. "When the insurance company for the tavern sees your name on the pleadings, it will have a huge impact on settlement prior to trial."

"I appreciate the compliment, but I'm not in the business of attaching my name to a lawsuit solely for purposes of ginning up a settlement. I'm a lawyer, not a poster boy."

"Parker can tell you I'm not afraid of the courthouse," Greg said, bristling.

"That's right," Parker added.

"And I'd want you to help try the case if it doesn't settle," Greg said.

"I understand, but if I'm not a significant part of trial preparation, I'm not comfortable walking into the courtroom. Depending on another lawyer's work, even if it's top-notch, is outside my comfort zone. I have to live with a case to get the right feel for what will work when it's time to stand in front of a jury."

"Of course," Greg replied. "That's acceptable."

Blocker was silent for a moment. "Parker, what do you think about the merits of the claim?" the trial lawyer asked.

"Me?" Parker replied in surprise.

"If we end up working together, I'm interested in your impressions of how best to proceed, especially as to the emotional side of the case. You're uniquely qualified to offer that perspective."

"Because of what happened to my parents?" Parker asked in shock.

"Yes."

Blocker's knowledge about Parker's past was creepy. He shook his head in disbelief.

"Go ahead," Greg said. "Answer him."

"Uh, I believe we need to leave room for the jury to develop its own sense of outrage at the defendant without trying to oversell it. Their sympathies will be fully engaged five minutes into the opening statement, and I suspect the defense lawyer will try to crawl in the jury box with them and agree that a tragedy occurred while planting a few small seeds of doubt about liability. He'll spend the rest of the trial watering those seeds."

"What is the most dangerous seed to the plaintiff in this case?" Blocker asked.

"Did you read my memo?" Parker asked.

"Yes."

"Then you know about the empty beer cans the police found in the defendant's vehicle. Walter Drew would have been drinking beer from a mug at the Calloway Club, which raises the question of when and where he got drunk. Could the bartender tell Drew was visibly intoxicated when he ordered the last round of drinks at the club or not? Or did Drew get drunk after leaving the bar?"

"We'll get to the bottom of that when I take the bartender's deposition followed by Drew's deposition," Greg said.

"And the depositions of as many of the patrons of the club as we can locate," Blocker added. "Have you hired a private investigator to collect that information?"

"Not yet," Greg replied. "That's on my to-do list for next week."

Parker doubted Blocker was fooled by Greg's false answer. Immediately after their initial meeting with Chet Ferguson, Parker had suggested they hire an investigator while the evidence was fresh, but his boss dismissed the idea.

"There's a former police detective from Charlotte named Ken Williams who has worked a few dramshop cases for me in the past. He'd be my choice to help."

"It sounds like you're in," Greg said with a satisfied nod of his head at Parker. "How would you propose we split the costs and fees? We have the case on one-third contingency if it settles prior to trial and forty percent if it goes to trial."

"Before we get to those details, I have another precondition to my involvement."

Parker leaned forward to listen.

"And it's nonnegotiable," Blocker continued.

"What is it?" Greg asked, shifting in his seat.

"I want Parker as my primary contact and liaison with your firm. If that's agreeable then we can split the attorney fee fifty-fifty, and I'll advance all the costs of litigation, assuming the client doesn't have the financial capability to do so. We'll also reduce the maximum potential fee to the client to one-third. I think forty percent is oppressive absent unusual circumstances that aren't present here."

While Blocker talked, Parker watched another rapid range of emotions flash across Greg's face. His boss's face ended up red.

"Why Parker?" Greg asked, glaring at his associate as if it were Parker's idea.

"My guess is that you're snowed under, and even though this is a big case for your firm, it's tough for you to consistently devote the time it deserves and needs."

"Even if that's true, you're busier than I am."

"How do you know that? At this point in my career, I'm very selective of the cases I accept, which keeps me from overcommitting my time and resources."

To actually hear a lawyer say what every lawyer dreamed of being able to do blew Parker away.

"Half the attorney fee is a lot to ask when we're the ones who brought in the case," Greg said, moving to a different point.

"How many dramshop cases have you tried to a jury?" Blocker asked.

Greg paused before answering. "None."

"How many have you settled?"

"None, but I've been in the six-figure range several times in other tort actions."

"But not several times a month and never over a million dollars, correct?"

It was a humiliating beatdown, but Parker knew Greg had brought it on himself.

"That's true," Greg replied.

"I know it's early, but what is your preliminary valuation of the claim?" Blocker asked.

"Four hundred thousand," Greg replied without hesitation.

Parker wasn't surprised at the quick response. Greg was always thinking about a case's monetary value.

"And that's without the benefit of an economist to testify about the value of Jessica's life or digging up and destroying the seeds of doubt Parker mentioned in his memo," Blocker said.

"You asked —" Greg retorted.

Parker knew Greg was about to lose his temper, which might not be a bad thing, because a cocounsel arrangement with Thomas Blocker was not a good idea.

"And you gave a reasonable answer," Blocker interjected evenly. "I think we have a reasonable chance of recovering around eight hundred thousand. Given that valuation and my willingness to advance all expenses of litigation, can we agree on splitting the attorney fee fifty-fifty?"

"Done," Greg said so fast that he almost spit into the phone.

"With Parker as my liaison."

"Yes, yes. You're right about how busy I am. The tyranny of the urgent can overwhelm the important."

"Then I look forward to working with you on the case," Blocker said. "I'll send over a cocounsel agreement. Parker can arrange a time for me to meet with the client and obtain his consent to my involvement."

The call ended. Greg lowered the receiver and looked at Parker.

"Well, what do you think?" he asked.

"Does it matter?"

"Not really," Greg said as he lifted one shoulder. "But I'm curious. Why would Blocker want you to be his primary contact with the firm?"

Parker's immediate thought was that the super-successful trial lawyer recognized his potential, but he doubted that was the idea at the front of Greg's mind.

"You tell me. You're more experienced in dealing with other lawyers."

"It's easy. He thinks he can manipulate you and do whatever he wants to do in the file. But there's no way Blocker is going to squeeze me out of the best case in the office."

"Why bring him in in the first place if you're not going to let him call the shots?"

"He'll call the shots when there's a need for him to hit the target, but Ferguson is my client. I'm going to soak up everything I can from Thomas Blocker so that next time I have a big case like this, associating him as cocounsel won't even pop up as a distant image on my radar."

CHAPTER 20

"Is that your lucky fishing hat?" Parker asked as he held open the car door for Layla.

The photographer was wearing light blue shorts and a white top along with a multi-colored floppy hat on her head.

"If SPF 50 is lucky, then yes. I don't mess with the sun."

Parker walked around the car and slipped behind the steering wheel. He didn't start the engine.

"Am I right that you like spontaneity?" he asked.

"Yes."

"Here's your first surprise of the day. We're going to have a stowaway on the boat this morning."

"A stowaway?"

"Not exactly, but that made it sound more exciting than it is. My grandfather is going to join us. Don't ask me how or why, but he manipulated the conversation when I called to borrow the boat into an opportunity for him to volunteer as our fishing guide."

"Does that mean he's a better lawyer than you are?" Layla asked with a smile.

"He won his case."

"Fine with me." Layla sat back in her seat. "I'd like to meet him."

They left New Bern and turned onto a ramp for the bridge over the Neuse.

"Do I need a fishing license?" Layla asked as they passed the city limits.

"Yes, we always fish legally. We're stopping at a bait-and-tackle shop along the way to take care of that and buy bait shrimp."

The windows of the car were cracked open and wisps of Layla's blond hair kept whipping up and out before dropping back into the car and then making another circuit. They came to the bait store and pulled into the parking lot.

While Parker selected the shrimp, a male clerk in his twenties meticulously explained the different types of fishing licenses to Layla.

"You need one that includes saltwater species," Parker said when he came up to the register.

Layla swiped her debit card to pay for a license that the clerk printed out and handed to her.

■ ■ ■ ■

It was a clear, cool morning with low humidity, a rarity on the coast. The two-lane road took them southeast and parallel to the river that was out of sight a mile to the right.

"Stop!" Layla called out. "Pull over!"

Parker slammed on the brakes and turned the steering wheel so the car went onto the shoulder of the road.

"What's wrong?" he asked.

"Did you see that tree?" Layla said, pointing to the right.

There was a small grove of stubby trees covered with scraggly leaves.

"Which one?" Parker asked, mystified.

"The interesting one. I'll only be a second."

Layla grabbed her camera and got out. There wasn't much traffic on the rural road, but Parker pulled farther onto the shoulder to be safely out of the way. Layla crouched down and pointed the camera through the limbs of a completely dead tree.

"That was an amazing tree," she said when she returned to the car.

"It was dead."

"But not its shape." Layla handed Parker

the camera. "Scroll back about ten frames and see what I got."

Parker held the camera in front of him so he could see the photos.

"Wow," he said, stopping at the third one. "It looks like it's reaching out with arms toward a cloud in the sky."

"Yeah, I think that's my favorite one. It brings together earth and heaven."

"You're right," Parker admitted. "How did you see that while we were driving down the road?"

"I saw the trees and thought there might be a photo waiting to be discovered."

They continued down the road.

"I wish I'd taken my camera inside the bait shop so I could photograph the clerk who sold me the fishing license," Layla said, staring out the window.

"He would have loved that," Parker replied.

"Did you get a good look at him?"

"Enough to know that he couldn't quit looking at you."

"He's a guy doing what guys do. I was interested because he wasn't a stereotypical redneck even though he talked like one. His teeth were perfect, and I bet he's never seen the inside of an orthodontist's office. And his eyes were the deepest brown I've ever seen. Maybe he has a Native American background, which would make sense since his hair was so straight and black."

"Do you want me to turn around and go back? You should take him outside and get him to pose like the tree with his arms reaching up to the sky."

Layla smiled. "That would work, but I'd rather get on the boat."

They reached the sandy parking area near the dock.

"That's my grandfather's car," Parker said, pointing to an aging white sedan. "He's probably down at the boat getting it ready."

Parker always relaxed when his feet touched sandy soil. Maybe it had something to do with the steady breezes caused when water and land met. He took in a deep breath.

"This is a gorgeous day," he said.

Layla was leaning over with her hands in her backpack. She looked up. "Yes, it is. Do you need my help carrying anything?"

"No, I'll grab the cooler."

Parker opened the rear door of the car and lifted out an oversized cooler with two wheels on one end. It was slow going in the sandy soil, but once they reached the wooden dock it rolled along easily.

"That's his boat," Parker said, pointing to a shiny white center-console skiff. "It looks like he's cleaned it up for you."

His grandfather stood up. In his hand was a long-handled brush. As they got closer, Parker could see a plastic bucket at his feet.

"Good morning, Opa," Parker said. "This is Layla Donovan."

Layla and Frank stared at each other for a second.

"You're the man from the church!" she exclaimed.

"Church?" Parker asked his grandfather.

"Yes," Frank replied. "And I'm very glad I went. Come aboard."

Parker hoisted the cooler onto the boat and then jumped on board. He held his hand out to Layla, whose long legs easily made the transition from the dock to the gently rocking vessel.

"I love your accent," Layla said to Frank. She followed up with several sentences in rapid-fire German. All Parker could decipher was the word for "good" and a number that he wasn't sure about. His grandfather listened before he gave a longer response in the same language.

"How's my accent?" Layla asked in English.

"Very good for an American," Frank answered.

"I hope we're not going to turn this into a New Bern Oktoberfest," Parker said to both of them.

"This is a US vessel," Frank said to Layla. "English is the primary language spoken here, but if you need to tell me something that you don't want Parker to know, feel free to use German."

Layla replied with another smattering of German that made Frank laugh.

"What did you say?" Parker asked her.

"Only what I don't want you to hear," Layla replied with a smile. "And it was complimentary, wasn't it, Mr. Haus?"

"Yes," Frank said. "But I'm not Herr Haus or Mr. House. Why don't you call me Frank?"

"Okay," Layla said.

They spent the next few minutes readying the boat for the trip. Parker stowed the cooler in a storage area under the deck while Frank snapped the fishing poles into brackets beneath the gunwale on the starboard side. Layla had her camera out taking pictures. When Frank started the boat's motor, it roared to life before he throttled it back to idle speed.

"Cast off," he said to Parker, who untied

a rope from a broad cleat on the dock.

"How fast do you want to go?" Frank asked Layla.

"Slow for now. The last bits of mist on the water won't last long, and I want to take advantage of them. It will be tougher to get nice pictures once the sun climbs up in the sky."

They left the dock, creating very little wake. Usually they took off at top speed to get to their fishing destination as quickly as possible. Layla's presence forced them to dial it back.

Clicking photos from various places on the boat, she ended up leaning so far over the bow that Parker took a step forward in case she started to tip overboard. She saw him when she straightened up.

"Hold it!" she said. "Don't go anywhere. Stay here while I give the camera to your grandfather."

Puzzled, Parker obeyed and watched as Layla handed the camera to Frank, who put the strap around his neck and received what appeared to be a quick tutorial. Layla returned to the bow.

"Ready for your *Titanic* moment?" she asked. "You know, the scene where Jack and Rose are on the front of the boat facing into the wind."

"I'm not sure this qualifies."

"Trust me."

"But why?"

"It's for your grandfather. He asked for it."

"He asked for a picture of the two of us together?"

"You sure ask a lot of questions. Strike a pose."

Layla faced downriver. Out of the corner of his eye, Parker saw his grandfather leaning against the gunwale with the camera raised to his right eye so he could capture their faces in the frame. The boat, which allowed the captain to lock the rudder in position, continued to motor forward.

"Look that way." Layla nudged Parker and pointed across the water at the distant shore. "And imagine we're heading toward a place you've always wanted to visit but never had the chance to until today."

Parker had always wanted to take the boat to Ocracoke Island, one of the most beautiful barrier islands on the entire eastern seaboard. He'd visited many times but always via the state-run ferry service.

"Okay, I have a place."

"Now imagine it's across the water at the edge of your vision."

In his mind's eye, Parker thought about

the stunning, unspoiled white beaches that looked the same as when Blackbeard the pirate and the British privateer Sir Francis Drake sailed the waters of the Outer Banks.

"Okay, we're done," Layla said after a few seconds passed.

"I'm just getting used to my happy place," Parker replied.

Layla took the camera from Frank. Parker watched as she scrolled through the photos until his grandfather stopped her with a nod of his head.

"That's my favorite too," Layla said. "You have a good eye."

"Let me see." Parker held out his hand for the camera.

Layla positioned the camera so the glare of the rising sun didn't wash out the image. In the photo, Layla was standing with her chin slightly extended. Parker had the confident look of a young man who knew where he was heading in life. The few clouds in the sky behind them softened the visual impression.

"Nice, Opa," he said.

"I agree," Layla said and then turned to Frank, who had returned to his place behind the wheel. "The sun is up in the sky. Could we go fast?"

Frank pushed the throttle forward. As they

quickly picked up speed, the powerful motor lifted the bow of the boat out of the water. Layla returned her camera to her backpack and stood by Frank. Parker stayed in the bow to watch the water rushing by. He never tired of leaving the safety of land to venture on the water. His summer on the *Aare* had been a lifesaving distraction. He could still remember the pungent smells of the sea and the nets that hung from booms and made the boat look like a crab on its back with its claws in the air.

They came into a section of chop that made the boat bounce up and down. Parker turned around. Layla had a grin on her face. Parker made his way to the stern and joined her.

"The water can change very quickly out here!" he yelled over the roar of the engine behind them.

"I like it!" she replied.

The chop increased, which made Layla laugh. His grandfather pointed to the place where a creek flowed into the water. Turning the wheel, he headed at top speed toward the mouth of the creek. He didn't slow down until he was within a few yards of the spot where it spilled into the river, when he suddenly cut the throttle. The friction of the water brought the boat to a rocking stop.

"A hundred yards up that creek is our first fishing hole," he said. "Hopefully there are some nice speckled trout hanging out there."

They slowly made their way forward. The creek was about seventy-five feet wide. Small, bushy trees clung to the bank, and a few dipped their branches into the water.

"How deep is it?" Layla asked, peering into the opaque water.

"Ten to twelve feet," Parker replied, pointing to the depth finder on the console. "There's not a lot of deep water within fifty miles of here."

Frank cut off the engine. "Drop the stern anchor so we don't drift into the bank," he said to Parker.

The boat had two anchors on narrow-link chains. Parker released the mechanism that held the one at the rear of the boat. Within seconds it hit the bottom of the creek.

"See," he said to Layla. "You could easily dive off the boat and grab a handful of mud."

"Too bad I didn't bring my bathing suit," Layla replied, making a face.

Parker was wearing his swim trunks beneath his shorts. He took off his shirt.

"Is it okay if I take a dip, Opa?" he asked.

"Sure, especially if you noodle a flounder off the bottom."

"Noodle?" Layla asked.

"Catch it with my hands," Parker replied.

"Is that possible?" she asked.

"Let's find out. Get your camera ready. It will be a fast shot. The fish don't like being grabbed."

CHAPTER 21

Parker stepped onto the deck beside the engine and dived into the water. There was no use opening his eyes as he swam straight down into the opaque water. The bottom of the creek was a mixture of sandy mud and underwater grass that was a favorite fall habitat for speckled trout. He ran his hands over the bottom until he found a nice-sized seashell that had traveled in with the tide and made its way up the narrow inlet. He stayed underwater as long as his breath allowed to increase the level of suspense for Layla on the surface. When the demand for air from his lungs couldn't be denied, he pushed off with his feet and rose up to the boat. As soon as he popped into the air, he shook his head to knock the water from his eyes. He held up the shell, which was an attractive cream and rose color.

"No flounder, but I brought you this," he

said, tossing the shell to Layla, who caught it.

Using a fold-down ladder at the rear of the boat, Parker scrambled on board and grabbed a towel from a storage bin near the engine to dry off.

"Thanks for my seashell," Layla said.

"You can put it in the glass bowl you have in the center of your kitchen table," Parker replied.

"How did you know about that?" Layla asked in surprise.

"Every woman has one," Parker answered.

Frank took the rods from their holders and laid them on the deck beside a large tackle box.

"Let's set up two with live shrimp and the other with an artificial fish lure so we can find out what's working," he said to Parker.

While the two men worked on the rods, Layla took pictures. Once the rods were ready, Frank showed Layla where to cast.

"This time of the year, the trout are just beginning to move into the creeks," he said. "They like the saltier water toward the bottom."

Layla's first cast came within inches of causing a massive line tangle in a tree limb.

"Easy," Frank said. "Not quite so forceful."

"That's the only way she knows to roll," Parker said.

"I take pictures of babies all the time without making them cry," Layla replied.

"On a day like this, the fish are more likely to be in the grassy channel than along the bank," Frank continued.

They stepped to different parts of the boat to avoid getting in one another's way.

"How cold was the water?" Frank asked Parker.

"Not too bad after the first shock," he replied. "The fish should still be active."

No sooner were the words out of his mouth than Parker felt the tap against his line that signaled the presence of a hungry fish. He quickly raised the rod tip and set the hook. The fight was on.

"It's a keeper," he said as the fish made a run, dragging out line.

"And it hit the live shrimp," Frank said. "That's what you have at the end of your line, Layla."

Parker played with the fish until it tired and then reeled it in. It was a healthy twenty-incher, perfect for eating. Layla laid down her rod and came over for a closer look. Parker held up the fish and carefully removed the lure from its lower jaw.

"Nice one," Frank said.

"Are you going to set it free?" Layla asked.

Parker and Frank both turned and stared at her.

"This is your lunch," Parker said.

"What if I'm feeling vegan today?" Layla replied, pressing her lips together.

"You're not a vegan. You loved the mango fish entrée you ate at the restaurant. All you left on the plate were the bones."

"Yes, but I wasn't there when my dinner was caught. I can see into your fish's eyes. It's pleading for its life."

Without a word, Frank took the trout from Parker and lowered it into the water, where it swished its tail once and disappeared.

"This is going to be a catch-and-release trip," he said.

"What about lunch?" Parker persisted.

"We can dock at Oriental and buy some fresh fish at one of the marinas."

"Is that okay?" Layla asked anxiously. "I don't want to ruin this for you and Parker."

"We like catching fish even if we don't eat them," Parker said. "And we never keep fish unless we intend to eat them. Opa has a freezer full of —"

"Maybe now isn't the time to bring that up," Frank interrupted.

"No, it's okay," Layla said. "I'd enjoy eating fish at your house. It's just that I wasn't ready for the thought of killing a fish I'd met in person."

Parker burst out laughing but tried to stifle it at the expression on Layla's face.

"Death is a hard reality when it's personal," Frank said in a serious tone of voice. "I'm glad you can care about a fish. We'll make this a trip for photos and fun, not for dinner."

Over the next hour, Parker caught four fish, Frank brought three into the boat, and Layla struck out.

"It can be a subtle bite," Parker said as he laid down his pole and stood beside her. "More of a tap than a hard-charging gulp."

In direct contradiction to his words, a fish suddenly hit Layla's lure with such force that it almost jerked the pole out of her hands.

"She's on!" Parker called out.

Frank, who was about to toss out his line, propped his rod against the gunwale and came over.

"Let it run!" Parker said, resisting the urge to take the rod from her hands. "The drag will slow it down a little bit."

There's nothing like the sound of a fish taking out line. The zing made Parker's heart race. Suddenly the fish stopped.

"Start reeling!" he yelled.

Layla looked at Frank. "Is that right?"

"Yes, yes," Frank said. "You can trust Parker."

Layla turned the crank on the reel, and the line quickly became taut.

"Not too fast," Parker said. "And keep the rod tip up in the air. That will maintain tension on the hook."

Layla raised the rod and slowly brought in line. The pole bent sharply.

"Let him run again," Parker said.

Layla removed her hand from the reel, and the line zipped out again.

"This could take awhile," she said. "The fish is getting farther and farther away from the boat."

"It's great if it takes a long time," Parker replied. "That means it's a fish worth catching."

Over the next ten minutes, Layla went back and forth with the fish as she brought it steadily toward the boat, only to see it take off on another run.

"It's hooked solid," Parker said to Frank, who nodded.

"Why do you say that?" Layla asked. "Am I doing something wrong?"

"No, but don't try to muscle it in. That could break the line."

"I'm stronger than I look," Layla replied.

"I don't doubt it," Parker said. "I bet you played volleyball on your high school team."

Layla glanced at him. "I did. For four years."

The fish came to the surface and flopped around for a moment. Parker's eyes widened at the scope of the splash.

"Wow," he said. "Be calm."

"I am calm," Layla replied.

"I'm not," Parker said.

Frank picked up the long-handled net he used to capture fish. The trout was about six feet from the boat when it took off on yet another run.

"He hasn't given up yet," Parker said.

"How can you tell it's a male?" Layla asked.

"You're right. Based on the way it's misbehaving, it's probably a female," Parker said, correcting himself.

"Girls don't like to get caught against their will," Layla said.

Layla brought the fish closer. This time its desire to fight was gone. Frank expertly scooped it up in the net.

"Woo-hoo!" Parker yelled. "Let's measure and weigh it."

Parker stepped over to the tackle box,

where Frank had a tape measure along with a scale.

"And bring my camera, please," Layla added.

Parker grabbed the backpack and laid it at Layla's feet. He started to take the rod from Layla, but she resisted.

"It's okay," Parker reassured her. "You can let go of the death grip on the rod. You've caught the fish."

"Sorry." Layla handed him the rod. "My hand is cramping."

Frank brought the fish into the boat. Parker dislodged the hook from the fish's lower jaw, attached the scale, and held up the fish while they all peered at the number.

"Six pounds seven ounces," Parker announced. "Awesome."

Layla snapped pictures. The fish was twenty-four inches long.

"She's chunky," Parker said.

"So if it's fat, it's a female?" Layla asked.

"No, but it is a female," Frank said. "They're called hens."

"Hens?"

"That's the term for a female trout."

"And a male is a rooster?"

Parker chuckled. "No, a male is called a jack or a buck. Give me the camera so we can forever record your first speckled hen trout. You started off with a trophy fish."

"Do I have to touch it?" Layla asked.

"Yes, and look into her eyes and imagine what she's thinking. It will add depth and emotion to the photo."

Frank handed her the fish and spoke in German.

"What did he say?" Parker asked.

"He told me I'd better squeeze her tight like I love her," Layla replied.

Parker took a succession of rapid-fire pictures. Layla's face revealed nothing about either love or imagination. All he saw was a desire to get this over with as soon as possible.

"Okay, let's release her," he said, lowering the camera.

Layla handed the fish to Frank, who stepped to the rear of the boat and slowly lowered the fish into the water. He held her so that she faced the slow current.

"What are you doing?" Layla asked.

"Letting the water flow over her gills to revive her. She's exhausted and out of breath."

"That's amazing," Layla said as the fish calmly stayed in Frank's hands. "She almost seems tame."

After a few moments, the fish slowly moved out of Frank's hands and swam away.

CHAPTER 22

Frank guided the skiff into Oriental. The clusters of sailboat masts at the town's six marinas made it look like an aspen thicket in winter. Frank drove slowly. Layla stood in the bow taking photos. The sun was directly overhead, and the corners of her floppy hat moved slightly in the breeze as she pointed the camera toward one of the marinas. They found two fishing vessels, neither as well maintained as the *Aare* in her prime. Frank and Parker stood beside each other in the stern by the wheel.

"I like her," Frank said to his grandson.

"I know why."

"Tell me."

"Because she speaks German."

Frank smiled but didn't respond. It had been a good day. His love of being on the water wasn't new, but there was a lightness in his spirit since going to church. The sun sparkled more brightly off the water, and the salt tinge in the breeze was fresher. Nothing had ever felt more alive to him than holding Layla's fish in the water waiting for it to catch its watery breath. Parker stepped to the front of the boat, and spoke to Layla.

"Head toward that vintage two-master!" he called out to Frank. "She wants a close-up."

Frank was familiar with the boat, an antique yawl formerly used as a commercial fishing vessel. The boat had a small mizzen sail aft of the rudderpost. The purpose of the secondary sail was to keep the boat steady when hauling in nets. Now it was a luxury craft with shiny wood accents and gleaming brass. Frank had always been curious about the interior restoration of the vessel. He throttled back, and they came to a rocking stop as Layla took pictures. A man in his fifties came up from belowdecks on the sailboat and saw them.

"I love your boat," Layla called out.

"Would you like to come aboard for a tour?" the man asked.

Layla glanced back at Frank, who nodded. He eased his boat closer, and Parker tossed a line to the man, who secured the skiff snug against a pair of protective bumpers. Frank cut the engine.

"Bring your whole crew," the man said.

They spent the next thirty minutes receiving a guided tour of the boat from one end to the other. Frank especially enjoyed the parts of the craft that hinted at its commercial fishing heritage. When they finished, Layla left with the owner's card and a promise to send him a computer disc containing a photo gallery of his vessel. They returned to Frank's skiff and cast off.

"That was fascinating," Parker said. "And we wouldn't have gotten a personal tour without Layla's help."

"That's not true," she replied.

"It is. For the same reason you received extra attention from the clerk who sold you a fishing license."

Layla smiled without answering. They pulled up to a marine fuel station.

"How many gallons do I need to buy to tie up for a couple of hours?" Frank asked the attendant who came out of a tiny shed at their approach.

Because the boat was designed to venture into the ocean for day trips, it had an extra-large-capacity gas tank. Frank bought enough fuel so there wouldn't be a charge to leave the boat in one of four short-term slips. He refused Parker's offer to pay for the gas.

It was a short walk along the water to a

commercial dock where fishermen off-loaded their catches. Layla was taking so many pictures that Frank was worried she'd miss a step and spill into the water. He walked between her and the river as a safety buffer. They entered a small building where freshly caught fish rested on beds of ice.

"Let's avoid the speckled trout," Frank said. "It will be at least a week before Layla wants to face a trout on her plate."

Frank spotted some flounder and showed them to Parker and Layla.

"You pick 'em, Opa," Parker said. "You know the best size to grill."

Frank selected three flounder that the owner put in a clear plastic bag.

"All right," Frank said. "I'll clean the fish on the boat while you and Layla take everything else to the park."

Frank's knife skills remained undiminished by age, and he sliced uniform fillets of flounder and then threw them into a bag containing a soy sauce and sesame oil–based marinade. The fish would soak in the seasoning while the coals in a tiny homemade grill heated up. Frank hummed an old German folk song as he worked. When he reached the chorus, he stopped. The song took him back to a place he'd not visited in a long time.

■ ■ ■ ■

Northern Italy, 1943

Late one night General Berg summoned Franz to a meeting in the general's quarters. Franz, who had already taken off his dress uniform, got ready as quickly as he could. He had a queasy feeling in his stomach as he arrived at the hotel that had been commandeered by the general. A guard snapped to attention before opening the door to an enormous second-floor suite. Inside, General Berg and an officer Franz didn't recognize were listening to a gramophone recording of "Ich hab die Nacht geträumet," a famous folk song. When the other officer stood, Franz saw from his insignia that he was a generaloberst, which meant he outranked a senior-division commander like General Berg, who was a generalleutnant. General Berg turned off the gramophone.

"Hauptmann Haus, this is General Krieger. He arrived earlier this evening from Berlin."

Surprisingly young, Krieger was handsome, trim, and athletic, with blond hair and chiseled features appropriate for a poster promoting Aryan supremacy. Franz guessed Krieger's career had been artificially accelerated by someone very powerful.

"General Krieger has a keen interest in the Medici period," General Berg said as he poured a glass of wine.

"Or any period in which there was an appreciation for fine art," Krieger added. "Especially if it involves fine workmanship in gold. Gold has the unique ability to maintain its worth, whether in raw form or shaped into something independently beautiful."

Since he'd been in Italy, Franz had learned a little about the House of Medici and its patronage of famous artists like Botticelli and Michelangelo.

"I'm not an art expert, sir," Franz replied nervously.

"But I told the general you might be able to suggest where he could find some objects of interest to him," Berg replied, sipping his wine. "You've had time to explore the area since we've been here, haven't you?"

"Yes, sir. Those were your orders."

"Give the matter consideration and let me know if you have any suggestions for the location of items of interest to the general," Berg said. "You're dismissed."

"That's it?" Krieger asked General Berg sharply.

"Yes, Herr General. Hauptmann Haus will

get back to us. Remember what I told you about his strategic assistance when we broke through the French sector in southern Belgium. I call him my Aryan Eagle."

Franz shifted his weight from one foot to the other. He suspected General Berg had already had too much to drink, which might explain his uncharacteristic boasting to General Krieger about Franz's ability to witness the future.

Krieger raised his voice. "This is absurd!"

"You're going to be here for a couple of days," Berg replied with a strained calm. "Let's see what develops."

Krieger turned his back on Franz.

"You may leave now, Hauptmann," Berg said.

Franz saluted, gave as emphatic a "Heil Hitler" as he could summon, and walked toward the door. When he had his hand on the knob, he stopped and didn't open it. He turned around.

"Herr General?" he said to Berg, who was now standing by the gramophone preparing to resume the recording.

"Yes, Hauptmann."

"There is a house on the Piazza del Campo in Siena. It might be worth looking there for art objects of interest to the general."

"Do you know the place?" Berg asked, his face lighting up.

"I will recognize it," Franz replied. "It has a cream-colored stone front that is different from other houses on the street."

"Items may have been moved there to get them out of Florence," Berg said to Krieger, who, wide-eyed, was now staring at Franz as if he had two heads.

"What do you suggest?" Krieger asked Berg.

"Send Hauptmann Haus with a detail of ten or so men to check it out."

"I wouldn't know exactly what we're searching for," Franz said.

"That's fine," Berg replied with a dismissive wave of his hand. "Oberst Adler, who is on General Krieger's staff, will be in charge. You just point out the house. He'll do the rest."

"I'll go as well," Krieger said, his eyes boring holes into Franz. "To verify the accuracy of the information."

"Certainly." Berg held up a full glass of wine. "And thank you, Herr General, for this excellent wine. Let's drink to a successful venture."

"This is not a joint business arrangement," Krieger replied, keeping his own glass lowered.

Berg's face suddenly became serious. "Of course not. I simply want to toast your success. A simple soldier like me can enjoy a good bottle of wine, but I lack the ability to appreciate art. I have no desire to be a collector."

Franz's palms were sweaty and his mouth was dry.

"Oberst Adler will let you know when to leave in the morning," Berg said to him. "Good night, Hauptmann."

Franz left the room. He now suspected General Berg's nonchalant attitude and apparent intoxication were feigned. His commander was afraid of Krieger and, for some unknown reason, desperate to curry the senior officer's favor. Franz paused at the top of a marble staircase. Failure to satisfy Krieger's expectations would likely have far worse consequences for Franz than for General Berg.

Parker had the fire going when Frank arrived with the fish. A red-and-white-checked cloth was draped over the concrete picnic table. Frank shook the bag of fish so the marinade could swirl around.

"The coals will be ready in about five minutes," Parker said.

"Where's Layla?" Frank asked.

"Looking for a Pulitzer Prize–winning photograph."

"I'm not sure she'll find a topic that serious in Oriental."

"But she'll try."

Frank placed the bag of fish on one of the benches for the table. "What do you know about Layla's background?" he asked Parker.

"Not a lot. She's divorced, and her father is a big-time trial lawyer."

"Where did she learn to speak such excellent German?"

"Why don't you ask her?" Parker replied, pointing toward Layla, who was approaching across the green grass. "In German, of course."

"I'm starving!" Layla said as she came up to them. "I've been taking pictures of people fixing food and eating here in the park, and my stomach just told my brain to ditch the camera and grab a fork."

Frank took the flounder from the bag and laid them on the grill. "In a few minutes we can satisfy your hunger," he said.

While Frank cooked the fish, Layla stood between him and Parker so they could see some of the pictures she'd taken since they left the dock.

"I've deleted a bunch already," Layla said

as she scrolled through them. "If you see any you like, I can give you copies."

"I want a bunch of them," Parker replied. "Why don't you organize the best?"

"Three-by-fives are fine with me," Frank said, poking the fish with tongs. "I don't need any big ones."

Several minutes later Frank watched Layla savor her third bite of hot flounder.

"This is better than cake," she said. "The fish is so delicate, and the marinade is subtle. You didn't overseason it."

"I would have," Frank answered. "It didn't marinate as long as I prefer."

"This is perfect," Layla replied. "Just like today."

CHAPTER 23

During the drive back to New Bern, Parker thought about telling Layla that Greg had associated her father as cocounsel in a big case, but he really didn't want to talk about the law. They crossed the bridge over Neuse River.

"Opa asked me where you learned to speak German," Parker said, settling on a safer subject. "I've never seen him enjoy talking with someone so much before."

"I didn't have a choice," she replied. "It wasn't an option with my father."

"Why?"

"Family history, which, as you know, is a huge deal to him. I'd want to forget about that sort of thing after settling in a new country, but my father is fascinated by anything that has to do with our German heritage. He forced me to go to meetings of German American groups when I was a kid. I even had a private tutor who taught me

German from age six on up."

"That's intense."

"But not unusual for us. Your grandfather told me he immigrated to the US from Switzerland after World War II."

"That's right."

"What did he do during the war?"

"He's never talked much about it," Parker answered. "But his entire family was wiped out during an air raid on Dresden."

"That's terrible."

To Parker's relief, Layla didn't press for more information. He pulled into the parking lot for her apartment.

"Will you have plenty of time to prepare for your engagement shoot?" he asked.

"Yes, and I had a great time on the boat. I'm glad your grandfather invited himself to come along too. I really like him."

"And he likes you. He's never shown much interest —" Parker stopped.

"In the girls you date?" Layla finished the sentence with a smile. "I'm not sure we've actually gone out on a date."

Parker turned off the car's engine. "Would you like to?" he asked.

Layla nodded her head. "Yes, I would."

The following morning Frank stood beside Layla at the church. He'd left his suit and tie at home and put on navy slacks and a white short-sleeved shirt. He enjoyed the sound of the voices singing but didn't try to join in the unfamiliar songs. Eric preached a message designed to encourage a person in their twenties or thirties to use their gifts and abilities for God instead of wasting them on worldly ambitions or burying them in the sand. The minister's text was the parable of the talents in the book of Matthew. To the young adults in the crowd, it was a spiritual pep talk. For Frank, it uncovered a layer of guilt he didn't know existed.

He'd thought his sins fit snugly within the basket of things he'd done to harm people without considering that what he'd failed to do in life might also be a wrong requiring repentance. At Frank's age, it was a message devoid of hope, and he regretted making the effort to drive into town to attend the meeting. He shifted uncomfortably in his seat. Layla, who was taking notes, didn't seem to notice.

Then, as Eric wrapped up the message, he turned to an earlier chapter in Matthew and read the parable of the workers in the vineyard. Frank followed along as the words from Scripture appeared on a screen at the front of the room: "For the kingdom of heaven is like a landowner who went out early in the morning to hire workers for his vineyard. He agreed to pay them a denarius for the day and sent them into his vineyard."

Frank didn't know the story. More and more workers went to work in the vineyard. Frank was intrigued by why, at five in the afternoon, the owner of the vineyard hired a last batch of laborers who would work for only one hour. When he operated his fishing boat, Frank never would have considered hiring a man who wasn't willing and available to put in a full day's work.

When evening came, the owner of the vineyard said to his foreman, "Call the workers and pay them their wages, beginning with the last ones hired and going on to the first." The workers who were hired about five in the afternoon came and each received a denarius. So when those came who were hired first, they expected to receive more. But each one of them also received a denarius. When they received it, they began to grumble against the landowner. "These who were hired last worked only one hour," they said, "and you have made them equal to us who have borne the burden of the work and the heat of the day." But he answered one of them, "I am not being unfair to you, friend. Didn't you agree to work for a denarius? Take your pay and go. I want to give the one who was hired last the same as I gave you. Don't I have the right to do what I want with my own money? Or are you envious because I am generous?"

Eric finished and looked up. Frank's heart was beating a bit faster than normal.

"Given the generous nature of God," Eric said, "does anyone here have a reason not to ask the Lord to send him or her into the world to use the gifts God has given them for the time they have left?"

During the closing prayer, Frank prayed earnestly that God might use him, even at this late juncture of his life. No internal visions provided help or insight. The service ended, and they stood up.

"What did you think about the message?" Layla asked in German, patting him on the arm.

"Parker calls me Opa," Frank replied in the same language, "but when it comes to Christianity, I feel like a little child."

"You say that like it's a bad thing," Layla answered. "But that's how we all have to be if we want to enter the kingdom of God."

Monday morning Parker holed up in his office working on *Ferguson v. Callaway Club.* He'd received a detailed memo in his inbox from Thomas Blocker with twelve action steps. Parker was impressed. Greg would have launched into the case with legal guns blazing. Blocker took a different approach. The level of organization and attention to detail a premier trial lawyer utilized in setting up and investigating a potential lawsuit made the process used at Branham and Camp look like a preschool coloring book. Parker wanted to absorb Blocker's methodology through every legal pore in his body. There was a knock on the door.

"Come in," he said.

It was Dexter. "How are you doing?" the partner asked.

"Fine," Parker replied, pushing away some of the paperwork spread out on his desk. "Did Greg tell you we've associated Thomas Blocker in the dramshop case?"

"Yeah, he's pumped up about it. He believes we're going to hit a grand slam." Dexter held up a sheet of paper in his hand. "Uh, Donna McAlpine filed a complaint against you with the state bar. She says you failed to inform her that you'd never handled a DUI case before, and if she'd known about your lack of experience, she wouldn't have let you represent her."

Parker gritted his teeth for a moment before responding. "Did she also mention that I represented her pro bono and was able to get the assistant DA to agree to a plea deal that was five times better than what she deserved?"

"No, and there's no ethical requirement for you to reveal your level of experience to a client. You passed the bar, and you're licensed to practice law in North Carolina. Look, I'm the one who asked you to help her, and I feel lousy that she's done this."

"What do I do about it?"

Dexter took a step back and glanced down the hallway for a moment. "I've never had a complaint filed against me," he said. "But it's happened several times to Greg. You might want to look at one of his responses. Basically, I think you tell the bar what took place from your perspective and wait for it to go away."

"Does Greg know about this?"

"No, because I didn't want to get in an argument with him about asking you to represent her pro bono."

"And Donna got a great result." Parker shook his head. "She has nothing better to do than sit in her jail cell and think about blaming someone else for her problems. I'll ask Vicki to pull a couple of the grievances against Greg and look them over."

Dexter laid the sheet of paper on the front of Parker's desk and left. Parker read the complaint and resisted the urge to wad it up and throw it across the room. Instead, he slipped it into the top drawer of his desk. Pushing the bar grievance out of his mind, he went back to work on the Ferguson case. An hour later he took a break and walked down the hallway. Greg's door was open, and the lawyer had his feet propped up on his desk while he talked on the phone. He motioned for Parker to enter.

"We have a deal based on your last e-mail," Greg said to the caller on the other end of the line. "Send me a draft settlement agreement, and I'll go over it with my client."

He hung up the phone. "I've resolved the Bontemps case."

"How?" Parker asked in surprise.

"Both companies want to continue to do business together because they can make more money jointly than they can separately. They just needed help getting over the hurdle in front of them."

From what he'd seen in the file, it was hard for Parker to imagine the owners being civil at a cocktail party, much less cooperating in a complicated business venture.

"The desire to make money can create strange bedfellows," Greg continued. "What have you done productive today?"

Parker handed him the memo from Blocker. "I thought you might be interested in looking this over. He raises a bunch of good points about things we should do."

Parker watched as Greg quickly read it.

"Yeah, if this is the only case on your docket. The practice of law is art as well as science. Blocker is suffering from obsessive-compulsive disorder. Next time you talk to him, ask if he has to wash his hands three times every time he goes to the bathroom."

"I just thought —"

"I'm kidding," Greg said, cutting him off. "Thomas Blocker is the man. Is this my copy of the memo?"

"Yes."

"And remember that I told you to keep me in the center of the circle, regardless of what he said about dealing primarily with you."

"That's why I'm here."

"Good."

Frank picked up the Bible that lay on a small table beside his recliner. He'd been reading through the New Testament after drinking his morning coffee, and it was the day to begin the Gospel of John. He immediately recognized a difference in the way the apostle John presented the words and mission of Jesus compared with Matthew, Mark, and Luke. There was a somber majesty to the proclamation of the Word becoming flesh, but the passage that captured Frank's attention began later in the first chapter:

The next day Jesus decided to leave for Galilee. Finding Philip, he said to him, "Follow me."

Philip, like Andrew and Peter, was from the town of Bethsaida. Philip found Nathanael and told him, "We have found the one Moses wrote about in the Law, and about whom the prophets also wrote — Jesus of Nazareth, the son of Joseph."

"Nazareth! Can anything good come from there?" Nathanael asked.

"Come and see," said Philip.

When Jesus saw Nathanael approaching, he said of him, "Here truly is an Israelite in whom there is no deceit."

"How do you know me?" Nathanael asked.

Jesus answered, "I saw you while you were still under the fig tree before Philip called you."

Then Nathanael declared, "Rabbi, you are the Son of God; you are the king of Israel."

Jesus said, "You believe because I told you I saw you under the fig tree. You will see greater things than that."

Stunned, Frank left the book open in his lap. He might not be able to understand everything that happened in the Bible, but Jesus seeing Nathanael under a fig tree before they actually met made perfect sense to him. And Frank knew at least one talent he could try to use for God before his time in the vineyard came to an end.

An hour later he and Lenny stood in the open doorway of the shed where Frank kept his fishing tackle.

"Do you want to head down toward Oriental and try to catch some speckled trout?" Frank asked. "I had good luck the other day on one of the creeks with Parker and a friend of his, a young woman photographer."

"Photographer?"

"Yeah, she served on the jury for a case handled by Parker's firm. And then I met her when I went to church. Her German is way better than your Vietnamese."

Lenny took a light-action rod suitable for

trout fishing from its place on the wall of the shed. "You wouldn't know if I was speaking Vietnamese or faking it. Are she and Parker dating?"

"I'm not sure, but I'd like it if they did."

"Did you say that to Parker?"

"Of course not."

"You should," Lenny said. "Remember telling us that Chris should meet Sally Henderson?"

Frank paused. After reading about Jesus' encounter with Nathanael in John chapter 1, he saw the conversation in a new light.

"Yeah," he said.

"We invited her parents over to the house for hamburgers on Saturday afternoon, and Sally came with them. She and Chris ended up going for a long ride in that dune buggy he built last year. He drives like a maniac in that thing, and I'm not crazy enough to get in it with him, but she seemed to enjoy it. They're going to see each other again."

"Well, every once in a while I have a good idea," Frank replied with a smile. "Are you sure you want to catch some specs?"

"Yeah, it's been awhile since I ate any fresh trout."

While they organized the tackle, Frank told Lenny about the fishing trip with Parker and Layla turning into catch and release instead of catch and eat.

"And an old commercial fisherman like you kept his mouth shut?" Lenny chuckled. "I can't believe that."

"Lenny, when I looked in that fish's eyes, I had an incredible urge to let it slip back into the water."

Lenny laughed again. "Liar, but it makes a heck of a fish story."

Chapter 24

By midweek, Parker was beginning to wonder if Thomas Blocker was serious about coming alongside as cocounsel in the Ferguson case. After the initial surge of activity generated by his memo, the trial lawyer had canceled two appointments to meet with Chet Ferguson and didn't even call to apologize. Instead, he had one of his legal assistants do so for him. After they received news of the second no-show, Greg sat with his head down for a few seconds.

"One more chance," he said, looking up. "Then I'm going to be one of the few lawyers in the state who've fired Thomas Blocker."

"Even though there's a lot he can teach us, it may be for the best," Parker replied.

"Yeah, I've picked up that vibe from you since the first phone call we had with him about the case, but I think you're off base. Blocker intimidates you. He doesn't intimidate me. After you've been practicing as long as I have, maybe you'll realize that whenever you enter a room it's your chance to fill up the space."

"Do you want me to try to reschedule a third meeting?" Parker asked.

"It's up to him to call us. Let's put a five-day deadline on him."

The following day Greg was out of town for an oral argument at the court of appeals in Raleigh. Parker was in his office trying to unravel a complicated easement dispute between two neighbors who had been friends but were now enemies.

"I know you told me to hold your calls for an hour or so, but do you want to talk to Thomas Blocker?" Vicki asked.

"I'd be glad to talk to anyone."

He picked up the phone as the call came through.

"I've had some time open up today and can scoot up to New Bern and meet with Mr. Ferguson," Blocker began. "Any chance we can set it up on short notice?"

"Greg is in Raleigh for oral argument at the court of appeals."

"In *Sayers v. Burleson*?"

"Yes," Parker replied in amazement. "How did you know?"

"It's not the sort of initial meeting that

314

requires Greg's presence," Blocker answered, ignoring Parker's question. "And you'll be there on behalf of the firm."

Parker was unsure what to do. If he turned Blocker down, Greg might chew him out for not closing the deal. If he said yes, Greg could blow up because he wasn't invited to the party.

"Okay," he said slowly. "I'll give Chet Ferguson a call."

"Do it soon. My assistant says he has a teacher conference at his son's school around four o'clock."

Parker shook his head in disbelief. "Mr. Blocker, what did I have for breakfast this morning?" he asked.

"I have no idea. What did I have?"

"Granola cereal topped with banana and black coffee."

"You're right, except I had strawberries instead of banana. Let me know about the appointment ASAP."

Parker ended the call, not sure whether Blocker was lying or teasing about granola cereal and coffee.

Frank and Lenny were sitting on the screened-in porch drinking a second cup of coffee. A slight breeze slipped through the wire mesh.

"I was a deserter," Frank continued. "I abandoned my unit in June 1944 and fled to Switzerland."

"I've always wondered how the war ended for you," Lenny said softly. "I'm just glad you made it through alive."

"I doubt that would be the reaction of my comrades in Germany, even after all these years have passed."

"Did that come up with the man who visited you last week?"

Frank shook his head. "No, he wanted to thank me for saving his life, which I guess means I did something good."

"Why did you decide to desert? What caused it?"

Frank told him about the death of his family in Dresden.

"Were they killed as part of the firebombing the British did? I've seen pictures. It was terrible."

"No, it was a random, solitary hit several months before that happened, probably a plane with an extra bomb that dropped it to lighten its load before heading home."

Lenny shook his head. "There's no pattern for those who live and those who die, whether soldiers or civilians."

"That's not the only reason I deserted," Frank said. Then he told him about the impact General Krieger's possible visit to southern Germany had on Frank's decision to flee. Lenny's eyes widened.

"You think this guy was going to drag you to Berlin? How can you be sure?"

"I'm sure. At that point there was nothing and no one left for me in Germany. I knew we were going to lose the war, and the desire to fight was gone. If I'd gone to Berlin, I would have died in a bunker or been executed by the Russians. So I stole a motorcycle and made it across the Rhine by bribing a ferryman at Basel. I spent the rest of the war working as a fisherman."

"A fisherman?"

"I lived with an elderly man and his grandson." Frank stopped and smiled. "The elderly man was probably about your age."

Lenny laughed. "Ancient. And you came to New Bern after the war ended."

"Yes. The visit the other day by my former comrade stirred up memories from the war years that I'd pushed down and buried so deep I thought they were gone for good. Even though I never fired my weapon in combat, many, many people died because of my actions."

"I don't understand."

Frank stared out at the peaceful scene in his backyard for a moment before he answered. "I offered strategic advice to my commanding officers. Someone else fired the bullets."

"That's happened in every headquarters for any army over the past three thousand years. The ultimate goal of war is to defeat the enemy, which means people die."

"Not the way I did it," Frank replied, pointing to his head. "I knew things in here that didn't come from field reconnaissance, intelligence information, or the study of military history. I witnessed things before they happened."

"I'm not following you," Lenny said, a puzzled look on his face.

"Do you remember when I suggested to you and Mattie that Chris might want to get to know Sally?"

"Of course."

"The idea for that came from the same place inside me as the advice I gave General Berg during the war. I've kept my mouth shut for so long that I wasn't sure I still had the ability to see into the future or pull back the curtain on things hidden in the past. Being around Conrad Mueller stirred up —"

"Frank, you're freaking me out," Lenny said, cutting him off. "If I didn't know better, I'd think you had Alzheimer's or something."

Every reason that had kept Frank silent for decades rushed back into his mind. There was a limit to what he needed to reveal and confess, even to his close friend.

"Maybe you're right," Frank said. "Not that I have Alzheimer's, but it's crazy to think that I could predict what was going to happen back then, or now."

Lenny took a final drink of coffee. "You're a smart guy," he said, putting his empty cup on the wooden floor of the porch. "Everyone knows that. And if you have any ideas about how I can catch bigger fish, I'm listening. That's the kind of inside information I'm interested in. But you need to put what happened during the war behind you. Some of my buddies who coped pretty well when they were younger now have trouble with flashbacks and panic attacks. I don't want to see something like that happen to you. Whether we like it or not, age doesn't make us stronger; it makes us weaker."

While Lenny talked, Frank saw his friend wearing army fatigues with his face pressed tightly against the ground. Suddenly Lenny shut his eyes and fired several rapid bursts from an automatic rifle. An American soldier in front of Lenny and to his left fell forward as one of the bullets hit him squarely in the back, killing him instantly. Lenny didn't see it because he kept his head close to the ground.

"Yes," Frank said. "You're right. It's better to leave what happened during the war behind us and not bring it up."

Parker furiously took notes as Thomas Blocker talked with Chet Ferguson and discovered additional facts about the case Greg hadn't uncovered. Ferguson and Blocker clicked immediately. The trial lawyer knew how to catch and reel in a client's trust as effectively as Opa did a flounder on a hook. Over a ninety-minute time frame, Ferguson revealed that Jessica's father was an alcoholic who died from liver failure. His wife's response was to volunteer once a month at a local alcohol treatment center.

"What about your marriage?" Parker asked when Blocker paused for a moment.

"It was great," Ferguson replied. "Jessica was the love of my life and my best friend."

Parker wanted to retreat to his notepad but couldn't. He cleared his throat. "Was there ever a time when you were separated?"

Ferguson stared at Parker for a moment. "Not legally."

"Did you ever move out of the house?"

"I thought you were my lawyer. Who have you been talking to?" Ferguson asked sharply.

"We need to know everything so we don't get ambushed at trial," Blocker jumped in. "Every couple faces challenges."

Ferguson blinked his eyes a few times. "Like I said earlier, we married young. I was nineteen, she was eighteen. We changed a lot, and earlier this year I wasn't sure I could measure up to all she expected me to be. So I moved in with a single guy at work and stayed at his apartment for four months while Jessica and I went to a counselor at our church. But we were committed to making the marriage work, and not just for the sake of the kids. That had been one of our problems all along. The light came on for us when a counselor at our church told us that for people who marry young it's necessary to recognize and adapt to changes. The woman told me that I was married to Jessica 2.0, but I was stuck in Chet 1.0 and needed to catch up. Admitting that I needed to look in the mirror was a big deal for me. I moved back home three weeks before the wreck. It was like we were newlyweds, only better." Chet stopped as tears welled up in his eyes. "This happens to me all the time when I talk about Jessica."

"It's like she's still here, and you're planning a life together," Blocker added in a soft tone of voice.

"Yeah. I'm not one of those guys who loses his wife and wants to get involved with someone else as soon as a reasonable time passes. The tough times Jessica and I went through made me want to succeed in marriage, not give up. Moving on from that mind-set is going to be very hard for me."

"Chet, being honest like this will make your marriage real in the eyes of the jury and help them appreciate what's been taken from you," Blocker said before he turned to Parker. "Thanks for asking the tough questions and not giving up."

Blocker moved on to questions about Jessica's relationship with her children and other members of her family.

"Here's how it will work," Blocker said as he began to wind down. "Greg and Parker are your lawyers, but so am I. They've brought me into the case because I've handled several of these types of cases, and we believe you and your children have a legitimate claim against the defendant."

"I get it. You're a specialist," Chet said. "Like a doctor who treats the heart."

"The state bar doesn't recognize a specialization in dramshop cases, but I have experience to bring to the table. Carl Bruffey, the lawyer who usually represents the insurance company that issued the policy to the tavern, knows who I am."

"And you've beaten him?" Chet asked.

"Yes, and he's beaten me. But the last couple of times I've come out on top. One of those cases involved a settlement in excess of a million dollars after we selected a jury and delivered opening statements. It's too soon to predict what's going to happen in your case."

Looking at Parker, Blocker asked, "Unless you already have a sense of how this is going to turn out?"

Parker's fingers froze to the pen, and he quickly looked up to find Chet staring at him and Blocker eyeing him with a hint of a smile on his face.

"Uh, no," Parker replied. "But I'm glad to have you involved."

After Ferguson left, Parker and Blocker stayed in the downstairs conference room.

"Seeing you talk to the client was an education," Parker said. "You really listened to him and drew things out of him that went way beyond the legally relevant facts. You had him at ease within five minutes by asking open-ended questions that made him feel in charge of the conversation even though he wasn't."

"But you hit the home run when you pried the truth out of him about his relationship with his wife."

"Greg would have tried to hide it," Parker replied. "I mean, he might have taken that approach."

"Chet's story shows that Jessica's death snuffed out their hope for the future. I believe every woman on the jury will devour what he has to say, and woe to Bruffey if he tries to make our client look like a villain."

Parker walked Blocker out of the office to his black Mercedes.

"Where did Greg Branham find you?" Blocker asked when they reached his car.

"I was glad to get a job."

"Have you talked any more to Layla?" Blocker asked.

"Yes, she met my grandfather, and they enjoyed speaking German, which left me out of the conversation."

"Don't forget, I'd really like to meet your grandfather. Would you be able to arrange a time for us to get together?"

"Uh, probably."

"Sehr gut," Blocker replied with a smile.

Chapter 25

The following morning Parker told Greg about the meeting with Thomas Blocker and Chet Ferguson and then held his breath as he waited for Greg's reply.

"Good initiative," Greg said with a nod of his head. "You don't need me to hold your hand twenty-four seven."

"And a follow-up memo from Blocker dropped into my in-box around midnight last night," Parker said. "The guy is a machine. I've been working on it this morning."

"Okay, the more you work on the case, the stronger our position regarding attorney fees."

"What do you mean? The split is set. Blocker only gets paid if we recover at least eight hundred thousand dollars."

"That's in the paperwork, but whenever there's a cocounsel situation, you have to watch your back in case the other lawyer tries to snake the case. If that happens, you can end up in a hearing before a judge arguing quantum meruit, which means the lawyers with the most time in the case get the lion's share of the fee."

"If you don't trust Blocker, why did you associate him?" Parker asked, perplexed.

Greg shrugged. "I don't trust anybody. But that doesn't mean I won't take a chance on a joint representation, especially when the reward exceeds the risk. Remember what happened in the Bontemps case? People work well together when it's mutually beneficial. Get back to Blocker as soon as you can on the memo. Copy me too."

Northern Italy, 1943
Franz stood on the sidewalk in front of the hotel that served as General Berg's headquarters and waited anxiously for Oberst Adler and the detachment of soldiers to arrive. He heard a commotion behind him and turned around. It was General Krieger and two aides descending the steps. Franz jerked to attention.

"Hauptmann, I am here to accompany you and observe," Krieger said. "You have piqued my curiosity."

"Does General Berg want to increase the size of the detail to ensure your security,

Herr General?" Franz replied.

"Actually, I've reduced the size of the detail myself," Krieger replied. "Too many eyes and ears can create problems on a mission like this. Do you anticipate any unforeseen problems?"

Franz felt a sour sickness in his stomach but didn't know exactly what it meant. "Uh, I'm not sure, sir," he managed.

Krieger leaned closer so that only Franz could hear him. "You'd better be sure that I'm not wasting my time, Hauptmann. Is that clear?"

"Yes, Herr General," Franz replied, trying to keep his voice from trembling.

Oberst Adler arrived in a staff car followed by a covered truck with five soldiers riding in the back.

"Ride in the truck and lead the way," Krieger said to Franz. "We'll follow in the car."

Franz climbed into the truck beside the driver, a large man with thick, meaty arms. It was a forty-five-minute drive to Siena through the beautiful low hills of Tuscany. Franz had been to Siena on two occasions, but the precise location of the cream-colored house had not been part of his vision. They reached the outskirts of town.

"Turn left at the next intersection," Franz

told the driver.

They drove eight blocks, drawing closer to the center of town and the famous Siena Cathedral, a twelfth-century duomo that was one of the greatest examples of the Romanesque-Gothic style in the entire country.

"Turn here!" Franz called out.

"Which way?" the driver replied as he slammed on the brakes.

Franz heard several thuds as the soldiers in the rear of the truck were thrown from the benches.

"Left," Franz said.

A hundred meters down the narrow street Franz saw the cream-colored house on the right-hand side of the road.

"That's it," he said with relief, pointing it out to the driver. "Stop there."

There was a narrow alley on one side of the house. The driver stopped the truck, blocking it. Weapons on ready, the troops hopped out and took up positions on the sidewalk. The car rolled to a stop behind the truck. Krieger and Oberst Adler got out.

"Quite dramatic," Krieger said to Franz as the general looked up at the house. "You've never been here before?"

"Twice to Siena but never on this street."

Krieger gestured to Adler, who approached the door and banged on it with a gloved fist. Franz remained on the sidewalk looking up at the windows of other houses on the street. He caught glimpses of faces peeking down from above. Each window could be transformed in an instant into a gun turret. Adler banged his fist again. The door opened, and an elderly man wearing a black beret appeared. He spoke in Italian, and Adler answered. Franz didn't know what was said, but the oberst briskly pushed the man aside and, with the soldiers trailing behind him, entered the house. Franz remained on the sidewalk with Krieger and a single guard.

"Are you proficient with your weapon, Hauptmann?" Krieger asked, pointing at Franz's sidearm. "Or is it just for show?"

"I am certified as a marksman with the Luger, sir," Franz replied.

"And how many times have you fired it in battle?"

"Never, sir."

Krieger looked at the houses that hemmed them in on the narrow street. "Let's hope today isn't the first."

Adler came out of the house and approached the general. "The servant claims he's living there alone while the owner is in Rome," the officer said. "But we found a man and two women hiding in a closet in an upstairs bedroom. Also, there is an attic filled with large wooden crates."

"That's what I saw," Franz said before Krieger could respond. "Check the crates."

"Do it," Krieger said to Adler. "And set a guard on the man and two women. I want to see them before we leave."

Adler returned to the house, and Krieger turned to Franz. "What will we find in the crates?" he asked.

"I'm not exactly sure, sir," Franz replied. "But I hope it will be worth the trip."

"Good," Krieger replied. "You're doing well. Quite well. I understand the value General Berg places on you."

A group of young Italian men turned onto the street. When they saw the Germans on the sidewalk they stopped, talked for a moment, and retreated.

"They could be a threat," Franz said to Krieger.

"Were they armed?" the general replied.

"No, sir, but they have access to weapons and know how to use them."

Krieger stepped to the door of the house and yelled up for Adler to hurry. Less than a minute later, two soldiers emerged carrying a large crate. Adler was behind them. He and Krieger stepped a few feet away from Franz and spoke in whispers. Franz saw Krieger's eyes widen. The general nodded.

"Excellent," he said to Franz when he returned to his side. "This is definitely not a wasted trip."

Over the next thirty minutes more than twenty crates were removed from the house. Some were obviously heavier than others and took four men to carry. The combined weight of the crates caused the truck bed to lower onto the wheels.

Adler came up to Krieger. "That's all, sir. I checked each container in private to make sure they were worth removing, then sealed them myself."

"Very well."

Two soldiers emerged from the house, their machine guns trained on a man in his twenties and two women who looked like twins in their late teens. The soldiers brought the young people before the general. The man spoke in Italian. Adler translated for Krieger.

"They claim to be visitors from Milan," the oberst said.

A window opened in a house across the street. One of the soldiers turned and aimed his weapon.

"Juden! Juden!" a woman's voice called out.

The window closed. One of the girls began to shake uncontrollably. Suddenly the young man leaned over and pulled a knife from his boot. Before he could step forward, Franz heard the quick retort of a machine gun. All three of the young people fell to the pavement. A soldier standing behind the officers lowered his weapon. Two other soldiers quickly ran forward and fired several more shots into the young people's bodies. Franz closed his eyes.

"Drag them into the alley," Adler said to the soldiers.

Franz had seen death on the battlefield but never on a city street. And never women. He felt himself begin to tremble and desperately tried to stop.

"That was close, Feldwebel," Oberst Adler said, turning to the sergeant who had fired the initial burst of bullets. "You could have hit the general."

General Krieger removed his hat for a moment and then straightened it. "But he didn't, and there are three less Jews to contend with. Feldwebel, you will receive a commendation for what you did today. Let's go."

Franz remembered little of the return trip

to General Berg's headquarters. He spent much of the time with his eyes closed trying to erase from his mind the image of the three dead people lying on the sidewalk. Later that evening General Berg summoned him to his suite. Still deeply upset, Franz entered the same room where he'd first met General Krieger.

"Hauptmann, you saved a lot of lives today," the general said.

"No, sir," Franz protested. "Three civilians were shot outside the house in Siena."

"I know, but that's not important. General Krieger is going to recommend that our division be assigned to a new army group tasked with the defense of southern France. Otherwise, within a month we'd have been on a train heading east to face the Russians. Krieger has the ear of men at the top levels of the high command in Berlin. A suggestion from him is as good as a direct order. Somebody has to serve in the west, but it's not an easy assignment to secure. The contents of those crates paid the ticket to France for the men of this division."

"I didn't see inside the crates."

"It doesn't matter," General Berg replied. "And I didn't want to know any more details of the operation."

General Berg coughed violently several

times and then began to wheeze. When he finally caught his breath, he looked at Franz through rheumy eyes.

"Am I going to survive the war, Haus?" he asked.

Franz shifted nervously. "I don't know, sir."

"Never mind," Berg said with a wave of his hand. "It shouldn't make any difference whether or not a man knows the hour of his death. Until that day comes, our only job is to do our duty."

Early Friday morning Parker called Thomas Blocker. "Do you have a few minutes to talk about the Ferguson case?" he asked when the trial lawyer came on the line.

"Certainly," Blocker replied in a friendly voice. "I had it on my calendar to call you this afternoon."

"You were going to call me?" Parker asked.

"Trying to stay ahead of the game is what we're all about. And that's an extra challenge when dealing with you, isn't it?"

Parker shifted in his seat.

"But let's get right to it," Blocker continued.

For the next hour, Parker and Blocker discussed the facts uncovered thus far, the new information gleaned from the interview with the client, possible legal theories for recovery, and the measure of damages. Once again, Parker was impressed by the amount of information Blocker already had at his fingertips. The trial lawyer's memory was impressive.

"Of course, one of the keys will be identifying the best experts to testify," Blocker said. "We need to give the jury as many reasons as possible to award damages and not rely on their outrage over the basic facts. There are often one or two scientific types on a jury who have to be convinced that all the dots connect before they'll sign off on a big verdict."

"Yes, sir," Parker replied. "I think we might want to hire someone who could testify about the effect that much alcohol in the bloodstream would have on a person's mental capabilities based on an individual's weight, et cetera."

"Excellent," Blocker said. "We can't let the driver get on the witness stand and claim he can 'hold his liquor' without it affecting him. A man on the jury might agree. Running that down will be one of your responsibilities."

Parker appreciated Blocker's confidence in him but wasn't sure exactly where to look.

"Did you have a chance to research any of

the accident reconstruction experts I sent you?" Blocker asked.

Parker glanced down at the list of eleven men and women who'd earned more advanced degrees among them than the entire faculty at a small college. "No, except to skim over the qualifications for a few of them."

"Any impressions?" Blocker asked.

"Well, they're not retired police officers like the guy Greg used in a case shortly after I came to work here."

"Hiring someone like that might be appropriate in some cases, but not one where the road conditions are an issue due to the amount of rain that fell within an hour of the collision. We need someone who can talk about the coefficient of friction for tires on wet payment and plot the range of visibility for drivers approaching the intersection. We can't let Bruffey convince the jury that Jessica's death was the fault of a thunderstorm."

"Okay," Parker replied as he checked the list again. "Maybe we should start with Dr. Cavendish."

"Why Cavendish? What made him stand out?"

Parker wrinkled his brow. "He has a degree from Stanford, which is a pretty good school."

"So are Ohio State, Georgia Tech, and Northwestern, where some of the other experts studied. Tell me more."

"I think Dr. Cavendish might be the kind of witness who can make complicated things simple enough for a jury to understand. I mean, you'd have to interview him to make sure —"

"Very accurate," Blocker broke in. "He testified in a case for me eighteen months ago, and that's exactly what he did. He has an engineering degree, and he's worked with several governmental agencies on auto safety and highway design. Even though he lectures all over the world to professional associations, he doesn't talk down to the jury. He grew up in Alabama and has an accent that instantly sets a southern jury at ease."

"So you've already made up your mind?"

"No. Let's set up another conference call. How about next Wednesday afternoon at three thirty?"

Parker checked his calendar. He had nothing to do that day except grind out work for Greg.

"That works," he said. "Besides the alcohol expert and the other accident reconstruction candidates, is there anyone else you want me to research?"

"Surprise me," Blocker replied. "But I have to warn you, I'm not often caught off guard."

The phone call ended with Parker more convinced than ever that Thomas Blocker was a genius.

Frank came inside from trimming the bushes in front of his house, grabbed a bottle of water from his refrigerator, and sat down to check the soccer scores for the Bundesliga. He then switched over to his e-mail account. Included in the usual batch of spam ads for free vacations and miracle diet plans was an unnamed message from a no-reply address in Germany. Frank clicked it open. It included a single line of text:

Greetings, Hauptmann.

CHAPTER 26

Parker sat across the table from Creston as they shared an onion ring basket and waited for the waitress to bring each of them a pair of gourmet hot dogs.

"Are you sure there is such a thing as a gourmet hot dog?" Creston asked.

Parker pointed to the menu on the wall. "What else would you call a hot dog topped with borracho beans, fire-grilled salsa, red onion, cilantro, and goat cheese? And I'm glad you were able to get away from school for lunch. I bet you get sick of cafeteria food."

"It's better than when we were there," Creston said and shrugged. "The faculty line has a decent salad bar. And this semester I have one less class on Wednesday because I'm coaching the cross-country team. However, the fifty minutes they give me is gobbled up by the two and a half hours I spend with the team three afternoons a week."

"You'd be running even if they didn't pay you," Parker replied, picking up a slender onion ring and dipping it into a mixture of ketchup and horseradish sauce. "Are you still running with Belinda?"

"It's Melinda, which I expect you to remember when I introduce her to you. And we're running down the same path. How about the blond photographer? Have you convinced her to go to the playground and swing like a monkey?"

"Not yet."

Parker gave his friend a brief summary of the boat trip to Oriental.

"You know what I like about that?" Creston asked thoughtfully when Parker finished.

"What?"

"That you've brought your grandfather in as chaperone and wingman. He's always looked at me as if he was seeing right through me. If he doesn't like a woman, you should probably run as fast as you can in the other direction."

"I didn't know you felt that way about my grandfather."

Creston nodded. "Oh yeah. He never said a lot, which always made me think he knew a lot more than he let on."

Parker took a sip of his drink and stared at Creston.

"What is it?" Creston asked after a few moments passed.

"I'm trying to look through you," Parker replied.

"You're weird."

Parker took a bite of his hot dog that was topped with grilled onions and peppers. "I know what you need to do," he said.

"What?"

"Invite Melissa to go kayaking with you," he said. "Maybe take her to the marshy area upriver where we used to camp when we were in high school. Build a fire on an island and roast marshmallows. The bugs are dying off with the cooler weather. She'll love it."

"Melinda has never mentioned anything about liking kayaks, campfires, or marshmallows."

"Which will make it that much more impressive when you suggest it."

Switzerland, 1944
After crossing the Rhine, Franz spent the rest of the night walking the streets of Basel as a deserter in a new country. The following morning he slipped out of town and headed west.

One night he slept in an orchard; the next he hid in a hayloft. During the day, he walked about half a kilometer away from the road. Shortly after sunset on the fifth day, he went down to the river for a drink of water and to fill an empty wine bottle in case he got thirsty during the night. He was lying on his stomach in a brushy spot when he heard a man's voice in Swiss German.

"Otto, drag the boat out of the water and onto the bank. My leg is hurting too much to help."

Franz lay still as he heard the sound of grunts and cracks of small branches from nearby bushes.

"Careful!" the man called out. "It's about to tip on its side!"

The next sound Franz heard was a loud splash in the water. Still lying down, he scooted away from the river.

"Help!" he heard a muffled voice cry.

Franz jumped up and forced his way through the bushes. After a few meters he burst into a narrow clearing at a spot where the bank sloped gradually down to the river. Standing in the mud at the water's edge was a young boy who looked about ten years old. A small wooden boat was a few feet away from him and beginning to fill with water. Nets and fishing paraphernalia had spilled out and were drifting away in the slow current.

"Where is he?" Franz asked.

"Opa!" the boy wailed as he pointed to a spot not far from the front of the boat.

Franz quickly took off his shoes and stripped down to his underwear. In the fading light it was impossible to tell the depth of the water. He stepped off the bank and immediately went all the way under. He came up with his arms flailing and steadied himself by treading water. There was no sign of the man who had called out for help. Franz kicked away from the bank and reached the boat. When he touched it, his foot hit something solid beneath him that moved. Turning loose of the boat, Franz dived down into the water. His fingers felt hair, and he grabbed it. He tried to pull the man to the surface, but he barely moved. Franz's lungs were about to explode, and he had to let go of the hair.

Popping to the surface, he took a couple of deep breaths. The boy on the bank was sobbing loudly. Franz dived again. This time he managed to grab a piece of cloth and, with all the strength he could muster, kicked to the surface. He knew that if this didn't work, he wouldn't have the strength to try again. His hand felt the side of the sinking boat that was still above the surface enough that Franz could pull himself toward shore. With the man still submerged and in his grip, Franz moved along the side of the boat toward the bank.

"There! There!" the boy screamed and pointed to Franz's right.

Franz maneuvered in the direction where the boy pointed and suddenly felt the bottom of the riverbed beneath his feet. There was a shelf. Letting go of the boat, he stood up. The water was waist-deep. Taking hold of the man's shirt with both hands, he pulled him to the surface and pushed him toward the bank and the hysterically crying boy. With great effort, Franz was able to roll the heavyset man onto the bank and climb out after him.

The man was lying on his back with the boy at his feet. The older man wasn't breathing. Turning the man's head to the side, Franz pushed on his chest and water poured out of the man's mouth and down his stubbly gray beard. Then, to Franz's amazement, the man made a choking sound. Franz pushed again and forced out a much smaller amount of water. The man coughed again but weaker. The young boy was now almost on top of Franz trying to touch the old man's face.

"Get back!" Franz pushed him away roughly.

Franz leaned over and put his ear in front of the man's mouth. Hearing nothing, he pressed again on the man's chest. No water spilled out, but the man choked and coughed two times and then stopped. He waited and watched anxiously for another sign of life. The sobbing boy came close, reached out his hand, and gently touched the old man's face.

"Opa!" he cried out again.

The man's eyes fluttered and tried to open but failed. He choked once and gasped for breath. Franz didn't know whether he should raise the man's head so he left him alone. The boy called out again, only not quite so loud. The old man sucked in a deep breath and coughed several times. His eyes opened and tried to focus on Franz's face. Seeing his grandfather alive, the young boy pressed his head to the old man's chest and wrapped his arms around him.

"Opa, Opa," he repeated over and over. "Please don't die!"

Franz sat up. He could see the gentle rising and falling of the old man's chest. The boy's voice and touch were more powerful than anything Franz could do. The man coughed several times again and raised his hand to his mouth. He turned his head toward Franz and tried to sit up.

Franz reached out to him. "Easy, easy."

"Boat," the man managed to say before another coughing fit hit him.

Even in the fading light, Franz could see the old man's face turning red. It was a beautiful sight.

The boat was barely above water but only a few feet from the bank. Franz eased over to the spot where the muddy shelf lay beneath the water and stepped into the river. He eased along the shelf, reached out, and grabbed the bow of the boat. Inside was a rope. Taking hold of the rope, he returned to the bank and hauled the boat close enough that he could tip it on its side and empty it. Then it was easy for Franz to drag it out of the water. Once the boat was on dry ground, the old man closed his eyes for a few seconds.

"Thank you," he said softly.

Parker read over the short list of potential neuropsychiatrists in the Ferguson case. He'd never heard of a neuropsychiatrist until he started practicing law, and now he had the responsibility of evaluating them. The candidate with the best academic credentials had the least experience in the courtroom. However, being fresh could be a good thing because it would be hard for a defense lawyer to find examples of inconsistent testimony in other cases. Another option was a female medical school professor who took time off in the summer to ply the expert witness circuit. She conducted evaluations only in June, July, and August and made herself available for depositions on Saturday or Sunday. However, the professor assured prospective clients that when it came to testifying in person at trial, she could make arrangements due to her tenured teaching schedule. A third contender was an elderly man who had by far the most practical and trial experience. He was a retired physician who'd worked for a major medical center in Nashville, and Parker suspected the man's expert witness career enabled him to take an extra cruise or two on the Mediterranean.

Vicki brought in the morning mail and laid it on his desk. On top was a letter from the North Carolina Bar Association. She waited while Parker picked it up.

"Is this what I think it is?" he asked.

"Probably," Vicki replied. "Let's keep our fingers crossed that you don't have to go to Raleigh for an in-person interview."

"In-person interview?"

"Oh, I know how it works," Vicki said confidently. "Greg isn't the only attorney I've worked for who got hit with a grievance. I know the drill."

"You must be bad luck," Parker replied grumpily.

"Statistically, a lawyer has one bar complaint and one act of malpractice per decade of practice. You have one of the two out of the way quickly."

"And I'm not planning on committing malpractice anytime during the next nine years. I'd rather skew the statistics higher."

Parker waited. Vicki didn't move.

"Aren't you going to read the letter?" she asked.

"Eventually, and you want to watch my reaction."

Parker ripped open the envelope and read it without changing expression. "Okay," he said to Vicki. "I've read the letter."

"And?"

Parker grinned. "They're going to close the file. Thanks for your help. I really appreciate it. They'll let Donna McAlpine know I did nothing unethical. She gets out of jail at the end of the week. Maybe that will help her forget about me and concentrate on staying off the road when she's been drinking, especially with her little girl in the car."

Vicki left, and Parker double-checked the system he used on his computer to make sure he didn't miss a deadline and commit malpractice. Then, as he returned to the list of potential experts, an item on one of their résumés suddenly caught his attention.

Frank pushed his chair away from the dinner table at Lenny and Mattie's house.

"Mattie, your German potato pancakes are fantastic, better than any I ate growing up. They're crispy on the outside and creamy on the inside with enough spice to make them interesting."

Mattie laughed. "And you know how to give a compliment better than most men born in America."

"I compliment your cooking all the time," Lenny protested, patting his stomach. "And I carry the proof around with me wherever I go."

"Yes," Mattie said as she picked up a couple of plates to take into the kitchen. "But Frank doesn't make me feel guilty. I hate being responsible for the size of your stomach."

Mattie left and Lenny turned to Frank. "What kind of friend comes over and makes me look bad when I try to praise my wife's cooking?"

"The kind who brought the fresh fish we grilled."

"Yeah," Lenny said and nodded. "That was tasty fish. Low on the calories too."

"Which we made up for with everything else we piled on our plates." Frank glanced past Lenny toward the kitchen. "I'll let you score a few points by helping Mattie clean the table while I go outside and make sure the grill is closed up tight."

A side door led to the rear of the house. The fish cooked so quickly that it would be a waste to let the charcoal briquettes turn to ash. Frank closed the dampers.

The lighthearted conversation around the dinner table hadn't totally banished the tightness in his gut that had plagued Frank since receiving the e-mail from Germany. The dinner was Mattie's way of rewarding him for the matchmaker role he'd played in suggesting that Chris get to know Sally Henderson. The two young people had been inseparable for weeks, and the more Mattie got to know Sally, the better she liked her.

Frank went back inside the house. Lenny and Mattie were still in the kitchen, so he sat down in the living room and closed his eyes for a moment while he waited for them to finish. When he did, he instantly found himself in an unfamiliar place. At first he thought it was a well-decorated living room in a nice home, but then the floor moved beneath his feet, and he wondered if he was in the middle of an earthquake.

Then a voice without a face said, "Herr Haus? I'd like to talk to you about Siena."

Frank's blood ran cold. He was aware of the presence of other people in the room, and he strained to bring the face into focus. The floor shifted again.

"Frank, would you like to play a few hands of UNO?" Lenny's voice caused the image to suddenly compress and vanish like a photo being deleted from a digital camera. Frank opened his eyes and looked irritably at Lenny.

"Couldn't you tell I had my eyes closed?" he asked.

"Yeah, and if this was after Sunday lunch, we'd all be looking for a place to nap. But you mentioned getting together to play UNO the other day, and I told Mattie about it out in the kitchen. She's brewing a pot of the black tea you like so much, and we thought we might play a game while you drink your tea. You know how much she likes card games. But if you want to head on home, it's not —"

Frank passed his hand over his eyes. "I'm

sorry. I was thinking about something and didn't have a chance to finish my thoughts."

Lenny gave Frank a puzzled look. Frank closed his eyes again for a moment. The memory of the shifting room was vivid, but he doubted he could force it to come back to life.

"Where should we sit for the game?" he asked, opening his eyes again.

"The dining room table," Lenny replied. "Mattie has a bunch of craft stuff spread out on the kitchen table and doesn't want to disturb it. Are you sure you're all right?"

"As good as a man my age deserves to be," Frank replied, trying to sound more relaxed than he felt. "And this time I'm not going to forget to say UNO when I'm down to my last card. Do you know how to say UNO in German?"

"No," Lenny answered.

"Correct. You can't," Frank replied. "It's Spanish."

Lenny balled up his fist and shook it at Frank with a grin.

"Don't start the game without me!" Mattie called out from the kitchen. "The tea is still brewing."

Frank stood up. When he did, he felt slightly dizzy and gripped the top of the chair with his right hand. Lenny reached out to steady him. Frank leaned into his friend for a moment and then straightened up.

"I'm okay," Frank said. "Sometimes I feel light-headed when I get up too fast. It happens to everyone."

"Well, promise you'll let me know if you need me to drive you home or take you to the doctor."

Frank held up his left hand. "I swear."

"That's the wrong hand, but I'll accept it," Lenny replied.

CHAPTER 27

Parker spent an hour preparing for his phone conversation with Thomas Blocker. He'd printed out his notes, which were now neatly organized on his desk. One of his biggest challenges would be to keep the sheets of paper from becoming a jumbled mess five minutes after the conversation started. His phone buzzed precisely at the appointed time.

"I'm ready, Vicki," he said. "Put him through."

"It's not a him; it's a her."

"I can't take the call. Thomas Blocker is —"

"I know. You've reminded me about it three times today. Once at ten thirty this morning —"

"Okay," Parker cut in before she could go on. "You win, but take a message from the caller."

"Even if it's Layla Donovan."

"Yes, especially if it's Layla Donovan."

"You don't mean that," Vicki shot back. "But I'll let her know you're busy. When should she expect to hear from you?"

"As soon as I finish talking to her father."

Vicki was silent for a split second. "Thomas Blocker is Layla's father? Why didn't you tell me? Is that why he's associated you on this case?"

"What do you mean?"

"So he can get a chance to check you out before you get tangled up in a relationship with his daughter."

"No way," Parker replied, but he immediately realized he wasn't sure that was correct.

He hung up the phone. Thirty seconds later it buzzed again.

"Mr. Blocker is on line 2," Vicki said. "And I told Layla that you'd call her back before you left the office."

Parker waited a few seconds for the call to be transferred. Branham and Camp didn't have the most sophisticated phone system on the market, but at least it was reliable.

"Hello, Mr. Blocker," Parker said.

"I think it's time you started calling me Tom," the lawyer replied affably. "It will be a good habit to develop, especially when we're interacting with other people about the case. I don't want a witness or opposing counsel to get the impression that you're not an important cog in the machine."

"Thanks . . ." Parker hesitated. "Tom."

"Good, now that that's out of the way, I have some good news. Dr. Cavendish is on board as our accident reconstruction expert. Once I outlined the facts to him, he was confident there's a strong case for liability. Where do you stand in the search for an expert to unravel the misfiring synapses of Walter Drew's alcohol-soaked brain?"

Parker summarized his research regarding the three possible candidates.

"Who makes the final cut?" Blocker asked.

Parker stared at the sheet of paper in front of him for another moment before he spoke.

"I believe we should hire Dr. Cheshire, even though as a full-time professor her availability makes me nervous."

"I would have graded her as a C-plus," Blocker replied slowly. "At best."

"I agree, but I believe she'll go out on a limb with her opinion if that's what we need her to do."

"Why do you say that?"

"Her response to criticism of a technical paper she wrote on the effect of alcohol on the brain that was later slammed by some of her colleagues, including the professor who supervised her PhD program. She didn't back down and continued to defend her analysis. I don't know if she was right or wrong, but that's the kind of moxie an expert witness has to possess."

"Send me your research and I'll see what I think."

"Yes, sir."

"Oh, and I'm coming to New Bern on Saturday. Could we get together sometime late in the afternoon? Say, five o'clock at your office?"

"I guess so," Parker said slowly.

"But only if we can talk in private. I don't want to involve Greg Branham in our conversation."

Something about the way Blocker spoke made Parker's stomach suddenly knot up. "Do you want Chet Ferguson to be here?"

"No, that's not necessary."

"Okay," Parker said with relief. "I'll have to check Greg's schedule to see if he'll be here. He usually works a full day on Saturday."

"Do it. And be discreet."

Parker hung up the phone and stared out the window into the neighboring backyard for a moment. Greg was naturally paranoid and had zealously cultivated that tendency for years. The likelihood that Greg would blow up if he found out Parker met with Blocker a second time behind his back for any reason was extremely high. Parker thought about calling Blocker back and suggesting a place to meet other than the office. Parker swiveled in his chair and clicked open the task list on his computer. It was already 4:00 p.m., and it would be tough to finish what he needed to do before going home for a late supper. His phone buzzed again.

"Yes," he said after pushing the button to talk to Vicki. "You'd better hold my calls for the rest of the afternoon. I've got to get through the first draft of a set of interrogatories that have been glaring at me from the corner of my desk for over three days."

"It's Greg."

"Okay."

Parker accepted the call.

"How full is your plate?" Greg asked.

"Overflowing," Parker answered and told him what he had on his task list.

"You have to learn to work faster and smarter."

"I know," Parker said, glancing up at the ceiling. "What do you need me to do, and I'll find a way to work it in."

"I'm going out of town through the weekend and need you to do the prep work for the depositions scheduled next week in the Calypso case."

Parker barely knew anything beyond the exotic name of the lawsuit and that it involved a contentious fallout between two men who jointly owned several restaurants. Parker furiously took notes while Greg rattled off information. The depositions were scheduled to start on Tuesday and last through midday on Thursday.

"That sounds like the whole case," Parker said when Greg finished.

"Except for the fat lady singing. Pull the file while I'm on the phone and take a quick look so I can answer any questions you have. I'm going to be out of pocket for a few days after this phone call."

Parker left his office and approached Vicki's desk. "Greg is on the phone and wants to talk to me about the Calypso case."

"I have it," Dolly said, raising her hand. "I'm putting together our responses for some overdue requests for production of documents that Greg wants mailed today."

Dolly handed Parker an expandable folder that was shockingly thin for litigation that undoubtedly involved a considerable amount of financial records. Parker returned to his office. He found the file marked "Depositions." The contrast with Tom

Blocker's work product couldn't have been more dramatic. Greg had scribbled five or six pages of barely legible notes based on interviews with the client and the primary witness, an accountant.

"Got it," he said to Greg when he returned to his office.

"Do you see my notes?"

"These handwritten sheets of paper?"

"Yes, what do you expect me to do? Set it up for you in a PowerPoint presentation? Those notes will get you started in the right direction. Dolly has the financial records from our client. Unravel them. I want to review everything early Monday morning when I return to the office."

"All right." Parker turned one of the sheets of paper to the side and read a sentence written down the margin. "Have a good time in Freeport."

"How did you know I was taking a quick trip to the Bahamas? If Vicki spilled the beans —"

"No, no," Parker said, wondering where he might have heard about an impending trip. "Didn't you say something a few weeks ago about wanting to fly over there for a long weekend?"

"Yeah, but that was to Dexter. I don't remember you being there."

"Anything else on the Calypso matter?" Parker asked, changing the subject back to the case.

"Uh, not now, but I may think of something later."

"I'll be at the office all weekend," Parker replied.

Parker hung up the phone and tried to recall if he had really overheard a conversation between Greg and Dexter about the Bahamas. Pushing the thought to the side, he knew his task list had just blown up. He would have no option but to work faster and smarter. However, there was at least one flower on the mountain of work that faced him. He wouldn't have to worry about Greg barging into the middle of his meeting on Saturday with Tom Blocker.

Exhausted, Parker was about to leave the office later when he remembered that he hadn't returned Layla Donovan's phone call. He stood up to stretch for a second before dialing the number.

"Are you still at the office?" Layla asked.

"Yes."

"Working on the case my father associated with your firm, I bet."

"No, Greg is way more effective at dumping stuff on me at the last minute than your father could ever dream of doing."

"I doubt that. If I called Tom on his cell phone right now, I could almost guarantee he's at the office."

"Tom?"

"Hasn't he used that one on you yet? Asked you to call him by his first name so you'll feel like part of the inner circle?"

"Yes," Parker admitted. "I tried it, but it felt kind of weird. I'm as much a part of his inner circle as Neptune in the solar system."

"Good. The gravitational pull if you get too close to the sun can be hard to handle. Listen, do you have time to grab a cup of coffee? I have something important I want to talk to you about."

"What?"

"Your grandfather."

"Only if it's important," Parker sighed. "If you're looking for a two-way conversation, I'm too beat to do much more than grunt."

"That works."

Layla named a popular place on Middle Street.

"It'll be crowded," Parker warned.

"I've done some photography work for the owner. If I call him, he'll clear a table for us."

"You took pictures of coffee?"

"With a live black bear in the background. Check it out on their website. I think it turned out great."

"Okay. Fifteen minutes."

On his way out the door, Parker stopped by the bathroom and splashed cold water on his face. When he looked at his reflection in the mirror, his eyes betrayed fatigue.

Regardless of the day of the week, parking on Middle Street could be a challenge. There were a limited number of spots along the curb, and Parker had to walk a couple of blocks to the coffee shop. Along the way, he passed an ice-cream parlor that was always crowded regardless of the season of the year. As soon as he entered the noisy café, he saw Layla seated at a small round table against the rear wall. She was wearing a fancy blue dress, and her hair was styled into two braids that crowned her head. Parker straightened his tie that had drooped down the front of his shirt.

"You look nice," he said when he sat down.

"Thanks. I've been taking pictures at a fancy corporate cocktail hour down on the river." Layla pushed a stray strand of blond hair away from her face. "I worked fast. Candid shots of people who are intoxicated usually aren't very flattering, so it's best to photograph them near the beginning of a party. What would you like to drink?"

"I'm not sure." Parker glanced over his shoulder at the list of drink offerings on the wall. "I don't want anything to keep me awake or put me to sleep."

A young waitress with green and purple hair came over to them. Layla ordered a complicated-sounding concoction. Parker listened.

"Does that have any caffeine in it?" he asked the waitress.

"No," she said, giving him a look that reminded him of the reaction he'd received from a doctor to a question during a medical deposition less than a month after Parker started practicing law. The doctor didn't try to hide his condescension that Parker could pose such a stupid, juvenile inquiry.

"Then give me the same thing," he said.

"Have you ever had one?" the waitress asked.

"No, but I'm feeling wild and crazy tonight."

The waitress rolled her eyes and left.

"Why did she give me that look?" Parker asked Layla, who was grinning at him.

"I'm not sure, except that I ordered mine with a shot of a liquefied herb designed to promote better hair and nails and a few drops of an extract that helps control a woman's mood swings."

"Well, in a few minutes this is going to be a happy table," Parker replied with a grin.

Layla laughed.

"Okay," he said. "What's this important topic related to Opa? Is he confiding in you instead of talking to me?"

"No, I haven't talked to him since I saw him in church. What I wanted to talk to you about was the chatter I discovered on the Internet about him."

"What sort of chatter?"

Layla leaned forward.

"After we went on the boat trip to Oriental, I was curious to find out more about him. I wasn't trying to be nosy," she explained and then paused. "Actually, I was snooping around because he's such an interesting man, and I wanted to find out anything I could about his background without bugging him about it."

"He wouldn't tell you," Parker replied. "He's very reserved, and I've always respected his privacy."

"Anyway, I knew he'd been in the army, and he told me that he'd been a hauptmann in Army Group G stationed in southern Germany in 1944."

"He did?" Parker didn't try to hide his surprise.

"Yes, it was during one of our talks in German."

Before Layla could continue, the waitress brought their drinks. Parker took a sip. It was bitter, and he wrinkled up his face.

"This is going to make me happy?" he asked.

"It's an acquired taste," Layla said, noticing his expression. "Don't give up on it."

"How did you get my grandfather talking about the war?"

"The two of us were standing at the back of the boat, and you were fishing off the bow. He smiled and said you looked a lot like he did when he was in the army. I asked him where he'd served, and he mentioned his last assignment. Do you know how the war ended for him? He deserted and fled to Switzerland, right?"

Parker took another sip of the bitter drink before he answered. "Yes. I think he swam across the Rhine in the middle of the night, or something like that. Anyway, he lived in Switzerland until the war ended, then immigrated to the US and settled here, where he met my grandmother. He doesn't like to talk about those days, and I hope you're not going to drag it up. He really likes you, but it would bother him regardless of the reason."

Parker remembered his own futile efforts to research his grandfather's background after Conrad Mueller's visit. He couldn't exactly criticize Layla for doing the same thing. Her proficiency in German enabled her to understand what she was reading; however, he still felt a strong responsibility to protect his opa.

"I'd never want to do that, but I think I should let him know what I found out. All of the information was in German, of course, and it was like a puzzle trying to figure it out. At first I thought your grandfather was some kind of spy or secret agent, but it turned out he was an officer on the staff of a general named Berg. Your grandfather even had a nickname — the Aryan Eagle."

"Aryan Eagle?"

"He was almost legendary. The whole reason behind the interaction about him on the Internet relates to insight that he provided to his superiors for battles from the beginning of the war until he fled to Switzerland. It was like he knew where the enemy was going to be before they did anything."

"We were the enemy."

"I know, but not from his perspective at the time. Because he was considered a traitor, nobody in Germany was interested in him for years and years. However, men who served with him during the war mentioned him to others, and his name came up in connection with a reunion of veterans from his unit. Now people are trying to track him down and learn more about his role. I guess his desertion happened so long ago that it's no longer an issue for folks interested in finding out more about who he was and what he did. I wrote an e-mail to a journalist named Gerhardt who very much wants to interview him before, you know, your grandfather dies."

"That's morbid."

"I know how it sounds," Layla replied. "And I admit that I got caught up in what I was reading and lost sight of the fact that your grandfather is a man with feelings and a right to privacy. But I exchanged e-mails with Gerhardt, who was super excited when I told him I believed I might know the man he's looking for."

"Did you tell this Gerhardt guy where my grandfather lives?" Parker asked.

"No, no. All he knows is that I'm in the US and may be able to help. Gerhardt doesn't even know your grandfather changed his name from Franz Haus to Frank House."

Parker shook his head. "I'm not sure that's

true. A man named Mueller who served with my grandfather recently made a trip over here from Germany to thank Opa for saving his life. It had something to do with advice my grandfather gave that convinced Mr. Mueller not to request a transfer to a unit that ended up decimated in a battle near the end of the war. If Opa didn't want to meet with Mueller, I can't imagine him wanting to speak to a journalist who's going to pry into things my grandfather wants to forget."

"Well, I think it should be his choice. And I wanted to run it by you first."

"Are you going to tell him even if I don't think it's a good idea?"

"No," Layla responded immediately. "If you tell me to drop it, I will."

They sipped their drinks in silence for a minute.

"This concoction hasn't done its work on me yet," Parker said, putting down his cup. "I don't have a more positive outlook on life or sense a need to trim my fingernails."

"Your hair is shinier," Layla joked.

When they finished their drinks, they left the coffee shop together and walked slowly down Middle Street.

"Let me think some more about talking to my grandfather," Parker said.

"That's fine," Layla replied.

They reached a stoplight and waited for it to turn green so they could cross.

"Did you know your father is coming to town on Saturday?" Parker asked.

"No. But he probably wants to see you, not me."

Parker glanced sideways at Layla, who was staring straight ahead. They reached her car.

"Would you like to get together again?" Parker asked.

Layla faced him. "Yes, but I'm feeling as uneasy about you and my father as you do about your grandfather and Gerhardt."

"What do you mean?"

"I know it's a cocounsel arrangement on a lawsuit. It's just —"

"That it feels uncomfortable because your husband worked for your father?"

"Did he tell you about that?"

"No."

"But it's easy enough for a lawyer like you to find out," she said.

Parker didn't correct her. Layla continued, "It's none of my business what you do with your professional career. And I don't want to come across as trying to make our spending time together something that it's not."

"Please, it's obvious that I like you and want to get to know you better. But we're adults on our own. Let's leave your father out of it."

"I'm not sure that's possible."

CHAPTER 28

Shortly before the time for Tom Blocker's arrival at the office, Parker went downstairs and unlocked the front door. Dexter had come in earlier in the day but left around noon, saying he wouldn't be back. Parker spent most of his time focusing on the depositions in the Calypso case. It was a grinding process; Parker was flexing legal muscles he didn't know existed when he graduated from law school. Greg would be asking the questions, and it would be up to him to recognize unanticipated avenues of fruitful discovery. But Parker had to deliver his boss to the intersections in the road.

It was cloudy outside, and several short thunderstorms that produced big drops of rain had punctuated the afternoon. Parker opened the door and smelled the ozone lingering in the air from the latest downpour. Blocker's long, dark Mercedes turned a corner and rolled to a stop behind Parker's car. The trial lawyer got out and raised his hand in greeting. As Parker watched him stride up the sidewalk, he could see a similarity with the determined way Layla walked after a camera shot. Blocker climbed the steps and entered the house.

"Where's Greg?" Blocker asked, looking around.

"In the Bahamas for a long weekend."

"Are you sure?"

"I didn't put him on the plane, but he left me a ton of work to do while he's gone."

Blocker nodded. "All right. Let's go to your office."

"I thought we could meet in the downstairs conference room." Parker gestured toward the open door. "That's where we usually meet with clients and it's a better place to —"

"I prefer your office," Blocker said, cutting him off. "Lead the way."

Parker climbed the stairs and gave a forty-five-second tour of the second floor. "It's cozy," he said.

"Are you familiar with the house for rent on Pollock Street?" Blocker asked.

Parker knew the former residence. It was exquisitely restored on the outside, but he'd not been inside and had no idea how much the owner was seeking to lease it.

"The white one with the beautiful wood-work on the front porch?"

"Yes, I toured it a few minutes ago."

"Why?" Parker asked in surprise.

"Where is your office?" Blocker asked in return, ignoring the question.

They were standing in front of the closed door. Parker opened it. "Here," he said.

Blocker brushed past him. "Is that your grandfather? The one from Germany?" he asked, picking up the photo of Parker on the *Aare* with his grandfather.

"Yes," Parker answered. "That's on his fishing boat."

"The *Aare*," Blocker read. "I assume it's named for the river that begins in the Ober-aar glacier in the Bernese Alps and flows through Brienz, Thun, and Bern."

"I have no idea," Parker replied. "My knowledge of Swiss geography is worse than my German."

"It's beautiful. It's the longest river wholly in Switzerland. If you ever see it, you won't forget it."

Blocker didn't comment about the photo of Parker and his parents. He sat in the single chair across from Parker's desk. Parker slipped behind his desk, which made him feel like a school principal who'd called a student into the office. Blocker pursed his lips for a moment but then relaxed into a slight smile.

"Do you know why I wanted to talk to you?" he asked. "And don't be reluctant to guess."

An unanticipated thought shot through Parker's mind, but there was no way he was going to express it openly. He swallowed and stared across the desk at Blocker.

"I'm waiting," Blocker said.

"And I'm listening," Parker replied, still feeling a lump in his throat.

Blocker leaned forward and tapped the front of Parker's desk with his index finger a couple of times. "I'd like to open a New Bern office and want you to come to work for me."

Parker coughed into his hand. He didn't know whether to be shocked by the offer or by the fact that he knew it was coming moments before the words left Tom Blocker's mouth.

"Mr. Blocker," he began. "I'm not sure what —"

"Remember, call me Tom," Blocker interrupted. "And that part is nonnegotiable."

"Tom," Parker said, even though it felt unnatural. "It's an incredible honor for you to offer me a job. I mean, you barely know anything about me. I graduated in the middle of my law school class, and I didn't serve on the staff of the law review."

"But what I do know is more than enough. You have abilities that can't be taught in a classroom. And when I meet a lawyer who has the innate ability to see around the corner before the evidence has arrived in the courtroom, it gets my attention."

"I'm not sure what you mean by —" Parker began.

"Don't play coy with me. I saw what you did in the Mixon arbitration. That wasn't the result of detailed preparation. Greg kicked you out of the room because you were on to something that neither one of you knew when we started the hearing. Am I right or wrong?"

"You're right."

"And that wasn't the first time something like that has happened since you started practicing law. Am I correct?"

Parker didn't respond.

"Give me examples," Blocker continued. "Include details without compromising client confidentiality."

Something about the way Blocker spoke demolished Parker's resistance. He told him about several instances, including the bluff he ran in the DUI charge against Donna McAlpine. Blocker listened and didn't interrupt. Finally, Parker stopped.

"Is that all?" Blocker asked.

"Yes."

Blocker shook his head. "I think you're wrong."

Parker mentally ran through the other cases he'd worked on and came up empty. "I'm sorry," he said. "Other than the Mixon arbitration, that's all I can remember."

"What about insisting that Layla serve on the jury in the case against the lumber company?"

"Oh yeah." Parker nodded. "There was no real reason to lobby so hard for her based on voir dire. And we had no idea the reason you were in the courtroom was because she's your daughter."

"Who told you that's why I was there? Layla?"

Suddenly Parker realized she'd never confirmed his assumption.

"No. But if you weren't there to see her and didn't have a case on the docket, why were you in the courtroom?"

Blocker looked at him in a way that made cold chills run down Parker's spine. He wasn't sure if they were good or bad, but he couldn't deny that he'd suddenly stepped into unfamiliar territory.

"Can I have some time to consider your

offer?" Parker asked after a few moments passed.

"Of course, and all I'm asking is whether you're interested in the possibility. We'd still need to discuss salary, profit sharing, benefits, and so on. Although I'd guess the total package would be significantly more than what you're currently making."

"Okay."

"And will you agree to keep this conversation confidential between us?"

"Yes, sir."

After Blocker left, Parker gave up trying to work anymore on the Calypso case. He went home, changed into his exercise clothes, jogged to the park, and threw himself into an exhausting workout that left him red-faced and breathing heavily. He bent over and put his hands on his knees as he tried to catch his breath. Returning home, he took a shower and plopped down in front of the TV, but nothing on the screen was able to hold his interest.

Parker needed someone to talk to, but he didn't want to violate his agreement with Blocker to keep their conversation confidential. He knew the primary reason for secrecy was Greg. If Parker abruptly abandoned the firm, Greg would consider it a personal affront and slander him all over town.

Parker could bounce ideas off Creston without mentioning specifics, but his friend wasn't likely to be a helpful option. He had no frame of reference for the legal world Parker lived in. Parker ran his fingers through his hair and turned off the TV. He knew who he needed to call, but speaking with her would be even tougher. Without formulating a plan, he picked up his cell phone and scrolled down to Layla Donovan's number.

"I'm at a wedding reception that's going to last at least another hour and a half," Layla said. "After that, all I want to do is go home and crash. I'm as beat as you were the other night."

"I wasn't sure you could get together," Parker said. "I know it was a spur-of-the-moment thing."

"Did you meet with my father this afternoon?"

"Yes."

"Is that what you wanted to talk to me about?"

Parker paused. "Yes."

"Did he offer you a job?"

Parker couldn't believe how quickly Layla had destroyed his promise of confidentiality to her father. "I can't answer that," he replied cryptically.

379

"You just did, and you want to know what I think about it. Why don't you meet me at church in the morning? Maybe your grandfather will be there, and we can eat lunch together. Your grandfather is a wise man. His advice will probably be better than mine. Also, have you decided to tell him about my contact with Gerhardt on the Internet?"

"Church?" Parker asked.

"Yes, it's the place where people go to worship God."

Parker laughed. "Okay. It would probably be a good idea for me to go to church. I went for a while after my parents' deaths, and it helped me a lot."

"See you then," she said.

The following morning Parker shaved and selected a charcoal gray suit and yellow tie. He inspected himself in the mirror. At least he looked the part of a man on his way to a religious service. The church was a ten-minute drive from his apartment. When he pulled into the parking lot, he almost turned around and went home. There wasn't a sport coat in sight, much less a full business suit. The most common item of clothing for both men and women was blue jeans. Parker was going to stick out worse than a man with cut-off shirtsleeves and his arms covered in tattoos. At that precise moment, a bearded man in his forties got out of a black pickup truck with the multicolored artwork on his arms fully displayed.

Parker took off his tie and unbuttoned the top of his shirt. As he walked into the building, he looked around for Layla or his grandfather but didn't see them. He walked up several rows before he saw a place where they could sit together. A band began playing softly. Parker felt someone touch him on the arm. It was Layla.

"Sorry I'm late," she said, leaning close to whisper in his ear. "There was a car wreck in the intersection at the end of my street and I had to take a detour."

"What about Opa?" Parker asked.

"I thought you might call him."

"I should have but didn't," Parker replied as the volume of the music increased and the band began to lead the congregation in a song.

"You're just like him," Layla said in a slightly louder voice.

"How?"

"He wore a fancy suit the first time he came, but he didn't ditch the coat and tie before he walked inside."

Parker listened absentmindedly to the

unfamiliar songs. The church he attended as a teenager was more traditional; however, the youth minister had spent a lot of time with Parker and pointed him in the right direction during the first stages of grief. Parker still read the Bible on occasion and prayed a silent prayer or two when under pressure at work.

Because he didn't know the songs, he focused on some of the people sitting nearby and wondered what brought them to the service. He decided the woman beside him was going through a divorce and experiencing difficulty due to her kids' choosing sides in the domestic breakup. In front of him sat a family of four: husband, wife, and two boys, one a teenager and the other a preteen. As Parker watched them, he suspected the older of the two boys couldn't wait for the service to end so he could sneak away from the house for the rest of the day and hang out with a group of older boys who were going down a negative path strewn with illegal drugs. The younger brother leaned against his mother, who put her arm around him. Parker had the impression the boy was being bullied.

When he was in school, one of the things Parker hated most was a bully. He'd always been part of a clique of popular boys so it never touched him directly, but he occasionally used his social standing to bring a more marginal boy into the protection of the larger herd. As he watched the younger boy, Parker thought about Reggie Richardson, a target of bullying in the eighth grade until Parker, Creston, and a couple of their friends invited him to sit with them during lunch. Parker wasn't sure what happened to Reggie after graduation. He'd have to ask Creston if he knew.

Frank wasn't surprised when he entered the back of the crowded room and saw Parker and Layla standing together a few rows in front of him. All morning he'd been thinking about the three of them together in the church service. Twice he'd started to call Parker and invite him, but he stopped both times. His grandson worked so hard during the week that he didn't need something else to do and somewhere else to go on Sunday morning. Now Frank realized a phone call was unnecessary. A smile on his face, he stood in the rear until the music stopped and then made his way forward to join them.

Layla noticed Frank and stepped back so Parker's grandfather could sit next to him.

"No," Frank protested in a soft voice. "I don't want to sit between you."

"It's okay, Opa," Parker replied. "That way we won't know who's your favorite."

Eric's sermon continued his series on talents and gifts regardless of age and experience. The primary biblical example he used was Timothy, with an emphasis on how Paul encouraged his protégé to follow God. The third of the pastor's four points focused on 2 Timothy 1:5: "I am reminded of your sincere faith, which first lived in your grandmother Lois and in your mother Eunice and, I am persuaded, now lives in you also."

The words reached out and grabbed Frank's attention. He glanced sideways at Parker, who was checking something on his phone as the minister talked about the importance of a spiritual legacy. Frank was forced to realize he'd done virtually nothing to pass along what his own grandfather had given him, another example of failure that could be inscribed on his tombstone.

For his last point, Eric read 2 Timothy 1:6: "For this reason I remind you to fan into flame the gift of God, which is in you through the laying on of my hands." Then, while the minister talked, Frank left New Bern.

A long meeting ended on a balmy night. Eight-year-old Franz fell asleep curled up in a chair in the corner of the room. His mother gently woke him, but instead of sleepily making his way upstairs to bed, he stayed behind at his grandfather's request. It was only the two of them in the downstairs area with chairs scattered about from the gathering. With his grandfather's full attention directed at him, Franz rubbed his eyes.

"Franz, did you see anything during the meeting before you fell asleep?" his grandfather asked.

Franz didn't have to think about his answer. "I saw snow coming down on people," he responded.

"Even though it's warm outside and snow doesn't fall inside the house?"

"Yes, Opa. It wasn't real snow."

"Was it falling on everyone or just a few people?"

Franz remembered several people, including a family of four, who were sitting near the front of the room. He related what he saw.

"They didn't feel the snow," he said when he finished.

"Yes, they did," his grandfather said with

a smile. "Did it stay on them or disappear?"

Franz rubbed his eyes again as he tried to remember. "It stayed for a little bit but then melted. Their faces looked shiny."

His grandfather nodded. "I saw that part, but not the snow. Do you know what the snow means?"

"That they like snow?"

"Everyone likes this kind of snow, and it can fall anytime of the year."

"How?"

His grandfather leaned in closer. "Because this is the kind of snow that covers people's sins. Are you thirsty?"

Franz's mouth suddenly felt dry. "Yes."

His grandfather went to the kitchen and came back with a glass of water. After Franz finished the water, his grandfather asked him a question.

"How did you like that water?"

"I liked it, Opa. But I didn't know I was thirsty until you asked me if I wanted a drink."

"Good." His grandfather nodded, looked directly into Franz's eyes, and then let out a long breath. "Would you like me to pray for you?"

Even as an eight-year-old boy, Franz knew it wasn't a casual question, and any prayer that followed would be different from the ones said before a meal.

"Yes, sir," he said timidly.

"Are you sure?" his grandfather asked with a voice that held a mix of opportunity and fear.

Extra glad that he'd had the glass of water to drink, Franz swallowed.

"Yes," he said, trying to sound confident and grown up.

His grandfather didn't say anything. Instead, he continued to stare at Franz while breathing in and out with loud sighs and an occasional groan. Franz began to squirm in his chair. He looked over his shoulder at the stairs that led to the upstairs bedrooms.

"Opa —" he started.

His grandfather didn't respond but slipped to his knees and pulled Franz down beside him. He then placed his right hand on Franz's head and began to pray. Franz heard snippets of sentences that sounded like words from the Bible, but what he vividly remembered was the pleasant sensation of warmth that flowed over him and made the room feel like a summer afternoon. The sensation of heat remained after his grandfather said, "Amen," and slowly got up.

"Why is it so hot in here?" Franz asked.

"Is it a good heat?" his grandfather replied.

"Yes, I like it."

"Water and fire and snow," his grandfather said. "For a little boy, you've seen and felt a lot tonight. And you're going to see a lot more."

The older man looked tired as he led the way upstairs. Franz followed. The next time Franz saw him, his grandfather was lying in an open coffin.

"Opa," Parker said.

Frank jumped at the sound of the word so closely linked in his mind with the memory of his own grandfather.

"Did you doze off?" Parker asked. "The meeting is over."

Frank glanced around as everyone around them was standing up. "No," he said, rubbing his eyes.

Parker looked at him skeptically. "I was worried you were about to snore."

Layla was talking to the mother of the two boys sitting in front of them.

"Can you come to lunch with Layla and me?" Parker asked.

"Sure." Frank stood up and stretched. "What did the minister say about Paul laying his hands on Timothy and praying for him?"

"That it's something the church has done ever since. He asked people who wanted someone to pray for them to come forward."

Frank saw a half dozen people at the front of the church. An equal number were praying for them.

"My grandfather prayed for me like that when I was a little boy," Frank said to Parker. "And it's something I should have done for you a long time ago."

"Why?" Parker asked with a puzzled look on his face.

"Because of the verses about Timothy's mother and grandmother."

Before Parker responded, Layla turned around as the woman moved away down the aisle. "You never know what someone who walks into a church meeting wearing nice clothes is struggling with," she said.

"Was it about her sons?" Parker asked.

"Yes," Layla answered in surprise. "They're going through tough times in different ways."

"Yeah, it was easy to see," Parker replied.

"Tell me," Frank said to him.

"Oh, you know," Parker replied vaguely. "The kind of stuff boys struggle with as they

grow up. Let's get out of here. I'm starving."

CHAPTER 29

Ten minutes later they were sitting in a local delicatessen that served an extensive array of meats, cheeses, and spreads. After the waitress brought them water to drink, Parker started focusing on his phone.

"What are you doing?" Frank asked.

"Checking on my fantasy football team," Parker answered. "All through the church service I was debating whether to start my backup quarterback because of a favorable matchup with the opposing team. I know soccer is your sport, but what should I do?"

"You should turn your phone off when you go to church and not look at it," Frank shot back. "If you were working for me on my fishing boat, I would have thrown that thing into the water."

"Hey, I was paying better attention than you were," Parker countered. "You dozed off, and I had to tell you what the minister said during the last ten minutes of the sermon."

"I was thinking about something important that had to do with the message," Frank replied.

Layla glanced back and forth between the two men. "Be nice," she said.

Parker refocused on his phone and pressed several buttons. "There, it's done," he said.

"You'll regret it," Frank mumbled.

They ordered their sandwiches.

"Put extra brown mustard on his and mine," Parker said to the waitress. "It's a German thing."

"Make mine with extra brown mustard, too, please," Layla added.

"Well, we agree on that," Parker said.

After the waitress left, Frank eyed the two young people. There was more to the lunch than discovering unanimous agreement about extra mustard. Parker cleared his throat.

"Is it okay to talk about something that's supposed to be a secret if everyone already knows about it?" he asked.

"What?" Frank asked.

"My father offered Parker a job," Layla replied, turning to Frank. "And he wants to know what we think about it."

"Is that true?" Frank asked.

"Yes," Parker answered.

"He's not moving here, is he?" Layla asked.

"He didn't mention it, but I'm sure he'll be here on a more regular basis."

Layla pursed her lips. Frank shifted uneasily in his chair. The mention of Layla's father caused his stomach to suddenly feel queasy.

"Working for Greg Branham is no picnic," Parker continued. "But at least it's a job, and I don't want to end up in a worse situation, even if I'm making more money. Layla's father wants to open a branch office in a house on Pollock Street."

"Which one?" Frank asked.

Parker described it. Frank nodded. "That's a showplace," he said.

"And it's recently been renovated."

"When do you have to give him an answer?" Frank asked.

"He hasn't given me a deadline," Parker replied. "At least not yet."

"He will," Layla interjected.

"Then don't decide before you have to," Frank said. "And it might be good if I met him in person before giving you my opinion."

"Oh, he'd like that," Parker replied. "He's mentioned a couple of times that he'd like to meet you. He's very interested in everything German."

Layla turned to Frank and said something to him in German. Frank nodded but didn't reply.

"What did you say?" Parker asked irritably. "When are you two going to realize it's rude to talk behind my back?"

"We weren't talking behind your back," Layla replied with a slight smile. "You watched every word come across my lips. I was simply pointing out that my father can be a hard man to read. He has such a thick shell that I'm not sure even he knows how to penetrate it!"

"I'd still like to meet him," Frank replied.

The waitress brought their food. The freshly baked bread used for the sandwiches made Frank nostalgic for the bakery where his mother bought bread when he was a child. Layla turned to him.

"I know you weren't dozing in church," she said. "What were you thinking about during the sermon?"

Frank told them about the evening when his grandfather prayed for him in Dresden.

"You've never talked about your childhood like that," Parker said when he finished.

"Now is the time," Frank replied. "Before

it's too late."

"Quit, Opa," Parker said. "I don't like it when you talk like that."

They sat in awkward silence for several moments.

"There's another important reason for lunch," Parker said. "Layla, tell him what you found out."

Parker watched his grandfather's face as Layla described her Internet exchange with Gerhardt, the journalist searching for the Aryan Eagle. What had seemed to Parker like an unwelcome intrusion into his grandfather's privacy at the coffee shop now took on a more sinister tone. Several times he saw the older man's jaw muscles tighten.

"Some things are better left unsaid and buried in the past," Frank said when Layla finished.

"And it's my fault all this is coming back into your life," she added. "I didn't tell this Gerhardt guy where either one of us live."

"And I'm not sure why anyone would care about me now." Frank shook his head.

"Conrad Mueller tracking you down," Parker said, "and now this. At the least, it's creepy. You know, attracting the interest of strangers on the Internet is never a good thing."

"I'm really sorry," Layla said apologetically. "I won't do anything else."

"Don't worry," Frank said to Layla with a kind expression on his face. "Ende gut, alles gut."

"Which means?" Parker asked.

"All's well that ends well," Layla replied. "That's what I hope for everything we've discussed."

Parker and Layla waved good-bye to Frank as he pulled out of the parking lot.

"I feel worse than ever about talking to Gerhardt online," Layla said. "I could tell the whole thing upset your grandfather."

"Yes," Parker answered. "But I don't think he can stay upset with you."

"Which makes me feel worse."

They walked over to a bench positioned near one of New Bern's ceramic black bears and sat down.

"What about the job offer from your father?" Parker asked.

"I've been down that road once, and it's not a place I want to go again," Layla said without hesitation. "For me, dating a lawyer who works for my father is a recipe for disaster."

It wasn't the answer Parker expected and caught him off guard. "But that involved someone else," he said.

Layla turned on the bench so she faced him. "But my father is the same person, and I know what being under his control will do to anyone."

Parker's backup quarterback in fantasy football threw three interceptions in the first half, and the head coach pulled him out of the game. But that wasn't the main worry on Parker's plate. His brief conversation with Layla on the bench had forced him to consider what he really thought about the blond photographer. And added another layer of uncertainty to the chance to work for her father.

Monday morning Parker was researching an issue on the computer when Greg showed up in his office doorway.

"How was the Bahamas?" Parker asked.

"What I can remember was great," Greg replied, rubbing eyes that were slightly puffy. "But I should have stayed away from a rum drink they were hawking at the resort. It had a wicked second and third punch that took me down for the count. How was your weekend?"

"Different. I went to church yesterday."

"What?"

"With my grandfather and Layla Donovan."

Greg's eyes widened. "Donovan? She's roped you in and tied you up if you're willing to do that. The one thing I can't handle in a woman is religion."

"Even if she had the good sense to keep you from diving headfirst into the rum and ending up with a level 10 hangover?"

"Maybe if she had other qualities, but I don't know anyone like that."

Greg handed him a file. "Here's some good news. I looked over your prep work for the Calypso case, and it's spot-on. I know I dumped a bunch of stuff on you at the last minute, but you came through."

It was a rare compliment.

"And how did your follow-up meeting with Thomas Blocker go on Saturday?" Greg continued.

Parker stopped and stared at his boss. "Uh . . . ," he started and stopped.

"Vicki drove by and saw him coming into the office to see you. I assume it was a positive meeting. If not, you'd better tell me now."

"Oh, it was positive," Parker said, trying to regain his footing. "He's pleased with the work we've done so far, and he's assigning me real tasks to perform, mostly related to finding and choosing experts who will give us the most bang for the buck."

Parker hoped his use of one of Greg's clichés would help end the conversation.

"Okay," Greg replied with a wave of his hand. "I'm not sure what else you're working on, but get to it. We'll circle back after I finish these depositions."

Greg left, and Parker closed his office door. As had happened repeatedly during the past eighteen hours, his mind returned to the dilemma of the job offer from Thomas Blocker and his blossoming feelings for Layla. After several minutes passed, Greg returned.

"Quit daydreaming," Greg said. "Just because I gave you kudos for your work on the Calypso litigation doesn't mean you can take the rest of the day off."

"I was thinking about what to do next," Parker answered truthfully.

Greg dropped a folder on Parker's desk. "I have the answer. Prepare the responses to interrogatories in this case. They're due Wednesday, and I don't want to request an extension."

Parker finished his initial phone call with Dr. Cheshire, the neuropsychiatrist. He was nervous when the call began, but Dr.

Cheshire didn't make him jump through any hoops to prove his qualifications to ask her questions. Once he laid out the basic facts, she rattled off a bunch of medical terms and tests that quickly left Parker behind, but before he could interrupt she set him at ease.

"Don't try to take notes and look up anything," she said. "I'll give you a glossary along with my analysis and opinion. We'll also discuss ways my testimony can be attacked and how to counter them."

They concluded the phone call with Parker's promise to send a contract to Dr. Cheshire agreeing to pay her hourly consulting rate but leaving the charge for testimony via deposition or in court to be determined later. The latter request made Parker nervous, but the professor wouldn't budge, which left Parker hoping Tom Blocker would know what to do if Dr. Cheshire tried to jack up her fees later on.

Parker then located an online legal seminar featuring Tom Blocker as lecturer. As he watched and listened to Blocker repeat the closing argument from a real case involving carbon monoxide poisoning, Parker was mesmerized. Carbon monoxide is a clear and odorless gas, but Blocker made Parker taste the fear the vapor could release as it

400

insidiously seeped into the unsuspecting lungs of a family of four as they slept in their suburban home. The Greensboro jury that actually heard the argument returned a seven-figure verdict.

"Wow," Parker muttered to himself when the presentation ended.

The possibility that he could sit at Blocker's feet and soak up the trial lawyer's wisdom and experience was tempting. But he wasn't going to let an online seminar make up his mind about his future.

CHAPTER 30

Parker checked his hair in the rearview mirror of the car on his way to pick up Layla. It had taken several minutes of persuasion to convince her to accept his dinner invitation for Thursday evening. In the end, his uncertain status with her father kept her resistance from becoming an impenetrable wall.

"Are you sure steak is okay?" he asked as they drove away from Layla's apartment.

"So long as I don't have to look in the cow's eyes," she answered.

The restaurant was dark on the inside. The only lighting came from sconces set in the walls.

"This looks like a meeting place for the mafia," Layla said as they stood at the hostess station and let their eyes adjust from the sunlight outside.

"Mr. Burnside, the owner, is an old friend of my grandfather. He's more of a pirate than a gangster. He used to sneak off and spend a day on the water when Opa owned the *Aare.*"

"Parker!" a man called out. "Welcome!"

A short, burly man with a gray beard and balding head came up and greeted them. Parker introduced him to Layla. The owner led them to a table in a quiet corner of the restaurant.

"You can look at the menu," Burnside said when they were seated. "But order the rib eye. The ones waiting to be grilled are as good as they get."

The owner left, and a waiter brought them water and menus. Along with the steaks, they selected creamed spinach and scalloped potatoes à la carte. Parker took a sip of water.

"If it's okay with you, I don't want to talk about anything that has to do with the law," he said.

"Agreed," Layla replied.

"Okay," Parker said, sitting up straighter. "You've never told me why you became a photographer."

Parker couldn't have predicted how much he would enjoy listening to Layla describe the creative journey that began with taking pictures of her friends in smeared makeup when she was a little girl to composing shots of immaculate brides with a rose-colored sunset as a backdrop.

"And I love going to movies," she said in a random comment when she finished. "I get ideas all the time for still shots from them."

"I was talking to a buddy the other day about movies and women," Parker said. "Have you ever noticed how in romantic comedies the guy and the girl keep getting thrown together, even if they aren't trying to make it happen?"

Layla nodded. "Yes. Tell me the name of the last romantic comedy you saw."

"Uh, I can't, but my friend Creston filled me in on the genre. Anyway, every time I think I won't see you again, something comes up and I do. Vicki claimed you were stalking me —"

"That's not true!" Layla interrupted.

"And I know that," Parker said and held up his hand. "But I can see how she reached that conclusion. Anyway, the more I've been around you, the better I like you and appreciate who you are as your own, unique person. And it helps that you're gorgeous."

"Don't mess with me, Parker."

"I'm not. I mean every word."

Their food came. Burnside was right. The rib-eye steaks were superb. Parker made

Layla laugh several times with stories from his childhood. When they were almost finished with the meal, he cleared his throat.

"Are you ready for another boat ride on the river?" he asked. "I'm sure I could borrow Opa's boat."

"I'm not sure," Layla replied.

"Why?"

"Because a different river is sweeping me along faster than I want it to go. I thought I could control the pace, but an evening like tonight makes me wonder if that's possible."

"That sounds like a fun river."

"Fun but serious."

The look in Layla's eyes made Parker want to kiss her and tell her he was going to turn her father down. But she glanced away, and the moment passed.

"Just consider my invitation a photo shoot," he said. "I'd like to hire you to take some pictures of the river and marsh that I can give Opa for Christmas."

"Strictly business?" Layla asked.

"Yes. I'll pay your top rate. If I'm satisfied with the results, of course."

"Okay," Layla replied. "But remember, you're dealing with a heart that has been broken, just like in so many of the movies you haven't seen."

"And I take that very seriously."

■ ■ ■ ■

"I can't go," Frank replied when Parker called the following morning and asked to take Layla out on the boat Saturday. "I promised Lenny that I'd help him replace some windows at his house that have been damaged by the salt air. If you need to borrow any fishing tackle, I can put together some rigs for you in advance."

"No, it's just us and Layla's camera. I'd like to take her farther down the Sound."

"Make sure you avoid the shoals, especially at low tide. The skiff can handle shallow water, but I don't want you to plow the propeller into a sandbar at thirty miles an hour."

"I'll be careful. Would it be okay if we came by the house around eight o'clock in the morning? Both of us like to get an early start on the day."

"I'll be up long before that."

"Thanks, Opa."

"One other thing. Have you set up a time for me to meet her father?" Frank asked. "I've been thinking about him a lot."

"Uh, no, but I'm supposed to talk to him in a few minutes. I'll find out when he's going to be in New Bern. Would you be willing to come to town?"

"Yes, whatever works best for you. It's important."

After the phone call with Parker ended, Frank left the house and drove to the dock. In the trunk of his car were the supplies he used to clean his boat. Even if he couldn't go, he wanted it to be pristine for Parker and Layla. Not that it ever got dirty; however, it was impossible to avoid some buildup of residue from the brackish water and exposure to the elements. He'd considered buying a custom cover, but that was for boats that spent months idle, and hassling with a cover was the last thing he and Lenny wanted to do when they were eager to get on the water and catch fish.

When he arrived at the dock, Frank recognized a truck driven by one of the other boat owners, a man name Kevin Hill who sold life insurance. For years Kevin had tried to convince Frank to buy a policy. More recently, the familiar sales pitch no longer made its way into their conversations. At his age, Frank was no longer a risk worth taking.

Like Frank, Kevin was there to clean his boat, a twenty-four-foot cabin cruiser. Kevin had his back to him spraying the side of his boat and turned the nozzle away for a moment, catching Frank in the spray as he approached.

"Hey!" Frank called out.

"Sorry, Frank," Kevin said, lowering the hose and turning off the water. "I didn't see you coming."

Frank wiped a few drops from his face. "That's okay, I'm about to get wet anyway."

"I'm almost finished with the hose," Kevin replied, laying it on the dock.

"I'm cleaning my boat before Parker takes it out tomorrow."

"Is he still in college?"

"No, he finished law school and is working for a firm here in New Bern."

"Which one?"

"Branham and Camp."

Kevin made a negative face. "Oh yeah, I've run into Greg Branham a time or two. But the way the economy is going, it's tough to get any kind of legal job, and I've heard there's a real glut of lawyers."

"Parker seems to be doing well."

"He's a good kid," Kevin said and then brightened up. "Hey, I'll call him up and invite him to lunch. His age is the best time to start thinking about life insurance. Is he married?"

"Not yet, but he's dating a woman who seems like a perfect match."

"Then it's a no-brainer to lock in a decent policy at a low rate that's guaranteed for as long as he wants the policy."

Frank knew it was pointless to protest on Parker's behalf.

"I'll bring the hose down to you in a couple of minutes," Kevin continued. "I just need to finish scrubbing the seats. My wife wants to impress her out-of-town sister from Kansas with our yacht tomorrow afternoon."

Frank continued down the dock to his boat. While he worked, he thought about Kevin and his family. A short time later he saw the insurance agent walking toward him with the hose.

"Are you going to tell Parker that I'm going to call him?" Kevin asked.

"No, I'll give you a fair shot at him."

Kevin smiled. "You know how the game works. I'm trying to earn a living."

"And Lenny Blackstock is satisfied with what you sold him."

"Yeah, he's had that policy for a long time. By now it has a nice cash value." Kevin handed the hose to Frank. "Do you need me to give you a hand with anything?"

"No, I can handle it if I take my time." Frank laid the hose on the boat deck. "Is your sister-in-law having any health problems?"

"Yeah," Kevin replied. "That's why she's made the trip. She's not sure she'll be able to do it if she waits much longer, and we want her to have a good time. Her husband passed away a couple of years ago, and she's been down in the dumps ever since. Then she found out she has this condition in her lungs that will eventually require her to use an oxygen tank, and it sent her even deeper into depression."

Frank adjusted the cap on his head. "Maybe you could take her to church while she's here."

"My wife would love that," Kevin said. "But I play golf with clients on Sundays. The problem is, my sister-in-law is bitter about all that's happened to her, and I don't think she'll want to go."

"If you invite her and agree to go, she'll say yes," Frank replied.

"Me?"

"Pretend you're trying to sell her a policy."

"That's a good way of looking at it," Kevin said, grinning. "My wife will freak out when I bring up going to church as a family. It will be worth watching her reaction even if her sister turns me down."

After Kevin left, Frank found himself whistling while he cleaned his boat.

Chapter 31

Parker's weekly phone conference with Thomas Blocker was set for Friday afternoon. In the meantime, his turmoil about what to do about the job offer increased by the minute. The time set for the call passed. He could distinctly remember Blocker saying he would initiate the call, but it would be easy for the busy trial lawyer to forget such a minor detail. Deciding it was better to act than be late, Parker picked up the phone and entered the number.

"Mr. Blocker, please," he said to the receptionist who answered. "It's Parker House. I have a call scheduled with him at three o'clock this afternoon."

"Mr. Blocker is out of the office and won't be returning until Monday," the woman replied.

"Is there a conference call with me on his calendar?" Parker asked.

"Let me check," the woman replied and

put Parker on hold. A moment later she returned. "No. Do you want me to take a message in case he checks in?"

"Yes, just tell him I'll be in the office the rest of the afternoon and available to talk."

After he hung up, Parker checked the calendar on his computer screen and verified the hour he'd blocked off for the conversation about the Ferguson case. His phone buzzed.

"Mr. Blocker is here for his meeting with you," Vicki said.

"He's here?"

"No, he went to the restroom, but he was standing in front of my desk about thirty seconds ago. Are you okay?"

"Does Greg know?" Parker ignored Vicki's question.

"Not yet. He's meeting with a client in his office. Should I interrupt him or slip him a note?"

"No, I'll be there in a second and take Mr. Blocker downstairs to the conference room."

Parker hurriedly grabbed the information on the Ferguson case and went out to Vicki's desk.

"I can definitely see the family resemblance between Layla and her father," Vicki said in a low voice. "Have you met her mother yet?"

"No."

"Isn't it about time for that to happen? You've interacted a lot with her father, and her mother has a lot of catching up to do —"

"Please, Vicki," Parker said. "Not now."

The door to the upstairs restroom opened and Tom Blocker emerged. He was wearing a green golf shirt and khaki pants. Parker had straightened his tie before leaving his office. He loosened it as he stepped forward to shake the trial lawyer's hand.

"I was expecting a phone call, not a personal visit," Parker said. "Would you like to meet in the downstairs conference room?"

"No, your office is fine."

"Should I let Greg know where you are when he's free?" Vicki asked.

Parker turned to Blocker and waited. "Of course. I'll be glad to see him," Blocker said.

Parker led the way to his office. Blocker closed the door behind him and sat down.

"Have you checked out the house for sale on Pollock Street?" Blocker asked.

"For sale? I thought it was for rent."

"Most things for rent can be bought if the price is right."

"No, I've not seen the inside," Parker replied.

Blocker reached in his pocket and took out a key. "Would you like to? The spot I've picked out for your office doesn't have a view of the neighbor's backyard, but it would give you the chance to stretch out and think large. I'll never forget the first time I argued an appeal in the Eleventh Circuit Court of Appeals in Atlanta. The size of the courtroom made it easier to present big ideas about important issues."

"Don't you want to talk about the Ferguson case first?"

"We'll circle back here and do that later," Blocker replied. "I'm in town for the whole weekend, so I'm not in a rush."

Parker and Blocker emerged from the office. Vicki raised her eyebrows as they passed her desk.

"We'll be back in a few minutes," Parker said.

"Maybe more than a few," Blocker added and then stopped. "What's your name again?"

"Vicki Satterfield."

"And what's your work experience?"

Parker shifted nervously on his feet and glanced several times at the door to Greg's office as Vicki provided a quick verbal résumé.

Blocker nodded when she finished. "Impressive. You've thrived in several different types of legal environments."

"Including here," Parker said. "Vicki is the glue that holds this place together."

"I look forward to learning more about that," Blocker said as he moved on toward the stairwell.

They walked downstairs in silence. Parker didn't speak until they were outside on the porch.

"Was that a job interview?" he asked.

"First steps," Blocker replied, raising his index finger. "Of course, I'll rely on your recommendation about actually hiring her; however, a person with experience running a law office is important when the lawyer in charge is young. That's probably one reason why Greg hired her. What's he paying her?"

"I have no idea. I don't know what anyone else makes at the firm."

They reached the sidewalk and headed toward Blocker's car.

"What's your salary?" Blocker asked.

Slightly embarrassed, Parker told him and watched the trial lawyer's face for his reaction.

"Thank you," Blocker replied, unlocking

the doors of his car.

"Why?" Parker asked as he slipped into the passenger seat.

"For telling me the truth. It would have been easy to inflate the figure to make sure I offer you more to join me."

The possibility of lying hadn't crossed Parker's mind.

"But you didn't even consider doing that," Blocker continued. "You'll get a hefty raise, but working with me isn't about what you'll make now. What's more important is your potential down the road."

The car pulled away from the curb. Parker's head was spinning with thoughts of what "potential" meant, along with Greg's likely reaction if Blocker lured both Parker and Vicki away from the firm. If that happened, every time Parker left the new office he would have to look up and down the street to make sure his former boss wasn't preparing to drive his vehicle onto the sidewalk and run him over.

And then there was Layla.

Frank finished cleaning his boat and turned off the hose. No one else was on any of the other boats that quietly rocked at their moorings. He was alone except for a pair of seagulls loudly calling to each other as they circled overhead. Taking a dry towel, Frank dried off the seat in front of the console in the middle of the boat and sat down to enjoy a few moments of a late-afternoon breeze. The seagulls moved down the shore in search of dinner. The wind on Frank's face had a familiar yet ancient feel.

Rhine River, Switzerland, 1944

The cool breeze ruffled Franz's hair that hadn't been cut since he crossed the Rhine. He was in the boat with Otto, a ten-year-old boy, and Alfred, the boy's grandfather. They were fishing for perch to sell the following day in the local fish market.

"Opa, if I catch a pike, will you take it off the hook?" Otto asked.

"Yes. If you can land a pike without it sawing through your leader, I'll take it off the hook and cook it for your supper," Alfred answered.

Franz was sitting in the back of the boat with his line drifting from the stern. He'd learned more about fishing during the past five months than he had in his entire life. Alfred had grown up fishing with his father along the river when the Upper Rhine still teemed with millions of salmon in midsummer and early fall.

Otto's parents were killed in a house fire

when the boy was two years old. Rescued by a neighbor, he was sent to live with his grandfather in a two-hundred-year-old cottage not far from the river. Otto's frantic reaction to his grandfather's near drowning was understandable under any circumstances, but it made even more sense when Franz learned about the boy's tragic background. Otto hated to be apart from his grandfather for a single day, but attendance at the local school was mandatory. Once a month, Alfred let Otto skip school and join them on the water.

They were fishing with river crustaceans that made up a large portion of a perch's diet. In a mesh basket attached to the side of the boat were fifteen fat fish they'd caught since heading out while mist still hovered over the surface of the water. Ten of those fish had come off Franz's line. He'd shown a quick aptitude for fishing, which extended his stay with Alfred and Otto from a few days to several months. Alfred didn't raise questions about Franz's past and spread the word around the village that the young German was a second cousin who had been living in Basel since before the war began. As time passed, Alfred added more details to enhance the story. Franz was impressed with the creative details in the fake narrative.

"My grandfather was a great storyteller," Alfred said with a smile when Franz asked him about it. "He could entertain me for hours on the river with tales about fish who talked and otters who lived like kings in their dens. And he would have been furious if I let a good fisherman like you slip through my net. We've more than doubled our production since you came to stay with us."

Franz kept up with the war news by listening to a French-speaking radio broadcast that came from a station on the other side of the river. A few weeks earlier, in a mixture of tears and patriotic outbursts, the announcer had proclaimed the liberation of Paris from German occupation. Franz knew the occupation of German cities would soon follow.

"Fish on," Franz said at the telltale jerk of his line.

Otto watched wide-eyed as Franz quickly reeled in another fish, the largest of the day, and dropped it into the wire basket.

"Is Franz a better fisherman than you, Opa?" the boy asked.

"No," Franz answered. "And your grandfather is a great teacher. I knew nothing about fishing until I came to stay with you.

Every fish I catch is because he taught me the right way to do it. That's why he makes you go to school. He wants you to learn so you can be successful in life."

"But all I want to do is fish," Otto protested. "I'm wasting time in school."

"You're already a good fisherman," Franz replied. "But you're going to be an even better engineer who will help save the river from those who might destroy it."

Otto turned away. Alfred eyed Franz.

"Why do you say that?" the old man asked.

"The manufacturing debris being dumped in the river is killing —"

"I know about that," Alfred interrupted. "I'm talking about Otto's future."

"I believe you are right to make him go to school," Franz answered evasively. "And from the work he's brought home, he's very good in math. That's what it takes to be a good engineer."

"Do you know what his father did for a living?"

"No."

"He was a civil engineer in Bern."

Franz was putting new bait on his hook and looked up. "There. It's in his blood."

Alfred caught a fish and reeled it in. "What about you?" he asked. "What do you want to do?"

"Maybe I'll become a fisherman," Franz said with a smile. "I hated math in school."

"Would you like to stay and work with me? We could get a bigger boat and expand the business."

"Yes, I want to stay here and be a fisherman with you," Otto replied, speaking over his shoulder. "And we don't have to get a bigger boat. I like this one."

"Being an engineer doesn't mean you can't fish," his grandfather replied. "But taking care of the river will help every fisherman. And the fish."

Otto hunched over and didn't reply. Alfred looked at Franz.

"Well?"

"I can't say right now," Franz said slowly. "But I appreciate you letting me stay with you and Otto."

"You saved my life."

"And you saved mine."

"How did Opa save your life?" Otto asked, turning around. "You pulled him out of the river."

"There are other ways to save someone."

Otto rolled his eyes. Alfred and Franz laughed.

That night while Franz was listening to the French radio station, the announcer played a message in English from General

Dwight D. Eisenhower, the commander of the Allied forces in Europe. Franz didn't speak English and without a French translation wouldn't have understood the speech by the American general. But as he listened to the unfamiliar words, Franz felt a churning in his stomach and an undeniable pull across the Atlantic.

Leaving the cottage, he walked in the light of a full moon to the riverbank and sat down. As he watched the double-reflected light bounce off the surface of the water, he decided two things — he would become a fisherman and he would go to America.

CHAPTER 32

"What do you think?" Blocker asked Parker as they stood in the foyer of the house on Pollock Street.

"Wow," Parker said. "I had no idea they'd spent so much time and money on the renovation. It's probably better than when it was brand-new."

"Back then they didn't know about telecommunication switch-boxes, internal cable connections, or central air-conditioning. Let's go upstairs to see your future office."

Parker was uncomfortable with Blocker's unquestioning confidence that Parker was going to accept the trial lawyer's invitation to become an associate. However, as they climbed the stairs, Parker had an unusual experience. In a matter of seconds he witnessed himself climbing the stairs hundreds and hundreds of times. His body was a blur as he ascended to the second floor of the building.

They reached a broad landing that dwarfed the one for Branham and Camp.

"Here it is," Blocker announced with a flourish of his hand. "It was the master bedroom suite for the house."

They stepped through a broad door into a long room with a fireplace, massive crown moldings, and multiple windows that generously welcomed natural light. An infant nursery attached to the master suite would be available for a secretarial space.

"Like I said, a big space helps germinate great ideas," Blocker added.

"It's beautiful," Parker said and then felt silly for not coming up with a different word.

"But you won't be able to stomp around," Blocker said. "My office in the former dining room is directly beneath this room."

Blocker checked his watch. "Let's go back to Branham and Camp for a few minutes to discuss the Ferguson case. Afterward, I need to call Layla. I've planned a surprise for her tomorrow and need to let her know when I'm going to pick her up."

"Uh, I need to talk to you about Layla," Parker responded. "We've been spending time together, and I really, really like her."

"Excellent." Blocker's eyes lit up. "I think that's great. She needs to meet someone like you who has integrity, brains, and a strong intuitive streak. And you can keep her interested. That's not easy."

Parker absorbed Blocker's rapid-fire analysis of his personality.

"Uh, thanks," he said. "But she's given me a nonnegotiable ultimatum. If I accept your job offer, she's not going to date me. It seems like an extreme position for her to take, but I guess it all goes back to —"

"The fact that she blames me for everything negative that's happened in her life," Blocker supplied, "which is ridiculous. You're a lawyer. You know there are two sides to every situation. Layla's mother and I split by mutual agreement, and Layla's marriage to Mitchell Donovan was doomed by their immaturity."

Even if Blocker withdrew the job offer, Parker wasn't going to drop the subject without seeing it through.

"Whether Layla is right or not, she believes it would be toxic for her to be romantically involved with another man who works for you."

"Do you agree with her?" Blocker asked.

"No," Parker blurted out. "I don't know anything about Mitchell, but I'm a different man, and this is a different relationship."

"I agree," Blocker replied with satisfaction.

Parker glanced at the stairwell, which in his mind's eye he'd already climbed hundreds of times, and strained for a moment to discern whether Layla ever accompanied him. She wasn't in the picture.

"And I'm confident you can work this out with Layla," Blocker continued. "You're strong enough to keep her from running over you."

Parker didn't agree with Blocker's assessment of his daughter but doubted there was common ground for additional discussion.

They returned to Branham and Camp. The firm was inexorably beginning to seem like Parker's former employer. He and Blocker climbed the stairs and reached Vicki's desk. Vicki greeted Blocker with an added dose of personal enthusiasm.

"I'm sorry, Mr. Blocker, but Greg had to leave," she said. "He apologized."

"We'll catch up later," Blocker replied.

Parker led the way to his office and spent the next thirty minutes trying to keep up with Blocker's constant stream of comments, questions, and suggestions about the Ferguson case.

"All right," Blocker said, taking a breath. "What are your action steps?"

Parker checked his notes and rattled off five items.

"You forgot one," Blocker said when he finished.

"What is it?" Parker asked, looking up.

"Give me an answer about the job offer."

"I'd like more time to consider —"

"You don't need it, and I'm not going to give it to you," Blocker replied briskly. "I've learned to read people pretty well, and I believe you made up your mind standing outside your new office a few minutes ago. Here's what I'm willing to do."

Blocker quickly summarized the terms of the offer, which included everything from free health care to a profit-sharing plan that would be fully vested within five years. Parker's salary would increase immediately by forty percent, with the "potential for the future" rising up before him like a lofty mountain whose summit disappeared in the clouds. While he listened, Parker tried to imagine himself saying no. He couldn't.

"Could I give Greg and Dexter Camp a two-week notice?" he asked when Blocker finished.

"Do you think that's necessary?"

"Yes."

"I don't," Blocker replied, standing up. "Most firms turn off a departing associate's computer as soon as he quits and escort him from the premises, especially if the attorney is going to work with a competitor."

Parker could certainly imagine a similar scenario with Greg. "Okay. I'll talk to him first thing Monday morning."

"Fine. That will give you a chance to move out over the weekend." Blocker pulled a key out of his pocket with a smile and handed it to Parker. "I was confident you would accept the job and already bought the house on Pollock Street. I'll need you there next week to oversee all the work that's going to need to be done to get it fully ready."

Parker almost felt like he was having another out-of-body experience.

"What if I'd said no?" he asked.

Blocker shrugged. "Every lawyer has contingency plans, but in this case it wasn't necessary to implement one."

"How will you handle Chet Ferguson's case?" Parker asked. "Do you think you'll be able to work out an arrangement with Greg to stay involved?"

"It will be more like Greg working out an arrangement with me. Mr. Ferguson and I have had several very productive conversations. He's willing to let Greg continue as cocounsel. The client's loyalty is more to you than Greg. If Greg has a problem with that deal, he'll be left with a quantum mer-uit claim that I can promise will net him a lot less."

Parker shouldn't have been surprised that a lawyer like Blocker, who thought of every detail in a case, would be just as prepared when it came to the business side of a practice.

"And Vicki?" Parker asked.

"I'll leave that up to you," Blocker replied.

"Are you going to say anything about this to Layla?" Parker asked.

"I'll be glad to."

Parker quickly debated the best course of action. "No, I should tell her," he said after a few moments passed.

"I completely agree. Oh, give me your personal e-mail address. I want to send you the employment agreement. Look it over and let me know if you have any questions. I'm sure you'll find it acceptable. Also, one of my assistants is going to send you sum-maries of several files for you to look over this weekend."

"I wouldn't be comfortable using Greg's account if there's any legal research in-volved."

"You won't need it for what I'm looking for. These matters are ideally suited for your abilities."

Parker stayed late at the office. After waiting until everyone was gone, he packed his personal belongings in several empty cardboard boxes and took them down to his car. Even though working for Greg hadn't been a picnic, it was hard not to be nostalgic over leaving his first job. None of the office furniture belonged to him, but it had felt that way. He sat behind his desk and flipped through a few files that had been meaningful to him on a personal level. He picked up the photo of the *Aare,* which he knew would have a prominent place in his new office.

Parker heard footsteps in the hallway leading to his office. He placed the photo in the last box he was packing up. The thought of facing Greg without a weekend to prepare made him feel suddenly sick to his stomach.

Frank had enjoyed cleaning the boat for Parker and Layla. There was something about the prospect of the two young people spending time together that made his tired heart beat a little bit stronger. Each generation has the opportunity for new life regardless of the darkness from which it springs. Frank thought about the photo of Parker and Layla standing at the bow of the boat looking toward the future and resolved to

431

place the picture in a frame as a symbol of hope.

As he sat on his back porch in the fading light, Frank listened to the sounds of the night emerge from the shadows. A pair of fruit bats dived across the yard in pursuit of insects awakening for the night's activities. Nature's sonar still exceeded anything man could manufacture, and the bat's gift reminded him of his own. Like the bats, Frank had a kind of sonar, and now the same capability was obviously stirring in Parker's life. The thought that his grandson would have to wrestle with how to handle witnessing the future made Frank shift uncomfortably in his chair. He closed his eyes and offered up a quick, simple prayer for help, for both Parker and himself. Before he reopened them, a scene from the past rose to the surface.

Dresden, 1929
The exact time gap between the night his opa placed his hands on Frank's head and prayed for him and the older man's death was hazy, but Frank could vividly remember his mother picking him up and holding him for a moment so he could peer down into the casket at the lifeless body that he knew, even at his young age, no longer contained

432

the essence of the man who'd ministered with love and authority to the people who visited the little house in Dresden. After his mother lowered him to the floor, Franz stood at the head of the casket and refused to move when his mother urged him to. Lowering his head, he stared at the floor and shook his head when she touched his shoulder.

"I want to stay here," he said.

"But, Franz," she began, but she stopped when he looked up at her with stubborn determination in his eyes. "All right. I'll be with your aunt Elise."

Franz stayed put while other people passed by to pay their respects. Then the hair on his neck suddenly stood up, and he involuntarily shivered. Franz was conscious of a presence, not seen, but nonetheless there. Not scary in a bad way, but fearful in a good one. He glanced up and focused on a spot beyond the casket in the corner of the room. There was nothing to see, but he knew with certainty there was a power or force or person present that was more aware of him than he was of it. Then a calm peace and pure love flowed over him and enveloped him. And Franz remembered a strange thing, his grandfather's best smile, the one that made him feel like he was the most important, most special boy in the whole world.

Frank opened his eyes, but his skin still tingled as the past intersected with the present. He needed to give that smile to Parker, and he hoped that somehow his grandson might be bathed in the same peace and love that had washed over him, only to be lost in war, then finally regained in old age. With Parker he hoped there wouldn't be such a long detour from the right path.

"What are you doing here?" Dexter asked when he appeared in the doorway of Parker's office.

"Daydreaming about boats," Parker answered, holding up the photo of the *Aare*. "And you?"

"I was in the middle of supper and suddenly realized I hadn't sent a document to a client that they need first thing Monday morning."

Parker saw Dexter glance past him with a puzzled look. "Where are the other photos you had on your credenza?"

"Uh, I'm giving the one with my grandfather on his boat a rest."

"Okay," Dexter said and nodded. "How late are you going to be here? I know Greg can be a slave driver, but you need a life outside the office."

"I do."

"Well, let me know if he needs to back off. I'd hate to lose you."

Parker swallowed. He felt terrible not telling Dexter about his plans, even though it was bad news.

"And I've enjoyed practicing with you," he managed before he realized he'd inadvertently slipped into the past tense. "Except for Donna McAlpine."

"What's the status of her complaint?"

"I forgot to tell you. It was dismissed by the state bar at the first level of review."

"Good."

Dexter hesitated at the door. Parker held his breath and hoped his face didn't reveal the tension he felt.

"See you later," Dexter said. "I'll be in my office for a few more minutes."

As soon as Dexter left, Parker waited until he heard the door to Dexter's office close. He quickly slipped out of the office and didn't look back.

CHAPTER 33

Arriving at his apartment, Parker tossed Bosco a treat and walked up the stairs. Tom Blocker and his daughter, Layla, shared one characteristic — a strong, inflexible will. Parker's phone rang, and he took it out of his pocket. It was Layla.

"Where are you?" she asked as soon as he answered.

"At my apartment."

"You're not at the office talking to my father?"

"He left hours ago. He told me he was going to see you."

"He did and wanted me to cancel my boat trip with you tomorrow. I told him no."

"Why?"

"Is that what you wanted me to do?"

"No, uh, yes. I mean, he told me he'd planned a surprise for you."

"Oh, he wants to buy me a townhome overlooking the river. It's always bothered

436

him that I rent an apartment. He believes a townhome would be a good investment, so we went to see it after we ate supper."

"Congratulations."

"I turned him down."

"What was wrong with it?"

"Nothing. It was gorgeous, but I'm not going to do it."

"Why not?" Parker asked, confused.

"Because I'm trying to live a more independent life. And for me that means keeping a healthy distance between me and my father. It's a commitment I made last year, and so far it's been one of the best decisions of my life."

Parker swallowed as he thought about the news he would deliver the following day.

"I'll see you in the morning," he said. "Can I pick you up around eight o'clock?"

"Yes."

"I'm glad we're still on for tomorrow."

"Me too. See you then."

Parker arrived at Layla's apartment at 7:55 a.m. The complex was in a less desirable part of town. A car parked next to Layla's vehicle was sitting up on blocks with two of the tires removed. Next to it was a car in which the rear window glass had been completely shattered as if hit by a baseball bat or, worse, blown out with a shotgun blast. Layla came out wearing white shorts, a green top, and simple sandals. She had a beach bag in her hand and her camera over her shoulder.

"This area has gone downhill since I was in high school," Parker said when he got out to open the car door for her. "Do you feel safe here?"

"Not always," Layla replied as she settled into the passenger seat. "But it's under my budget while I grow the business."

"I can understand why your father wants to get you out of here. I'd feel the same way if you were my daughter."

"And if you're going to think about me as your daughter, let's end the day right now, and I'll go back to my apartment," Layla replied.

"You win," Parker responded. "But there's nothing wrong with wanting you to have a nice, safe place to live."

"It's not that bad. A police officer and his family live in the apartment across the hall from me. It helps that his car is usually parked out front."

"Do you want to stop for breakfast?" he asked as he turned onto a street that led to one of the highways that crossed the Neuse River on a long bridge.

"A sausage biscuit would be nice," Layla answered.

"Really?"

"Or a slice of fresh quiche with fruit on the side. Your call."

Parker glanced sideways at Layla's face for a clue as to her preference. He knew they would pass a coffee shop that served a morning quiche on their way to the bridge. And nearby was a locally owned restaurant that offered the best sausage and biscuit in the area. He turned into the parking lot for the sausage-and-biscuit spot.

"You guessed right," Layla said.

"I did?"

Layla patted him on the arm. "I would have been happy either way, but I wanted you to choose for me. It's a tiny way of letting you know I don't have to control every minute detail of my life."

"That's good news," Parker replied, thinking about her father's comment.

"And that I trust you," Layla continued. "Baby steps."

Parker licked his lips. Five minutes later they were back on the road with a cup of coffee each and two sausage biscuits. Layla made several contented noises as she ate her food.

"I didn't picture you as a sausage-and-biscuit girl," Parker said, glancing sideways at her.

"I'm constantly full of surprises."

They crossed over the river and twenty minutes later arrived at the dock. Parker took a cooler and a plastic bag of snacks from the trunk of his car, and Layla secured her camera strap over her shoulder.

"I brought drinks and a few things to munch on," he said. "I thought we would find a place on the river to eat lunch."

"I may not be hungry after that sausage and biscuit."

They walked down the dock to the boat. After they hopped aboard, Parker untied the immaculately clean skiff, started the engine, and backed into the river. The sky was overcast, but the edges of the clouds hinted at sun, not rain. As soon as they were in the river, Parker opened the throttle, and the boat rose higher and cut through the water. Layla stood in the bow. The wind blew her hair behind her in a tangled swirl that she made no effort to control. Parker took in deep breaths of air tinged with a taste of spray. He liked going fast on the boat and was glad the water was smooth enough that Layla wasn't unsteady on her feet. He divided his time between watching the scenery on the bank and admiring

Layla's wild hair.

They ran wide open down the river for forty-five minutes before Parker backed off the throttle and headed toward shore. Layla took a hat from her beach bag and crammed it on her head.

"I loved that," she said as the sound of the wind rushing across the boat decreased. "Even if my hair didn't."

Parker eased the boat next to a small marshy area and dropped the anchor. They were a hundred yards out of the main channel and completely alone. The boat rocked a few times before it became still. Parker left the stern and sat on the gunwale. Layla took several photos of the river, the marsh, and the scrubby trees along the shoreline.

"What's special about this place?" she asked, lowering her camera.

"That you're here with me."

He knew his words were at odds with what he was going to have to tell her later in the day, but during the boat ride his confidence that he could persuade Layla to change her mind increased. What was the point of being a lawyer in the first place if he couldn't convince her about something that should be obvious?

"Nice," Layla said with a smile. "And

what makes it better is that I believe you. Would you be willing to tell me why you feel that way?"

Parker went back to the first day he saw her in the courtroom and told Greg to leave her on the jury.

"My head knew you needed to be on the jury, but it took me awhile to realize my heart was also interested. That started when I saw you at Chip and Kelsey's wedding. You were both professional and graceful at the same time. But I backed off when you analyzed Greg's performance at the trial."

"Why?"

"What man can be around a woman that smart?"

Layla laughed.

They spent a leisurely couple of hours watching the hidden activity of the marsh unfold before them. Several blue herons were fishing in the reeds nearby. Layla had her camera ready, and when one caught a fish, she captured several images as the bird speared the fish with its bill, then skillfully flipped it into its mouth for a final wiggling journey down the heron's neck and into its stomach.

"That bird didn't have a problem eating what it caught," Parker said as he watched Layla scroll through the images.

"It didn't look into the fish's eyes."

"So you'd do better if you fished blind-folded?"

"I think a better solution for me is to go to the fish market."

The tide went out, exposing several spots of black soil inhabited by villages of miniature crabs that scurried in and out of tiny burrows.

"There are tons of larger crabs on the bottom," Parker said. "Did you ever catch crabs by luring them to a net with chicken necks tied to string?"

"Yes."

"Did you cook and eat any of them?"

"A few times, but I hate the sound they make when you drop them alive into a pot of boiling water. It sounds like a scream."

"You're going to make a vegan out of me before you know it."

Around 11:30 a.m., Parker pulled up the anchor and restarted the boat's motor. They continued downriver along the edge of the marsh at a much slower pace. Layla left her place in the bow and stood beside Parker at the console, which gave him a chance to study her long, graceful fingers.

"Do you play the piano?" he asked.

"No, but I can juggle five tennis balls. Anything over three is tough."

Parker burst out laughing.

"What's so funny?"

"I knew you were a juggler the first time we went to dinner. I'd love to see a demonstration."

They continued along the marsh until a larger tributary spilled into the Neuse. Parker turned into the side water that was moving slightly faster than the main channel.

"There's a resort a few miles upriver where we can eat lunch. The restaurant is open to the public."

"Does it have tennis courts?"

"Yeah, I think so."

"Maybe I can borrow a few old tennis balls and give you a juggling exhibition."

They coasted into the small marina for the resort. There was a mixed assembly of motorboats and sailboats. Parker found a place near the gas pump. A young man in his twenties came out of the main resort building as they approached.

"If I fill up with gas, can I tie up while we eat lunch at the restaurant?" Parker called out.

"Yes, let me swipe your card, and I'll have a receipt ready for you when you leave."

They reached the main building for the resort, a single-story stucco-covered structure that seemed to grow out of the sandy soil. The light brown building was surrounded by dune grass, palmetto trees, and an array of fall flowers. Layla snapped a few pictures.

"I need to learn more about the flowers that grow around here," she said. "It's more fun to know what I'm photographing."

The restaurant was close to the water and featured a row of picture windows on the side facing the river. A hostess seated them so they could see the marina. They each ordered a seafood salad. While they ate, Parker learned that in college Layla had auditioned to be the school mascot at football games.

"I would have made a terrible eagle," she said. "The costume didn't fit me at all."

"Your legs are perfect."

"I don't think that's a compliment."

"Hey, there's a guy on my boat!" Parker said, looking out the window.

Layla turned in her chair. "And he has a gas nozzle in his hand. Maybe he works for the marina."

"Yeah." Parker nodded his head. "I shouldn't be paranoid about it, but Opa is so particular, and it's a big deal that he trusts me enough to take the boat out on my own."

"It's okay. I know what violation of trust

looks and feels like."

And with that, Layla launched into a comprehensive explanation for the breakup of her marriage. Parker was immediately uncomfortable, and when he realized she was being vulnerable, he felt even worse.

"My father sent Mitchell on the road to take depositions and try cases all the time. There would be stretches of seven to ten days or longer when I wouldn't see him. Mitchell kept reassuring me it was only temporary and necessary to advance his career. I felt abandoned. When I complained to my father about it, they both got mad at me for butting my nose into business."

"Maybe it really was just temporary."

"I knew better," Layla replied. "It's the same thing my father did to my mother, and every lawyer in his practice racks up tons of frequent-flier miles. I know what a big deal it is for other firms to associate my father on their cases, and that's never going to stop. Just because he's thinking about opening an office in New Bern doesn't mean he's going to be spending much time here with me or anyone else. It's just another place from which to send people out. Did he tell you that when he talked to you about a job?"

"No," Parker replied truthfully.

"He should have. But it wasn't just all the

446

hours away that killed my father's marriage to my mother, and my marriage to Mitchell. That —"

"Layla," Parker jumped in. "You don't have to tell me."

"Why?" she asked, raising her eyebrows. "Do you already know?"

"No."

Layla blinked her eyes several times as she studied him for a moment. "Have you already accepted the job?" she asked.

Parker shifted nervously in his seat. "I haven't signed an employment agreement."

"But you told him you'll accept," she finished flatly.

"We visited the new office on Pollock Street, and it was as if I'd already been working there for years," Parker replied, trying to sound calmer than he felt. "It's hard to explain, but I knew it was a step I was supposed to take."

"Supposed to take," Layla repeated with emphasis. "Or were you just seeing yourself doing something that you wanted to do and convinced yourself it was the right thing?"

Layla's question stopped Parker in his tracks. "I'm not sure," he admitted.

"Well, I am," Layla said. "I want you to take me home."

"But Mitchell and I are different men —"

"Of course you are, but my father isn't, and I'm not willing to risk tearing my heart in two again." Tears appeared in the corners of Layla's eyes. "I can't sit at home waiting and worrying about whether the man I love is cheating on me with a woman he meets in one of the cities where he's cooped up in a hotel room night after night. That life destroyed my mother, and I deceived myself into thinking it wouldn't happen to me."

"I'm sorry —" Parker started.

"But it did." Layla spoke like a freight train that couldn't be stopped. "With God's help, I'm finally getting back on my feet, and I'm not going to go down that road again with you or anyone else!"

CHAPTER 34

During the return trip to New Bern, Parker ran the boat wide open. Layla stayed in the bow with her back to him. This time her hair swishing in the breeze was a symbol of how the day had ended up completely out of control. By the time they reached the dock, Parker hoped she would be willing to talk. After all, they were at the beginning of a relationship, not on the verge of marriage. Recognizing that distinction should make a difference. The boat slowed. As soon as it touched the dock, Layla jumped out.

"Hey, I could use a hand here!" Parker called after her, but she didn't turn around as she walked rapidly toward the shore.

Parker cut off the engine and tied the boat to a weathered post. He methodically went through the process of preparing the skiff for its next outing. He knew Layla was waiting at the car, but he wasn't ready to face her. He hoisted the gear onto the dock and lugged it to his vehicle. Layla was nowhere in sight, and the thought shot through Parker's mind that she'd decided to hitch-hike to town. He quickly threw everything into the rear seat of the car and jumped behind the wheel. Looking up, he saw Layla emerge from behind a large clump of dune grass along the edge of the parking lot. She walked over and got in.

"Were you going to leave me?" she asked as soon as she was seated.

"No, I was worried you might have started hitchhiking back to town."

"Hitchhiking? Do you think I'm crazy?"

"No, it's just —"

"Please take me home and don't try to talk to me. I need to be alone as soon as possible."

After Parker dropped Layla off in silence, he trudged up the steps to his apartment as Bosco settled down to munch on the treat Parker had tossed to him. Following a hot shower, Parker tried to relax, but his mind was churning faster than the prop on his grandfather's boat at full throttle.

Turning on his laptop, he checked his e-mail. Toward the top of the queue was a message from an unknown name; however, the subject matter grabbed his attention: "Cases for Immediate Review." He clicked it open. It was from one of Tom Blocker's assistants, a woman named Sandy Stumpf. Attached was a list of six cases, each summarized in two or three paragraphs with a specific question at the end. She'd sent a copy of the e-mail to Blocker and directed Parker to send his responses to both of them before 9:00 a.m. on Monday morning.

Needing something to distract him from thoughts of Layla, Parker read about the first case, a lawsuit against the manufacturer of autopilot devices for yachts. He was familiar with the sophisticated equipment that could plot a precise course from New Bern to the Bahamas. The autopilot in question linked to a sonar system intended to keep the big boat from running aground or into another vessel. Blocker's client left the wheelhouse for a few minutes one evening and the boat plowed into a smaller yacht, causing several million dollars in damage. Parker's first thought was that the owner of the yacht was contributorily negligent because he left the wheelhouse and trusted the system. But that wasn't Blocker's question. He wanted advice about the best expert to analyze the autopilot's software system. All he gave Parker was a list of six names. No credentials, no summary of each person's experience.

Parker spent the next hour trying to track down the candidates on his own. He was able to locate four of the six and learn a few basic facts about their training, but two eluded him. Of the four he found, nothing stood out in a way that caught his attention. He raised his head and looked up at the sharply sloping ceiling. This was random guesswork, not legitimate research. Glancing down, he saw the name of one of the candidates, Pamela Pyke, PhD, who had worked for a few years at a Silicon Valley start-up before branching out as a software consultant. He clicked on a small picture associated with her online bio. Then he suddenly saw her sitting in an office with an autopilot navigation device on her desk while she ran some sort of scan on her computer. Parker blinked his eyes. The scene dissolved. Parker stared again at the photo and with a surprising level of confidence answered the question: Pamela Pyke, PhD.

Over the next four hours he worked his way through the other cases. The questions included whether to depose a former company officer in an intellectual property dispute and whether a defense lawyer in a large personal injury action was bluffing when he claimed he could contradict several key elements of the plaintiff's claim. Parker concluded it would be a bad idea to depose the former officer because the man would provide information the company's lawyer didn't know about that would hurt the lawsuit. Parker believed the defense lawyer wasn't bluffing in the personal injury action; however, the witness he was going to rely on could be impeached because he had several felony convictions in the remote past and had been a client of the lawyer when the defense attorney first started practicing law.

When he finished, Parker sat back and rubbed his tired eyes. He then reviewed his responses for typos and grammatical errors and prepared to send the file to Ms. Stumpf and Mr. Blocker. Suddenly he stopped and studied the computer screen again. His eyes went to what seemed like the most straightforward case in the group, a lawsuit involving the breach of a contract between a computer equipment manufacturer in Alabama and a well-established Belgian company. The Alabama company shipped the equipment and didn't receive payment. Blocker wanted to know if it would be better to sue in the United States or in Belgium. Parker didn't attempt to engage in a crash course on Belgium's laws and immediately chose the US as the best venue. Now he wasn't so sure. He deleted his previous response and typed in "Belgium — The judge assigned to the case will have prior knowledge of the company and its dealings and will be favorably disposed to our client's interests." Both intellectually and emotionally exhausted, Parker pressed the Send button and crawled into bed.

Parker woke Sunday morning, groaned as he recalled the previous day with Layla, and finally rolled out of bed. He went to the playground for an hour of intense exercising. The workout helped clear his mind.

After returning to his apartment, his BlackBerry rang and an unfamiliar number appeared.

"Good morning, Parker. This is Tom," a male voice said. "I hope I didn't wake you up after you stayed up late working on the memo Sandy sent you."

"No." Parker sat up straighter in his chair. "I've already spent an hour exercising and fixed a cup of coffee."

"I wanted to touch base with you on your responses."

"Yes, sir. I tried to do what you asked. There wasn't much to go on with some of the questions, so I'm sure you'll need to do some additional research and give thought to other options that might be —"

"Actually, that's not necessary," Blocker said. "It would be a waste of time at this point in the litigation."

"A waste of time?" Parker asked with a sinking feeling in the pit of his stomach.

"Yes, all those cases are closed files. They've either gone to trial or settled."

"Then why did you ask me —" Parker stopped as he suddenly suspected Blocker's motive. "It was some kind of a test."

"Yes, and you did quite well if three out of six is a passing grade with one unclear. Do you want me to run down the list?"

"I guess so."

"Good news or bad news first?"

"Uh, I'm curious what you mean by 'unclear.' "

"That was the choice-of-jurisdiction question between the US and Belgium. I retained local counsel in Alabama, and we filed suit in Birmingham. There was a prolonged fight over preliminary matters, and my client got tired of the hassle and expense of litigation and settled for an amount that barely covered its cost of goods sold. So we'll never know if you were right about the favorable judge in Belgium, but it was an intriguing perspective."

Parker heard Blocker clear his throat and say something he couldn't hear to someone else who was apparently in or near the room.

"You were right on the money with Dr. Pyke," Blocker continued. "She was the key witness in the auto-navigation litigation. Once she testified about a serious glitch in the software, the insurance company for the manufacturer made an offer at trial that my client accepted. You whiffed in the intellectual property case. I deposed the former corporate officer and obtained crucial information; however, it was a gutsy call on your part to recommend caution. A knee-jerk response would be to depose everyone in sight and sort it out before trial."

While Blocker talked through the cases, Parker pulled up the e-mail and his responses on his computer so he could follow along.

"Finally," Blocker said, "you nailed what happened with the defense lawyer's supposed key witness in the personal injury case. By the time I finished unpacking the guy's criminal record and links to the defense lawyer going back twenty years, the man's credibility was completely blown. The jury threw out his testimony and returned a very nice verdict. Overall, your performance was impressive."

"But nothing that careful research couldn't have uncovered," Parker replied. "Except, I guess, for the Belgian judge. It wouldn't be possible to investigate him until the suit was filed and he was assigned to the case."

"But pointing me in a potentially fruitful direction is very valuable," Blocker responded. "I'm looking forward to you firing your gun with real bullets in a live case. We'll talk again tomorrow after you meet with Greg Branham and give him the news. Don't mention the Ferguson case. We'll address that issue later."

"What if he asks me about it? I'm sure it will come up."

"Think of something creative. Oh, I have a trip coming up to Spokane in a couple of weeks, and you're joining me."

"Spokane, Washington?"

"Yes, beautiful area. You'll like it."

The call ended, and Parker looked down at his phone.

Frank arrived at the church early and picked a row with several empty chairs. He kept looking over his shoulder as the music began. When Layla arrived, he raised his hand to get her attention.

"Good morning," he said in German

when she came up to him. "Is Parker coming?"

"I don't know," she replied in English. "I didn't talk to him about it."

Layla sang with her eyes closed, and a couple of times Frank saw her wipe them with a tissue. When the music ended and they sat down, he leaned over to her.

"Are you okay?" he asked.

She simply nodded. Frank suspected something was wrong, but he didn't know what it might be. Eric got up to speak. He opened his Bible and the words of Matthew 16:24–25 appeared on the screen: "Then Jesus said to his disciples, 'Whoever wants to be my disciple must deny themselves and take up their cross and follow me. For whoever wants to save their life will lose it, but whoever loses their life for me will find it.' "

The minister looked over the congregation for a moment before he spoke.

"These words in virtually the same form appear five times in the New Testament," Eric said. "Which makes them the most often quoted statement Jesus made during his earthly ministry. I believe there's a reason for that."

The minister launched into a description of the Christian life as a journey marked by

458

self-denial, not self-effort. He also emphasized daily cooperation with what it meant
to be a new creation in Christ Jesus. As Eric
talked, Frank recalled faint whispers of
similar statements by his grandfather during the home meetings in Dresden. Then,
the words had sounded esoteric and beyond
the comprehension of a small boy, but now
they came forth with undeniable clarity.
Frank touched his chest as if awakening his
spirit to listen and learn. The time flew by,
and he was disappointed when Eric delivered the closing prayer.

"Wow," Frank said to Layla when the
service ended. "That was amazing."

Layla studied him for a moment. "I believe
you because your eyes are shining," she said,
"but I'm not exactly sure why."

Frank was disappointed that the message
hadn't transported Layla to the same place
he'd gone. He paused for a moment.

"I've seen death, and at my age I'm a lot
closer to natural death than you are, but
this was about a different type of death that
isn't the end of life but rather the doorway
to the kind of life God intends us to live. It
blew me away."

Layla smiled. "Maybe you should be a
preacher. You summarized half the sermon
in one sentence."

They left the church together. Frank lingered with Eric for a moment at the door to let him know how meaningful the message had been to him. The minister listened and politely nodded, which left Frank with the odd sensation that he might have received more from the sermon than the man who delivered it.

"Did you and Parker have fun on the boat yesterday?" Frank asked as soon as he and Layla were outside in the sun. "It was cloudy, which should have been good for taking pictures."

"No, we didn't," Layla replied.

Frank, who was walking beside her toward his car, stopped and faced her. "Would you like to tell me what happened?" he asked.

"No." Layla pressed her lips together tightly and shook her head.

"Are you sure?" Frank persisted.

"He's your grandson, and I'm barely more than a stranger," Layla answered. "It wouldn't be right —"

"That's not how I feel about you," Frank replied forcibly. "In fact, I want you to start calling me 'Opa.' "

Tears suddenly burst from Layla's eyes. She turned away and ran to her car. Frank stood still and watched her leave the parking lot. Deeply troubled, he drove by Parker's apartment to talk to him, but his grandson's car wasn't in its usual place along the street.

The following morning Parker lingered longer than normal at home to make sure Vicki arrived at the office before him. He didn't want to face Greg alone in the office. He paced back and forth in his apartment while drinking three cups of coffee. His phone rang. It was his grandfather.

"What happened between you and Layla on the boat?" his grandfather asked as soon as Parker answered.

"Did she call you?" Parker asked.

"No, I saw her at church. She wouldn't tell me anything except that it hadn't been a good day."

"That's true."

Parker told his grandfather about his decision and Layla's reaction. He considered leaving out her personal history but couldn't because the story wouldn't make sense.

"That's where it is," he said when he finished. "I'm sorry I hurt her feelings, but if she's not going to change her mind about my working for her father, it's better for us to part sooner rather than later. Not that I wanted it. I still hope she'll come around, but it's up to her to open the door since she

461

slammed it in my face."

He heard his grandfather grunt on the other end of the line.

"Opa?" he asked. "Did you hear me?"

"Oh yes. I heard every word, and you sound like the man who used to work on my fishing boat when he described a hydraulic leak. I thought you were going to let me meet Layla's father before you made a decision about working for him."

"Yes, but it didn't work out. I'm sure you'll meet him soon."

"Bye."

Before Parker could say anything else, the call ended. He looked up at the ceiling. Now he had to deal with his opa being upset with him too. He pushed that thought aside and called Vicki at the office.

"Hey," he said, trying to sound nonchalant, "what time will Greg be getting into the office? I know he has a luncheon appointment with Quentin Cutler because he mentioned it the other day."

"He's here now, and he's been bugging me about what time you're going to get here. Some fire has flared up regarding discovery in a case he should have been keeping tabs on, and you're the fireman who's going to put it out."

"Which case?"

As Parker listened, he remembered asking Greg about the requests for production of documents at least a month earlier and pointing out that it was going to be tricky deciding what was subject to discovery by the other side and what could be withheld because of trade secrets not relevant to the litigation.

"I'll put you through to him," Vicki said.

She transferred the call before Parker could stop her. In a moment of split-second panic, he abruptly ended the call, then turned off his phone. He left his apartment and quickly descended the steps to his car. During the short drive to the office, he ran a stoplight, then checked in the rearview mirror to make sure a cop didn't see him. Parker's brain was a jumbled mix of caffeine overload and multisource anxiety. He took the stairs two at a time to the office.

"What's wrong with your fancy phone?" Vicki asked. "We got cut off and neither Greg nor I could reach you."

"Is he available now?" Parker replied, hoping his eyes didn't look too wild.

Vicki glanced down. "Maybe."

Parker knocked on the closed door and entered before Greg responded. Greg was sitting behind his desk and gave Parker a startled look.

"I'm glad you're finally here," he began. "Vicki has the discovery file in the —"

"I'm not going to be able to help you," Parker said. "I've accepted a job offer from Tom Blocker beginning immediately. I cleaned out my desk Friday evening before I left."

Parker paused to take a breath. Greg was staring at him with a shocked expression on his face.

"Why would Tom Blocker offer you a job?" he asked.

The condescension in Greg's voice reinforced Parker's resolve that he'd made the right choice.

"He's opening a branch office in New Bern and bought the newly renovated house on Pollock Street," he replied in a calmer tone.

"I heard a rumor last week that the place was under contract," Greg said, shaking his head. "But I had no idea Blocker was the buyer. They say it's a real showcase."

Greg stopped talking but continued shaking his head. Parker waited and braced himself for the impending explosion he knew was around the corner.

"Well, I can't blame you," Greg said without looking at Parker. "I don't know what he's going to pay you in salary, but the upside to linking your car to his train is way beyond anything Dexter and I could offer you here. I knew it was a mistake to bring him in on the Ferguson case and let him treat you like his own associate. He's too smart not to see your potential and snatch you up for himself."

Parker felt like he was listening to someone talk about him as if he weren't there. He cringed at the mention of the Ferguson case but didn't have the courage to tell Greg that Blocker had the upper hand in that as well.

"The good side for me is that this opens the door for ongoing cooperation between the two firms on major litigation," Greg said, thinking out loud.

"Blocker has had a chance to see you in action," Parker said noncommittally.

"And you're not going to work out a notice?" Greg's eyes narrowed. "Don't you care that you're leaving me completely in the lurch without any backup? I'm staring down three or four gun barrels at the same time."

"I asked if I could give you another two weeks, but Blocker nixed it. I have responsibilities at the new office beginning today."

"Yeah," Greg replied with resignation in his voice. "I'd do the same thing if the shoe was on the other foot."

"Thanks for understanding."

"Oh, I understand. I have no choice if I don't want to burn any bridges for the future. Are you going to tell Dexter?"

"If you want me to."

"No, he never wanted to hire you in the first place. And I'll break the news to Vicki and Dolly."

Walking down the stairs to the main floor, Parker's primary emotion was relief. No one knew what he'd put up with at Branham and Camp, not his grandfather, not Layla, and it was nice to be free. Getting in his car, he didn't look back as he drove out of the lot on his way to Pollock Street.

CHAPTER 35

Parker pulled his car into a courtyard finished with paving stones behind the house on Pollock Street. Taking out his phone, he called Tom Blocker. The receptionist put Parker on hold while she transferred the call.

"Have you had a busy morning?" Blocker asked when he came on the line.

"Yes."

"Give me a condensed version. I only have a few minutes before I need to leave for a motion hearing."

Parker summarized his conversation with Greg as succinctly as he could.

"Did you advise Greg about the status of the Ferguson case?"

"No, and he's already angling for ongoing interaction between the two firms on future cases. As he would say, he's 'trying to make lemonade out of lemons.' "

Blocker laughed in a way that reminded

Parker of Layla. "And what do you think about that?" he asked.

"It would have to be on a case-by-case basis."

"Can you give me an example of the type of litigation in which you'd recommend associating Greg because of his particular skill and expertise?"

Parker thought for a moment. "No," he said.

"That's what I thought. And don't worry about the Ferguson matter. I'll take care of it in a way that won't be any harder on Greg than a trip to the dentist."

Parker wasn't sure how painless that would be, but he was relieved to have the burden off his shoulders.

"Oh, and there's a new laptop in your office. Sandy is going to send over a packet you need to complete so we can set you up on the firm payroll and for medical insurance, benefits, et cetera. You'll also receive a memo later this morning about a research project. And this one won't be a theoretical exercise."

"I never received the employment agreement."

"That will be included as well."

Parker had the building to himself. He wandered through the rooms and noticed many details he'd overlooked during the quick inspection the previous week. He ran his fingers along the chair rail molding in the conference room and imagined what it would be like taking a deposition beneath a shimmering brass chandelier while sitting at a long wooden table with a top that glistened. It was impossible to absorb.

Climbing the broad steps of the curving staircase to the second floor, he couldn't help but contrast it to the narrow steps at Branham and Camp. He was surprised to find that furniture had already been delivered to his office. In place was his new desk, a massive piece of wood the size of a small aircraft carrier that had an inlaid leather top enhanced by an embossed design around the edge. The leather chair reminded him of the one Judge Murray used in the main courtroom, only Parker's was a bit higher and had more shiny brass buttons. He opened the new laptop that he immediately recognized as one of the newest, fastest models on the market. While he waited for the computer to boot up, he decided this wasn't a desk he'd ever prop his feet up on — at least for the next five years.

Frank and Lenny had been out on the water since shortly after 7:00 a.m. They had four poles in the water, hoping to convince a big flounder to suck in the live shrimp bait. There was a twitch on the end of one of Lenny's rods. He was pouring a cup of coffee from a thermos and didn't notice.

"You may have one," Frank said, pointing to the rod.

Lenny picked up his rod, held it lightly in his hand for a few seconds, and then jerked it up sharply.

"Got him!" he cried out as he began reeling in the fish.

In a couple of minutes, Frank scooped up the fish in his big net and placed it on the deck.

"I think he's a keeper," Lenny said, peering into the net.

"We'd better measure to be sure," Frank replied. "If we don't, the game warden will."

Frank laid the fish on top of a cooler with a measuring scale printed on its surface. The minimum length for a keeper was fifteen inches.

"Sixteen and one-quarter inches," Frank announced.

"And it's a fat one," Lenny added. "If such a thing can ever be said about a flounder."

Lenny picked up the fish and put it in the live well they'd filled with water from the Sound earlier in the morning.

"Mattie will be happy," Frank said. "She's been over the moon ever since Chris and Sally announced their engagement."

"Engagement?" Frank replied. "That was quick."

"You shouldn't be surprised. You're the one who said they should get together in the first place."

"I didn't know —" Frank started to say but stopped before he told a lie.

He watched Lenny put a shrimp on his hook and let the weight on the line take it straight to the bottom.

"I really liked the young woman Parker was seeing," Frank said, shaking his head.

"The one you took to Oriental on the boat?"

"Yeah. She goes to the church I've been attending. But I'm afraid Parker has messed it up."

"How?"

"He accepted a job working for her father, and she doesn't think it's a good idea."

"Hmm," Lenny replied. "Sounds like maybe he should have listened to her."

"I agree."

They fished in silence for a few minutes.

"Tell me more about the girl," Lenny asked.

Frank tried to be objective, but it was

471

impossible not to praise Layla.

"Any young woman who's made that sort of impression on you is someone I'd like to meet. Parker would be an idiot not to make things right with her. Do you think they would be willing to come over to the house for a peacemaking dinner? Mattie would love to check her out."

"If Mattie fixes seafood stew, I'll make them come," Frank replied and then paused. "Only in my heart I know I can't."

One of Frank's lines twitched, and he picked up the rod. A few minutes later he added a seventeen-inch flounder to the live well.

"Sorry about my fish being so much bigger than yours," he said to Lenny.

"Liar," Lenny replied with a smile.

Frank replaced the bait on his hook and lowered it over the side. "Would you and Mattie be willing to pray for Parker and Layla?" he asked. "I'd really appreciate it."

"Yes," Lenny said, "it would be an honor."

Parker sent a long text message to Creston and a few of his other friends. As soon as Creston had a break between classes, he replied, demanding more information.

"Congrats. This is better than winning your fantasy football league," Creston wrote.

Close to noon, Parker went downstairs to check out the kitchen, which had been downsized from its original dimensions but was furnished with top-of-the-line equipment. Included were two different kinds of coffeemakers, a device Parker had never heard of that brewed hot tea, and a warmer to assist caterers who brought in hors d'oeuvres for firm-sponsored events. The door chime sounded. He rapidly walked through the reception area to the front door and opened it. He was shocked to see Layla standing on the front step.

"Come in," he managed.

"What's that beeping noise?" she asked.

"Oh, the alarm system," Parker replied quickly. "And I have thirty seconds to deactivate it."

Parker hurried over to a former coat closet beneath the stairway and opened the door.

"I wrote the code on a slip of paper," he said, rummaging in the left-front pocket of his pants. "I need to enter it in my phone."

He withdrew his hand without a slip of paper. He tried the other pockets of his pants and shirt and came up empty.

"I don't want you to feel like we're in a movie in which the hero has to disarm a bomb and the red numbers on the detonating device are ticking down to zero," he said.

473

"That's exactly how I feel," Layla responded.

"Here it is!" Parker exclaimed as he extracted a piece of paper from his wallet. He quickly hit several buttons on the control panel. The beeping stopped.

"We didn't blow up," Layla said.

"Yeah, and I'd hate for the police to be our first visitors. After you, of course," Parker added quickly.

"Actually, I'm here on business," Layla said.

"Business?"

"Yes, my father called this morning and hired me to take photos for an open house he's going to host in a few weeks. He asked me to check it out in advance."

"Would you like a tour?" Parker asked, still unsure how to act.

"That's why I'm here."

They went into the kitchen. Layla looked around.

"That's the same hot tea machine my father has at his beach house on St. John's."

"Your father has a house in the Virgin Islands?"

"Yes, he has to spend his money on something. I went once but won't be going again."

Parker didn't know enough about the

house to give a proper tour and simply followed Layla around as she checked it out. She stood in the doorway of his office for several seconds taking everything in but didn't comment. Parker was more tongue-tied than he'd been in years. They ended up at the front door.

"Would you like to grab lunch?" he asked.

"Nothing's changed between me and you," she replied. "And agreeing to do the photo shoot for my father is all about dying to self."

Parker had no idea what she meant. "Thanks for coming by," he offered lamely.

He reluctantly watched Layla walk down the steps. Passing by on the street was a large new white BMW. Parker saw an older man wearing sunglasses and sitting in the passenger seat glance at him and then quickly look away.

The man looked a lot like Conrad Mueller.

CHAPTER 36

It was early afternoon when Frank and Lenny returned to the dock. They'd each caught their six-fish limit of flounder.

"I'm going to invite my favorite relatives over this evening for a fish fry," Lenny said as he opened the live well and prepared to scoop out some fish with a small net. "What are you going to do with this haul? It would be a shame to freeze them."

Frank was standing over Lenny, who had knelt down beside the live well.

"First, I'm going to make sure you only take the fish you caught."

Lenny glanced up. The holding tank for the fish was crowded with the dark gray fish.

"How do you plan on doing that?" he asked. "Did you tag and name them when we caught them?"

"Trust me," Frank replied.

Lenny shook his head. There were two five-gallon buckets beside the live well. He captured a fish in the net and held it up.

"Yours or mine?" he asked.

"Yours," Frank answered.

Lenny dropped the fish in his bucket. They repeated the process until the fish were evenly divided.

"Satisfied?" Frank asked.

"Sure, although the biggest one was yours."

"That's what we thought at the time, but you came over the top near the end."

They finished straightening up the boat and got in Lenny's truck.

"I like your idea," Frank said. "I think I'll see if Parker wants to invite a bunch of his friends over this evening for a fish fry. Most of them would drop everything to dig into fresh flounder. And it will give me a chance to pull Parker aside and talk some sense into him about Layla."

As soon as he got home, Frank put the flounder on ice in a cooler beside the cleaning sink and then washed his hands and called Parker.

Parker was sitting in the kitchen at the new law firm when he received the call. Tom Blocker had stopped on his way to Wilmington following a deposition in Raleigh. Apparently unannounced visits were part of the trial lawyer's standard practice.

"It's my grandfather," Parker said, covering the phone's microphone with his hand. "I'll call him back later."

"No, take it," Blocker replied, leaning back in the chair. "He's important. I can wait."

Parker didn't want to have a private conversation with his grandfather in front of his new boss, but that didn't appear to be an option.

"Hey, Opa," he said, answering. "I'm sitting here with Mr. Blocker —"

"Tom," Blocker interrupted him. "And I like that you call him Opa."

"I mean Tom," Parker continued. "We're sitting in the kitchen of the new firm in the restored house on Pollock Street."

As he listened to the purpose of his grandfather's call, Parker tried to figure out how to respond.

"Can I get back to you on that?" he asked. "I'm not sure everybody can get together on such short notice."

"Is there a chance for me to meet him?" Blocker interjected. "I can delay my return to Wilmington until later in the evening. He might be able to help me with something too."

Parker had the phone to his ear but didn't

hear his grandfather's response to his previous statement. He told his grandfather about Blocker's suggestion.

"And I know you've wanted to meet him as well," Parker continued. "Maybe we should limit it to the three of us."

When Parker heard his grandfather's next suggestion, he wished he'd kept his mouth shut and had tried to send multiple text messages to his buddies. He put his thumb over the speaker again so his grandfather couldn't hear him.

"He wants to invite Layla."

"How does he know Layla?" Blocker asked in surprise.

"They met independently of me at church."

"Oh yeah, I knew she was dabbling with that," Blocker said. He hesitated for a moment before adding, "If he wants to include her, I won't object."

"I'd rather keep it to the three of us," Parker replied to his grandfather. "We'll be there about six thirty."

Frank wasn't surprised that Parker didn't want to include Layla. Whatever the wounds between them, they were still fresh.

He carefully cleaned and filleted three flounder. Two of the large fish could provide more than enough fillets for a generous fish fry, but he decided to increase the menu by adding four small pieces from a third fish topped with a crabmeat stuffing. His hands were deep into the stuffing as he mixed the meat and seasoning together when there was a knock on his door. He wasn't expecting anyone to arrive for another hour. Quickly rinsing his hands, he went into the living room to find out who it was. It was Layla.

"What are you doing here?" he asked.

"I felt bad about running off on Sunday and wanted to talk to you," she replied. "But it looks like a bad time if you're fixing supper?"

"Not really. Your father and Parker are coming over in forty-five minutes to eat with me. I'd love for you to stay —"

"No, I can't." Layla turned to leave.

"And I understand why. Parker told me."

Layla hesitated. "Did he seem sorry about it?"

"Not as much as he should have, but I'm hoping he'll come around."

"You don't think he should go to work for my father either?" Layla asked in a hopeful voice.

"I honestly can't say," Frank replied. "All along I believed I needed to meet your father before I could offer an opinion. Now it may be too late for my opinion to matter."

"They're both hardheaded," Layla answered. "Maybe they deserve each other."

"There are plenty of hardheaded people in both our families."

Layla gave him a slight smile. "Which is good if you're right about what you believe," she said.

"I agree." Frank motioned to the kitchen. "Will you stay a few minutes and help me fix the asparagus?"

Layla checked her watch. "Okay, but I want to be out of here before they arrive. I don't want to be in the same room with both of them."

Frank led the way to the kitchen. "I thought we would have grilled asparagus tips with the fish," he said. "I know it's not a southern staple, but I bought them the other day not knowing I could use them tonight. Here's the recipe for the sauce. Take a look at it and tell me what you think."

Frank resumed his work on the crabmeat stuffing while Layla read about the sauce.

"My father will like this," she said when she finished. "Asparagus is his favorite vegetable. Make sure he knows the sauce has German roots. That will ramp it up even more in his eyes."

Frank told Layla where to find the ingredients for the sauce. It felt natural to have her in the kitchen helping him.

"What about hush puppies?" he asked her. "Does your father like them?"

"Not really."

"Parker does. When he was a little boy, he could make an entire meal out of a bowl of hush puppies."

Frank put the crab-topped flounder on a large plate in the refrigerator to stay cool. "I'll broil the flounder after they get here," he said.

"Opa," Layla said, putting down the wooden spoon she was using to stir the sauce.

Before Layla completed her thought, there was another loud knock at the door.

"Oh no," she said. "What am I going to do?"

"Stay here," Frank replied.

He left the kitchen, went to the front door, and opened it.

"Who's your company?" Lenny asked.

Frank glanced over his shoulder. Layla had obeyed his request and stayed in the kitchen.

"Layla Donovan," Frank replied.

"The girl you picked out for Parker?"

"Keep it down," Frank whispered, raising his index finger to his lips. "What do you want?"

"Oh, I was returning the set of putty knives you loaned me for the bathroom remodeling job."

Lenny handed Frank a small box with the knives neatly organized.

"And I cleaned 'em up," Lenny continued, trying to look around Frank's shoulder. "I know how you like everything better than new."

"You're welcome."

"Can I come in and meet her?" Lenny asked. "If I don't, Mattie will give me a hard time."

"Suit yourself," Frank sighed and stepped to the side.

He led Lenny into the kitchen and introduced him to Layla. Lenny's eyes opened wider at the sight of the blond photographer.

"Frank is crazy about you," Lenny said.

"Lenny!" Frank exclaimed.

Layla laughed and spoke to Frank in German.

"Yeah, that's part of it," Lenny said. "You remind him of what was good about where he came from."

Layla turned to Frank. "Is that true?" she asked.

"Yes, but I don't know how Lenny knew since I've never mentioned it to him."

"Frank and I have been buddies for so long that we think the same thing without even telling each other."

Frank shook his head. "We're not that close."

"Yes, we are," Lenny said to Layla. "Nice meeting you. I told Frank the other day that you have an open invitation to a fish stew dinner with my wife and me."

"Thanks," Layla replied.

Lenny turned to leave but stopped. "Oh, what did you say in German a minute ago to Frank?"

Layla looked at Frank, who spoke. "She told me that you looked like a very nice man and wanted to know if you liked to fish as much as I did."

"You didn't answer her question, so I will," Lenny said as he faced Layla. "Thank you and yes."

After Lenny left, Frank caught Layla smiling several times out of the corner of his eye. She turned down the heat beneath the sauce for the asparagus.

"I'd better go," she said. "The next knock on the door will surely be my father and

Parker."

"I can't talk you into staying?"

"No, but I'd love to sample thc fish stew Lenny's wife makes sometime soon."

"I can make that happen."

Frank escorted Layla to the door. She stepped outside and then turned around and gave him a quick hug.

Parker and Tom Blocker rode together in the trial lawyer's Mercedes. When they were still a few miles from Frank's house, Parker noticed a familiar car passing by, going in the direction of town.

"Was that Layla's car?" he asked Blocker.

"Uh, I don't know. I've tried to get her to trade that piece of junk for something better."

Parker realized his own car probably fell in the same category as Layla's vehicle. He was about to tell Blocker to turn onto the sandy unpaved road that led to his grandfather's bungalow, but the lawyer had already flipped on his blinker.

"How did you know you needed to turn here?"

"Research."

Parker glanced sideways, but Blocker's face revealed nothing else. He pulled into the driveway for Frank's house without any

prompting from Parker. They parked beneath the large live oak tree and got out.

Instead of barging in, Parker knocked on
the door. His grandfather appeared wearing
a nice but rumpled shirt and khaki pants.
The older man was way overdressed for a
fish fry.

"Opa, this is Tom Blocker. He's Layla's
father and my new boss."

The two men shook hands.

"Come in," Frank said.

They entered the living room.

"Why don't you stay in here while I finish
up in the kitchen?" Frank suggested.

Parker wanted to join his grandfather in
the kitchen and help, but he and Blocker
sat down in the living room. A few moments
later Frank stuck his head through the
opening into the kitchen.

"We're having asparagus and hush puppies, so both of you should be happy," he
said.

"You like asparagus?" Parker asked
Blocker.

"My favorite vegetable."

"How would my grandfather know that?"

"You tell me."

They sat in silence for a couple of minutes.
Parker shifted uncomfortably in his chair.
Socializing with Tom Blocker was not going

to be relaxing.

"I left something in the car," Blocker said, getting up from the sofa. "I was going to bring it in later, but I'll get it now."

After the door closed, Parker jumped up and went to the kitchen. His grandfather was taking a thin fillet of flounder from the fryer and putting it on a paper towel to drain.

"He went to get something from the car," Parker said rapidly. "When can we eat? I'm dying out here sitting in silence."

"He's toying with you, waiting for you to say something stupid," Frank replied.

"Why would he do that?"

"Because he always tries to establish himself as the most powerful person in any relationship."

"You could tell that by shaking his hand?"

Frank took another piece of fish from the fryer. "And a lot more."

They heard the door open as Blocker reentered the house. Parker left the kitchen. Blocker placed a folder on the sofa where he'd been sitting.

"What's in there?" Parker asked.

"Something I want to ask your grand-father about after supper," Blocker replied. "You might be able to help too."

Parker could see that there was writing in

German on the outside of the folder.

"My German is terrible," he said.

"I don't need a translator," Blocker replied. "I'm looking for a more specialized kind of assistance."

CHAPTER 37

"Flounder two ways," Frank announced as he carried a platter of fish into the room and set it in the middle of the dining room table. "Broiled and stuffed with crabmeat and fried in peanut oil."

The sweet crunchiness of the hush puppies diverted Parker's attention from his curiosity about the contents of the folder. He glanced at it several times before he stopped trying to guess what it contained.

"Opa, these hush puppies are the best ever," Parker said, holding up a tiny golden ball before popping it in his mouth.

"And the asparagus is superb," Blocker added. "Tell me about the sauce."

Frank explained the German origin of the recipe. Blocker answered in German, and the resulting conversation left Parker alone with his thoughts and the flounder.

People who universally condemned fried foods had never eaten his grandfather's fresh-caught flounder fillets. The delicate flavor of the white fish was enhanced, not destroyed, by its brief bath in hot oil, and the breading added just enough extra flavor to make every bite an invitation to another.

"And this broiled fish is better than any I've had in the best restaurants in Charleston," Blocker said. "The crab mixture on top is a delight."

"Thank you," Frank said with a smile. "And I'm glad that Parker has gone to work with you."

"You are?" Parker asked, returning a hush puppy to his plate.

"Yes."

Parker was dumbfounded, especially after hearing his grandfather's summary of Blocker's personality a few minutes earlier in the kitchen. In the back of his mind, he'd been uneasy about accepting the job without his grandfather's approval. The older man's simple endorsement was more important to him than thousands of dollars in additional salary. Parker picked up another hush puppy and enjoyed it more than any of the others he'd eaten.

"The patriarch's blessing is powerful, isn't it?" Blocker said to Frank. "Tell me about your family in Germany. Parker just provided a tidbit."

Frank shared a brief summary. He didn't even mention the war years. The conversation then moved to life in Germany during the 1930s while they finished the meal.

"And I immigrated to America in late 1946," Frank said.

"Why New Bern?" Blocker asked.

"I knew I was going to be a commercial fisherman, and coming to New Bern from Bern seemed the logical thing to do. Also, it's the place where I could meet Parker's grandmother."

"Can you tell me more about the war years?" Blocker asked.

"No, that's a time I don't like to remember."

"Of course."

"What do you already know about him?" Parker asked.

Blocker gave Parker an irritated look and then turned to Frank. "Parker knows I extensively research parties to lawsuits, expert witnesses, the lawyers on the other side of a case, and anyone else of interest to me."

"Why would you be interested in me?" Frank asked.

The way his grandfather asked the simple question made the hair on the back of Parker's neck stand up. He watched Blocker blink his eyes a couple of times.

"Let's circle back to that topic after supper," Blocker said.

They spent the remainder of the meal in small talk that failed to hold Parker's attention. Listening with half an ear, he learned that Blocker had been to Germany over ten times during the past twenty years. Many of those trips had to do with genealogical research.

"I saw the house where my great-great-grandfather lived in a village not far from Stuttgart," Blocker said. "His son went into manufacturing and owned a business in the city."

"Stuttgart?" Frank replied. "I had relatives on my father's side of the family who lived there."

"Have you tried to maintain contact with them?" Blocker asked.

Frank looked intently at Blocker for a moment. "I'm more interested in the current generation than the past ones," he said.

After they finished eating, Parker stood next to his grandfather at the kitchen sink as they rinsed dishes to put in the washer. Blocker was in the living room. Parker glanced over his shoulder to make sure they were alone.

"What's going on?" Parker asked. "Are

you going to keep answering his questions about your past?"

"Do I have to?"

"Of course not." Parker placed a plate in the dishwasher. "And what changed your mind about me working for him? I thought you disagreed with my decision."

"I said I was glad you're working for him," his grandfather replied. "Which doesn't mean it's a good idea except that you're supposed to learn something from it. The lesson, though very painful and hard, will be valuable to you in the future. I just hope you're a faster learner than I was."

Parker put the last fork in the part of the dishwasher basket reserved for eating utensils with tines.

"What exactly do you mean? I want to know."

His grandfather took his hands from the water in the sink, dried them on a towel, and turned sideways so he faced Parker.

"One of the biggest mistakes of my life was misusing the gift God gave me," Frank said. "And I can't blame General Berg, or the war, or anyone else for what I did. It was my choice, and it's taken me a lifetime to realize my sins and face the truth. I pray it won't be the same for you."

Parker felt like the breath had been

knocked out of his body. "I'm just trying to help us better represent our clients," he said.

"And I don't have the right to lecture you. But I hope you'll figure out the right path before you go too far down a wrong one."

Parker suddenly saw his grandfather as a young man wearing a spotless uniform and sitting erect at a shiny conference table along with a group of high-ranking German officers. He blinked his eyes and immediately returned to the kitchen in the fishing bungalow where his opa, a sorrowful expression on his face, stood slightly stooped before him, wearing a wrinkled blue shirt and tan pants.

"Would you tell Layla you believe I made the right choice?" he asked. "I really want to patch things up with her."

"Layla is the only one who can convince Layla of anything."

Parker knew his grandfather was right. They joined Blocker in the living room. Parker sat beside the trial lawyer on the couch, and Frank positioned himself in his recliner. Blocker held up the folder.

"I'll get right to the point. Several months ago I was contacted by a German lawyer who found me on a genealogy website and asked if I'd be interested in helping him find someone for a client. I agreed to help, and he sent me a generous retainer. My search led me to Parker."

"Me?" Parker asked in surprise.

"Through a paper you wrote in law school about the legality of German reparations after World War I."

"For my international law class," Parker said. "The professor gave me an A, but the paper was never published in a legal journal."

"Maybe not, but he liked it enough to mention a few statistics you reported in an article he wrote about postwar legal remedies that appeared in the *Virginia Law Review.* You received credit for the information in a footnote, and he entered your paper into the database for your law school."

Blocker reached in the folder and took out several sheets of paper stapled together. He handed them to Parker. "Here," he said.

Dumbfounded, Parker read the familiar words of the first paragraph he'd slaved over during his third year in law school and never thought he'd see again.

"But why did this pop up in your search for the rich German client?"

"Read the bio at the end."

Parker turned to the last page, where he read, "Parker House is a second-generation American whose grandfather, Franz Haus, immigrated to North Carolina from Switzerland after World War II."

"Yeah, I remember telling the professor about my background when we first discussed the topic, but I didn't put that information in the paper."

"Then he did it on his own. When I searched for anyone in the US named Franz Haus, the bio for your paper was one of the hits. From there it was easy to track you to New Bern. It was a bonus when you were in the courtroom on the day I came to see if Layla would be picked for a jury. After that, I checked the active files in our office and saw we'd been retained in the Mixon arbitration, and your firm was on the other side. It was a small case, and one of my associates was going to handle it, but I saw it as a chance to get to determine whether your grandfather was the man my client was looking for. The unexpected bonus for me was discovering how talented you are as an attorney. Finding you turned out to be much more important to me than locating Franz Haus."

Parker looked at his grandfather, who was sitting motionless in his chair with his lips tightly pressed together. Parker pointed to him. "Is he the Franz Haus you're looking for?"

"If your grandfather has the ability to witness the future before it occurs, then the answer is yes. The man I'm looking for served on the staff of a general named Berg in southern France. Hauptmann Haus had an uncanny insight into strategy and tactics that earned him the nickname the Aryan Eagle. Apparently he was never wrong."

Northern France, 1941
Franz and his division were serving as an occupying force in the hedgerow region of Normandy. The common rumor among the lower-ranking staff and troops was that they were going to be the tip of the spear for the impending German invasion across the English Channel. The broken remnants of the British Expeditionary Force had struggled home in a makeshift manner from the beaches of Dunkirk, and despite Winston Churchill's public bluster, the English were soft and could be defeated easily. The Channel coasts were not heavily fortified, and some officers, including Franz, started to learn English in preparation for their interaction with a subjugated British population.

One evening after dinner, General Berg summoned Franz to his quarters and told him he needed to know the location of any resistance units made up of French soldiers or civilian partisans that were operating in the area. Twice before, Franz had provided accurate information in similar circumstances. The general ordered him to deliver the intelligence first thing the following morning.

What transpired for Franz was a night of torment. At first he found a quiet spot and waited for insight to bubble to the surface. When that didn't work, he tried to fall asleep and dream. Anxiety trumped sleep, and he tossed and turned for several hours. Finally, he got up and spent the time left until dawn poring over military maps of the area, pausing at the names of tiny towns, and waiting a moment to see if he had an impression. Nothing came. After drinking two cups of black coffee, he shaved and pressed his dress uniform. Thirty minutes before his meeting with the general, Franz decided it wouldn't hurt to take one last look at the maps to see if anything jump-started a helpful impression. When he did, he saw the name of a provincial town, Lisieux, and quickly committed it to memory. He then went to see General Berg.

"Well, Hauptmann," the general said when Franz stood at attention before him. "What do you have for me?"

"I recommend a patrol be sent two kilometers west of Lisieux," Franz said, trying to sound more confident than he felt.

"Be more specific," the general demanded. "I'm not sending troops on a sightseeing visit to old Catholic churches."

"Not in the town, Herr General, two kilometers to the west," Franz said, hoping the general wouldn't be offended because he merely repeated himself. "That's the best I can offer."

"Dismissed," the general said grumpily with a wave of his hand.

Franz left not knowing if the general would do anything with the information. The following day he received another summons to headquarters. He stood before General Berg, who couldn't speak at first because he was experiencing a coughing fit. Two of the general's aides stood beside him. Finally, red-faced, General Berg looked at Franz.

"The patrol sent to Lisieux was ambushed two kilometers east of the town and suffered eight dead and twelve wounded. They killed three partisans who were French soldiers still in uniform. That's not how to win a war."

Franz was speechless. He braced himself for the next words from the general's lips —

an order for his immediate court-martial.

"Don't ever do that again," the general said, his hand covering his mouth. "Do you understand me, Hauptmann?"

"Yes, sir."

Trembling, Franz left.

"Never wrong?" Frank asked softly. "What does 'wrong' mean? Was it wrong when I provided information that resulted in the deaths of thousands of Allied soldiers? Was it wrong that I let my ability be used for greedy ends by evil men? Was it wrong when I pretended to know something I didn't and as a result soldiers in my own unit were killed?"

Parker stared at his grandfather as if seeing him for the first time. Blocker, too, was speechless.

"So it's true," Blocker said, shaking his head. "I thought it might be a wartime myth blown out of proportion by the passage of time and faulty memory."

"It's not a myth or a fairy tale," Frank replied. "But whatever I've done in the past, I want to be left alone now."

Blocker had the folder open on his lap. He glanced over at Parker, who was holding his breath. The trial lawyer looked down for several moments, carefully turned over several sheets of paper, and then closed the folder.

"Very well," Blocker said. "I think it's a reasonable request. I don't know why the German lawyer hired me to find you, but I'm going to refund the retainer and tell him I can't help."

"Thank you," Frank replied.

"No, thank you for the delicious dinner," Blocker replied. "And for the influence you've had on Parker. I believe he's going to be a special lawyer, and I want to be a part of making that happen."

CHAPTER 38

Early the following morning Frank sat on the back porch cradling a cup of coffee in his hand. After Parker and Blocker had left, he'd spent a restless night trapped in random wartime images that flashed through his mind without forming a cohesive narrative. He took a sip of coffee, but the rich beverage didn't bring the usual satisfaction. Placing the cup on the floor, he went into the living room and got his Bible.

He'd finished reading the Gospel of John and was now deep into the Acts of the Apostles, which he quickly realized wasn't limited to the lives of a few men but represented the broader experiences of an explosively vibrant new church. His bookmark was at Acts chapter 21, where he'd been following Paul's trip from Greece and Asia Minor to Jerusalem:

Leaving the next day, we reached Caesarea and stayed at the house of Philip the evangelist, one of the Seven. He had four unmarried daughters who prophesied. After we had been there a number of days, a prophet named Agabus came down from Judea. Coming over to us, he took Paul's belt, tied his own hands and feet with it and said, "The Holy Spirit says, 'In this way the Jewish leaders in Jerusalem will bind the owner of this belt and will hand him over to the Gentiles.' "

When we heard this, we and the people there pleaded with Paul not to go up to Jerusalem. Then Paul answered, "Why are you weeping and breaking my heart? I am ready not only to be bound, but also to die in Jerusalem for the name of the Lord Jesus." When he would not be dissuaded, we gave up and said, "The Lord's will be done."

Frank stopped and flipped over a few pages where, sure enough, Paul ended up arrested by Roman soldiers in Jerusalem. Frank looked up from the pages of the book.

What happened in Caesarea was another Bible story that moved seamlessly across two thousand years and into Frank's present. Hearing, knowing, warning, and witnessing were parts of the lives of the early disciples with which he could totally identify. There were the four daughters of Philip, probably no older than Layla, who prophesied. And there was Agabus, who issued a warning to Paul that came true. But the twist that caught Frank's attention was the apostle's refusal to change his plans because of the threat of imprisonment. There was something greater at work in Paul's life than self-preservation and personal safety. He had an awareness of God's will for his future that trumped every competing influence or source of pressure. Frank had never considered that there was something beyond knowledge and wise reaction to it. He stared through the screen wall of the porch and into his backyard.

And wondered what that greater will might be for him.

When Parker arrived at the house on Pollock Street, a familiar car was parked along the curb. Inside sat Vicki Satterfield. Taking a deep breath, he approached the vehicle from behind and gently knocked on the driver's side window. Vicki jumped and quickly lowered the window.

"Why did you sneak up on me like that?" she demanded.

"Because I wanted to scare you. Would

you like a tour of the office?"

"Yes."

As he showed Vicki around, Parker tried to decide if he wanted to broach the subject of a job to the receptionist/bookkeeper/pseudo lawyer. He didn't have to debate very long.

"Is there a place for me here?" she asked when he showed her where the receptionist would sit.

"I can mention it to Mr. Blocker," he said noncommittally. "But the decision will be his."

"And he'll rely on your recommendation," Vicki replied. "Mr. Blocker is going to have you flitting around all over the place, and you'll need someone here who can watch your back. Remember how I helped you when Donna McAlpine filed the grievance against you with the state bar."

"And I appreciated it."

"There's no use trying to cushion the blows to Greg. He's already past the boiling point, and my leaving won't make the pot spill over any faster."

"He's mad at me?"

"Furious, of course, but so far his desire for self-preservation and the chance to eat the crumbs that fall from Tom Blocker's table have kept him chained to his desk.

Otherwise he'd be over here yelling his head off."

"What about Dolly?"

"She's on her way out once she marries Barry, who's interviewing this week for a new job in Charleston. If he gets it, they're going to set a date and load up a moving van. With her skills she won't have a problem finding a position with another law firm."

In spite of Greg's conduct over the past few months, Parker couldn't help feeling sorry for the challenges facing Branham and Camp.

"And you feel sorry for Greg and Dexter, don't you?" Vicki asked. "I can see it in your eyes."

"A little bit."

"Which is why I'd really like to work for you."

Parker had never heard Vicki indicate she worked for him; it had always been working with him.

"Okay," he said. "I'll give it serious consideration."

"I'll be waiting to hear from you."

Vicki left, and Parker went upstairs to his office. The weight of responsibility for the expectations of other people was a new and unpleasant experience.

By midafternoon a local office supply company had stocked the shelves downstairs, the communications workers had finished and cleared out of the house, and the company delivering the furniture was in high gear. It was a six-person setup crew, and Parker was impressed with how quickly they filled each room. After they finished, Parker walked through the house. The exquisite decor made him feel like a visitor in an antique museum.

Frank spent the remainder of the day at the dock working on his boat. He'd learned how to do basic mechanical maintenance on the *Aare* as a cost-cutting measure when he was making a living on the water, but now he didn't attempt any boat or engine repair that required heavy lifting. After making sure all the electrical switches on the boat were functioning properly, he checked for loose or corroded connections in the system. An electrical failure on the water could bring the most modern boat to a standstill and result in an oppressive tow bill. Frank methodically moved his volt meter from spot to spot and checked the lines. He located a couple of wires that were beginning to show signs of corrosion and replaced them.

Close to noon he finished and ate lunch, a slightly green banana and a North Carolina-grown apple. Frank wasn't in a hurry and took his time nibbling the apple until only the seeds and stem were left. Gathering up his toolbox, he made his way slowly along the dock to the shore. He had to decide if he wanted to go home and take a nap or spend a couple of hours organizing the fishing tackle in the shed behind his house.

The following morning Parker continued the process of settling in as the only person in the new office. He was surprised how much he missed being around other people. Of course, the absence of Greg lurking down the hallway ready to dump a last-minute project on him made solitude more attractive. Around 10:30 a.m., he called the main office in Wilmington. He wanted to talk to Tom Blocker about *Ferguson v. Callaway Club* and Vicki Satterfield.

"This is Parker —"

"I recognize your voice," the perky receptionist replied. "When are you going to visit us?"

"Soon, I hope. Is Mr. Blocker available?"

"He's on the phone if you want to hold."

"Yes."

"Good morning, Parker," Blocker said when he picked up. "I don't have time to talk now, but I'm driving up to see you this afternoon. Any chance we could swing by and see your grandfather again?"

"Uh, maybe. I can check."

"Do it. See you at four o'clock."

After the call ended, the doorbell chimed, and Parker went downstairs expecting a delivery person. Instead, he saw Creston peering through one of the glass sidelights.

"What are you doing here?" Parker asked when he opened the door. "You're supposed to be teaching eager students about pi."

"Pi is amazing, but I left early because I have a training session at the central office and thought I would come check out your new digs."

"Come in."

Parker showed Creston around. His friend was duly impressed.

"Man, this is fancy," he said when they stood in Parker's office. "I feel like I should start calling you Mr. House."

"I agree, but you can wait until tomorrow."

"And does this mean you and your new boss's daughter are a legal item? Did he set you up because he wants his future son-in-law to provide for his baby girl in the man-

509

ner she's grown accustomed to?"

"That's about as far from the truth as possible," Parker said, shaking his head. "Layla told me if I took the job I could forget about dating her. And so far, she hasn't changed her mind."

"What?" Creston asked.

"There are some complicated family dynamics in play. How are you and Melissa doing?"

"Melinda and I are cruising along at a comfortable pace. I think she may be the one I want to run with for the long haul. If I decide to take it to the next level with her, I want you to be my best man. That's the main reason I stopped by."

Parker jerked his head back in surprise. "That's fast," he managed.

"I've always been faster than you," Creston replied with a grin. "But the old saying that you'll know when it's the right one is true. Will you do it?"

"Of course. Have you shopped for a ring?"

"Yes, and I need a loan from my future best man."

Parker pointed to his shiny new desk. "If we can get this down the stairs and to the pawnshop —"

"No need, but I wanted to make sure of your level of commitment. Do you think

Layla would give us a break on the wedding photos?"

"Why don't I cover the cost of that for you?" Parker replied. "I'd be glad to do it."

It was Creston's turn to give Parker a shocked look. "You'd pay for it? Do you realize how much that can cost?"

"It doesn't matter," Parker replied. "And if you want Layla to be lurking in the bushes to snap a few pictures when you pop the question to Melinda, I'll toss that in too. Engagement photos are included in any wedding package I purchase."

After Creston left, Parker went back upstairs with a smile on his face. It was the first time one of his hunches had cost him money, and for some reason it felt great.

Frank shaved and took a shower when he returned from working on his boat. After two days' labor it was in faultless condition and ready for anything. He was eating a sandwich in the kitchen and thinking about taking it over to Ocracoke Island when the phone rang. It was Lenny.

"Do you want to motor down the river late this afternoon and see if we can find some spots that are hungry?" Lenny asked.

"No, but I've been working on the boat so we won't get stranded next time we go out."

Frank paused. "Swing by tomorrow around nine in the morning, and we'll go wherever you want."

"Deal."

After the call ended, Frank changed into one of his nicer shirts and a pair of pants and sat on the back porch. The phone rang again. This time it was Parker.

"Opa, Tom Blocker is coming through town again and wanted to see you. Could we swing by your house? Not to eat, but to talk."

"What does he want to talk about?"

"I don't know," Parker replied. "It was a quick call."

"No," Frank said as he glanced down at his clothes.

"That's okay," Parker quickly responded. "I need to establish boundaries for people who come into town to bug you, even if it's my —"

"Don't drive here," Frank cut in. "I'll come to your office. I was sitting on the back porch all dressed up with no place to go when you called. What time should I be there?"

"Around four. Are you sure?"

"Yes. Have you ever read about Agabus?" Frank asked.

"Who?"

"Agabus. He's in the Bible toward the end of Acts. You should check him out."

"Uh, okay. I'll do that. Maybe we can eat supper together after we meet with Mr. Blocker. I'll pay."

"I'd expect you to."

Frank chuckled as he hung up the phone. However, when he returned to the porch his mood changed as quickly as a squall racing across the surface of the sea. Puzzled, he returned to his chair. As if to mirror his feelings, the sun, which had been shining brightly, disappeared behind a cloud.

Parker and Tom Blocker were sitting in Parker's new office.

"How do you like your digs?" Blocker asked.

"It's hard to believe this is where I get to practice law," Parker replied truthfully.

"Get used to it."

Parker checked his watch. "My grandfather should arrive in a few minutes. Before he does, I wanted to talk to you about the Ferguson case."

"Go ahead."

"It's about Greg's involvement. I'm not comfortable jerking the rug out from under him."

"Oh, I'll honor my commitment to him

on the attorney fee," Blocker replied. "But he's not going to be close enough to the case to mess it up. Admit it. Greg can be toxic, which is not a good quality for successful litigation."

"But —"

"I appreciate your loyalty," Blocker said. "But that loyalty needs to shift from Branham and Camp to this firm. Will you be able to do that?"

"Absolutely."

"Good. I haven't talked to Greg yet, but I will. Maybe you should be there so you can watch and learn."

Parker wasn't sure it was a class he wanted to attend.

"Uh, the other thing is Vicki Satterfield," he said.

Parker told Blocker about his encounter with Vicki, and the receptionist/bookkeeper's desire to switch firms.

"That's your call," Blocker said. "I gave that responsibility to you the other day."

Parker paused for a moment. "I don't think we should hire her," he said.

"I agree," Blocker responded immediately, "but you needed to figure that out on your own."

"I'm not sure what I figured out."

"That experience isn't the only factor to

consider in hiring an employee. The ability to learn a job and perform it in the way you want it done is even more important. This is your chance to mold an assistant to do that."

"I barely know what to do half the time myself."

"That will change quickly working for me. The crushing weight of responsibility is about to be lowered onto your young shoulders," Blocker said with a smile. "And whether you survive will be determined by how quickly you grow."

The doorbell chimed.

"That's probably my grandfather," Parker said. "I'll let him in."

Frank stood outside the front door of the house on Pollock Street. The sense of foreboding he'd felt on his back porch diminished the farther he drove away from his house. A slightly frazzled-looking Parker opened the door.

"Come in," he said. "We're going to meet in the conference room."

"Are you okay?" Frank asked.

"Yeah, great," Parker replied and then paused. "No, actually I've bounced around so much the past few days that I'm out of sync."

They entered the conference room where Blocker waited for them. The shiny wooden conference table was surrounded by twelve ornate but sturdy chairs covered with brocade fabric. A long mirror hung on one wall, and graceful vases rested on delicate wooden side tables at either end of the room. The beautifully decorated space reminded Frank of a European drawing room where money and power met.

"What do you think?" Blocker asked him. "This is where Parker is going to be taking depositions within the next few weeks."

Frank nodded as he tried to recall when he'd been in a similar place. "Impressive."

"Have a seat," Blocker said.

Blocker sat at the head of the table with Parker to his right and Frank to his left. He turned toward Frank.

"As promised, I returned via overnight courier the retainer paid by the German lawyer who hired me to track you down. I then followed up with a phone call telling him I wasn't available to offer any further assistance. He didn't seem upset, and as we talked, he shared more information about his interest in the Aryan Eagle. Would you like to hear about it?"

"Not really," Frank replied.

"But you probably should," Parker advised. "I mean, there's never any harm in having more information."

"You're wrong," Frank said. "If I never hear the words *Aryan Eagle* again, I will be a happy man."

"I respect that," Blocker said. "But it was odd that the German lawyer also asked me about Parker."

"Me?" Parker asked in surprise.

"Yes. Your name was added to our firm letterhead as soon as you accepted the job, and it appeared on the cover letter sent with the retainer. The lawyer asked me if your last name was an anglicized version of Haus."

"What did you tell him?" Parker asked.

"That I'd talk to you about it, but I didn't make a commitment to get back to him."

Parker was silent for a moment. "If you made the connection between me and Opa based on the paper I wrote in law school, someone else could too."

"Possibly, but the lawyer didn't indicate he'd done that, and his questions about your grandfather didn't involve you," Blocker said.

"Go ahead," Parker said. "You may as well tell us what he asked."

"All right," Frank sighed.

Blocker cleared his throat. "He's accumulating information about a secret World War II military operation in northern Italy at a place called Siena. The lawyer's client is interested in finding out what happened there and believes you were involved."

The sense of foreboding Frank had felt on his porch descended on the fancy conference room. Both Blocker and Parker stared at him.

"There's no use talking about Siena," Frank answered with a heavy heart. "I saw many horrible things during the war. That was one of the worst."

"Enough then," Blocker replied. "I wanted to make sure you didn't want to connect with the lawyer about it."

"Absolutely not."

"Should I know about Siena?" Parker asked his grandfather.

"No!" Frank responded.

CHAPTER 39

Frank and Parker ate a quiet meal at a local Italian restaurant.

"I wish we hadn't come here," Frank said when they finished.

"Why? You wolfed down all your spaghetti."

"Because of the Italian town your boss mentioned when we were at the office."

"I didn't think about that when I suggested coming here." Parker hit his forehead with his hand. "It must have been a subliminal thought. You should have told me no. We could have gone someplace else."

"You're paying, so you had the right to decide where we ate."

"Then may I order you tiramisu for dessert? I know you like it."

"No," Frank said and shook his head. "I should go home. I've not felt right most of the afternoon. Be glad that you're young and don't know what it's like to feel less than one hundred percent."

"I am."

The waitress brought the check, and Parker handed her his credit card.

"Would you please tell me about Siena?" Parker asked after she left.

"No."

"I believe I'm supposed to know," Parker persisted.

Frank studied his grandson for a moment. "Why?"

"Because I haven't been able to get it out of my mind ever since it came up at the office."

It was Frank's turn to be persistent. "What's been in your mind?" he asked.

Parker glanced around to make sure no one was close enough to hear what he had to say. "I saw something. It only lasted a second or two, but the detail was incredible, and I can still remember it."

"I'm listening."

Parker took a deep breath. "It was a street scene in a city somewhere in Europe. There was a house built with light-colored stone on a narrow street."

"Cream colored," Frank cut in.

Parker nodded. "Yeah. And the house suddenly blew up and flames were shooting everywhere. At first I thought it might be your parents' house in Dresden, but then I wondered if it had to do with Siena. Were you part of a commando team that blew up a house?"

"Not literally, but for all practical purposes that's what happened," Frank replied with a reluctant shake of his head. "If you make me tell you about this, it will change our relationship forever."

"Please, I want to know the truth."

And so Frank told Parker what happened on the narrow street in Siena almost sixty years earlier. When he got to the part about the murder of the three Jewish young people, Frank had to stop and use a napkin to wipe his eyes.

"Now do you understand why I said you won't ever be able to look at me the same again?" he asked when he finished.

Parker started to speak but didn't.

"That's right," Frank continued. "You can't try to make me feel better by arguing it wasn't my fault. I didn't pull the trigger, but I took the general and his men to the house. I wish I'd died instead of the young people, but that won't bring them back to life. I've had the chance to grow old; they didn't."

"Why would I see this if it happened a long time ago?" Parker asked.

"I don't know, but it's still a bloody stain on my soul."

Parker was restless when he returned to his apartment. He paced back and forth and then turned on the TV, but the images didn't distract him. An extra set of exercises didn't help, and he resumed pacing. Stopping and staring out the dormer window into the gathering dusk of evening, he closed his eyes for a moment, but the inner image of the burning building was so intense that he quickly opened them. He picked up his cell phone and called Layla.

"Thanks for taking my call," he said quickly. "And please don't hang up."

"You have five seconds."

"This isn't about me. It's about Opa. Please, hear me out?"

The phone was silent for a moment.

"Layla?"

"Yes."

Parker told her about the conference room conversation and about the revelation from his grandfather at the restaurant.

"He would be furious if he knew I told you this, but I had to talk to someone, and you're the one who came to mind."

Parker thought he heard sniffles on the other end of the call.

"Are you crying?" he asked.

"Of course I am. What would you expect? It's terrible in every way."

"Was I wrong to call you?"

"No, it doesn't keep me from loving him, but I'm not sure how to help him."

"You love my grandfather?"

"You didn't know that? We had an instant connection, just like —"

Parker knew the rest of the sentence had to do with the two of them.

"Would you be willing to go see him together tomorrow evening?" he asked. "Maybe we could grab some take-out food."

"He's been craving Greek food."

"How do you know that?"

"It came up one Sunday after church. You could be a part of that time with him if you wanted to."

"Yes, I know. And it's one mistake I can correct."

"All right. Pick me up at five to deliver the meal. And don't let my father keep you from doing it."

"Okay."

"And, Parker, this had better not be an attempt to spend time with me using your grandfather as an excuse."

"No. I was going crazy worrying about him and wanted to come up with a way to do something positive."

"What are we going to do when we get there besides eat?" Layla asked.

The answer came out of Parker's mouth before he had time to think about it. "Save his life."

The following day Frank and Lenny returned from their fishing trip around 5:00 p.m. and tied the boat up to the dock.

"I should have stopped off at the Little River Marina and filled it up with gas," Frank said as he turned off the engine. "There's barely enough in the tank to make it down there the next time we go out."

"After the day we had, I was ready to call it quits and go home." Lenny shrugged. "I can't remember when we've been totally skunked like that."

"At least there are fish in the freezer and we're not trying to make a living on the water," Frank answered.

"Yeah, but I can't figure out why nothing was biting anything we offered. It's not like we're first-timers who don't know the difference between a bloodworm and a night crawler."

"Does Mattie know the difference?"

"She's not touching a worm no matter where it came from."

Lenny stepped onto the dock and held his hand out to Frank to help him onto the wooden planks. Frank hesitated.

"Go ahead," he said. "I ought to run down to the marina and fill up before it closes. You head home. It won't matter since we both drove."

"Suit yourself," Lenny said. "I'm so out of sorts that I'd be lousy company."

Frank watched his friend trudge down the dock toward the shore with an empty five-gallon bucket in his hand. Being a commercial fisherman for so many years gave Frank perspective. A disastrous day on the water when he owned the *Aare* meant hundreds of dollars out of his pocket to pay crew and fuel. Now the only loss was a few gallons of gas and personal frustration. As he untied the boat, he saw Lenny returning with his hand raised in the air.

"I almost forgot," Lenny said as he handed Frank a couple of crisp twenties. "You shouldn't bear all the costs."

"Keep one of those," Frank replied, holding out his hand with his palm up.

"No, consider it penance for having to put up with me most of the afternoon. I know I was a grouch."

"Then I'll accept," Frank said with a slight

smile. "And maybe you should add another one."

Lenny grinned. "I wasn't that grumpy. And your head was in another place too."

Lenny left, and Frank cast off. It was true that he'd been wrapped up all day in his own thoughts, and the absence of fish on the end of their lines had seemed insignificant. It was a five-minute ride to the marina. It had been a warm day, but as the sun crept lower, the air temperature rapidly dropped. He reached in the console, took out a navy windbreaker, and slipped it on. Pulling into the marina, he asked the young attendant on duty to fill up the fuel tanks.

While he waited, Frank saw one of the larger boats he'd seen before this far up the river slowly motor past, heading toward the Sound. It was a true oceangoing vessel that could make it to the Bahamas or the Caribbean without refueling. Among the several flags and pennants flying from the mast was the German national flag.

Frank looked past the yacht toward the east. The field without gravestones and the stream of clear water hadn't touched the guilt he felt over Siena. Thousands of miles and multiple decades separated him from the evil that occurred at the house with the cream-colored stone facade. But even though he got on his knees and asked God to forgive him when he returned from New Bern the previous evening, the stain remained on his soul. Frank resolved to ask Eric about it on Sunday, even if he had to reveal to the minister what he'd done. After paying for the gas, Frank returned to the dock. The sandy parking area was empty except for his car.

At home, he had a message from earlier in the day on his answering machine in the kitchen.

"Opa, this is Parker. Layla and I would like to bring you dinner this evening around six o'clock. Would Greek be okay? We'll come even if I don't hear from you since I know you and Lenny may be out on the water. Oh, you heard me right. Layla and I are coming together, but nothing has changed between us. It's just that we both care about you."

The last two sentences of Parker's message touched Frank deeply. All day he'd felt unworthy of continuing to take oxygen from the atmosphere. He sniffled and wiped his right eye. Checking the clock, he realized he needed to shower and clean up quickly.

Parker and Layla stopped by a well-known Greek restaurant near the multicolored

Tooth Beary ceramic bear. They ordered a dinner for three that included a variety of salads and grilled lamb.

"Let me call him again," Parker said when they were in the car. "A lot of times he doesn't check his messages and may already have eaten supper. But once he smells the onions on the salad and the Greek dressing, his appetite will revive."

Parker dialed the number again. When there wasn't an answer, he left another voice mail.

"It's possible he's out someplace or at Lenny's house," he said when he finished. "I hate to waste a trip."

"We should go anyway," Layla said. "I've been worried about him all day. It was hard for me to focus on my work."

"Same for me," Parker replied.

Frank got out of the shower and dressed. His hair was still damp when he went into the kitchen. He'd missed another call from Parker. He picked up the phone to return the call when there was a knock on the door. Glad that Parker and Layla had arrived, he went to the front door and opened it.

Two large, muscular men in their late twenties or early thirties burst into the house and grabbed his arms.

"Come with us," one of the men said in German.

"Why? Who are you?" Frank vainly tried to jerk his arms out of their grasp.

"We're not going to harm you," the other man said, also in German. "But you must cooperate."

Both men were dressed completely in black — shirt, pants, socks, and shoes. One of the men, with dark hair, took a thick plastic tie from his pocket and bound Frank's wrists together behind his back.

"That will hurt him," the other man said. "Do it in the front."

"Why do we care?" the first man said.

"Don't argue with me," the other said brusquely.

The first man pulled out a military-grade knife with a seven- or eight-inch blade and sliced through the plastic tie. He took another tie from his pocket and bound Frank's hands in front of him.

"Satisfied?" he asked.

"Where are the keys to your car?" the blond-haired man asked.

"Why do you need my car keys?"

"We're not a chauffeur service," the blond man answered with a smile. "You're driving yourself home when we're finished."

Frank pointed to the peg by the door

where he hung his car keys. The dark-haired man slipped them into his pocket. Then the two men each grabbed an arm and easily carried Frank out of the house between them.

"Where are you taking me?" Frank demanded.

"Be patient," the blond-haired man answered. "Your questions will be answered."

A white BMW sedan was parked outside under the live oak tree. They put Frank in the rear seat. The light-haired man joined him and buckled the seat belt around Frank's body. Frank noticed that the driver was wearing a black cap, but he couldn't see his face. The dark-haired man got in Frank's car.

"Drive," the blond-haired man said.

The windows were heavily tinted, but Frank could still see outside. The men made no effort to conceal their route. Once the car reached Highway 70, the driver turned away from New Bern. They were going downriver toward the Sound.

They drove for thirty minutes before turning onto a road that Frank knew ended at the river. They passed several sandy, unpaved roads before taking one that snaked through a pine thicket. The blond man took out a blindfold used by airplane passengers who wanted to sleep during a flight and slipped it over Frank's eyes. Frank's world turned utterly dark.

"This may not be necessary," he heard the blond man say, "but it's a preliminary precaution. I trust you'll make sure it remains secure."

"I can't see a thing," Frank said in German.

"Good."

The car continued on for several minutes. Then, to Frank's surprise, they were on smooth pavement. Somehow they'd made a turn, and now he didn't know where they were. After four more turns and a short trip on a rough road that made the car bump up and down, they stopped.

"We'll open the door and guide you," the blond-haired man said. "We don't want you to trip and hurt yourself."

Frank felt a hand on his shoulder that guided him out of the car. He could tell from the sounds and smells that they were near the river.

"What about my car?" he asked.

"It will be waiting for you at the drop-off spot when we finish."

"We're going to get in a small boat that will take us to a larger one," the blond-haired man reported.

Two men walked on either side of Frank and guided him down a sandy path until he felt his feet on the wooden planks of a dock.

"Here we are," the blond-haired man said. "The easiest method for us to make the transfer is by picking you up."

Before Frank could respond, the two men lifted him in the air. His feet landed on the deck of a boat where another set of hands steadied him. He heard the sound of the other two men as they boarded. A moment later the engine started, and the boat rapidly accelerated. Frank knew they were in a speedboat that was rocketing down the river. Without being able to see, he was unsteady on his feet and reached out, hoping to grab a railing.

"We have you," an unfamiliar voice said in German. "Step this way and hold on to the pole."

A pair of hands guided Frank to a spot where he could grab a metal pole that he guessed was near the steering wheel. After several minutes, the boat suddenly slowed. From the sound of the water lapping against the side, Frank guessed that they'd slipped into one of the many creeks that flowed into the river. Even though they'd taken a circuitous route in the car, Frank was confident that without the blindfold, he could identify where he was within fifteen or twenty seconds.

"Don't touch the blindfold," the new voice warned. "We'll make sure you don't trip and fall."

A set of hands on either side of Frank half guided, half carried him to a spot where a gangplank had been lowered into the speedboat. They walked Frank up the plank and onto what he immediately could tell was a substantial vessel. The deck beneath him wasn't moving, and when he reached out with his hand, he felt the side of an enclosed cabin. He remembered the oceangoing yacht that had passed by the marina earlier, but he'd not paid attention to it beyond noticing the small German flag. He couldn't recall the name of the craft that would certainly have appeared someplace on the vessel. He heard the footsteps of several people around him, but no one spoke as the hands continued to guide him forward.

"We're going belowdecks," the new voice said. "However, there's plenty of room. You won't need to lower your head."

They walked down eight steps to a very cool area. The only sound in the cabin was the subdued hum of the ship's air-conditioning unit. They walked about twenty feet, turned left, and went another ten feet.

"Please, sit down," the blond-haired man said. "There's a chair behind you."

Frank sat in a comfortable leather chair. Suddenly he felt the cool blade of the knife against his wrists. A moment later the plastic tie fell off.

"You may take off the blindfold," said the man who'd joined them on the transfer craft. "We appreciate your cooperation."

Frank reached up and slipped off the blindfold. The yacht's lounge was brightly lit, and it took a few seconds for his eyes to adjust. When they did, he took in a sharp breath.

Parker and Layla didn't talk during the drive to his grandfather's house. As they neared the turnoff for his road, Parker's phone, which was resting on the console, rang.

"I don't recognize the number," he said.

"I do," Layla said, glancing down. "It's my father."

"Should I answer it?" he asked.

"Your choice," Layla replied, looking away.

Parker picked up the phone and answered the call.

"Parker, I need you at the office as soon as you can get there," Blocker said. "I had a voice mail from Chet Ferguson. There's a problem, and you need to calm him down in person."

"What sort of problem?" Parker asked.

"Greg has filled his head with a bunch of nonsense by claiming that with you leaving the firm, Ferguson's case isn't going to get the attention it deserves. Greg quoted some saying to Ferguson about a man with one racehorse taking better care of it than a man with a stable of thoroughbreds. Anyway, you need to reassure the client that his case is better off with us than anyplace else. He trusts you."

Parker looked nervously at Layla, who continued to stare out the window.

"Did you talk to Chet?" he asked.

"No, I'm in the middle of something else and can't break away. Sandy Stumpf called him and told him we'd get you down there as soon as possible. I'm sending her an e-mail right now to set up the meeting within the next thirty minutes."

"I can't do it," Parker replied. "I'm with Layla on my way to see my grandfather and take him dinner."

"That's a nice thing to do, but this is priority one. Taking control of the Ferguson case is a major reason why I hired you."

Parker felt like he'd been punched in the

stomach. Stunned, he didn't respond. Taking the BlackBerry away from his ear, he stared at it for a second, terminated the call, and turned off the phone.

"What's going on?" Layla asked, facing him.

Parker gripped the steering wheel tightly. "I think I just quit my job."

"What?" Layla asked, her eyes opening wider.

Parker briefly explained the part of the conversation she hadn't heard.

"Are you sure you don't want to call him back? I can deliver the food to your grandfather and try to cheer him up. Once you're finished in town, you can come back and get me."

Parker's head was spinning. "Is that what you want me to do?" he asked.

"It's what you want that's important. But I never would want you to think you made a hugely important decision like this because I was with you."

Parker hesitated. "All I know for sure is that I have to see Opa, at least for a minute or two."

Pulled in opposite directions, Parker turned into the driveway of Opa's house. His grandfather's car wasn't in its usual place.

CHAPTER 40

Frank rubbed his eyes. Several men stood in a semicircle in front of him. Standing beside the blond-haired man was a familiar face.

"Conrad?" Frank asked in German. "What are you doing here?"

"I'm here to help," the former private replied, putting his hand on the shoulder of a distinguished-looking middle-aged man beside him. "And I hope you will too."

Frank stared again at the middle-aged man. Something about him seemed vaguely familiar.

"Krieger?" he asked.

The man looked at Conrad Mueller and shook his head.

"The Aryan Eagle," the man said in German. "He's remarkable."

Mueller shrugged. Krieger addressed Frank: "My grandfather was the general you met during the war."

"Are you the one who sent me the e-mail?"

"Not directly. I wouldn't be that indiscreet, but after Conrad and Attorney Blocker confirmed your identity, I reached out to you via e-mail."

"Blocker? I didn't think he responded to your lawyer."

"He didn't have to. We were able to obtain the results of his research through other means."

"You broke into his office?"

"No, of course not. But that's not important for our purposes now."

"And what is your purpose in kidnapping me?"

"You haven't been kidnapped. You'll be free to leave when we're finished," Krieger answered, turning to the man with blond hair.

"Yes, sir," the man replied. "That's what I told him at his house."

"Which is the truth," Krieger replied, refocusing on Frank. "You're here because I'd like to see an injustice made right. My grandfather obtained some items from a residence in Siena during the war, and I want to see them returned to their rightful owners."

"And you don't have them?" Frank asked.

"The crates from the house in Siena were stolen by someone toward the end of the war and have never resurfaced, which makes me believe they've been kept intact." Krieger held up a folder. "My grandfather made a detailed inventory. There are paintings by Giorgione, Lippi, gold work by Cellini, two small sculptures by Bernini, and multiple gold and silver pieces. It was an amazing collection brought together by several wealthy families from Florence and Venice for storage in a nondescript house in Siena. Museums all over Europe would be thrilled to have any of these items on display."

"What about the true and rightful owners?" Frank asked. "Wouldn't they have a say in that?"

"The Jews?" Krieger asked. "No heirs exist. I've done my research. All members of the families perished. There were no survivors."

Frank felt like he was about to throw up.

"I am aware there was unexpected violence when three residents of the house tried to kill my grandfather," Krieger continued. "Their blood is on their own heads."

"No!" Frank replied. "I was there! They were gunned down on the sidewalk!"

"Many unfortunate things happen in a war," Krieger replied calmly. "Millions of men are swept up in events over which they, as individuals, have no control."

"Not in my war," Frank said. "We all made choices."

"Partly true," Krieger responded with a nod. "You chose to desert your unit and flee to Switzerland. And that choice caused Conrad to barely escape with his life."

"How? Why?" Frank asked.

Mueller stepped forward with his fists clenched. Krieger easily restrained the older man by holding out his arm and blocking him.

"Conrad, please. There are no enemies here. Don't open old wounds."

Frank looked into Mueller's eyes, but the former private's countenance didn't reveal the truth.

"I was blamed for your desertion," Mueller said, "and sent to the Russian front where I lost two fingers, half of my left foot, and suffered the unbearable pain of frostbite over much of my body." Mueller raised the remaining fingers on his left hand and pointed them at Frank. "And it's your fault!"

"When you said I saved your life —"

"In your arrogance you believed me," Mueller said, cutting him off. "It should have been you, not me, who was sent to his death!"

"Enough!" Krieger raised his hand, and Mueller moved back a step.

Frank looked at Mueller's hand. "I'm sorry," he began. "If I'd known —"

"We've all suffered here," Krieger snapped. "The Russians shot my grandfather in the middle of a Berlin street and dragged his body behind a truck until his face was unrecognizable. I wouldn't want anyone to share his fate. But this is our chance to make many things right. If you want to compensate Conrad, I have a way for you to do so. We're not the only people trying to locate the treasures of Siena. There are those who want to profit for themselves, but with your help we can keep that from happening."

"How?"

"Tell us where to find what we're looking for, Hauptmann, and we will all share in the reward."

"I've not been a hauptmann for a long time," Frank replied.

"It was a slip," Krieger said with a slight smile. "I've thought about you in that way for so long it's hard to adjust. But unlike when you stood before my grandfather, I have no authority to order you to do any-thing."

"You mentioned a reward," Frank said. "What do you mean?"

"A finder's fee would be in order so long as it is reasonable. The amount would depend on the condition of the artifacts and their value. If you like, we can prepare a written agreement —"

"I'd want my grandson to do that," Frank said. "He's a lawyer. Conrad met him."

Mueller nodded. "We can prepare a short-form memorandum now that your grandson can formalize in a document acceptable to you," Krieger said with a satisfied smile. "I suggest we agree on a percentage of value based on the average of three independent appraisals. All we're asking you to do is tell us where to look. We'll do everything else and cover all costs of the operation. Once recovery occurs and value is confirmed, you'll be notified immediately."

"Thirty-three and a third percent," Frank said. "You know I could ask for more, because without me you have nothing."

Mueller looked at Krieger, who ignored him.

"I was thinking more along the lines of ten percent," Krieger responded smoothly. "I agree your role is key, but my people will bear all the risks inherent in a treasure hunt like this."

Frank paused for a few moments. "Twenty-five percent, which is nonnegotiable."

"Agreed," Krieger replied immediately.

"No!" Mueller said. "That's more than twice what you promised me if I —"

"And you accepted," Krieger cut in. "You made your deal and should be grateful for it."

Krieger called over the blond-haired man and whispered instructions in his ear.

"Gerhardt will prepare the memorandum for us to sign," he said to Frank.

"Make sure it includes everything found in Siena," Frank added.

"Of course, that sets the boundaries," Krieger said. "In the meantime, I suggest you begin the process of determining where the treasure is located. Would you like something to drink? We have a fully stocked bar. Do you need to be alone in a quiet place? That can be arranged. Virtually anything you need is at your disposal."

"That's not necessary," Frank replied.

"Why not?" Krieger asked, a surprised look on his face.

"Because I already know the answer."

■ ■ ■ ■

Parker and Layla stood on the front porch. Parker used his key to unlock the door.

"Where do you think he is?" Layla asked.

"He could be out on the water night fishing with Lenny. Sometimes one of the men who worked for him on the *Aare* will swing by and take him out to dinner."

"Opa!" Parker called out as soon as they were inside.

It took only a few seconds to confirm that the house was empty.

"Even though I'm sure he's okay, he ought to get one of those things he can hang around his neck in case he needs to push a button and call 911," Parker said.

"Would he agree to do that?" Layla asked.

"No," Parker replied. "And if I tried to make him do it, he'd wear it on his boat, drop it in the water, and claim it was an accident."

"What should we do now?" Layla asked.

"We can put his meal in the fridge. He'll enjoy it later."

"You should probably call my father now," Layla said after they divided the food and put some in the refrigerator.

Parker took out his phone and turned it

on. He'd missed three calls. "Should I listen to the messages before I do that?" he asked her. "A call at this point may be a waste of time."

"Don't drag me into this, Parker."

"You're the one who brought it up —"

The phone in the kitchen rang.

"I'm going to answer that call first," Parker said.

Going into the kitchen, he picked up the receiver.

"Frank?" a male voice asked when Parker answered.

"It's Parker."

"Oh, this is Lenny. I was calling to check on your grandfather. We spent the entire day on the water, but he was so distracted that he wasn't even there. And not just because the fish weren't biting. Something else was really working on his mind."

"Well, he's not here now," Parker replied. "I brought him a surprise dinner to cheer him up, but I don't know where he is. His car is gone. Did he mention going out with anyone else this evening?"

"He didn't say anything to me. He dropped me off at the dock late this afternoon. After that he was going to run down to Little River Marina and tank up with gas."

"So he may not have come home yet?"

"Possibly, although that was a couple of hours ago, and it's dark now."

"Is there a chance he went night fishing?"

"No way," Lenny answered. "After the day we had on the water, he doesn't want to see a fishing pole for at least twenty-four hours to get the bad memory out of his mind."

The mention of bad memories made Parker's stomach suddenly knot up.

"Okay, thanks," he said.

"Call me when you find out where he is," Lenny said. "I'll be worrying until I hear from you."

"Sure, thanks for checking."

Parker hung up the phone. He rested his hand against the wall and tried to figure out where his grandfather might be.

"Parker! Come here!" Layla called out.

Parker joined her in the living room.

"Look what I found behind the door."

In Layla's hand was a thick black plastic connector that had been fastened together but then cut in two.

"Should this be here?" she asked, handing it to him.

Parker turned the tie over between his fingers. "This is heavy-duty, but I'm sure he has things like this in his tool kit."

"But what would he use it for in the living room?"

"I don't know. And he never leaves anything on the floor. Believe me, I know. Picking up after yourself isn't an option in this house."

Parker checked the door to see if something was broken and the tie was an effort at a temporary fix. Nothing seemed out of order.

But in his heart, Parker knew that wasn't the case.

CHAPTER 41

Every eye in the room was trained on Frank.

"We'll wait for the agreement," Frank said calmly. "I want everything confirmed in writing."

"Yes, yes," Krieger said impatiently and then motioned for another man to come over to him. Krieger spoke to him, and the man left.

"The treasure is somewhere that will make it difficult for you to recover it," Frank said while they waited.

"As I mentioned earlier, that's not your concern," Krieger responded. "Once we know where to look, the problem is ours, not yours."

Gerhardt returned with a single sheet of paper in his hand and handed it to Krieger, who quickly scanned it.

"This is clear enough," Krieger said before handing the sheet to Frank.

It was in German and succinctly set out

the terms of their agreement. There were signature lines for Frank and Krieger.

"Where does Conrad sign?" Frank asked when he finished reading it. "I want his commitment too."

"It's not necessary," Krieger replied with a dismissive wave of his hand. "I'm in charge."

"I want Conrad to sign it," Frank insisted.

Krieger's face turned slightly red for a moment before the German regained his composure.

"Very well."

He took the paper from Frank, drew another line on the bottom with a pen, wrote "Conrad Mueller" beneath it, and handed it back to Frank.

"There, it's done," Krieger said. "Satisfied?"

"Yes."

Frank signed his name and watched as Krieger and Mueller did the same.

"Copies for all of us, please," Frank said. "I'll need two so I can give an original to my grandson."

The blond-haired man left the room, and Krieger fidgeted while they waited.

"It would be a good idea to fax a copy to my grandson's law office," Frank said. "That way he'll already have one when I call him about it."

"Gerhardt will take care of that later this evening," Krieger replied.

The blond-haired Gerhardt returned and distributed the copies of the agreement to the three men. Krieger then dismissed everyone except Frank and Mueller from the room. Krieger and Mueller pulled up chairs and sat in front of Frank. Up close, Frank could see that Krieger was wearing an expensive watch, and a diamond-encrusted thick gold ring circled one of his fingers.

"It's an incredible honor to be part of this venture with you," Krieger said, not able to hide the excitement in his voice. "Now, what can you tell us?"

"First, what happens with me is not a science."

"Understood," Krieger replied.

"And I don't know the condition of any of the items stolen, I mean confiscated, by your grandfather."

"There's no use focusing on the unknown," Krieger said impatiently. "Tell us what you do know."

Frank spoke calmly. "I know that I'm not going to help you. There was a time when I would have done what you've asked without questioning and not given much thought to the consequences. But I'm not that man anymore. Much has changed in what I believe and what I'm willing to do in life. Herr Krieger, what happened in Siena wasn't a part of a war. It was a war crime. And for those reasons, I'm not going to reveal anything."

The veins on Krieger's neck bulged out, and he jumped to his feet. Red-faced, he jabbed his finger in Frank's face. "I didn't come halfway around the world to waste my time debating the past with you! You will tell me what you know! And you will do it now!"

At the sound of Krieger's voice, the other men came running back into the room.

"Is there a problem, sir?" Gerhardt asked.

Krieger kept his attention riveted on Frank. "Don't push me, Haus," he said. "My family has spent decades in this search. And you're going to help me finish it. Out with it!"

Frank felt the strange calm of a man who considered his life over. No threats could touch him. No reservoir of fear remained in his soul.

"I did a great wrong in Siena," he said. "And I will not add new guilt to the old. Do what you want to me. I won't change my mind."

"Why did you ask for an agreement and sign it?" Mueller asked.

"That wasn't for me," Frank replied, turning to his former comrade. "It was for you. Someday soon you're going to remember this moment in a time and at a place when it will mean something very different to you. When that happens, my words will be written like fire across your heart, and you will have one last chance to repent. In the only way that truly matters, I am giving you a chance to save your life."

Mueller's face was pale.

"You're an old fool. Both of you," Krieger replied as he motioned to a man who was standing in a dark corner of the room.

The man was about six feet tall with close-cut brown hair and blue eyes. He stepped over and slipped a fresh black plastic tie around Frank's wrists and cinched it down extra tight. When he did so, Frank saw a swastika tattooed on the man's forearm.

"Krieger, no!" Mueller protested.

"This is not your decision," Krieger responded. "If he's not going to cooperate, there's no reason to keep him around. If he'd been captured when he deserted in 1944, he would have been shot, no questions asked. There's no statute of limitations on treason."

Frank looked at Mueller, who was anxiously glancing back and forth between Krieger and the man who'd bound Frank.

"Just do what he asks," Mueller said.

"If I cooperate, do you believe Herr Krieger is going to let me go?" Frank asked. "Is he going to honor the worthless sheet of paper we signed? Is he going to risk me telling someone else where the treasure of Siena is located? What if I do and they solve the riddle of recovery before he can? How does he know I haven't already made arrangements for the information to be released if something happens to me?"

"I'll accept that risk," Krieger replied, staring coldly at Frank. "And do you think I would have gone into this without a backup plan?"

Frank gave Krieger a puzzled look. Then, in an instant, Frank's calm acceptance of his fate was blown into a million pieces.

"No!" he cried out.

"Where are we going?" Layla asked.

"To Opa's boat."

It was dark by the time they reached the sandy lot and parked the car. There was only a thin sliver of moon in the sky.

"His car isn't here," Layla said. "He must have gone out with someone else."

Parker had a physical reaction to Layla's words identical to the way he felt when Lenny had mentioned a bad memory.

"No, there's something else going on," he replied. "We're going out in the boat."

"Why? What are we looking for?"

"I don't know!" Parker banged his fist hard against the steering wheel. "But there's no way I can leave!"

"Okay, okay."

They got out of the car. Parker used the light on his cell phone to guide them along the dock to the boat. Once there, he flicked on the running lights and took a powerful flashlight from the console below the steering wheel. He turned on the flashlight and shined a long, straight beam across the rippling water of the river.

"That's a strong light," Layla said.

"It can be seen over a mile away."

Parker retrieved the spare key from its hiding place beneath one of the life jackets stored in a cabinet along the gunwale.

"Can I ask where we're going?" Layla asked in a timid voice.

"Yeah, there's a spot along a creek several miles downriver that I can't get out of my mind. I want to check the river from here to there."

"Do you think that's where your grandfather might be?"

"I hope not, because there's nothing at the creek except a private boat ramp and water. But maybe this is a way to get us out on the river in the direction we're supposed to go."

"Parker, are you so upset that you can't think straight?"

He stopped and faced her. "Maybe," he said, his voice shaking. "I'm scared to death that I'm wrong and we're wasting time that should be spent doing something else to find him. But I don't know what that is. If we don't see anything at the creek, we'll come back and file a missing person report with the sheriff's department."

"I'm fine with that," Layla said.

Layla sat in one of the seats behind the steering console while Parker started the boat's motor and cast off. They pulled slowly away from the dock and headed toward the river.

"Have you been out on the water at night before?" she asked.

"Plenty of times. As long as we stay in the main channel there shouldn't be a problem, and the sonar doesn't need daylight to work."

Parker didn't push the throttle forward but proceeded at a slow pace. From time to time, he shined the flashlight along the bank. There weren't any other boats on the water. Once, the light picked up the reflection from the eyes of a deer that was walking along the edge of the water. The animal froze until the light started moving away.

"Your grandson's talents haven't gone unnoticed," Krieger continued. "It was a surprise when it surfaced. We didn't realize these sorts of things could be passed down through the generations. Based on the information we obtained, his new employer is proud of Parker's ability, even though he had no idea how significant the information was to me."

Frank gritted his teeth and kept his mouth closed.

"So here are your options," Krieger said. "You can cooperate with us and hope we let you go, or you can refuse to help, in which case both you and your grandson will suffer the consequences."

"Give me a sheet of paper and a pen," Frank replied after hesitating for a few moments. "And free my hands so I can write."

"Tell us. We'll write it down for you."

"That's not how it works with me," Frank answered.

Krieger nodded to Gerhardt, who cut the

tie. Frank rubbed his wrists. Gerhardt handed Frank a pen and paper and stepped back.

"The items taken from the house in Siena are in the Ukraine," Frank said to Krieger. "They were seized by the Soviet commander who interrogated your grandfather before ordering that he be shot. The Soviet officer later bought a chateau, and the treasures have been there ever since."

"What is the officer's name?" Krieger asked.

"I don't know, and I suspect he's dead. The property is in a secure location, and even if you present evidence, no Ukrainian court is going to order that the items be turned over to you."

Frank began to sketch on the sheet of paper. Krieger stepped forward and peered over his shoulder.

"The chateau is near the place where a road, river, and train track intersect. The river flows down from the Carpathian Mountains in eastern Ukraine and is a tributary of the Dniester." Frank continued to draw lines on the sheet of paper. Then he stopped and made a dot that he enlarged. "The chateau is near a town called Nad-something. The word is unfamiliar to me. The main structure for the residence has a brown roof and beside it is a large horse barn. That's it."

Krieger took the sheet of paper from Frank and studied it. "And are you sure you don't know the name of the Soviet officer?"

Frank hesitated. "Kuznet —" he started to say, then stopped. "I'm not sure."

"Kuznetsov." Krieger completed the word with a shocked expression on his face. "It means 'blacksmith.' He was a colonel in the unit that captured and killed my father."

"What do you think?" Mueller asked Krieger.

"This is enough," Krieger said. "We should be able to find it. If the courts are closed to us, then we'll have to use alternate measures."

Krieger looked down at Frank. "How can we succeed in recovering the treasures?"

"You won't," Frank replied flatly. "But I've done what you asked, and I'd like to go back to my home and live out my life in peace. You don't have to worry about me talking to anyone else. I don't want to think or talk about Siena ever again."

"Very well," Krieger said, motioning to one of the young men. "Thank you for your help. I'm sorry for my threats, but often the ends justify the means."

"Conrad and I have both heard that argument before," Frank replied, looking at the former private.

Parker pulled back the throttle on the boat and turned closer to shore. He handed the flashlight to Layla.

"It's not far to the creek," he said. "But all these inlets look alike in the dark. Shine the light along the bank until I see the right spot."

The light illuminated an area of marsh and reeds. A heron that had been fishing in the dark slowly flapped its wings as it took off.

"Can herons fish in the dark?" Layla asked.

"Yes, there's a whole species of night herons."

The light moved past the marshy area to an opening.

"There's the creek," Parker said. "Please shine the light higher."

Layla directed the beam upward.

"Oh my —" Parker began.

"It's a boat," Layla said. "A big one."

"Lower the light!" Parker ordered. "And turn it off."

Parker killed the running lights for the boat, and Layla quickly flipped the switch on the flashlight. The night went dark except for tiny lines of light that were now visible from the shaded windows of the vessel in the creek.

"Do you think Opa is on that boat?" Layla asked in a whisper that was unnecessary given their distance from the creek.

"Maybe. I don't know. I hope so. I hope not," Parker said in rapid succession.

"What are we going to do?"

"Wait," Parker replied.

"Why?"

"Because that's all I know to do."

"How long?"

"Please don't push me," Parker said in frustration. "I'm doubting myself anyway."

"I'm sorry. It's just —"

"I'm worried about him too," Parker said, finishing her thought.

They waited in the dark. There was no breeze, and the boat sat motionless in the water. Parker moved to the bow. Layla joined him. Together they stared into the night. There was no sign of activity on the boat moored in the creek. Then a door on the vessel opened, and Parker saw a young man come out onto an open deck area toward the stern. He strained his eyes in an effort to see more clearly. Another figure emerged.

Parker didn't have to squint to identify

who it was.

Frank took a deep breath as they stepped into the night air and quickly looked around. It was a cloudy night with virtually no moon, which made it tougher than he'd expected to identify the yacht's location. The vessel had slipped into a creek off the main channel of the river, but there were a score of places that fit that description. He followed the brown-haired man to the rear of the yacht. The man swung a short gangway over and lowered it onto the small boat that had brought them over from the shore. He stepped back and motioned for Frank to go first.

Up close, Frank could see that the small boat was the kind of craft often hung from the deck of a large yacht. It was finished in smooth wood with two short bench seats and a single seat where the pilot sat to steer it by moving a rudder pole. The man signaled for Frank to sit on one of the benches and then started the boat's oversized motor. Frank wasn't sure how far they'd have to go up the creek to the spot where they'd boarded the small boat for the transfer to the yacht, but he estimated the previous ride had lasted less than five minutes. To his surprise, the man at the tiller turned away from the creek and toward the main channel of the river. There was a small red light on the bow of the craft.

"How far is it to the place we'll take out?" he asked in German.

"Not far," the man replied. "There's a boat ramp there. That's where your car is waiting for you."

Instead of hugging the shoreline, the boat ventured farther into the channel. They were near one of the widest parts of the river between New Bern and the Pamlico Sound. Now Frank knew exactly where they were. The creek where the yacht stood anchored was a familiar place. He and Lenny had fished for trout there within the last month. The yacht was anchored about six miles downriver from the dock where Frank kept his boat.

It was only a few hundred yards to the boat ramp. When they got closer, Frank could see the ramp, which was illuminated by a single light on a ten-foot pole. His car wasn't in sight.

"I don't see my car," Frank called out to the man at the rudder.

The man didn't answer. Frank swung his legs over the bench so that he faced the brown-haired man controlling the boat. The man hit the kill switch on the motor, and the boat quickly drifted to a stop. They were still a hundred yards from shore.

"This is where you get out," the man said.

Frank leaned forward, but in the dark he couldn't make out the expression on the young man's face.

"It's a hundred yards to the bank," Frank said.

"Get in the water, or I will throw you in," the man replied matter-of-factly. "Your car is already on the bottom of the river at the end of the ramp. You're going to join it."

Frank hesitated for a moment, but then he lunged forward and tried to get his hands on the man's throat so he could push him over the stern. Frank's hands got only as far as the man's upper chest when he felt a vise-like grip on his wrists. The man sharply twisted Frank's arms in opposite directions, and Frank cried out in pain. The next thing he knew, Frank was being pushed toward the left side of the boat. He managed to jerk his left arm free and land a feeble blow against the side of the man's head. A more violent twist of his right arm caused Frank to cry out again in pain as the brittle bones in his arm cracked and snapped in protest.

In one smooth movement, the man in the boat hoisted Frank over the side and dumped him headfirst into the water. Wearing clothes and shoes, Frank immediately sank beneath the surface. Sharp pain again shot through his right arm as he flailed about trying to turn around, and he gagged on a mouthful of water just before his head broke into the air. He choked as he came up beside the boat and tried to kick off his shoes. Looking up, he saw the man in the boat with an oar raised in the air. The man slammed the oar directly down onto Frank's forehead.

And everything went black.

Chapter 42

Parker gently eased the boat forward, which slightly decreased the sound generated by the engine as the prop engaged the water. None of the running lights were on, and he kept the bow pointed toward the red light of the small boat that they'd been following since it left the large vessel anchored in the creek. Parker had instantly recognized his grandfather's gait as the older man walked toward the yacht's stern. The small boat had stopped in the water. Layla came back to the console and joined him.

"Can you see anything else?" Parker asked her.

"No."

The light on the small boat was beginning to move back and forth.

"Someone stood up and the two people are close together," Layla said.

That was it. Parker threw the throttle wide open, and the skiff raised up out of the water as it shot forward.

"What are you going to do?" Layla called out.

"When I say so, turn on the light."

The boat bounced up and down on the water as it reached top speed. The light on the small craft continued to bob up and down as they got closer and closer.

"Now!" Parker called out.

Layla turned on the powerful lantern. The beam shot across the water and framed a man with an oar in his hands who was about to thrust it down into the water. When the light hit him, he looked up in shock as Parker and Layla bore down on him.

"Drop the light and hold on!" Parker yelled at Layla. "I'm going to ram him!"

Layla grabbed a metal bar that ran alongside the console. Parker flipped on the boat's main lights. The man standing in the boat took a step toward the side to dive overboard, but it was too late. Parker crashed into the bow of the boat and spun it around in the water. Layla lost her grip on the bar and slammed against the seats behind the console. She staggered to her feet.

"Are you okay?" Parker called out as he jerked the wheel to the right and sent the boat into a sharp turn.

"Yes."

"Where's the lantern? Opa is somewhere in the water."

Layla dropped to her knees, retrieved the lantern from beneath the rear seats, and turned it on. The front section of the wooden boat had been ripped off, and what was left pointed up in the air as the weight of the motor dragged it down. The light danced across the water. Parker raced up to the wreckage and cut back the throttle.

"I don't see anyone!" she called out.

Parker left the console and ran to the bow of the boat. All he could see to the right were pieces of wood floating in the water.

"Shine it over there!" he called out, pointing to the left.

Layla did as he directed, and Parker saw a flash of color about ten feet away. Without waiting for a second look, he kicked off his shoes and dived into the water. He came up from his dive and saw nothing. The water was completely opaque, but he lowered his head and kicked down a few feet, extending his right hand in front of him. His hand touched cloth, and he grabbed it with his fist and kicked toward the surface. His face barely came above the water, but he managed to turn his head and see who it was he'd grabbed.

It was his opa.

"Throw me the lifesaver," he sputtered to Layla, who was now standing where he'd been at the bow of the boat.

The circular ring hung on the front of the console and had always been more decoration than anything else. Parker went beneath the water as the weight of his grandfather pulled him under. Flailing with his free arm and kicking as hard as he could, he again reached the surface. His hand touched the life ring, and he hooked his arm around it.

"Pull us in!" he called out.

They were only a few feet from the boat. Layla tugged on the rope and brought them to the side.

"Get us around to the ladder," Parker said as he repositioned his arm around his grandfather's chest.

Layla dragged them to the rear of the boat.

"Cut the engine!" Parker yelled as they got closer. "It could chew us up."

"Where?" Layla asked in panic. She disappeared, and a few seconds later the engine died.

Parker kicked his way to the rear of the boat and put his hand on the lower rung of the ladder. Layla was looking down and crying.

"He's unconscious," Parker managed. "I

need your help getting him out of the water."

Layla reached down with both arms and grabbed Frank's right arm. Parker felt the older man move slightly.

"He's alive! Hold tight."

While Layla held on to the right arm, Parker scrambled up the ladder. He then turned and grabbed his grandfather's left arm.

"Pull," he said.

Together they dragged Frank onto the rear of the boat. Parker immediately dropped to his knees and began to perform CPR. Tears streamed down Layla's face and fell from her cheeks as she knelt beside them. Frank coughed weakly and water ran out the corner of his mouth.

"Opa! Opa!" Parker called out as he sat up for a few seconds.

Layla touched the old man's white hair. Parker leaned over and blew another breath into his grandfather's lungs. Frank sputtered and choked again, followed by a deeper breath. He began breathing on his own.

"Thank God," Layla said.

Parker relaxed. Watching the slow but steady rising and falling of his grandfather's chest was the most beautiful sight of Parker's entire life.

"Parker!" Layla screamed. "The ladder!"

Parker's head shot around. The man who had been in the small boat had both hands on the bottom rung of the ladder. Blood was pouring from a gash on the side of his head. Instinctively, Parker raised his right foot and slammed it into the man's face. The man lost his grip on the ladder and fell back into the water.

"Hold on to Opa!" Parker yelled as he jumped up and started the boat's motor.

Parker threw the throttle forward. Layla had her arms wrapped around Frank to keep him from sliding off the rear of the boat.

"Where is the other man?" Parker called out.

"I don't see him," Layla said.

Parker turned the wheel of the boat in a tight spin.

"What are you going to do?" Layla asked. "Run over him?"

"Shine the light and find him," Parker replied, grim-faced.

After a moment's hesitation, Layla turned on the lantern and shined the beam on the water.

"There he is," she said, pointing to the end of the light.

The young man was slowly moving his

hands across the top of the water. Parker headed directly for him but swerved at the last moment and stopped the boat. Grabbing a life jacket from beneath the console, he threw it in the water. The life jacket landed a couple of feet from the man, who managed to reach out and grasp it with his hand.

Parker hit the throttle and sped away.

Parker and Layla sat beside each other on orange plastic chairs in the waiting area of the ER. Parker's clothes were still damp from his unexpected swim in the Neuse River. Layla's cell phone rang.

"It's my father," she said, glancing down at the number.

"Please, you tell him what happened to Opa," Parker said. "I don't want to talk to him."

Layla answered and listened for a moment before she left the waiting area and stepped outside. Parker closed his eyes and leaned his head against the wall behind the chair. Several minutes later a woman's voice caused him to open his eyes.

"Mr. House?" she called out.

"Here," Parker said, raising his hand.

"You can see your grandfather now."

Parker stood up and got Layla's attention

through the glass wall beside the ER doors. She ended the call and joined him. They followed the nurse down a hallway into a triage room. Frank was lying in a bed with the head slightly elevated. There was a large purplish bump on his forehead, and his right arm was wrapped in a rigid foam brace.

"Cracked, not shattered," Frank said, pointing to his arm when they entered the room. "The doctor only needed to immobilize it. And I can still cast a rod with my left arm until it heals."

"What about your forehead?" Parker asked.

"Harder than a boat paddle, I guess."

Parker glanced at Layla, whose tears had returned. Frank reached out with his left hand toward her, and she grasped it.

"I'd tell you not to cry," Frank said softly to Layla, "but your sweet tears are a balm to my soul."

The old man's words unleashed a fresh torrent from Layla. Parker wiped his own eyes.

"I don't know what to —" Parker started.

"I do," Frank said. "Things in life have a way of circling back to the beginning. It's odd, but I heard you calling my name from a long way off when you pulled me onto the boat. Have I ever told you about the old man I saved from drowning in the Rhine in 1944?"

"No."

Parker and Layla sat beside the bed while Frank talked. It was another open window into the vast reserve of the old man's memory and experience.

"And I stayed with Alfred and Otto until the end of the war. Alfred showed me great kindness and mercy." Frank closed his eyes for a moment. "What happened to the young man who tried to kill me? Did you see him after you pulled me from the water?"

Parker told Frank what he'd done to protect him and about tossing the life jacket to the man in the water before they sped away.

"You did the right thing," Frank replied with a look of relief on his face. "I've carried too many deaths on my conscience, and I don't want you to labor under that heavy burden."

"I'll reimburse you for the life jacket," Parker said.

"You'd better," Frank said, managing a small smile.

CHAPTER 43

After they left the emergency room, Parker spent the night with Frank at the older man's house. Layla arrived early the following morning. She and Parker cooked breakfast together in the kitchen.

"Has he told you anything else?" she asked.

"No, but he insisted on coming home and claimed it was safe. I barely slept. Every time he snored, I thought someone was breaking into the house. I checked on him several times, but he slept soundly through the night."

"He snores?"

"Yes."

"Do you?"

"Not once in my life," Parker replied as he poured eggs into a skillet to scramble them.

Frank appeared. He was still wearing his pajamas.

"Two of my favorite people on earth," he announced with a smile.

"Don't do that," Layla said, touching her eyes. "I can't handle it."

"Yes, you can. And it's good for you. Say something cheery to me in German."

Layla paused and then rattled off a few sentences. Frank nodded and replied in the same language.

"What did she say?" Parker asked.

"She wanted me to tell her how loudly you snore when you sleep, and I told her," his grandfather said.

"He wasn't under oath, so you can't be sure he was telling the truth," Parker replied as he vigorously stirred the eggs with a white plastic spatula.

They ate breakfast together on the back porch. Parker found some TV trays in a closet and set them up. Frank said a blessing that made Layla cry again.

"I'm a total mess," she said, wiping her eyes.

"This isn't all about me," Frank said. "You're letting go of a lot that's been pent up inside."

Layla nodded. As they ate, they listened to the sounds of morning on the coast. When their plates were empty, Frank took a long sip of coffee.

"Who brewed the coffee?" he asked.

"Layla," Parker answered.

"Loving hands," Frank said with a smile that caused Layla to tear up again.

While they sipped coffee on the porch, Frank told them what had happened from the time he was abducted until they pulled him out of the water.

"Are you sure you don't want to file a police report?" Parker asked when the old man finished. "The longer you wait, the less chance they can find the yacht and the men on it."

"They wouldn't have caught them if I'd let you notify them as soon as we got to the dock. And Krieger and his men aren't a threat to me. Soon they won't be a threat to anyone."

Layla's eyes widened. "Do you mean they're going to die?" she asked.

"When I told them they wouldn't recover the treasure of Siena, that wasn't all I saw."

"What about Conrad Mueller?" Parker asked.

"I'm not sure," Frank said and shook his head. "He could be a pawn or a player. The full nature of his involvement with Krieger isn't clear to me. But I believe he'll have a chance to repent. However, I don't know everything. I thought the man in the boat was going to bring me home."

They continued to enjoy the peaceful morning and one another's presence.

"There's something I need to do," Frank said when he finished drinking his coffee and set the empty cup beside his chair.

"What's that, Opa?" Parker asked.

"It'll be easier to explain if I tell you another story."

And while Parker and Layla listened, Frank told about the night his grandfather placed his hands on eight-year-old Franz's head and prayed for him. It was the night of fire, water, and snow. As Frank talked, the air on the back porch began to feel heavy and rich.

"I'd like you to pray for me like that," Parker said when Frank finished.

Without another word, Parker got up from his chair and knelt down in front of Frank. Looking at the curly brown hair on top of his grandson's head, Frank suddenly wondered if he could do what he wanted to do. After all, his sins stretched out in an unbroken line for so many years that the beginning point was lost in the mists of the past. He wasn't worthy to lay his hands on anyone's head and impart a divine gift. His hands had shed too much blood to hold a blessing. He took a deep breath and prepared to tell Parker to stand up and return to his seat.

"Paul once described himself as the chief of sinners." Layla's quiet voice interrupted his thoughts. "And he laid hands on Timothy."

"How did you know what was bothering me?" Frank asked, turning toward her.

"You and Parker aren't the only people on the planet who have hunches."

Frank took another deep breath and refocused his attention on Parker, who hadn't moved an inch.

"And I'm not getting up until you do what you're supposed to do," Parker said. "Even though this hard floor is eventually going to destroy my knees."

Frank smiled and was suddenly flooded with such an overwhelming sense of the favor of God that it swept away every barrier of opposition in a torrent of grace. He placed his left hand on Parker's head and effortlessly released the promise of heaven's will fully into the life of his grandson. When he finished, Layla was once again in tears. Parker stood up. He wasn't crying. Instead, Frank saw a resolute strength in his grandson that, if nurtured by faith, would last a lifetime.

Layla left shortly after breakfast. Parker

stayed. He couldn't bear the thought of being away from his grandfather, but when midafternoon came, the older man insisted Parker go home.

"I need time alone to think through a few things," Frank said. "Don't forget to pick me up Sunday for church."

"I'll be here."

As he was driving home, Parker's Black-Berry rang. This time he recognized the number. It was Tom Blocker. Parker answered the call.

"I drove up this morning to New Bern to check on you and Layla. She and I are at the office. I know you've been through a lot, but could you join us for a few minutes?"

"I'm pretty drained. It's not a good time for us —" Parker stopped.

"Please," Blocker replied. "But I'll understand if you say no," he added.

Parker paused for several moments. "Okay," he said. "I'm on my way."

He parked his car behind Layla's vehicle on Pollock Street. The front door was locked, and he didn't have his key. He rang the chime and waited. Layla opened the door for him. From her face, he couldn't tell exactly how she felt.

"We're in the conference room," she said.

Tom Blocker was sitting at the end of the table where he'd talked to Parker and Frank the day before. Now that seemed like another lifetime. He stood when Parker entered.

"I want to apologize," Blocker said before Parker could say anything. "If you'd done what I told you to do and come to town for a meeting with Chet Ferguson, your grandfather would have been murdered."

Parker searched Blocker's face and found nothing but sincerity. "I accept your apology," he said simply.

They sat down. Layla selected a chair beside Parker.

"And I want to straighten out another matter with you," Blocker continued. "I shouldn't have said I hired you to get the Ferguson case. It was a way to manipulate you to do what I wanted in the moment; however, it wasn't true then and it isn't true now. You're a talented young attorney who would be an asset to any law firm."

"Thank you."

Blocker took a deep breath. "And Layla and I have spent the past three hours talking about things we should have discussed and worked through over the past fifteen years. I've admitted some of my flaws" — Blocker paused — "and told her I want us to get to a place where she can forgive me. I realize this isn't going to happen overnight, but once I commit to something, I don't quit."

Parker turned to Layla.

"I will do my part," she said.

"Parker, I want you to continue to work for me," Blocker continued. "I'll still be your boss who has the right to tell you what to do, but my commitment today is to shift the paradigm of my approach so you and Layla can be free to explore a relationship with each other."

Parker eyed Blocker for a moment. "That sounds good," he said. "But I'm not sure it's possible."

"Why not?" Blocker asked, a surprised look on his face.

"Because to make that radical a change in your life, you're going to need God's help. Are you willing to go down that road?"

Blocker blinked his eyes a few times. "I'm not sure how to begin," he said.

Parker put his left hand on Layla's shoulder. "Let me introduce you to someone who can help."

CHAPTER 44

Six months later, Parker, Tom Blocker, Greg Branham, and Chet Ferguson walked out of the courthouse. Ferguson stopped at the bottom of the steps and shook hands with the other men.

"Thank you," he said. "I'm glad we were able to settle the case before trial. It would have been tough to relive everything that's happened since Jessica's death in front of the jury."

"I was ready to go to the mat," Greg said belligerently and then glanced at Blocker. "But with Tom on our side, we were able to get a great result without the fight. Nine hundred thousand dollars is more than I thought possible."

"And my children won't have to worry about choosing a college based on the cost of tuition or stress about making a down payment on their first home," Ferguson said. "I'll also be able to fulfill Jessica's dream to make a big gift to the treatment center for alcoholics where she volunteered. They're going to expand their services for teenagers struggling with addiction problems."

When they finished talking, Ferguson turned away and began walking toward his car. Greg spoke to the other two men.

"I met with a new client the other day. It's a product liability claim against the manufacturer of those autopilot gizmos they put in big boats. This one malfunctioned and caused a collision with another vessel that resulted in almost a million dollars in damage. I'm calling it the fender bender on steroids. Would you be interested in taking a look at it?"

"I handled a similar case in the past," Blocker said.

"Why am I not surprised?" Greg responded. "What do you say?"

"Send it over for Parker to evaluate," Blocker said. "He's in charge of the New Bern office."

It was a Saturday evening in early summer when Creston and Melinda jogged, hand in hand, from the wedding reception to a car that Parker and the rest of the groomsmen had decorated with cheesy sayings about running and love. Creston's rush to the altar had been slowed by Melinda's desire for her dream wedding. Or as Creston described it to Parker, preparing for the wedding had turned out to be a marathon, not a sprint. Parker watched as Layla crouched down to get a different angle on the couple as they approached the car. For any other woman it would have looked awkward, but to Parker, Layla was eminently graceful.

After the newlyweds drove off, Parker helped Layla gather up her equipment. It was the same wedding venue where Chip and Kelsey had tied the marital knot the previous year. They loaded the camera gear into Layla's car.

"Thanks," she said after they finished. "I'm way behind with editing and may try to review these photos while it's all fresh in my mind before going to sleep. Will I see you tomorrow morning? Opa sent me a text message that he's coming to church. Can you believe he sent me a text from his new cell phone?"

"Yes, because it's you; no, because it's him. Do you have time for a quick walk along the river?"

Layla hesitated. Even though it had been a warm day, the weather along the coast could change moods faster than a three-year-old child, and an approaching storm was causing a stiff breeze to blow off the water. Parker took off his jacket and wrapped it around her shoulders.

"Any other excuses?" he asked.

Layla smiled. "No."

They walked slowly away from the pavilion toward the river. When they reached the water there was a momentary lag in the breeze.

"Do you want your coat back?" Layla asked.

"No, it looks better on you."

Layla pushed a strand of hair away from her face. She was wearing black slacks and a yellow sweater.

"I've been working," she said. "You're the one who's all dressed up for a wedding."

They walked hand in hand along the river to a small park. Several decorative street-lamps cast a soft yellow glow. They stopped and looked out over the water in the fading light.

"What's wrong with your hand?" Parker asked, releasing Layla's left hand and holding it up in the light.

"Nothing," Layla replied.

Parker kissed her hand and then reached in the pocket of his pants, took out a small black box, and got down on his right knee.

"Parker!" Layla said when she saw what he was doing. "We haven't gone to the jewelry store to look at rings. You know how picky I am."

"They have a liberal return policy, and you're not helping the mood," he said, looking up into her eyes.

"I'm sorry," she replied, putting her right hand over her mouth.

Parker opened the box. The oval diamond in the delicate setting gently sparkled in the diffused light from the lamps. He took it out and held it at the end of Layla's left ring finger.

"Will you marry me?" he asked.

"Yes," Layla whispered as she nodded, her eyes brighter than the diamond.

Parker slipped the ring on her finger, stood, and kissed her. When they parted, he held her left hand gently in his and inspected the ring.

"It looked bigger and brighter under the lights in the store," he said.

"I love it," Layla said. "And we're never going to exchange it for another one. How in the world did you know what kind to get?"

"I stood in the store looking at the insane number of options in the case and went with a hunch."

"That's the kind of hunch I like." Layla smiled.

Frank sat on his screened-in porch in the soft morning light and sipped a cup of coffee. Release from his guilt over Siena had been a gradual process. No act on his part could atone for what took place. But he'd prayed. He'd confessed his sin to Parker, Layla, and Eric. And he'd ended up accepting a simple, profound truth that made no logical sense — forgiveness was an undeserved gift.

His right arm occasionally ached if he performed too many chores around the house or made one too many casts with a heavy fishing pole, but he was grateful. A close call with death, whether at twenty or eighty-two, makes life, even if not perfect, precious. And the opportunity for a few final minutes in God's vineyard caused thankfulness to well up inside Frank's heart each time his eyes opened to a new morning.

The previous night he'd dreamed about his grandfather. When he awoke, he wasn't sure if what he'd experienced was a dream or a repressed memory. In the vision, Frank was sitting in the corner of the living room of the house in Dresden while his grandfather spoke to the people assembled to hear him. As he listened, Frank sensed a sweetness on his lips he could literally taste with his tongue. Even in the dream, he knew it wasn't possible for this to happen in real life, but he couldn't deny the vibrancy of the message his taste buds sent to his brain. It was a sensation that would never grow old. Light, yet satisfying. Rich, yet ephemeral. Sitting on the porch, Frank licked his lips again at the memory but came away with only the taste of coffee mixed with cream.

Frank arrived early at the church and reserved two chairs for Parker and Layla. The young couple was reason to hope for the future. And Frank knew one of his primary jobs in the vineyard was to pour into his grandson all the wisdom he could. Watching Parker come into manhood was a joy to behold. And Layla was a kindred spirit. Every time she spoke to him in German, Frank felt a connection to the good things he'd left behind.

Parker and Layla arrived late, after the music started, and slipped in beside him. Parker patted him on the shoulder. Layla reached across Parker and held her left hand in front of Frank's face. He saw the glittering ring on her finger, looked into her shining eyes, and smiled.

"Congratulations," he said to her in German.

"Thank you, Opa," she replied in the same language. "You saw this day a long time before Parker and I did."

"But you'll be the ones to enjoy it."

The music ended, and it was Eric's turn to speak. His topic for the morning focused on the ways God reveals himself to his people. Partway through the message, a Bible verse popped up on the screen that made Frank sit up straighter in his chair.

Eric spoke: "Psalm 34:8 says, 'Taste and see that the LORD is good; blessed is the one who takes refuge in him.' "

Frank touched his tongue to his lips. And tasted something sweet. He closed his eyes and let the awareness of God's goodness seep into the hidden crevices of his soul. He nudged Parker and spoke in a whisper. "I know exactly what the psalmist means."

"It's a metaphor," Parker replied.

Frank nodded. "Maybe, but God's children get to witness every promise."

DISCUSSION QUESTIONS

1. What were your first impressions of Franz Haus during the opening scenes? Were you sympathetic or not? Did that section of the story remind you of any other books or movies?
2. When Franz escaped to Switzerland, what did you think might happen next? Were you surprised by the jump forward in time? How soon did you suspect a connection between Parker and Franz/Frank?
3. What do you think or believe about the influence of our ancestors on our lives, both for good and for bad? Are there Bible verses that mention this? Can you think of examples from your life?
4. What were the issues Parker was dealing with in the early stages of the novel? Answer the same question for Frank as an older man.
5. Have you had a relationship with a grandparent similar to that of Parker and Frank?

Have you ever had anyone pray for you the way Frank's opa did for him? Would you like to?

6. If you've read other Robert Whitlow novels, how was this one similar and how was it different?

7. What did you learn about World War II, German language/customs/military, boats, coastal fishing, and the legal system in this book?

8. How did your opinion of Thomas Blocker change over the course of the novel? What were some milestones in the arc of his character?

9. What would your answer be to Creston's question: "Are you sure there is such a thing as a gourmet hot dog?"

10. Did you think Layla was a good match for Parker? If so, why? What aspects of her character did you find interesting?

11. In the parable of the workers in the vineyard, do you think the owner's treatment of the workers is fair? What does this parable teach us about grace?

12. What was your reaction to Frank's vision of the meadow, stream, and hidden graves?

13. What did you find interesting about Frank's relationship with Lenny?

14. What was the origin of Frank's and

Parker's abilities to witness things before they happened?

15. How did you react to Layla's decision not to see Parker if he was going to work for her father? Explain what was going on in her mind and heart.

16. What was your reaction to the closing scene in the church when Frank experienced a unique aspect of God's goodness? What does it mean to "taste and see that the Lord is good"?

ACKNOWLEDGMENTS

Special thanks to Becky Monds, Deborah Wiseman, and my son, Jacob Whitlow, for their expert editorial advice. This is a much better story because of your guidance and suggestions. And thanks to my wife, Kathy, who, after listening to me relate a dream, encouraged me to write this book.

ABOUT THE AUTHOR

Robert Whitlow is the bestselling author of legal novels set in the South and winner of the Christy Award for Contemporary Fiction. He received his J.D. with honors from the University of Georgia School of Law where he served on the staff of the *Georgia Law Review.*

Visit him online at www.robertwhitlow.com
Twitter: @whitlowwriter
Facebook: robertwhitlowbooks